WELCOME TO MY WORLD

Miranda Dickinson has always had a head full of stories. From an early age she dreamed of writing a book that would make the heady heights of Kingswinford Library. Following a Performance Art degree, she began to write in earnest when a friend gave her The World's Slowest PC. She is also a singer-songwriter. Her first novel, *Fairytale of New York*, was a *Sunday Times* top ten international bestseller. *Welcome to My World* is her second novel.

To find out more about Miranda visit www.miranda-dickinson.com

By the same author

Fairytale of New York

MIRANDA DICKINSON

Welcome to My World

AVON

This novel is entirely a work of fiction.
The names, characters and incidents portrayed in it are
the work of the author's imagination. Any resemblance to
actual persons, living or dead, events or localities is
entirely coincidental.

AVON

A division of HarperCollins*Publishers*
77–85 Fulham Palace Road,
London W6 8JB

www.harpercollins.co.uk

A Paperback Original 2010

3

A catalogue record for this book is
available from the British Library

ISBN-13: 978-1-84756-166-4

Set in Minion by Palimpsest Book Production Limited,
Falkirk, Stirlingshire

Printed and bound in Great Britain by
Clays Ltd, St Ives plc

Mixed Sources
Product group from well-managed
forests and other controlled sources
www.fsc.org Cert no. SW-COC-001806
© 1996 Forest Stewardship Council

FSC is a non-profit international organisation established
to promote the responsible management of the world's forests.
Products carrying the FSC label are independently certified
to assure consumers that they come from forests that are managed
to meet the social, economic and ecological needs
of present and future generations.

Find out more about HarperCollins and the environment at
www.harpercollins.co.uk/green

Wow. You mean I get to do this again? Blimey . . . First of all – and most importantly – I'd like to thank you, for picking up my book today. You're amazing. I still can't quite believe that people other than my family and friends want to read my stories. Thank you!

Thanks as ever to the fantastically talented Authonomy.com community and the lovely Clive, Laura and team who run the site. Here's to many more Authonomy successes!

A massive thank you to the Avon team at HarperCollins, for believing in me and making the whole experience so fun and fulfilling. I hope this book is just reward for your faith in me. To my brilliant editor, Sammia Rafique, for not only being the very best editor any writer could wish for but also a true friend. To Caroline Ridding, Claire Bord and Kate Bradley, for supporting me so much, and Tara Hiatt and the Rights team at HarperCollins for all their hard work on my behalf. Thanks also to Yvonne Holland and Anne Rieley.

Being a bit of an armchair traveller myself, my experience of the world is somewhat limited. So I'd like to say a huge thank you to the people who shared their worlds with me: Laura Goss (New Orleans), Kim Curran and Dan Holloway (Pad Thai), Phil and Jo White (Kefalonia – in particular, the goat bells!), Victoria Connelly (Venice), my bestest chum Helen Smith (for inspiring Stella and Harri's friendship), and Phil Henley (Thailand and the inspiration for Alex's story). I'd also like to thank the very lovely Alison Howell from www.foot-trails.co.uk, for inspiring Emily's story – she's a shining example of what can happen when you take a chance on your dream.

For excellent Mini spares knowledge for Jack's car (and for generally being brilliant), grateful thanks to Phil Jevons, Dan Guest and Dave Jevons. Big thanks to my dedicated posse of writerly superstars – Kim Curran, Danielle Derry and Linsey Pearson – for your honesty, enthusiasm and all-round fabulousness in reading the various edits of this book.

I'd also like to thank the fantastic people I've met on Twitter, especially the six superheroes who flew to my rescue when I needed colour suggestions for Harri's wardrobe: Melissa Dixie, Rin Simpson, Sarah Siddons, Leigh Fenn, Jane Colston and Mandi Millen.

Thanks as always to my wonderful family and to my awesome friends for just being the best mates in the world and inspiring me in more ways than they realise. Also, big thanks to Siobhan Brown at Stourbridge Yoga – www.stourbridgeyoga.co.uk for much-needed relaxation and unending thanks to my family at Calvary Church, Kingswinford, for all your support and love. For everything that's been and is to come, thanks to the Master Storyteller, who knows it all.

Finally, to my lovely Bob: knight-in-shining-armour, support team, book widower and the man of my dreams. Thank you for loving me.

It's still a dream come true to be able to create worlds for other people to wander in. Thank you for choosing to step into mine!

For Phil Henley – who travelled round the
world to find his heart.

CHAPTER ONE

How It All Began . . .

Right at the start, there are two things you should know about Harri: one, she doesn't usually make a habit of locking herself in toilet cubicles during parties; and two, she is normally one of the most sane, placid individuals you could ever meet.

But tonight is an exception.

Because this evening – at exactly 11.37 p.m. – the world Harri knew ended in one catastrophic event. In the space of three and a half minutes, everyone she loved collided in an Armageddon of words, leaving mass carnage in its wake – sobbing women, shouting men and squashed vol-au-vents as far as the eye could see. Powerless to stop the devastation, she resorted to the only sensible option left available – seeking refuge in the greying vinyl haven that is the middle cubicle in the ladies' loo at Stone Yardley Village Hall.

So here she is. Sitting on the wobbly toilet, black plastic lid down, head in hands, life Officially Over. And she has no idea what to do next.

It was all Viv's idea. Harri should have said no straight away but, being Harri, she decided to give her first Sunday school teacher the benefit of the doubt.

'You know how useless Alex is at finding suitable girlfriends,'

1

Viv said, lifting a steaming apple pie from the Aga and inadvertently resembling a serene tableau from *Country Life* as she did so. 'He's hopeless! I mean, twelve girlfriends in the last year and not two brain cells between them. Danielle, Renée, Georgia, Saffron, two Marys, three Kirstys, an *India*, for heaven's sake – and the last two I can't even remember . . .'

Harri smiled into her mug of tea. 'Lucy the weathergirl and Sadie the boomerang.'

Viv looked up from her flour-dusted *Good Housekeeping* recipe book. 'The *boomerang*?'

'Yeah, you know, the one who keeps coming back when you chuck her,' Harri grinned.

'Harriet Langton, you can be awfully sharp for someone so generally charitable.'

Harri gave a bow. 'Thank you, Viv.'

'So, anyway, about Alex . . .' Viv smiled – and then presented her Big Idea. So subtle in its introduction, it seemed so innocuous that nobody could have predicted the devastation it was about to cause.

It began with a nib feature in *Juste Moi*, Viv's favourite women's glossy magazine. Between articles on the latest fashions that Hollywood starlets were scrapping over, and scarily titled features such as 'Over 50s and the Big-O', was a small column entitled 'Free to a Good Home'.

'People write in,' Viv explained, 'and nominate a man they know, to be recycled.'

'Recycled?' Harri repeated incredulously. 'Into *what*? That sounds horrific.'

'It's not like going to the bottle bank, Harri. It's presenting a man who's been unlucky in love – you know, divorced, recently separated or just plain rubbish at finding the right girl – to a whole new audience.'

'I can't believe that works,' Harri giggled. 'I mean, who writes in to a magazine to ask out a guy they've never met?'

Viv shot her a Hard Paddington Stare. '*Plenty* of people, apparently. You would be amazed at how many responses this column gets. Listen to this. "Our February 'Free to a Good Home' candidate, Joshua, received over two thousand letters from women across the UK, all keen to prove to him that true love is still very much alive and well. Josh thanks all of you who replied, and is currently whittling the responses down to his top ten, whom he will contact shortly to arrange dates. Good luck, ladies!" How about that? What does that tell you, Harri?'

Harri wrinkled her nose. 'It tells me that there are too many desperate women out there. Two thousand sad, lonely and deluded individuals letting their dreams get abused in the name of journalism.'

Viv's enthusiasm was unabated. 'It does not. It means that concerned friends and mothers – like, well, *me*, for example – can have the opportunity to find someone truly worthy of the men they care about. After all, we mothers know our sons better than anyone else, so who better to pick the perfect girlfriend for them?'

'It sounds kind of creepy to me. And what about the women who write in? How do you know that the guy you're pinning your hopes on isn't some sad loser who's single for a very good reason – like halitosis, or strange hobbies, or an unhealthy aversion to personal hygiene?'

'It's all very well for you, Harriet, you have a lovely boyfriend. You've been in a relationship with Rob for so long that you've forgotten the pain of being single. Alex doesn't have that luxury, remember. So I'm just acting in his best interests.'

'You aren't thinking about nominating Alex, are you?' Harri

3

felt like her eyebrows were raising so high they would soon be visible above her head, making her look like a Looney Tunes cartoon character. 'No way, Viv! How would he feel if he knew his own mother had put him up for auction in this meat market?'

'I'm not suggesting *I* nominate him, sweetheart,' Viv said with a reproachful motherly smile.

'I'm glad to hear it.'

'I'm suggesting *you* nominate him.'

The suggestion hung in the air between them, sparkling in its audacity. Harri needed a few moments to take it in.

'*Sorry?*'

'Well, I can't do it, can I? Al would instantly dismiss the notion on the grounds of me being an interfering mother.'

'And he wouldn't do the same with an interfering best friend?'

Viv looked sheepish and folded her hands contritely. 'Harri, I honestly wouldn't ask you if it wasn't the only way to help my son. I'm worried about him – despite what he thinks about me being a nosy old busybody.'

'It's a really bad idea. He'd be mortified by it – I know I would.'

'But he doesn't need to know about the magazine part. And we could vet all the replies he gets.' She pointed at the picture of the last successful candidate. 'Over two thousand replies for him – and, let's face it, he's not exactly a supermodel. Just imagine the choice we could have for Alex!'

Harri had to agree that Joshua the 'Free to a Good Home' nominee had a face only a mother could love. Alex, on the other hand, had no problem attracting the opposite sex. It was just attracting the right kind that he struggled with.

'I know he needs help, Viv, but is this really the best option?'

'You know better than most how woefully inept my son is at forming meaningful relationships. You've had the pleasure of living through each disaster with him. I know he confides in you.'

'All the same, it sounds like a nutty idea to me.'

'Well, my son seems to live his life by nutty ideas. You don't just walk out of a perfectly good job and go travelling around the world for ten years if you're in any way sane, do you? The point is, Harri, Alex is a lovely, honest, good-looking young man and he will be a fantastic catch for the right young woman. Besides, you're always saying that he goes for the wrong sort of girls – so this is the perfect opportunity to find the *right sort of girl* for him. Don't you think?'

Viv had definitely missed her true calling, Harri mused. She would have made a great prime minister, or UN negotiator, or crazed terrorist . . . But despite it all, Viv was right: Alex possessed a near legendary bad taste in women. It was also true that Harri suspected Alex deliberately pursued women he had little intention of settling down with.

Of course, if Harri could have seen into the future, she would have refused, point blank. She would have laughed it off, changed the subject, or just grabbed her coat and left. But right then, she decided it was better to be involved and keep Viv in check than it was to risk Alex's mother doing it alone.

So Harri said yes. And that's when the trouble started.

CHAPTER TWO

Best Friends

'Harri? Are you in there?'

Behind the locked cubicle door, Harri remains silent. There is an awkward pause on the other side, and the sound of kitten heels nervously tapping, as the woman standing by the basins appears to be debating her next line.

'Um . . . listen, Harri, this probably isn't as bad as it looks right now. I mean . . . um . . . OK, it does look pretty bad, actually, but if you just come out I'm sure we can discuss this calmly and rationally with everyone . . . um . . . well, with the people who haven't left yet or . . . um . . . gone to hospital . . .'

Another pause. Then a large sigh.

'Well, OK, I'll . . . I'll leave you to think about it, hon.'

The ladies' loo door opens and the kitten heels beat a hasty retreat.

Harri shakes her head.

Stella Smith was Harri's oldest and dearest friend.

They met on Harri's first day at school, in the small playground at the front of Stone Yardley Village Primary. Harri was five and a half, and was beginning her schooling there six months later than most of her classmates, having recently moved to the area from her birthplace in Yorkshire.

Her first memory of Stella was of a tall, dark-blonde-haired girl in a red polo-neck jumper – which appeared both to accentuate her long fingers and elongate her neck like a Masai tribeswoman – heading confidently towards her, clutching a large bag of crisps.

'Shall we be friends?' Stella asked (although it was more of a command than a question).

'Yes,' Harri replied.

Stella smiled at her new friend. 'Good. Have a Monster Munch then.'

And that was it.

Twenty-two years later, their taste in refreshments had matured from Irn-Bru and Wagon Wheels to lattes and Starbucks' Skinny Peach and Raspberry Muffins, but Stella and Harri's friendship remained strong as ever.

To the casual observer, Harri and Stella's friendship might have appeared to be a strange mix. Stella was well-known for commanding attention wherever she went (now being nearly six feet tall with long bottle-blonde hair, cheekbones to die for and practically no inhibitions makes that easy). Harri, on the other hand, was quietly confident and assured; barely five feet four with wavy auburn curls, big blue eyes and more than a healthy dose of common sense. But when they were together, something magical happened. In Stella's company Harri found she could be herself, whilst Stella felt safe, accepted and loved. It was, in many ways, the perfect combination.

Harri chose one of their frequent coffee-shop visits to tell Stella about Viv's Big Idea.

'She wants you to do *what*?' Stella spluttered, almost choking on her macchiato.

'Hmm, that was pretty much my reaction,' said Harri.

'No flippin' way on this earth!' Stella's shoulders rocked

wildly as she let out a huge guffaw. It was a truth universally acknowledged that Stella's laugh had the potential to stop traffic.

'Oh. My. Life! I hope you said no?'

Harri looked down into the foam of her cappuccino. 'I *should* have said no . . . But she had a point.'

'Her point being?'

Harri sighed. 'Alex is rubbish at dating. No, actually, he's very good at dating, it's just that he's rubbish at finding the right sort of women to date.'

'Or brilliant at finding weird and wonderful bunny-boilers,' Stella suggested.

'Yeah, absolutely.'

'It's quite a skill he has there. Maybe he could offer his services for rooting out strange women. He could make a fortune!'

Harri grinned. 'Honestly, Stel, I love Al dearly, but I've seen him devastated by his nightmare love life so many times . . .'

'Usually at three in the morning, by the sounds of it.'

'Don't worry, after the last time he did that I made it perfectly clear that my emergency heart-to-heart service was only available during daylight hours.'

'All the same, H, most people would've called time on him by now.'

'Probably. But the problem remains that he doesn't ever seem to learn from his mistakes. So maybe this crazy idea is worth a try. At least if Viv and I are vetting the candidates we can make sure the oddballs don't get through.'

Stella snorted. 'Oh, Viv's promised to help you, has she? Well, I'll believe *that* when I see it.'

'No, she will, it's all sorted.'

'Yeah, *right*. I think I just saw a pig in a Spitfire overhead . . .'

Harri giggled. 'You're so cruel. I believe her this time.'

'Good for you. But what happens if Alex – your Official Best Male Friend in the Whole Wide World – disowns you for nominating him in the first place, eh? I would be *livid* if I found out my best friend had put me up for a magazine love auction.'

'I know. But knowing Viv she'll concoct an even dafter plan than this if I don't stop her. At least if I'm there to steer her I can protect Al from the wild vagaries of his mother's imagination.'

During the following week, Harri mulled the Big Idea over and over, as she sat behind her desk at Sun Lovers International Travel.

The scratched metal name plaque on her MDF desk read 'Travel Advisor', but a more truthful (if prohibitively longer) description might have been 'Travel Advisor Who Tries in Vain to Get Stone Yardley People to Visit Amazing Places She Longs to Go to Herself'.

Sun Lovers International Travel was not as grand and corporate as its name suggested. In fact, SLIT (as it was affectionately known by its owner – and acknowledged with a whole different connotation by its staff) was a small, single-fronted shop in Stone Yardley High Street. In its only window, carefully placed posters promised exotic adventures across the globe: Australia, Thailand, India and the USA, by luxurious air travel; whilst the handwritten offer cards Blu-Tacked to the window suggested altogether homelier destinations: Blackpool, Weston-super-Mare and Rhyl – usually by coach.

Business had been slow all week, and by Friday morning, with all of Harri's jobs ticked off her list, she took the opportunity to lose herself in a glossy brochure for Venice.

Venice. The place that had started it all . . . She smiled as familiar images of the city she'd loved from afar for so many years met her eyes. Grand *palazzi*, elegant buildings reflecting in the deep green-blue canals, brightly attired carnival-goers milling amongst tourists and city dwellers, as if being swathed head to toe in opulent velvet was as commonplace as buying your daily coffee . . . She could almost hear the sounds of the city wafting up from the brochure pages, almost taste the plates of delicious *cicchetti* snacks or the tangy limoncello . . . *One day*, she promised herself, as she had done a million times before, *one day I'll be standing there* . . .

She was brought sharply back to reality by Tom, SLIT's trainee travel advisor and cultivator of some of the most impressive acne ever seen in Stone Yardley, who let out an enormous, adolescent sigh and flopped down on the chair opposite Harri's desk.

'Bored, bored, *bored*,' he chanted, Buddhist-style, staring wide-eyed through his mop of oily, blond curls.

Harri quickly closed the brochure and smiled at him. 'Loving your work again, Tom?'

'Oh, totally. "Come and work in the travel industry, Tom, you get to see the world!" Yeah, right.'

'Welcome to Sun Lovers International Travel,' Harri smiled, reaching across to pat his hand. 'So tell me, what exciting destinations have you dealt with today?'

Tom groaned. 'Barmouth. Isle of Wight. And I almost sold a flight to Dublin.'

'Dublin? Wow! What stopped the sale?'

'Mrs Wetton didn't realise it was outside England. She doesn't believe in travelling abroad.'

Harri laughed. 'Hmm, well, *Dublin*, that's almost another *time zone*. I mean, they have different money and everything.'

Tom shifted his lanky frame awkwardly in the chair. At six foot four, he was almost a foot taller than anyone else on the staff, so wherever he stood or sat he appeared to have outgrown his environment like Alice in her Wonderland.

'Why do you do this, Harri? I mean, you've been here for – how long?'

'Nearly eight years.' She could hardly believe it was true.

'Yeah, exactly. And in all that time what's the most exotic destination you've sold a holiday to?'

What was so sad about the question was that Harri didn't even have to think about the answer. 'Morocco. And the Harpers didn't like it because it was "too foreign".'

'What is wrong with people in this town? If it isn't a coach tour, they don't want to know.'

'*Luxury* coach tour, thank you,' Harri corrected him with mock disdain.

'Oh, yeah, luxury coach travel. Would that be Somers Travel Direct coaches, by any chance?' Tom smirked. '*STD* coaches – they didn't think about that one, did they?'

Harri laughed. She was certain that Albert Somers, local businessman, who had run his family coach firm for forty-five years, had never thought twice about the unfortunate initials. Yet it was a constant source of amusement to the staff when prim and proper elderly residents of Stone Yardley said things like, 'We love STDs,' or, 'I don't know what we would have done without STDs all these years!' or, 'I just couldn't imagine a holiday without STDs.'

'I guess we're just unfortunate to be working with the most unimaginative travellers in the entire world,' Tom sighed, stretching out his impossibly long legs and knocking over a pile of brochures by a neighbouring desk. 'Oh crap!'

Harri left her chair to help him retrieve the brochures,

casting a cursory glance across each shiny exotic cover as it passed through her hands: India, the Far East, the Caribbean, Hawaii . . . A brochure on Trinidad and Tobago fell open at a page of colonial houses surrounded by lush green palms and azure waters. Harri and Tom paused almost reverently and shared an unspoken moment of wistful awe.

'I can't understand why these people want to stay in the UK all the time when there's this big amazing world out there,' Tom said, shaking his head. 'I just want to travel *anywhere* that isn't here. So far, I've only managed Spain, Italy and France, but I've got so many more on my list that I want to see before I'm twenty-five. And I'm glad you understand, mate. I mean – case in point: you understand travel, right? So – where's the most exotic place you've ever been?'

Harri winced. She hated this question and she felt her heart sinking to her toes. Because despite being so passionate about travel, despite knowing all she knew about destinations across the globe, Harri had only once set foot outside of the UK – on a day trip to Calais with her school. In fact, she had only ever been on a plane once: a small bi-plane that flew her round the local airfield on a half-hour trip, as a treat for her ninth birthday.

Tom's jaw made a swift bid to meet the brown carpet tiles. '*Seriously?*'

'Seriously. My parents were scared of flying, so we always had holidays in Yorkshire, Wales or the Lake District. I love it there – don't get me wrong – but I've always dreamed of travelling.'

'So how come you've never just done it?'

Harri loathed this question too. As usual, she dusted off the old excuses. 'Life just didn't turn out the way I planned it, that's all. I got too involved in college, then Dad got sick and

12

our holidays became respite care for him, with our relatives in Yorkshire and Cumbria.'

Tom flushed a spotty shade of crimson. 'Right, and then your mum . . .'

Harri swallowed hard and looked down at the stack of brochures on the floor. 'Yeah. So after everything with them I bought my house, got the job here and then I met Rob and started going camping with him.'

'*Camping?*' Tom laughed. 'Wow, your fella knows how to give you a good time, doesn't he?' He ducked expertly, as Harri made a swipe at him with the last brochure.

'Cheeky. I actually like camping, you know. Besides, Rob makes anywhere we go fun. I can't tell you how lovely it's been to have him in my life after feeling so alone without Mum and Dad. Yes, I'd love to travel, but right now, with Rob's job the way it is, plus the recession and everything, going abroad just isn't feasible for us. One day, it will be and then I'll be off.'

'Tell me about it. If I don't save some money soon, I'm never going to be able to get out of this dump,' Tom confided, lowering his voice in case their boss was earwigging from his office. 'I mean, Georgie Porgie in there isn't likely to give us a pay rise while he can use the "we're in an economic downturn" excuse.' His brown eyes twinkled and he jabbed Harri playfully with his elbow. 'You *really* go camping with Rob?'

Harri smiled. 'Yep. Every year.'

'Thomas! In the unlikely event that you actually decide to do anything resembling *work* today, that window display needs refreshing sometime before the end of the twenty-first century.'

'Yes, boss.' Tom winked at Harri. 'Ever get the feeling that George was trained by the interception squad at MI5?'

'I can hear your sarcasm from here, Thomas!'

'Right, *fine*. Sorry, H, better go before George busts a blood vessel or shops us to the KGB.'

Harri waved. 'Have fun.'

'Cheers. So – Rob does take you to *different* places camping, right?'

'Of course! We've been all over – usually the Lake District but sometimes Snowdonia or Pembrokeshire too. We just drive around until we find a campsite and then explore the area for a couple of days before we move on. It's nice to not be tied to a schedule, you know? And Rob's great at planning little surprises for us. There was one time when we were staying at a site on a hill farm near Troutbeck and Rob arranged a candlelit meal for us, snuggled under travel blankets watching shooting stars in the sky over the mountains. I honestly couldn't have been happier anywhere else on earth that night.'

Tom's spotty face was a picture as he walked away. 'Ugh. Pass me the sick bucket, *purrlease* . . .'

Harri's tales of Rob's makeshift romantic gestures were far better received by Stella, despite the fact that, as far as she was concerned, public displays of affection were nothing if they didn't include luxury, indulgence and a hefty blow on a credit card.

'I know your Rob is a sweetie, but why on earth hasn't he taken you abroad yet?' she asked, one Wednesday evening, when Harri had arrived for a chat after work. 'He's been in your life for seven years, Harri – you'd think he would've at least whisked you off to Paris or somewhere by now.'

Harri dunked a chocolate digestive biscuit in her tea. 'He says he just doesn't feel comfortable being somewhere where he can't speak the language. But I suspect it's because he doesn't like flying. His mum told me that a couple of years ago – I'm not supposed to know, but it makes sense when you think about it.'

'I suppose so. Hey, maybe he'll spring a big trip abroad on you when he pops the question.'

Harri raised her mug. 'I'll drink to that!'

Every year, Stella promised to take Harri abroad with her. Around January or February, she'd beg Harri to bring home the latest brochures from work so that they could spend happy evenings poring over impossibly gorgeous destinations. Over countless bottles of wine, takeaways and coffee-shop visits they would plan their Big Girly Adventure: 'like Thelma and Louise without the death or guns,' Stella would quip. But somehow, as summer approached, she would find a new man and get so caught up in romantic stuff that Harri would inevitably get invited for 'a really nice meal out' and receive a tearful confession somewhere around dessert. This would generally go something like: 'I know I promised I'd take you with me this year, but before I could say no I'd agreed to go with [delete as appropriate] Joe/Mark/Matt/Juan [yes, really], but I completely, honestly promise we'll go somewhere next year . . .'

Despite the annual let-downs, Stella's ill-timed romantic liaisons weren't the problem. Neither was the recession, the weak pound or the rising cost of airport taxes. And, despite what Stella and Viv said, Rob wasn't the problem, either. At the end of the day, it was down to *her*.

Every year, Harri would entertain the notion of choosing a destination from a travel brochure at SLIT, packing a case and heading off somewhere on her own. But when she thought it through, the reality of spending two weeks by herself began to tarnish the dream. What was the point of seeing wonderful places if you had nobody to share them with? Unlike Viv's son Alex, who seemed entirely at home in his own company, for Harri the prospect held no allure. Ever since her parents died, she had become all too familiar with the sense of aloneness – why

15

would she want to take that with her to another country? One day, she knew she would be able to do this and love it. But until she could overcome the fear of the unknown, she was content to stay as she was. Surely holidaying with Rob in the UK was far more fun than being abroad alone, wasn't it?

In Harri's world, there were two versions of herself: the confident, spontaneous one in her mind, who would throw caution to the wind and go wherever her heart desired; then the *real* Harri – thinking about things too much and planning imaginary journeys from the safety of her little cottage at the far end of Stone Yardley village.

One day, she frequently told herself, *one day I'll stop worrying about it and just go.*

So, instead, Harri would buy another travel book and spend hours poring over the intricate details of other people's adventures across the world. She became an armchair traveller – fluent in three languages and a dab hand at pub quizzes whenever travel questions came up. The world in her mind was safe, constantly accessible and, most importantly, just *hers* – a secret place she could escape to without anyone else knowing. For years, this had been her solitary pursuit. Until she met Alex. Then, all of a sudden, she wasn't alone.

CHAPTER THREE

All About Alex

A cold breeze blowing through the gaps in the grubby skylight above Harri's head increases and small drops of rain begin to hit the toughened glass. She shivers and hugs her thin cardigan round her, feeling goose bumps prickling along her shoulders.

Trying to take her mind off the cold, she looks around the vinyl walls of the cubicle, absent-mindedly reading the motley collection of graffiti. There's quite a selection of revelations ('Debbie is a dog', 'Kanye Jones luvs ur mutha' and 'Sonia likes it backwards', to name but a few), along with some startling creativity (one wit has written 'Escape Hole', with an arrow pointing to a Rawlplugged scar where a toilet-roll holder once was). Over in one corner of the cubicle, by a rusting chrome door hinge, one small message catches her eye:

ALex woz eRe

Harri catches her breath and shuts her eyes tight.

When Alex Brannan moved back to Stone Yardley, Harri's world suddenly became a whole lot bigger.

Viv's only son had always been around when Harri was

growing up, but she'd never really had that much to do with him; their paths rarely crossed. It was only when he returned from ten years of travelling the world that their friendship began in earnest.

It started with the closure of Stone Yardley's traditional tea rooms, three years ago.

When the Welcome Tea Rooms closed, many locals declared it a sad day for the town, bewailing the loss of an institution. The truth was, however, that most of those who complained had not actually set foot in said institution for many years, largely because it was anything but welcoming. The proprietress, Miss Dulcie Danvers, was a wiry, formidable spinster who had inherited the shop from her maiden aunt. No amount of scalding hot tea or stodgy home-baked scones that made your teeth squeak could combat the frosty atmosphere of the place: so you ordered (apologetically), you consumed your food in self-conscious silence and you got out of there as soon as possible. Finally, at the age of seventy-three, Miss Danvers admitted defeat and retired to a sheltered housing scheme in the Cotswolds.

For several months the former café lay empty and lifeless in Stone Yardley's High Street, a gaping wound in the bustling town centre, but then, at the end of October, the For Sale sign disappeared from the shop front and work began on its interior. Residents noticed lights ablaze inside and shadowy figures moving around late into the night. Three weeks later, a sign appeared on the door: 'New Coffee Lounge opening soon.'

A week after that, Viv asked Harri if she'd like to go to the launch party of her son's new venture.

'You remember Alex, don't you?'

Harri nodded politely, although what recollections she did possess were decidedly vague. 'He's in London, isn't he?'

Viv pulled a face. 'Well, he *was*, but the least said about *that* particular episode, the better. Anyway, the point is that he's moved back to Stone Yardley and he's starting his own business.'

'What's he doing?' Harri asked.

Viv beamed the kind of proud smile that parents wear when watching their children performing in a nativity play (even if they're awful). 'He's taken over the old Welcome Tea Rooms. It's going to be quite different and I think he's worried that nobody will turn up. Would you mind awfully?'

'No, not at all. Rob's away working this weekend so I have a free night on Friday.'

The moment Harri set foot inside Wātea, she felt at home. Alex had transformed the dark café into a relaxed, warm and welcoming coffee lounge. Large, comfy leather armchairs rested on a green slate floor, whilst a bar by the window – made from what looked like a large driftwood beam – offered a great view of the High Street outside. Travel books and magazines were stacked casually in wicker baskets by the sides of the chairs, and treasures from Alex's travels adorned the walls: South American paintings, an African mask, Maori figures and Native American blankets.

But it was the photographs that caught Harri's eye and made her heart skip. Beaches and rainforests, deserts and islands, snow-covered mountain peaks and azure ocean vistas. And the star of every picture, in various wildly dramatic poses – and always with a huge grin – was Alex.

While the other guests sampled coffee and ate tiny cocktail *quesadillas*, spicy chorizo and olive skewers, and shot glasses of intense gazpacho, Harri moved silently round the room, letting her fingers brush lightly against the richly woven textiles and ethnic sculptures as she gazed at the photos. She was looking intently at a picture of an Inca settlement when a deep voice close behind her made her jump.

'Machu Picchu. I loved it there. The altitude is amazing, though – you have to move really slowly so you don't get out of breath.'

Harri spun round. She came face to face with a wooden Maori-carved bead necklace and lifted her eyes till they met the huge-grinned star of the photos. Alex extended his hand quickly, suddenly self-conscious, running the other hand through his sandy-brown mop of hair. 'Hi. Sorry to make you jump there. I'm Alex.'

Harri smiled and took his large warm hand in hers. 'Hi, I'm Harri. This place is amazing . . .'

'Ooooh, fantastic! You two have already met?' Viv exclaimed, appearing suddenly between them, as if by magic. 'Al, darling, you remember Harriet Langton, don't you?'

Alex's large brown eyes widened in surprise as he took a step back and looked Harri up and down, almost as if he couldn't believe what he was seeing. 'No way! *Chubby Harri* with the pigtails?'

'Yes!' Viv beamed. 'Little *Chubby* Harriet!'

'But . . . but the last time I saw her she was, ooh, *this* tall?' Alex motioned to just above his waist.

'I *know*!' Viv agreed. 'She's a fair bit different now, though, eh?'

'She certainly is,' Alex replied, looking so intently at Harri that she could feel a blush creeping up the back of her neck.

Viv's eyes misted. 'Her mother would've been so proud of her. All grown up and standing in your new coffee lounge!'

Harri lifted a hand and waved weakly between them. 'Hello? I'm actually here. And may I just remind you both that I was given that evil nickname when I was *four years old*?'

'Aww,' Viv gathered her up into a hearty embrace, which nearly expelled all the air from her lungs, 'sorry, my darling. Harri works at the travel agent's a few doors down from here, Al. She knows everything there is to know about, well, just about anywhere in the world. You should ask her over and show her all that strange stuff from your travels. Ooh, and your photos too! Wouldn't that be lovely, Harri?'

It was Alex's turn to be embarrassed. '*Mum . . .*' he protested, rubbing the back of his neck and staring at the floor, 'I'm sure she doesn't want to see all that . . .'

'No, no, I would. Really. It would be great,' Harri said quickly.

Alex looked up at her, his expression a strange mix of amusement and genuine surprise. 'Seriously? Nobody's ever asked to see my stuff before – I usually just bore people to death with it whether they like it or not.'

Harri smiled. 'Trust me, I would love to find out where you've been and what you've seen. My boyfriend says I'm an armchair-travel junkie, so you'll be helping to fuel my addiction.'

Alex's eyes twinkled and the broad grin from his photographs made another appearance. 'Well, in that case I'd be happy to oblige. We'll co-ordinate diaries and do it!'

Harri told Rob the following Monday evening about Alex and his invitation to dinner. Over the weekend, she had suddenly started to worry that perhaps Rob wouldn't be pleased in this relative stranger's interest in his girlfriend, but her fears soon proved unfounded.

'I think it's a great idea,' Rob smiled over the top of *Survival Monthly*.

'Are you sure you don't mind that he's invited me for a meal?'

'Not at all.' He shook his head, lowered the magazine and

reached over to stroke her cheek. 'You haven't been worrying about that, have you?'

'A little.'

'Well, you don't have to. An evening of travel gossip sounds right up your street and it will be good to chat to someone who shares your travel thing. Let's face it – I'm not the best audience when it comes to that, am I?' He smiled that deliciously crooked smile of his, which never failed to make her heart skip. 'So you get a night of travel trivia and I get let off that duty for once. Everyone's a winner.'

Encouraged by her boyfriend's words, Harri began to look forward to the evening with Alex. But as the week progressed, a new concern began to root itself in her head: would they find enough to talk about for a whole evening? After all, she could barely remember Alex – for all she knew about him he might as well be a complete stranger. Added to this, how would she fare in the company of a bona fide traveller, when all of her knowledge was based on other people's experiences? Would she feel a fraud by comparison?

It was still playing on her mind when she arrived at her aunt's shop on Thursday lunchtime. Eadern Blooms had served as Stone Yardley's florist for thirty-five years and, with the exception of a new sign over the door and an A-board for the street (which Harri had persuaded Auntie Rosemary to invest in the year before), the shop hadn't changed. The sunny yellow tiles and white-painted walls were simple but perfect for making the flowers stand out – they were, after all, the stars of the show, as far as Rosemary was concerned. As she entered the shop, Harri said hello to Mrs Gilbert from the cake shop, who was leaving with a paper-wrapped bunch of deep purple lisianthus.

'Hello, Harriet, how's the world today?' Mrs Gilbert smiled.

'Quiet, as far as Stone Yardley's concerned,' Harri replied, holding the door open for her. 'Having a good week?'

'Manic! Dora's introduced her new Irish Coffee Cheesecake this week and we've been run off our feet. Sugarbuds hasn't been this busy since Christmas.'

Auntie Rosemary was in the workroom at the back of the shop when Harri approached the counter, so Harri tapped the hotel-style brass bell to summon her aunt's attention. It was something she had done since she was little, relishing the thrill of ringing the bell when her parents had brought her into the shop. She called out, just like her dad had done, 'Shop!'

Rosemary's flustered face appeared in the hatchway, which opened to the workroom. 'Hello, you. Let me just wrap this bouquet and I'll be right with you.'

Harri absent-mindedly turned the rotating unit on the counter that held a selection of cards for inserting into floral arrangements. Most of them looked as old as the shop: faded painted pink and yellow roses, watercolour storks carrying blanketed babies, white arum lilies bending their heads in sympathy and linked horseshoes surrounded by fluttering confetti. Harri wondered if anyone actually chose to use one of these cards, or if they, like the brass bell and sunshine-yellow vinyl floor tiles, were simply irreplaceable elements of the shop's heart.

Five minutes later, Auntie Rosemary bustled in, strands of silver-grey hair flying loose in all directions from the messy bun at the back of her head, and a roll of twine around her right hand like a post-modern bangle. 'I'm here, I'm here,' she exclaimed, placing her cool hands on Harri's cheeks and kissing her forehead, 'and so are you! So, the kettle's on and I've got some sandwiches from Lavender's – tell me all your news.'

They pulled up wooden chairs behind the counter and ate

their crusty sandwiches from Stone Yardley's bakery as Harri shared recent events with her aunt.

When she mentioned her concerns about dinner with Alex, Auntie Rosemary frowned and took a large gulp of tea.

'I don't think you need worry, Harriet, I'm sure you'll have plenty to talk about.'

'But he's actually *done* the travelling thing. I've just read about it. I think I'm just worried that he'll laugh at me.'

'Don't be so silly, sweetheart. From my scant experience of men, I can tell you that one thing they like is to be listened to. And if the person listening to them knows *less* about a subject than they do, then all the better. I would hazard a guess that Alex is no different. You're a fantastic listener and you'll be interested in all of his travel stories – what more could he want in a dinner guest?'

'You're probably right. I'm sorry, Auntie Ro. You know me, always thinking three steps ahead.'

Rosemary smiled and brushed crumbs off her fluffy grey cardigan. 'In that respect you're the spitting image of your mother. She was a born organiser – and so are you. Worrying ahead comes with the territory, I suppose.'

'So you think I'll be fine?'

Her aunt stood up and ruffled Harri's hair. 'I think you'll have a fantastic time.'

In the end, it was Stella who – in classic Stella Smith fashion – allayed her fears by summing up the situation in one sentence.

'He seems like a nice bloke, there's free food and you get to overdose on travel stories. It's a no-brainer: stop thinking too much and just go.'

So the next week Harri arrived at Wātea for dinner. Alex was just finishing for the day and looked shattered. She waited while he turned off lights and checked everything was ready for the morning.

'Busy day?' she asked, as he joined her by the counter.

Alex rubbed his forehead. 'Yeah. It's been crazy since we opened. I was worried people would stay away because we're not like the old place.'

Harri laughed. 'Did you ever *visit* the old place?' Alex shook his head. 'Then you don't know what you're missing! I mean, look around here: the place is far too welcoming. You should be putting the fear of God into anyone who dares set foot on the premises! And those sofas? Too comfy by far! What are you trying to do, make people *want* to stay here?'

'Blimey, was it that bad?'

'Yes, it was. Trust me, this place is just what Stone Yardley needs.'

'Thank you.'

'You're welcome.'

They exchanged shy smiles.

Alex pushed his hands into his pockets self-consciously. 'So – if you'd like to follow me, I'll sort out some food.'

Up in his flat above the coffee lounge, Alex made Singapore Noodles while Harri walked around, gazing at the photos that covered the walls. After they'd eaten, she sat cross-legged on the floor, cradling a steaming mug of jasmine tea and trying to contain her excitement like a kid at Christmas, as Alex produced box after box of treasures. Postcards, fabrics, sculptures, seashells and countless photo albums emerged and were spread out over the floor, while Alex recalled his travels and Harri listened, wide-eyed, her mind brimming over with images almost too wonderful to bear.

'This shell came from Philip Island, in Australia – you should see the penguins there, Harri. It's just mad to be surrounded

25

by them on a beach! . . . An old priest in Belarus gave me this icon – he said it would keep me safe on my journey. Then he prayed over the coach we were travelling in, except he had to use a prayer for blessing a horse and cart because it was the only one for a mode of transport in the prayer book.'

Harri picked up a picture of Alex standing next to a Maori man, easily half a foot taller and almost twice as wide, with an enormous white smile that dwarfed even Alex's grin. The smiley Maori had his arm slung around Alex's shoulders and they looked like they'd just heard the most hilarious joke.

'Who's this?' she asked, turning the photo towards him.

'Oh, wow, that's Tem – he's a great guy I met on South Island in New Zealand. He ran the local bar and he gave me a job for three weeks when my funds were running low. He taught me some Maori – that's where *Wātea* comes from. It means "to be open" or "free". He said I was a free spirit and I had to stay like that, wherever I went. I learned a lot from him.'

Harri looked at the collection of mementoes laid out before her and shook her head. 'Al, this stuff is amazing. How come you don't have it all out on display?'

Alex shrugged. 'Because, honestly, nobody wanted to look at them – until I met you again, that is.'

'That's crazy. This stuff is . . .' she struggled for a moment as all the superlatives that came to mind seemed suddenly inadequate. 'I think this is wonderful, Alex. You have no idea how lucky you are to have all these memories.'

Alex smiled, his dark brown eyes catching the light from the group of tealight candles on the coffee table. 'I think we're going to be great friends, you and me,' he said. 'Soul mate travellers, that's what we are.'

Harri wasn't exactly sure what a 'soul mate traveller' was,

but she was happy to be called one nevertheless. This, she was to learn, was one of the things that set Alex apart from the others in Stone Yardley: he had a vocabulary for his world that surpassed the horizons of anyone else. Looking through his eyes, Harri saw the world around her in a new, altogether more attractive light. Alex was the ultimate dreamer – hopelessly optimistic about everything he surveyed. Even the most mundane thing became a magical mystery tour when he was involved – like the time he turned mopping the floor into a game of curling, using two steel buckets as stones and mops like the brushes. And while his unrealistic view of life lay at the bottom of many of his romantic problems, often landing him with a broken heart, at least when Alex was around life was never dull.

Over the next year, their friendship grew with each Wednesday night meal. Alex cooked dishes he had collected during his ten years travelling the world and Harri listened to his stories as the scents of spices, meats, fish and fruit fragranced the flat above Wātea.

'Pad Thai,' he announced, one evening, as spicy cinnamon, chilli and allspice-infused steam filled Harri's nostrils. 'They cook this everywhere in Thailand – little street stalls serving this up on almost every street corner. I got the recipe from Kito, a Japanese lady who moved to Phuket twenty years before when she married a local man – she was the landlady in the hostel where I was staying. Her Thai mother-in-law had insisted that Kito master the dish before she gave her blessing to the marriage, "so I know my son won't starve" – and Kito had cooked it ever since.'

Meeting Alex was as refreshing as Welsh mountain air; his sense of humour, wry view of the world around him and intense interest in other people made him irresistible company.

And as the weeks stretched to months, Harri found herself increasingly opening up to him – more than she had to Stella, Viv or even Auntie Rosemary. In turn, Alex's trust in Harri grew – leading, eventually, to the subject of his not-so-wonderful love life one Tuesday evening when Harri received a text as she was about to go to bed.

Hey H, are you still up? Fancy a chat? Al ;)

Harri almost ignored it, the lure of her warm bed and favourite Venice book vying for her attention, but Alex had never contacted her so late before and that alone was enough to make her call him.

He sounded tired when he answered, the spark gone from his voice. 'Mate, I'm sorry for texting so late.'

'Is everything OK, Al?'

He gave a long sigh. 'I'm fine, really. I just had my last date with Claudia – you know, the accountant I've been seeing for a couple of weeks?'

'Oh, hon. What happened?'

'Man, I don't know. She just isn't the woman I thought she was. Turns out the only reason she agreed to date me was because she wanted to make her ex jealous.'

'Ah.'

'And, apparently, the plan worked. Hence my final date. After all that I just needed to speak to someone normal, you know?'

Harri laughed. 'Oh, let me guess: the normal person didn't answer their phone so you had to call me instead?'

'Yeah, something like that. No, actually, I value your opinion.'

Quite taken aback by this unexpected compliment, Harri took a few moments to respond. 'Oh – right – er, thanks, Al.'

The ice thus broken on the subject, discussions about Alex's love life began to pepper their Wednesday night conversations. Harri didn't mind, really – it was worth it for her armchair adventures traversing the globe.

It was about this time that Alex took the brave step of tackling the thorny subject of Harri's lack of travel.

'OK,' he said one Wednesday night as he passed a bowl of spicy, smoky Hungarian Goulash to Harri. 'Imagine right now I could give you a plane ticket to anywhere in the world.'

Harri tore a strip of still-warm walnut bread and dipped it in the paprika sauce. 'Then you'd be a millionaire and I doubt we'd be eating dinner in a tiny flat above a coffee shop.'

Alex pulled a face at her. 'Seriously, think about it, H: if you could pack a bag right now and just go anywhere, where would you go?'

'Well, it depends.'

'Depends on what? Come on, H, you don't need to plan an entire itinerary before you go. This is *make-believe*, OK?'

Harri scooped up a spoonful of goulash and blew on it, feeling cornered. 'I don't know how I'm supposed to just pick somewhere, Al. It doesn't work like that.'

'It does, Harri! I'm talking turn up at the airport – money no object – and choose anywhere in the world. Just like that.'

Harri dropped her spoon with a loud clank. 'See, that's so easy for you. Just pack your bags and go, without any thought for who or what you're leaving behind. I have responsibilities, you know: my job, my cat, Rob . . .'

Alex held his hands up. 'Whoa, Harri, my good friend, *it's not real.*' He observed her carefully. 'OK, seeing as you're so woefully inept at this, let me help you. Let's go for somewhere not too far away to start off with, like . . . like Italy, for example.' Harri felt her heart give a little leap and her face

29

must have betrayed this as Alex's smile broadened. 'Ah, good, Italy it is, then. How about Rome?'

'Maybe . . .'

'Florence?'

'I'd like to see Rome before Florence.'

Alex clapped his hands, clearly enjoying this new game. 'OK, good. Now we're getting somewhere. Er – Milan?'

Harri thought. 'I'd like to see Rome and Florence before Milan.'

'Excellent.' He drummed his fingers on the table. 'So, we need to find a destination to usurp Rome from the top spot.' He screwed his eyes up, then opened them wide, snapping his fingers. 'Aha! Got it! *Venice!*'

Harri recoiled. 'No. Not Venice.'

Surprised, Alex leaned back in his chair. 'Oh? Why not?'

She really didn't want to be drawn on this, especially as Alex didn't know about her secret longing to visit the city. 'Just not, that's all.'

'But it's meant to be beautiful, H.'

'I know, but . . .'

His eyes narrowed. 'What's Venice ever done to you, eh?'

She wriggled uncomfortably in her seat. 'Nothing. This is getting daft now. Can we change the subject, please?'

But her protestations were in vain. Alex had sensed the story beneath and wasn't going to let go without a fight. 'Nah. I want to know why not Venice. Let me guess: you don't like canals?'

'No.'

'You think it's too touristy?'

'Of course not.'

'You have an irrational fear of gondoliers?'

Harri had to laugh at that one. 'You're impossible.'

Alex smiled cheekily and took a mouthful of goulash. 'So tell me, why not Venice?'

There was no point arguing with him when he was in a mood like this. Taking a deep breath, Harri told him the truth. 'Because I don't want to go there on my own.'

'So get Rob to take you.'

She dismissed it. 'He wouldn't enjoy it, Al, you know that.'

He leaned closer. 'So, you *do* want to go to Venice?'

'Of course I do! I have so many books on the city that I could probably write a guidebook myself without ever having set foot there.'

He leaned closer. 'Really? So where's the first place you'd go when you arrived?'

Feeling her heart skip, Harri closed her eyes and she was there in the city she loved so dearly. 'Santa Maria della Salute church and the Dorsoduro, where the maskmakers have their shops,' she breathed. 'Or *anywhere*. I'd just step off the *vaporetto* onto the *fondamenta* and head off in a random direction, so I could get lost – then have fun finding my way back.'

'Blimey, you've really planned this, haven't you? So I still don't get it: if you love a place so much, why not head there first?'

Harri sighed. 'It's just that if I'm heading anywhere, like you say, leaving all my responsibilities behind, then that means I'm travelling alone, right?'

His expression clouded over. 'Er, yes, but . . .'

She stared at him. 'So why would I want to go to one of the most romantic cities on earth on my own? Venice should be somewhere you are *taken* to, by someone who loves you.'

'I see. And if the person you love doesn't want to take you there?'

Her heart sinking, she shrugged. 'Now can we change the subject, please?'

Alex agreed, but sadness filled his eyes as he watched her eating.

Two years since their first Wednesday evening – and countless whirlwind romances, acrimonious break-ups and midnight heart-to-hearts later – Harri was well versed in the Alex Brannan Rollercoaster of Life.

A week after his mother's Big Idea, Harri found herself rudely awakened by what sounded like a herd of frantic buffalo charging her front door. Struggling to focus, she grabbed her alarm clock and juggled it up to her eyes until its bouncing red numbers calmed down enough to make sense: 2.47 a.m.

Muttering murderously under her breath, she snapped on the bedside lamp (half blinding herself in the process), wrestled the duvet away from her legs and half ran, half fell down the stairs towards the unrelenting hammering of fists at the door.

'OK, OK, I'm here,' she grumbled, fumbling at the chain and wrenching the door open. 'What do you want?'

The sight of the sodden, sorry figure on her doorstep stopped her anger in its tracks as torrential rain blew into the hallway, lashing her legs. 'Alex? For heaven's sake, it's nearly three o'clock.'

'I'm sorry. I just – I didn't know where else to go . . .'

'Whatever, just come in.'

Harri turned and strode through into her tiny living room, turning on lamps as she went and cursing as she stubbed her toe on a pile of books in the dim light. Alex followed behind, his soaked jeans and sweater leaving a trail of muddy water in his wake. Wincing as the kitchen strip light blazed into life, Harri filled the kettle and noisily pulled out two mugs from the cupboard overhead, throwing haphazard spoonfuls of coffee into each one. She let out a sigh and rubbed her sleep-filled eyes with clumsy fingers. For a moment the only sounds in the kitchen were the low buzz from the strip light and the hiss of water boiling. Then, Alex spoke from the doorway.

'I'm sorry, mate.'

'Al – look, it's OK, just – just let me wake up for a minute, yeah?'

He sniffed and splodged over to the sink, twisting his sweater sleeve to release a thin stream of water. The pathetic sight made Harri laugh and Alex did the same, shaking his head as rain dripped off his brow.

'Loser,' she smirked, throwing a tea towel at him.

'Thanks,' he grinned, catching the towel and rubbing his hair with it.

Coffee made, they returned to the living room. Harri found an old T-shirt of Rob's (several sizes too small for Alex) and spread a towel on the sofa so he could sit down. With much protesting, Alex surrendered his sweater and T-shirt to the tumble dryer, peeled off his socks to hang them over the radiator and rolled up the legs of his jeans, before donning the too-small T-shirt.

'I look like a dancer in an Elton John video,' he whined, flopping down on the sofa. 'I'm going through a traumatic twist in my love life and you add insult to injury by making me wear *this*.'

'Consider it your penance for waking me up at this ungodly hour.'

'Fair enough.'

Harri sipped her coffee. 'So what happened?'

Alex's expression darkened and he stared at his bare feet. 'Ellie.'

'Who?'

'You haven't met her. She works for one of those citizen journalism websites, writing restaurant reviews.'

Harri stared at him blankly. 'Right . . .'

Alex rubbed distractedly at his hair with the tea towel and avoided eye contact. 'She wanted to review Wātea – you know, do an article on us – so I agreed. We've been meeting up for the past two weeks and it's been . . . *amazing*. Like when you just immediately connect with someone on so many levels, you know?'

'Um . . .'

'Work with me, Harri. I'm trying to set the scene.'

'Al, it's a miracle I'm awake at this hour. I don't do emotional empathy before the birds wake up.'

'Duly noted. Anyway, she came over late last Thursday and we had a meal. Then she tells me the whole interview thing was a ruse to get closer to me. She said she'd been watching me for ages and all she wanted was to be with me.'

Harri shook her head. 'Oh Al . . .'

'Seriously, though, what was I supposed to do? I mean, here's this – this *beautiful* woman, declaring her love for me . . . Well, one thing led to another and – let me just tell you – the *sex* was—'

'Thank you, I get the picture.'

Alex's grin was mischief personified. 'Sorry, mate. Damn fine, though.'

'So what went wrong?'

His expression clouded and his eyes dropped to the floor again. 'She called me last night and told me she couldn't see me any more. Just like that. Yet she's been with me every night this week and I wasn't aware of any problems. Every night, *in my bed* and then . . .'

Making a valiant effort to erase the unwanted mental image from her mind, Harri reached over and squeezed his arm. 'I'm guessing you went to see her.'

He nodded. 'I had to. I mean, I had to know. I arrived at her house and the lights were on downstairs, so I went to the door but, just as I got there, I saw *them* through the window. Her and some random guy—' He broke off, ran a hand through his damp hair and stared at the ceiling.

'Oh, Al . . .'

'I wouldn't mind so much if she'd just been honest, you know? Just wheeled out the old "it's been great fun but that's all it was" speech. But the stuff she was saying to me – even a few days ago – about me being the one she'd been looking for, about all the places we could go together . . . Why would she say all that if she had no intention of seeing it through?'

'Hun, some people just say things to get what they want.'

'Yeah, I know, but I thought she was different.'

'Evidently, she wasn't.'

Alex raised his head and looked straight into Harri's eyes. 'It's always the same. Why can't I find someone right?'

Watching her friend in the midst of dating agony, Harri thanked her lucky stars that she was so happy with Rob. Dating hadn't been a priority in her life when they met – in fact, it had come as somewhat of a surprise when she found herself falling for him. How much better to have it happen that way than to endure the constant rollercoaster of hope and disappointment! Knowing that Rob loved her, and feeling the warmth of her complete trust in him was wonderful and she wouldn't swap places with Alex for anything.

'Just chalk it up to experience and be more careful next

time,' she smiled, wrapping her arms around Alex as his face crumpled again.

'I can't do this any more,' he moaned against her shoulder. 'Help me, Harri, help me to find someone. I'm done looking for them. I'm officially rubbish. I need help.'

Viv's Big Idea appeared in her mind, sparkling like a Las Vegas sign. Harri knew she was going to regret what she said next, but she couldn't let Alex go through this again. So, squeezing his shoulders, she said: 'OK, Al. I'll help you.'

CHAPTER FOUR

Recycle Your Man

Harri can't think straight: too many voices competing for attention inside her weary mind. She looks down at her shoes – new and probably too expensive for her, bought especially for tonight – even though until the very last minute she wasn't even certain she was coming to the party at all. They are gorgeous – and they were meant to make her feel special, which they do – or did, at least until about an hour ago. *Sixty quid* for a pair of purple high heels – more than she'd ever spent before. How times change . . .

'That photographer bloke you like's got a new book out,' Rob said one Saturday morning as they were browsing the bookshelves in Bennett's Pre-Loved Books in Innersley, the market town that lay five miles from Stone Yardley. Rob and Harri had spent most of the weekends of their relationship here, mooching about the farmers' market, enjoying coffee at Harlequin Café or wandering round the various antique shops dotted along the main street, but since Rob's promotion last year to Sales Team Leader in the specialist hydraulics firm where he worked, he had been working away most weekends – so this occasion was a notable exception.

'I know, but it's forty quid,' Harri sighed. 'I can't justify that cost for a book. Even if it *is* Dan Beagle.'

Rob wrapped an arm around her shoulders. 'I know it's tough right now, but if I make good on the Preston job things'll start to look brighter.'

Harri slipped her arm round Rob's waist and leaned her head on his shoulder. 'Reckon we can scrape enough change together for a coffee?'

Rob kissed the top of her head. 'I think we can manage that. You go and grab a table and I'll buy the drinks.'

Harri walked to the side of the bookshop where a few small tables were nestled between the bookcases. Choosing one near the large window that looked out onto Innersley's Sheep Street, she sat down. The bookshop had a unique scent – dust, old leather, ink and coffee – and no matter how many times she came here, she was always bowled over by it. Watching the sun streaming through the window in swirling dusty splendour, she drank in the moment. It was days like this that she loved the most – just her and Rob, whiling away the lazy hours together.

As if he knew what she was thinking, Rob appeared, his figure cutting through the rays of sunlight as he walked towards her carrying a tray.

'Nigel took pity on us,' he grinned as he sat down. 'He said he needed help finishing off these muffins, so I volunteered our services.'

'Excellent. Good old Nigel.' As Harri took a bite of raspberry and white chocolate muffin, Rob slid a green and white striped paper bag towards her.

'And this is for you.'

Surprised, Harri stared at it. 'You haven't been spending money on me again, have you?'

Rob's eyes were full of sparkle. 'Might have. Open it and find out.'

Harri reached inside the bag and gasped. 'Dan's book! But – that's so much money, hon – you can't afford it.'

'Yes, I can. You've had your heart set on this book for months, so I wanted you to have it. No arguments, OK? If Tierney, Gratton and Parr want me to work all hours to win their precious Preston contract then I think the very least they can do is fund your travel book collection.'

Harri hugged the book to her chest. 'Thank you so much!'

'Ah, here they are!' boomed a deep voice as Nigel Bennett, owner of the bookshop, appeared by their table. Though it had been many years since he retired from the RSC in Stratford-upon-Avon, his theatrical Shakespearean delivery was still impressive – every word correctly enunciated and every 'r' rolled. 'Our semi-resident young lovers! How good to see the two of you – Lucien and I had all but given you up for lost.' He reached down and lovingly patted a doe-eyed chocolate Labrador by his side. 'Shall we imprison young Robert here to save him from Preston's clutches, Harriet?'

Harri smiled. 'Maybe we should. Thanks for the muffins – they're wonderful.'

Nigel flushed with pride and proffered a flourishing bow. 'My pleasure, dear lady. I shall leave you lovebirds to enjoy your Saturday. Adieu!'

Rob watched him go. 'Got to love Nigel.'

'Absolutely. It is great to have you all to myself this weekend, though,' Harri admitted.

'Yes, it is. Hey, I don't like working away all the time, you know.'

'I know.'

'But it's for us, Red, honestly. If I can land the Preston contract then it means we can start to think about – you know – the *future* and stuff.'

The sun streamed through the window of the bookshop in

39

swirling dusty splendour as Harri leaned against her boyfriend. It was days like these that she longed for – where anything was possible and they were together. If only Rob's company would grant him more free weekends . . .

In the past few months, Rob's mentions of 'the future' had become noticeably more frequent, fuelling Harri's hope that maybe he was leading up to formalising their commitment. He had occasionally alluded to them moving in together, but what Harri *really* wanted was for them to get married.

Truth be told, while Harri's regular attendance at Stone Yardley's parish church contributed to this decision, the main reason for her resistance to cohabiting was that she wanted to be *proposed to*. Old-fashioned it may be, but Harri maintained her hope that Rob would actually *want* to marry her. And despite the passage of seven years without any such monumental happening, Harri's hope remained. After all, Rob loved her and he was working hard to provide for their future. Therefore it was only a matter of time before he proposed. Wasn't it?

When Harri first met Rob, at a charity football match organised by Merv, Viv's on-off gentleman friend, she had been completely bowled over by him. And, it seemed, the feeling was mutual.

Rob had been talked into joining the football team by his boss at work and, hoping for a promotion, he agreed. His case was greatly helped by the fact that he was pretty nifty on the pitch, scoring three textbook goals against a team of weedy solicitors from several local law firms. Athletically built and fast on his feet, Rob ran rings around their defence and Harri couldn't take her eyes off him. He was perfect: his chestnut-brown spiky hair, hazel eyes and olive complexion, coupled with a smile that could melt chocolate, made for a killer combination. Harri couldn't help thinking he looked like Frank Lampard – the reason she had watched several televised matches, even though she possessed very little interest in the beautiful game itself. When Merv called him over to meet Harri, Rob Southwood had looked at her like all his birthdays had arrived at once.

'A redhead, eh?' he had smiled. 'I've heard they're trouble.'

'Well, you shouldn't believe everything you hear.'

'Oh, really? Then I wouldn't mind dispelling the myth with you sometime.'

'That sounds like fun,' Harri had replied.

'So how about this evening over a drink?'

'Perfect.'

So they arranged to meet, Harri hardly believing her good fortune at securing a date with the handsome stranger. Drinks had quickly become dinner, which turned into a lively, animated discussion at his house late into the night. When Harri finally stood to leave, Rob escorted her to the door, opened it and then surprised her by placing an arm across the doorway.

'You're amazing, Harri. I have to see you again.'

'I'd like that, Rob.'

Then he'd pulled her into his arms and kissed her in a way that made her toes tingle.

In the weeks and months that followed, Harri and Rob were practically inseparable. They spent every weekend together, exploring the local countryside, heading off on day trips to Cheltenham, Worcester or Oxford, walking, cycling or just sitting in coffee shops, talking for hours. Rob fascinated her – with his knowledge of nature and his endless opinions on just about everything. It became a kind of a never-ending game that Harri played, bringing up new topics to see how quickly he could form a viewpoint on them. Rob loved that she loved it too; he would answer her with a wry smile, his cheeks flushing slightly at her wholehearted interest in what he said. She still loved their discussions, but his workload had significantly lessened the times when they were possible. While her love for Rob burned as brightly as ever, she could feel a dark resentment at his growing obsession with work bubbling within her. Since the Preston contract had loomed large in their lives, their time together seemed to be dictated by the company that employed him, as it demanded more and more of Rob's time.

Of Harri's friends, Viv was the most vocal about Rob's job.

'Ooh, *that man*,' she glowered, when Harri went to visit her a few days later, slamming a large bone-china teapot onto a cast-iron stand in the middle of the large pine table in her kitchen to emphasise her disgust. 'If he put half the time he spends at that job into considering you, then you'd be married by now.'

Fearing for the teapot's safety, Harri reached across the table and gently rescued it from Viv's vice-like grip. 'I'll pour, shall I?' She was beginning to wish she'd never mentioned how much Rob's absence was upsetting her.

Viv grimaced, clearly rattled. 'Sorry. That poor teapot – it's a wonder it's still here.'

'Maybe we should get it some counselling,' Harri said, pouring tea into two china mugs.

'Do they do counselling for inanimate objects?'

'Maybe they should.'

'If they do then we can book your boyfriend in,' Viv replied with a wicked smirk. 'He's about as inanimate as you can get when it comes to proposing to you.'

'Viv, that's not fair. Rob is a fantastic boyfriend and he's working really hard for us. It isn't his fault he has to be away so often. I just miss him, that's all. And as for him proposing, well, I think that might be closer than we think. He bought me Dan's book the other day – that's the third present in a fortnight – and he keeps talking about "the future". I honestly think he might say something, once this horrible Preston stuff is over. Anyway, the way things are at the moment, he's fortunate to have a job at all, so I really shouldn't be complaining.'

Viv's expression softened and she patted Harri's hand. 'Oh, my darling girl, I only worry because I want you to be happy. It's what your mum would have wanted too . . .'

It was time to change the subject, as Harri was feeling decidedly queasy. 'So – I sent the letter.'

'Which one?'

'To *Juste Moi*. About Alex.'

Viv's eyes lit up. 'And?'

'I haven't heard anything yet.'

'Does Alex know?'

Hmm, interesting question. Alex knew that Harri was going to help him find somebody – he just didn't know *how* she was planning to do it. 'I'll tell him if they choose to feature him.'

'Excellent,' said Viv, rubbing her hands together like a silver-tressed, Laura Ashley-attired, fifty-something Bond villain. All that was missing was the large white Persian cat . . . 'Then our plan is officially in action.'

'Well, yes, *if* they accept him, that is,' Harri warned.

'*Of course* they'll accept him! He's gorgeous – way out of their usual league. I mean, you should see some of the sorry excuses for manhood they dredge up most months!'

'Let's just wait and see if they put our sorry excuse for manhood in their column, eh?'

Alex was back to his usual chirpy self when Harri arrived at

43

Wātea that afternoon – an amazing feat considering it was 'Mad Mothers' Wednesday', when the local young mums' group descended on the café. Harri picked her way carefully through the minefield of baby buggies to the counter, where Alex was filling measuring jugs with warm water and carefully balancing feeding bottles inside.

'Do me a favour, pass these to the table behind you, would you? Lady with the screaming baby.'

This description didn't exactly narrow it down, as almost every woman at the large table appeared to be wrestling a noisy bundle of animosity. In desperation, Harri held the measuring jugs aloft one by one.

'Purple stripe?'

'Over here.'

'Tommee Tippee?'

'That's mine, thanks.'

'Mothercare?'

'Which one?'

'Er – pink bunny and yellow teddy bear.'

'Bunny's mine and teddy over there.'

Alex looked appreciative when she turned back to him. 'You're a natural, mate. Are you sure you don't want to change your career and work for me?'

'What, and leave my exciting jet-set lifestyle at SLIT? No chance!'

Alex returned to the espresso machine, grabbed a coffee arm and banged out the spent grounds. Filling it afresh from the coffee dispenser and tamping it down, he reattached the arm and set a mug underneath to catch the thick brown liquid as it dripped lazily from the machine. No matter how many times Harri watched him do this it never failed to fascinate her. There's something incredibly powerful about watching someone work, Harri always found: Stella swiftly typing a letter without looking at the keyboard once; Viv cooking; Auntie Rosemary assembling a bouquet of flowers in one hand as she floated around her shop; even her completely barmy Grandpa Jim building some Heath-Robinsonish contraption in the small workshop at the bottom of his garden in Devon.

Alex poured milk into the long-handled steel milkpan and turned a handle on the machine to release steam into its base. It was such an evocative sound – bubbly, crunchy and metallic all at once. Once frothed, he let the pan stand for a while, before bumping the base smartly on the wooden worktop and pouring its contents into the mug, holding the froth back with a spoon and then scooping out snowy blobs onto the top of the cappuccino.

'There you go. I think you've earned that today,' he smiled, dusting the top with chocolate powder as he pushed the mug towards her.

'Thanks. So how's Mad Mothers' Wednesday going?'

'*Mad*. I swear there's more of them in here each week. I think they're cloning themselves. Honestly, it looked like a scene from *Ben Hur: The Early Years* in here earlier – all those chariots parked up everywhere. Some of the old dears couldn't even get in through the door. I've been a bit sharp with them, to be honest.'

'Ah. Not much chance of you scoring a date with a single mum anytime soon then?'

'Yeah. I think I might've burned my bridges on that one.'

Harri feigned disappointment. 'Oh, well, Plan B it is then.'

Amusement lit Alex's eyes. 'Excellent, maestro. So, what's the plan then?'

Harri looked around her like a shady informant in a thirties gangster flick, leaned closer to Alex and tapped her nose. 'Can't reveal my sources yet. Suffice to say that your name has been circulated in the right – er – circles. We should know more very soon. Until then, there are things only I know that you can't know until it's the right time for you to *know*, understand?'

Alex held his hands up. 'Crystal clear. Are you sure you're capable of the mission, though?'

'You doubt a woman of my obvious covert skills?' Harri feigned astonishment. 'I am a woman of infinite capabilities, I'll have you know. I am a woman on a mission.'

'With an unusual flair for dairy-related nasal adornment.' Alex reached out to wipe a large glob of milk froth from Harri's nose as they both descended into helpless giggles.

'He *is* going to kill you when he finds out,' Stella frowned, picking up a strange garment, allegedly masquerading as a T-shirt. 'Which way is this supposed to go?'

'I have no idea,' replied Harri. 'I think that's the arm-hole.'

'Oh, right,' replied Stella absent-mindedly, adding the unusual creation to the pile of clothes slung over her arm as the next offering captured her attention.

It was Saturday morning and, with Rob away again, Harri had found Stella's invitation to accompany her to the large out of town shopping centre appealing. And it had been fun, until Stella appeared to get stuck in TKMaxx. Harri loved shopping, but compared with her best friend, she was a mere amateur. When Stella was on a retail mission, nothing short of an act of God could move her from her path. Two hours after they first entered the store – and no closer to making a purchase – Stella and Harri made a slow advance along the narrow gap between the seemingly endless rails of clothes.

'You won't be able to take all those in with you, you know.'

'I'll leave some with the girl and keep swapping them,' Stella breezed, adding another two garments to the pile on her arm, 'and besides, you're coming in with me so you can bring some in.'

And so Harri dutifully followed her best friend into the cramped changing room cubicle, *oohing* and *aahhing* in all the right places in the hope that it might encourage a decision. While she waited, she consoled herself with the thought of the large caramel macchiato waiting for her when they were finally released from the store's clutches. *Only thirty-nine garments to go and then it's all mine . . .*

'Are you listening?' Stella barked, as the glorious daydream dissolved like a sugar lump in hot espresso, snapping Harri back to reality. 'I *said*, what do you think?'

It was the third pair of jeans Stella had eased her perfect figure into and Harri honestly couldn't tell the difference. 'How much are those again?'

Stella let out an exasperated sigh. 'I *told* you, fifty-two pounds. I *knew* you weren't listening.'

'Sorry, hon. They're nice, but I like the first pair the most.'

'Really? You don't think they make my bum look big?'

'You don't *have* a bum, Stella.'

'Yes, I do. That's why it's a no-carb week this week.'

'You're crazy. You look great, hon. And those jeans – any of them – make you look great. But do you really need any more jeans? You've got about fifteen pairs at home.'

'That's a complete exaggeration, Harri! It's only nine, and anyway these are Fornarina.'

It was going to be a long day, Harri groaned inwardly, as Stella rotated slowly, scrutinising every inch of her reflection from every conceivable angle. Harri closed her eyes and imagined herself alighting from a packed *vaporetto* water taxi into the buzzing throng of a Venetian quayside, then wandering through the streets, finding a pavement café and slowly sipping rich espresso as colourful waves of people washed past her . . .

'So when do you think you'll hear from *Juste Moi*?'

Daydream shattered, Harri shuddered. 'I don't know. Probably a few months or something. If they accept him, that is.'

'Of course they'll accept him,' Stella insisted, echoing Viv's words from earlier in the week. 'He is a gorgeous man. Irritating as hell, but gorgeous. You wait and see.'

Harri didn't have to wait long.

CHAPTER FIVE

The Point of No Return

The buzz from the fluorescent strip light above the cubicle seems to be getting louder as the rain on the skylight intensifies. The only other sound is the thumping of Harri's heart, loud in her ears. It's slowed a little since her flight into the ladies', wow, *thirty minutes* ago. She wonders if the survivors of the Stone Yardley Armageddon are still in the hall; or maybe Viv has moved the remnant on, like a brisk police officer shooing onlookers away from a crime scene – *OK, people, step away now, nothing to see here . . .*

One thing's for certain: Alex won't be there. Not after *that look*. Harri feels a stab of icy pain at the memory. *He hates me. I've lost my best friend.* In all the time she's known him, she's never seen him so hurt, so angry. And every last atom of it directed straight at her. No, Alex will be long gone by now. If only she'd listened to her conscience when the letter arrived from *Juste Moi . . .*

> *Dear Ms Langton,*
> *Many thanks for your nomination for our 'Free to a Good Home' feature.*
> *Everyone here at Juste Moi loved your letter – your friend Alex is exactly the kind of candidate we want to*

feature in the magazine.

If you could provide us with a few more details on the form enclosed, we'll set the wheels in motion to find the lady of his dreams!

Looking forward to hearing from you soon,
Chloë Sahou
Features Writer

'What's that?' asked Tom, peering over Harri's shoulder as she read the letter. It was lunchtime and Harri had finally plucked up courage to open the envelope with the *Juste Moi* frank that Freddie Mills, the friendly postman, had handed to her that morning.

'Looks like an exciting one,' Freddie had remarked, tapping the top of the envelope with a nicotine-hued forefinger. 'London postmark, that. One of them fancy magazines, I reckon – they're all there, you know. Any publication worth its salt is based in London.'

To Freddie Mills, a year and a half from retirement and the undisputed pub quiz champion at the Star and Highwayman – the small cosy pub at the far end of Stone Yardley – anything hailing from England's great capital was worthy of note and due reverence. In all his sixty-three years, Freddie had only ever made the journey to London once: an away match of the Stone Yardley Darts Club on which his brother had managed to blag him a seat.

A non-player, Freddie managed to convince Big Bruce McKendrick, much-feared team coach and owner of Long and Winding Road Motorcycles, of his suitability with a near-textbook explanation of the finer points of the game. The team enjoyed an afternoon's sightseeing and arrived at the match venue in Fulham, only to lose magnificently – but at least

Freddie was able to revel in the delights of the city he had dreamed about since childhood.

Unusually for a Wednesday at Sun Lovers International Travel, business had been brisk. Tom, Harri and new girl, Nusrin, barely had time to pause for breath between each new customer, exchanging incredulous glances as they passed one another carrying brochures or escorting customers to their desks. The reason for this unexpected influx of custom remained a mystery until the late entrance of SLIT's owner, George Duffield, just before midday.

'Ah, the unmistakable power of advertising,' he boomed, his thick Wolverhampton accent bouncing off the shabby travel-poster-covered walls. 'It's amazing what a little bit of local advertising can do for a reputable business like SLIT, you know. Best twenty-five quid I've spent this year.'

His mystified staff rewarded his enthusiasm with a selection of blank expressions.

'You *paid* people to come into the shop?' Tom ventured.

'Don't be ridiculous, Thomas. A successful local business like SLIT doesn't need to resort to bribery – and I resent the very implication, actually. No, I placed two hundred and fifty offer leaflets in the *Edgevale Gazette* yesterday. Twenty per cent off any booking made this week.'

'You put leaflets in the free paper?' Nusrin asked.

'The very same,' George grinned, his shiny, red head blushing with pleasure. 'Genius, eh?'

'I didn't think anyone read the *Gazette*,' Harri said. 'Mine goes straight into the recycling box.'

'Well, *apparently* there are people in Stone Yardley who don't follow your woeful example, Harriet,' retorted George, sailing into his office. 'I think the hustle and bustle of this travel agency speaks for itself, don't you?'

As he shut the door, Tom chuckled. 'Shame nobody actually booked anything today then, isn't it?'

'Apart from the Wilkinsons booking their annual coach trip to Rhyl,' Nusrin replied.

'But we've done a brisk trade in brochures,' Harri smiled.

Half an hour later, the impressive flow of browsing customers had all but vanished, allowing Harri, Tom and Nusrin to grab a well-earned lunch break. Nusrin had seized the opportunity to vacate the premises, ever-present mobile in hand and packet of cigarettes hastily shoved in her coat pocket, leaving Tom and Harri to eat their lunch in relative peace. And for Harri finally to read the letter. Trying to read its contents, Tom nodded knowingly. 'Top secret communications, eh?'

'It's nothing,' she said, folding the letter defensively to hide its contents from her prying colleague.

'Not judging by your face it isn't.'

'Seriously, Tom, it's nothing.'

'Liar.'

'Am not!'

'So if it's nothing you can tell me what it's about then, can't you?' Tom smirked, mayonnaise glistening on his chin as he pointed his half-devoured sub roll at Harri. 'Ha – get out of that one!'

Harri let out a sigh of resignation. 'It's something I'm doing for a friend.'

His eyebrows shot up as he lowered his voice. 'Mafia?'

'Sorry?'

'They've hired you as a hitwoman and the letter is details of your mark.'

'You watch far too many gangster films,' Harri laughed.

'My Uncle Jez says the Mafia has a base in Birmingham,' Tom retorted. 'It's common knowledge.'

'Oh, and your Uncle Jez is such a trusted authority on that kind of information, isn't he? I mean, wasn't it Uncle Jez who was convinced that the Ku Klux Klan were holding secret meetings in Ellingsgate last summer?'

Tom looked away. 'He *saw* them meeting in that field.'

'Hmm, yes, and when he called the police, what did they find?'

Tom's greasy cheeks flushed scarlet. 'Beekeepers,' he muttered.

'Exactly. Ellingsgate Beekeeping Society. So I don't think we need to listen to your Uncle Jez, do we?'

'So what is it you're doing for a friend, then?' Tom shot back grumpily.

Harri grimaced. 'Something he might not thank me for.'

'OK – interests. Um, travel, photography, dining out, cinema . . . Anything I've forgotten?'

'Bugging people. Alex is particularly interested in that,' Stella replied, emptying two sachets of sugar into her takeaway coffee cup.

Harri looked up from the form spread before her on the weathered wooden picnic table at which they both sat. 'Be serious, Stel.'

Stella picked up the flimsy plastic stirrer and stirred her coffee with intense irritation. 'I'm deadly serious. This is a bad idea. Alex is going to kill you,' she added for the umpteenth time since Harri had first mentioned Viv's Big Idea. This had become her mantra, destined to accompany every conversation.

'You're not helping, Stel.'

'I wasn't trying to. Can we talk about something else, please?'

Harri groaned and shoved the form back into her rucksack. 'Fine. I'll finish it later, when I won't annoy anyone.' She looked out across the country park at families enjoying the unseasonably mild March Saturday. Vale Edge Park was one of her favourite local places – a large area of woodland around a high sandstone hill about twenty minutes' drive from Stone Yardley. Here she had spent most Sunday afternoons with her parents during childhood summers, riding bikes, having picnics and playing games. It was a popular destination for families, mountain bikers and dog-walkers, its trails offering something for everyone. Many of her first dates had taken place here; shyly holding hands by the lake or stealing kisses along the woodland paths through carpets of bluebells and bracken. In the early days, this had been the scene of countless laughter-filled walks with Rob, Harri pointing out wildflowers or birds and Rob identifying them with that confident, completely gorgeous smile of his.

In their more adventurous moments, Stella and Harri ventured here to walk up onto Vale Edge, before returning to the welcome retreat of the tiny log cabin that served as a refreshment kiosk. This afternoon, however, any thoughts of such exertions had been banished by Stella's 'urgent cake and caffeine craving'.

'This chocolate cake is a-*mazing*, H. Are you sure you don't want to try some?'

'I wouldn't dream of parting you from it,' Harri replied, popping a piece of buttery flapjack into her mouth.

'You know, I hoped you were going to say that.'

'I thought as much.' They exchanged smiles. 'Look, Stel, I know this magazine column is a daft idea, but it might just work. Stranger things have happened.'

'You *honestly* think it might bring Alex the woman of his dreams?'

Harri did her best to look convincing. 'It *might* . . .'

'I don't know why you're doing this if you aren't one

hundred per cent sure about it,' Stella said, taking a long sip of coffee.

'Because maybe Viv's right that Alex needs help,' Harri said, smoothing down a strand of red hair that the wind had worked loose from her ponytail. 'I'd just like to see him happy.'

Two noisy children dashed past their table with a large dog, its fur dripping from a recent foray into the lake. Stella wrinkled her nose in disgust. 'It could be worse, Harri. You could own one of *those*.'

'A dog or a child?'

Stella pulled a face. 'Either. *Eeuwch*. I am *never* having kids or dogs. Imagine spending your life trailing after that lot. Horrible, messy creatures – why in the world anyone would want that mayhem in their lives is beyond me.'

A harassed-looking woman appeared, stopping at their table and gripping it with both hands like a desperate lunatic from the asylum. 'Have you seen them?' she demanded, her eyes wide from too many late nights and hectic days.

'Two screaming brats and a mangy mutt? They went that-a-way,' Stella replied, and the woman hurried away.

'Stella, you're awful. Poor woman.'

'Two words, Harri: "contraception" and "vet".'

Harri shook her head. 'You're unbelievable. And I know you don't mean it.'

Stella inspected her nails. 'Oh, yes, I do. You wouldn't catch me and Stefan signing up for that nightmare scenario.'

'Ah, Stefan. How is the latest flame?'

Stella's eyes lit up. 'Gorgeous, H. Not gorgeous like Jase or Andy, of course, but with Stefan it's the whole package, you know what I mean?'

'I think I can guess.'

'He's caring and thoughtful – and his house is just to die for!'

Hmm. What attracted you to the millionaire Stefan, Stella? 'Right, I see.'

Harri's sarcasm was not lost on Stella. 'His money isn't the important thing, whatever you think. Honestly.'

'Perish the thought.'

'You're such a cynic. This could be true love and all you can do is mock me. Just because you're all loved-up, doesn't give you the monopoly on happy-ever-afters.'

'Sorry.'

Stella took a sip of her coffee and pulled a face. 'This stuff doesn't get any better, does it?'

Harri smiled. 'Shh. Ralph will hear you.' She looked round to see if the short, white-haired proprietor of the Vale Edge café was listening. Thankfully, he was engaged in an extremely animated conversation with the leader of a group of local ramblers, who were laying siege to most of the picnic tables around where Harri and Stella sat.

'I don't mind if he does. It's high time our Ralphy learned about decent espresso.' Stella flapped her hands as a thought blew into her mind. 'Ooh, ooh, I meant to tell you, Stefan finally solved the problem of who you remind me of.'

Harri wasn't aware this was a problem. 'Oh?'

Clapping her hands Stella smiled triumphantly. 'Amy Adams.'

'I do *not* look like Amy Adams.'

'Yes, you do. All that annoyingly gorgeous red hair of yours and your amazing blue eyes – you're the total spit of her.'

Harri shook her head. 'Just because I have auburn hair and blue eyes does not make me Amy Adams. Anyway, last month you thought I looked like Debra Messing and last year you said I was a dead ringer for Julianne Moore. Aren't you just working your way through red-headed actresses?'

'Nope. Not this time. Stefan and I were watching *Enchanted* and he said, "She looks like your friend Harri."'

'Hang on a minute – you were watching a Disney film with Stefan?'

Stella jutted her chin out. 'He happens to be a fan of animation. There's nothing wrong with that.'

Harri held her hands up to call a truce. 'Hey, if your fabulously wealthy boyfriend wants to revere the House of Mouse, then who am I to question him?'

'Exactly. So when does this form thingy have to be back with the magazine?' Stella asked, expertly swinging the conversation back.

'As soon as possible. They really like him, Stel.'

'I told you they would. Of course, you could always just *forget* to send it back . . .'

The thought had crossed Harri's mind, but now the magazine knew about him they were likely to pursue Harri for information. It was too late to back out. 'That's not going to work, mate. I've got to do it.'

There is something to be said for careful consideration and thought. Since the loss of her parents, Harri had relied upon her head to lead the way for every decision she made. As far as Harri was concerned, it was a much better option than trusting her heart, which often sent her in a different direction entirely. Unfortunately, she was surrounded by an entire clan of heart-followers – Viv, Alex, Stella and even Tom at work – none of whom seemed to agree with her cautiousness.

'How are you ever going to do exciting things if you spend all your time just thinking about them?' Stella often asked.

Secretly, Harri longed to be the type of person who threw caution to the wind and just went with the flow. Like Alex was.

The tales of his spontaneity were nigh on *legendary*. He had just decided, one Monday afternoon thirteen years ago, whilst sitting at his desk in the large insurance firm he worked for, to quit and see the world. He typed out his resignation letter, walked straight into his boss's office and, five minutes later, cleared his desk and left the building forever. Four weeks later, he was on a plane to Australia with only the next four months of his life planned. From there he met a friend who was travelling to New Zealand, so that's where he went next, finding a job at a backpackers' hostel for six months, doing general chores at first, then working in the kitchens. One of the girls visiting the hostel was the daughter of a hotel owner in Singapore who just happened to be looking for a sous chef for his busy restaurant, so Alex packed up again and went to work there. And so it continued, year after year; one spur-of-the-moment decision after another, taking Alex all over the world.

'How do you do it?' Harri asked him one Wednesday night, as he expertly juggled steaming pans in the kitchen of his flat above the shop. This particular evening Malaysian Ginger Prawns were on the menu, stir-fried with fresh root ginger that made the tongue tingle and sweet honey to soothe the palate, served on a bed of fragrant jasmine rice. As Harri leaned against the breakfast bar, the aroma of the meal sent images of floating markets, bamboo houses and piles of multicoloured spices whizzing through her mind.

'How do I do what?' Alex replied through a cloud of ginger-infused steam as he lifted the wok lid.

'The whole spontaneity thing.'

Alex let out a laugh that filled the whole room. 'What kind of a question is that?'

'I'm just curious.'

'Considering becoming a spontaneity convert, eh?'

'I didn't say that. It's just that I seem to be the only person in the entire world who can't just *do* things.'

His eyebrows lifted slightly. 'And that bothers you?'

Harri felt her defences prickle. 'No, not really. It's just – something I was thinking about, that's all.'

Alex's grin was mischievous but not unkind. 'Ah, well, you see, *that's* where the problem lies, H: if you're *thinking* about being spontaneous then you've kind of missed the point.'

Harri shook her head. 'Very funny, Mr Seat-of-His-Pants-Flyer. Forget I said anything, OK?'

'Aw, mate, I'm sorry. You just make it too easy . . . Look, I can't explain how to be spontaneous. It's something you *do*, not something you psychoanalyse. Don't question, don't worry and certainly don't deliberate. If it feels right, you just go with it.'

'But don't you ever worry about it all going wrong?'

'Heck, Harri, you know me. Sometimes it does go wrong. Spectacularly wrong on several occasions, as you no doubt can recall. But I never worry about it: if it all goes belly up then I just deal with the consequences. If you think about things too much, you'll never do anything, or go anywhere.'

Harri could almost imagine a version of herself setting off happily into the unknown – but quickly the questions and contingencies returned, blocking out the possibilities. 'Well, who's to say that my way isn't the best?'

Alex thought for a moment, then lowered his voice as if to soften the blow of what he was about to say. 'Nobody, I guess. You may very well be saving yourself from a shed load of failure by being cautious. But look at it this way, mate: would you rather be walking along a gorgeous palm-fringed beach somewhere or reading about it?'

It hurt, of course, but he was right.

Sitting in the cosy living room of her cottage the following Sunday evening, Harri stared at the completed 'Free to a Good Home' form in front of her. Though she said it herself, she had done a great job: Alex was well and truly described on the single A4 sheet. The woefully single readers of *Juste Moi* were going to tremble in their fluffy slippers at the mere sight of him. In fact, reading her description of him, even Harri was impressed.

She was about to file it safely away behind the clock on her mantelpiece (just so she could have a final think about it that night to make sure she was doing the right thing) when a thought hit her. If there was ever a time to practise spontaneity, this was it. She *wasn't* going to post it in the morning, she was going to post it *right now*. True, no self-respecting postie was likely to be collecting mail from her local postbox at 11.30 p.m. but at least the form would be *in* the box and therefore safe from Harri's second thoughts, which would doubtless halt its progress if it remained behind the clock. Kicking off her slippers, Harri grabbed the envelope and purposefully licked the flap, sealing it with a confidence that shocked her. Then she pulled on her wellies (the closest footwear to hand – hey, that was spontaneity in itself, wasn't it?), threw on her coat over her pyjamas, grabbed her keys and ran down the stone path from the cottage, flinging open the small, white creaky wooden gate and walking the five steps it took to reach the small, red postbox nestled in the dry-stone wall over the road.

Five small steps for anyone else: five giant leaps for Harri-kind, she thought triumphantly, as she thrust the small white envelope decisively into the black abyss of the postbox . . .

. . . and instantly regretted her decision.

Harri stared at her empty hand, still hovering over the inky blackness of the postbox's opening, feeling her heart sinking to the furthest end of her pink and white polka-dot wellies. 'What have you done?' a little voice demanded inside her head, accusingly. Harri felt her heartbeat pick up and an icy-cold pang shudder down her spine. Suddenly, spontaneity didn't seem like the blinding idea it had been moments before.

Maybe, she thought in desperation, if she stared hard enough at the opening, the letter would magically reappear and everything would be fine. Perhaps the postman would just inexplicably miss the letter and it would remain forgotten at the bottom of the box for years to come. Or maybe she would wake up any second and find that it was all a terrible dream . . .

Harri's train of thought was brought to an abrupt halt as the heavens opened above her. Large spots of rain began to pepper her head and shoulders, catching the light from the streetlamp as they fell: a shower of shimmering crystals splashing around her as she remained frozen to the spot. *It's done now: there's no going back.* As if to underline the sense of dread pervading her soul, a deep rumble of thunder rolled across the distant sky. Slowly, resignedly, Harri turned and walked back home.

CHAPTER SIX

Hide-and-Seek

The door to the ladies' opens with an unwilling creak.

'Is she in here?' a female voice asks.

'No, I don't think so,' a young man answers from the corridor beyond, his tone uncertain. 'Maybe she's gone home.'

'Well, I never saw her leave, Thomas, and not much escapes my notice.'

'You can say that again – *ouch*!'

'Less of your cheek, sunshine, thank you very much.' The door opens a little wider and Harri can hear a step onto the dull magnolia tiles. 'Harriet? Am you in here, chick?'

Harri holds her breath. She can't face a conversation; not yet.

'She isn't there, Eth— Mrs Bincham,' Tom whispers, his embarrassment as obvious as the acne on his chin.

'Mmm. Well, maybe you're right, Thomas, maybe she's gone. Better just check the hall again then, eh?'

Harri breathes a sigh of relief as the voices disappear and the door closes.

Ethel Bincham was the cleaner at Sun Lovers International Travel. At least, that's what it said on her contract. However, with eyesight as bad as hers, coupled with her penchant for long chats with the staff, and George's unwillingness to let her go after her many years of more or less faithful service, cleaning was not exactly top of her list of priorities. She prided herself on her ability to listen and fancied herself almost a surrogate mother, provider of pure Black Country wisdom and nothing less than a soothsayer for the assembled workers each Monday, Wednesday and Friday morning, seven o'clock till nine. In days of yore, every village would have its local wise woman, a source of mystical wisdom, cures for all ills and an understanding ear in time of need; now, the fortunate residents of Stone Yardley had Mrs Bincham.

'Would you run the Hoover round this evening before Mrs B comes in?' George often asked Harri on a Tuesday afternoon (knowing full well that she would be the last person out of the office and probably the first in next morning).

The irony of the request was never lost on Tom. 'Doesn't that kind of defeat the object of having a cleaner?'

George couldn't really argue with this reasoning, but knew that his initial lack of courage to let Ethel go when he realised she could hardly see the *office*, let alone the dust, had inevitably made a rod for his own back.

The morning after her late-night bout of ill-judged spontaneity, Harri arrived at work to find Ethel attempting to water the artificial aspidistra in the window.

'It's looking a bit peaky,' Ethel informed her cheerily, 'and no wonder – it's bone dry!'

'It's artificial,' Harri began, but Mrs Bincham was having none of it.

'No, it's an *aspidistra*, Harriet,' she corrected, tutting loudly. 'You youngsters don't know anything about plants these days.'

Harri gave up and retreated to her desk. She switched her

computer on and began to leaf through the morning post, most of which seemed to consist of stationery catalogues nobody could remember requesting and offers of business loans from banks she'd never heard of. As she worked, she was aware of Mrs Bincham surveying her carefully, although exactly how much Ethel could see was anyone's guess.

Harri picked up a pile of new brochures and walked over to the display units, wistfully gazing at each cover as she restocked the shelves: azure harbours with dazzling white yachts and jade-green waves lapping against white sand beaches, as smug couples stalked possessively along the shore. A sharp razorcut of longing sliced through Harri's heart at their blissful expressions. If only *she* could step into the pictures and leave everything far behind . . .

'Thought you might need this,' Ethel's raspy voice said right by her ear, bringing her sharply back to reality. Harri jumped and almost knocked the mug of super-strong tea from Mrs Bincham's hands as she did so.

'Oh! I'm sorry, Mrs B, I was miles away.'

'I could see that,' Ethel replied as Harri accepted the mug. 'Where was it this time, eh?'

Harri looked sheepish. 'Grenada.'

'Don't they do *Coronation Street*?' Ethel asked.

Harri stifled a giggle. 'Um, no, that's—'

'No matter,' Ethel cut in, rummaging in her tartan shopping trolley and producing a large off-white Tupperware box that looked at least a hundred years old. 'I've been baking again.'

'Oh . . . you really shouldn't have . . .'

'Tsk, nonsense, I love it! My Geoff says I missed my calling in life – should have been a baker, he reckons. Mind you, he also used to fancy Margaret Thatcher, so what does that tell you? Now, clap your chops round one of these.'

Harri peered dubiously into the fusty plastic-scented depths of the box and selected an overly browned, crunchy square of *something*. 'Thanks,' she replied, hoping she sounded convincing.

Ethel's face was a picture of gleeful anticipation. 'Well, go on then,' she urged.

Harri took a bite. 'It's – um – different,' she ventured, uncertain whether the odd concoction of tastes was pleasant or not. 'What is it?'

Ethel's wrinkled cheeks flushed with pride and she patted her recently set blue-rinsed curls. 'My own recipe,' she grinned. 'I love Bakewell tart, see, and my Geoff's partial to Chocolate Crispy cakes – big kid that he is – so, I thought, why not combine the two? Proper bostin' stuff, that.'

Harri swallowed and reached for her tea. 'So this is . . . ?'

'Chocolate Crispy Bakewells!' Ethel proudly announced. 'Remarkable, eh?'

Harri couldn't argue with that. 'Absolutely.'

'Ta.' Ethel's smile morphed into solemnity. 'Now, are you going to tell me what's up?'

'I'm fine, Mrs B, just a bit tired, that's all.'

Ethel's eyes may have been lacking in physical performance but her perception was as sharp as ever. 'Don't give me that, Harriet. "Just tired" my backside. I know a troubled soul when I see one.' She parked her ample behind on the edge of Harri's desk and motioned for her to sit down. 'Now, why don't you just tell your Auntie Eth all about it, eh?'

In truth, Harri didn't quite know what to say. She *was* tired: her whole body ached from only an hour's sleep the night before and her eye sockets felt as if she'd been punched repeatedly in the face by a crazed boxer. Added to which, telltale shivers in her bones were heralding the unwanted onslaught of a cold following her late-night soaking by the postbox.

All night long she had wrangled with her thoughts, her

mind abuzz with worry upon worry as she cursed her spontaneity, finally succumbing to sleep curled up on her sofa under a travel rug (which, like its owner, had never actually travelled much further than her armchair).

Harri wasn't sure Mrs Bincham would understand (after all, this was the woman who thought an aphrodisiac was a flower, and the giant Egyptian statues in the Valley of the Kings were known as sphincters), but she found herself trying to explain it all anyway. Ethel listened calmly, nodding sagely every now and again as she munched a square of Chocolate Crispy Bakewell, her dentures clicking rhythmically as Harri recounted the events of the past few weeks.

'I don't know, Mrs B. Part of me still believes this could work for Alex, but since I actually posted the letter I can't shake the thought of what might happen if it doesn't. There's nothing I can do about it either way now: I just have to get on with it, I suppose.'

'I completely get you, chick. It's very simple, really: you've got the Big F at work here.'

Given her current sleep-deprived mind, Harri blocked out the many possibilities appearing before her and asked the obvious question. 'The Big F?'

Mrs Bincham peered carefully over her right and left shoulders as if checking for unwanted spies. '*Fate*, Harriet. You've trusted the situation to fate so's you're no longer in control. It's only natural you should be a bit jumpy while you're waiting to see what's in store for you. I mean, anything could happen next – good or bad.'

'You think so?'

'I know so, chick. I've a feeling about this. My mother always said I was *psycho*, you know. Swore it blind till the day she popped off. "Your gran was a psycho, your Auntie Lav was a psycho and now the Gift's passed to you, our Eth," she used to say to me.'

'Don't you mean "psychic" . . . ?'

'Now, I've never held much with all that mumbo-jumbo rubbish, to tell the truth. But every now and again I get my *feeling* and I have to say, *stuff happens*, like.'

Although Mrs Bincham was smiling, Harri didn't exactly feel reassured. 'So what do I do now?'

Mrs Bincham's grin broadened. 'Nothing you can do, our kid. Just got to sit it out, I s'pose. So you have another bit of Chocolate Crispy Bakewell while you're waiting and I'm sure that'll take your mind off it, eh?'

Harri surrendered to the inevitable and reached into the Tupperware box.

She should have been used to the Big F by now – although she had never really thought about it in that way before. She had become accustomed to the strange mix of joys and sorrows that twisted and twirled her from one event to the next, often unannounced. It was just life.

She remembered her grandma once saying: 'Life is like a wild pony – you can never tame it. But if you grab its mane and hold on with all your might, it will be the most thrilling ride you'll ever have.' Grandma Langton had lived in a tiny cottage on the edge of Dartmoor, where Harri and her parents would visit during the summer holidays. As a little girl, Harri had liked nothing better than to hold tightly on to Grandma's hand as they battled against the elements to climb the hill behind the cottage and gaze out across the windswept moor to where the wild ponies grazed. Even as a small child, she'd appreciated and envied the beautiful creatures' freedom, walking and cantering wherever they pleased. The thought of jumping on one of their backs and taking off across the wildly undulating moor towards distant hills was at once impossibly exciting and ridiculously scary, but Harri longed to be as carefree as they appeared to be. As for Grandma, her own 'thrilling ride' had come to an abrupt halt when Harri was eleven – life throwing her from its back for the last time.

Life, or fate – or whatever you chose to call it – had certainly taken Harri for more than one breathless ride over her twenty-eight years – although it had to be said that most had been brutally scary rather than exhilarating. Losing one parent to cancer was bad enough; losing both was cruel in the extreme, not least because her mother's malignant tumour was diagnosed while her father was enduring his last weeks of life. As Dad lay on the sofa in the family home, too weak to move, but still somehow able to smile and joke (which he accomplished with aplomb right up until he finally succumbed to unconsciousness), Mum made two sets of funeral arrangements – one for him, one for her – sitting at the kitchen table making copious lists for Harri 'for when the time arrives'.

Dad's cancer had taken him slowly, a long-drawn-out process over nearly six years, which crumpled the once strong and vital six-foot-three former rugby player into a pitiful heap of skin and bone arranged painfully across the old Dralon settee in the living room. In contrast, Mum's illness took hold at lightning speed: five and a half months from the diagnosis to her funeral at St Mary's, Stone Yardley's parish church. Five months after burying her husband, Mum went to join him and Harri was alone in the world. Of course, she had friends. Viv and Stella rallied round, cooking meals (Viv) and getting her out of the house to go shopping or for walks (Stella), whilst Auntie Rosemary came to stay for three months, helping Harri to put the family home on the market and, eventually, find the tiny, ivy-covered cottage that was to become her own, bought with the money left to her by her parents.

Her father's illness meant that holidays were spent near to home or at least a major hospital: the Lake District was about the furthest they dared travel and this was only because they had family living in Kendal, should an emergency arise. Towards the end, Langton family holidays became more like sofa transfers: Dad carefully transported from home in their old red Volvo to a different living room three hours away – the only difference being the mountain views from the window.

When Harri met Rob, just over a year later, she found herself returning to the Lake District for summer holidays. Rob viewed camping as 'the purest form of holidaying'. Understanding Rob's long-held passion for all things outdoors was part and parcel of loving him, as far as Harri was concerned. His father had been a scout master for years so Rob and his brother, Mark, spent weekends and holidays under canvas from an early age. When his father died five years ago, following the pursuits he had learned from him took on a whole new significance for Rob. It was almost as if being outdoors brought him closer to his father's memory. Watching him pitch a tent, knot guy ropes and make a fire was strangely comforting for Harri – Rob's capability and protectiveness made her feel safe.

'If he's so fond of camping, why don't you go to one of these new glamping sites, with yurts and wood-burning stoves?' Stella suggested during one of their many coffee-shop outings. 'Or do it somewhere warm, like France?'

'It just wouldn't be his sort of thing,' Harri replied, stirring her cappuccino with a wooden stirrer. 'And actually, that's OK.

It's just part of who he is – like me with my travel book addiction. I don't feel I have to like everything he likes and neither does he with me. We're settled and secure enough with each other to be able to have different interests. When we go camping it's like he feels he's fending for us, I think. It's that whole "protective caveman" instinct.'

Stella's eyes lit up. 'I have to admit, it's quite sexy when guys get like that – all rugged and strong.'

'Oh yes. I have *no* complaints there,' Harri agreed as they clinked coffee cups in a mutual toast.

'So I bet your beloved likes that Ray Mears bloke, doesn't he?'

Oh, yes. To say Rob worshipped at the well-worn survival boots of Ray would be putting it mildly. When his father was alive, Rob had taken him on several of Mr Mears' bushcraft weekends – something Harri was hugely relieved she hadn't been invited on. Camping in the great outdoors was one thing; eating bugs and making shelters out of twigs and tarpaulin was definitely above and beyond the call of duty.

So, whilst Rob would indulge in copies of *Survival Monthly* or his extensive collection of Ray Mears DVDs, Harri knew she could always escape into the welcoming pages of *Condé Nast Traveller* and *Lonely Planet* magazine – and, of course, her favourite books on Venice and the Veneto.

For as long as she could remember, Harri's imagination had been her sanctuary; she could escape into its endless possibilities whenever she wanted to get away. As a little girl she would dream herself cycling past tulip fields in Holland, or twirling round an opulent Viennese ballroom in a beautiful gown to the swirling strains of Strauss; in her teens she would rollerskate along the promenade at Miami Beach, or spot multi-hued parrots in Brazilian rainforests; by the time she reached her twenties, she would be backpacking across Australia, bridge-swinging in New Zealand's South Island, or riding galloping horses through the tide along Mexican beaches.

But Venice had always towered head and shoulders above the rest of her dreams. Its colour, opulence and uniqueness captured her heart and fired her imagination – her parents' own dyed-in-the-wool romanticism alive and well, and coursing through her own veins.

When her parents were resting, or she just needed five minutes to herself, escaping was as easy as closing her eyes or opening a travel magazine. For a few moments, she could go wherever her heart desired. It didn't matter that she couldn't actually jump on a plane and visit these places; it was enough to imagine herself there. Where others would choose chick-lit, crime thrillers or historical drama to provide their escape, Harri chose a travel book. No matter where it was, as long as she could learn something new about the world, Harri eagerly consumed its contents, each new glimmering scrap of information adding to the growing travel library in her mind.

Fuelled by her daydreams, Harri's longing to travel grew stronger as the years passed. The true extent of her desire to see the world was something she confessed to nobody but Ron Howard, the large ginger and white cat that had appeared in her front garden one December morning as a small, shivering kitten and stayed with Harri ever since. Harri had never considered herself a cat person, yet there was something she understood immediately about the tiny stray trying to shelter under the birdbath from the fast-falling snow. He was like her: adrift in a new, unfamiliar place, seeking refuge from the winter cold. Harri had not long moved into her cottage and was still feeling a stranger in her own home, surrounded by someone else's curtains, carpets and paint colours. From the moment he made his impromptu arrival in Harri's life, Ron Howard was a soul mate. Unlike Rob, Stella or anyone else, he didn't mind watching awful foreign soap operas like *Santa Barbara*, or endless travel documentaries on cable. He liked nothing better than to curl up on Harri's lap, purring or snoring loudly through hours of other people's experiences. There was something uniquely comforting about a creature that required nothing more than food and fuss; no expectations, no conditions, no arguments – simply feed me and love me.

In many ways, Ron Howard was particularly un-catlike. He liked to play fetch with his toys or bits of screwed-up paper; he rushed to the front door whenever someone new appeared; he loved to have his tummy rubbed and never once thought to use the opportunity to sink his considerable claws into the unsuspecting tickler's forearm; and he never, ever tucked his tail in – leading to many occasions where it was accidentally tripped over or stamped on. Washing, too, was something he took a long time to acquire the necessary skills for: Harri frequently had to wipe his nose and forehead after he had been eating his food, as it never seemed to occur to him to wash there. Auntie Rosemary once joked that he'd obviously left his mother before she could teach him all of these cat essentials. Harri was simply thankful he had turned up – the other stuff just made him who he was. Most importantly, he was a good listener. Well, as good a listener as a cat can ever be, snoring, purring and occasionally farting contentedly while Harri poured out her heart to him. Did Ron Howard understand? It didn't matter. What mattered was that he was *there* when she needed him.

After a day of trying to distract her mind from her posting Alex's profile to *Juste Moi*, Harri retreated to the safety of her cottage. With a bowl of home-made tomato, basil and chorizo soup (straight from the pages of her latest *Food & Travel* magazine) and a chunk of Gruyère ciabatta from Lavender's Bakery, Harri and Ron Howard snuggled down for a night of rubbish television. She had just taken her first mouthful of soup when the phone rang on the bookcase, just out of reach. Much to Ron Howard's disgust, she manoeuvred herself from underneath his furry frame to answer it.

'Hello, may I speak to Harriet Langton?' asked a well-spoken woman.

'Speaking.'

'Ah, Ms Langton, hello. Sorry to ring you so late, but it's Chloë from *Juste Moi*. It's just a quick call to check if you've sent us the form back for your friend Alex for "Free to a Good Home" yet?'

Harri felt the single spoonful of soup curdling in the pit of her stomach. 'Yes – um – yes, I sent it last night, actually.'

The sense of relief from the other end of the conversation was palpable. 'That's great, thank you so much.'

'I'm not sure he's what you're after, you know,' Harri began, hoping that Chloë would say something like, 'Oh I see. Best not to bother then, eh?' and end the call.

Of course, she didn't. 'I'm sure he *is*, Ms Langton. After all, you must think he's a worthy candidate, seeing as *you* nominated him.'

Touché. 'Right, yes, I suppose I did.'

'Trust me, Ms Langton, *everyone* has second thoughts about this. Believe me, I know. I've had more conversations with dithering best friends, sisters and mothers than you would ever imagine since we started this feature.'

Harri wasn't convinced by this. 'I'm just concerned that Alex might not be happy about it, that's all.'

Chloë gave a long sigh and lowered her voice. 'Look, I'll

level with you, OK? The feature is dying on its sweet arse here – my editor says I have to turn it around in the next two months or I'm back to "Celeb Gossip". Do you *know* how awful that is? Trust me, it's *death* to your career. I've been here for four years and *nobody* has ever *gone back* – do you understand what I'm saying?'

'I – er – think so . . .' Harri stuttered, momentarily stunned by the journalist's sudden change of demeanour. 'But I thought the last man got thousands of responses?'

'Like *crap* he did.' Another elongated sigh ensued. 'I'm sorry, Ms Langton, forgive me. It's just been a really long day.'

'*Tell* me about it.'

'OK, I'm being really honest here: your friend Alex is the first decent candidate we've had in two years. Most of the muppets who get nominated for this feature don't know one end of a woman from the other – hence the fact that they are still single . . .'

Harri suppressed a smile, recalling her previous conversation with Viv on the matter.

'. . . but Alex is – well, I mean, he's *hot as*, for one thing. Then there's the travel, the successful business . . . He ticks all the boxes, trust me. It's just possible that he could save my career.'

Despite her inner conflict of panic and mirth, Harri couldn't fail to feel compassion for the overstressed journalist on the line. 'I see. Well, that's OK then.'

'You honestly won't regret this, I promise! So your letter should arrive tomorrow and then it's all systems go, eh?'

'Great.'

'Have a super evening! Bye!'

Harri replaced the receiver and flopped back down on the sofa as Ron Howard slunk heavily back onto her lap. The bowl of soup on the coffee table remained there, its temperature dropping steadily; Harri's appetite had suddenly vaporised.

'Looks like it's happening, Ron,' she whispered, stroking his vibrating back. 'What on earth have I let myself in for?'

Ron Howard stretched his paws out and farted loudly. Enough said.

CHAPTER SEVEN

A Question of Priorities . . .

With all the excitement of tonight, Harri realises that she completely missed the buffet. Or, more precisely, the buffet completely missed her – considering that most of it was being requisitioned as ammunition at the point she fled the main hall. As the decision to attend the party was made at the last minute, there was no time for food beforehand, her time being taken up with trying to find a dress that wasn't too large for her. Looking down at her arms, Harri is surprised at how much weight she has lost during the past fortnight. Thankfully, an emerald-green halter-neck dress donated to her by Stella two years ago and relegated to the deepest, darkest part of her wardrobe on account of its being too tight, came to the rescue. Teamed with the too-expensive purple shoes she bought from the boutique shop in Innersley, and a thin purple cardigan she found stashed under T-shirts in the ottoman at the bottom of her bed, the overall effect with her long auburn hair is impressive, if not exactly the warmest option.

Harri is suddenly acutely aware of the hunger gnawing away at her insides. Reaching into her handbag, she sorts through the detritus of her everyday life – purse, phone, keys, tissues, receipts and old shopping lists – until she finds a treat-sized Mars bar. She has no idea how long it has lain in the depths of her bag, but needs must. Tearing open the wrapper, she takes a small bite and leans back against the cold ceramic cistern behind her.

'What are you doing this evening?' Viv asked as soon as Harri answered her phone.

'Um, I hadn't decided yet . . .' she began.

'Excellent!' Viv declared. 'Dinner at mine, seven thirty. OK? Good. See you then!'

Harri opened her mouth to speak, but it was too late. Viv had been replaced on the line by a monotonous buzz. Shaking her head, Harri put down the receiver and stared at Ron Howard, who was lying at an impossible angle on the very edge of the sofa cushion.

'Seven thirty? Let me just check my diary . . . Ah, yes, that should be fine. Thank you *so* much for the invitation . . . Honestly, Ron, it's a good job I don't have much of a social life. What would she do if I ever said no?'

Reluctantly, she picked up her bag and slung it across her shoulder.

'Oh, well, I suppose I'd better go and see what she wants. Unless you have any objections, Ron?'

Ron Howard purred loudly and fell off the sofa.

It wasn't that Harri minded doing things for Viv: she had known her for long enough to understand that beneath all the fuss and bluster lay a deep concern for her wellbeing. What Harri did object to was the way Viv assumed she had nothing better to do with her time than to jump at her every whim. Tonight would be no exception: whatever the reason for the urgent dinner invitation, it was bound to entail Harri doing something she wouldn't normally have chosen. That said, there

77

was something strangely comforting about having Viv in her life. Whilst Viv's ideas were often outlandish, her concern for Harri was unquestionable. In many ways, she was a surrogate mother for Harri and relished every intricacy of this role. And Harri loved her for it. So, quickening her pace under the dusky evening sky, she walked straight towards the next thrilling episode of Vivienne Brannan's Imagination.

To say Viv was excited would be like calling Everest 'a bit of a hill'. As Harri approached Viv's farmhouse on the long winding gravel drive that dropped steeply from the white gate at the roadside, she could see her friend standing in the front porch, peering impatiently out into the growing dark, arms folded like a shivering teacher on playground duty in winter. Her face lit up when she saw Harri approaching and she rushed out to meet her.

'Oooh, this is *so* thrilling!' she exclaimed, flinging her arms around Harri and expelling every last bit of air from her lungs in an enormous bear hug. 'Come inside, come inside! You *have* to see this!'

Winded from her overenthusiastic welcome, Harri fought to regain her breath and slowly followed Viv into the farmhouse. A wonderfully heady brew of roasting meat, baking pastry and steaming vegetables met her nostrils as she stepped through the doorway. One thing you could always count on with Viv was her ability to make any meal occasion into a *pièce de résistance*. Even snacks or impromptu lunches were transformed into show-stopping culinary events; there was no such thing as 'just a sandwich' as far as Viv was concerned. It was easy to see from where her son had gained his considerable catering skills.

'I didn't realise we were *banqueting* tonight,' Harri grinned as she entered the kitchen.

Viv dismissed the comment with a nonchalant sweep of her hand. 'Oh, *this*? It's nothing. Besides, you know me – I don't do low-key.'

'Couldn't have put it better myself.'

'I do hope you're not mocking me, Harriet Langton.'

Harri held her hands up. 'I wouldn't dare, Viv.'

Viv surveyed her with suspiciousness. 'Mmm. Anyway, it's not important. What *is* important is something that happened to pop onto my doormat this morning.' She opened a drawer in the vast central island of her kitchen and produced a magazine, then proceeded to perform a frighteningly energetic victory dance around the terracotta-tiled kitchen floor.

Harri saw the title *Juste Moi* and took a deep breath. 'Right then. Let's have a look.'

Viv could hardly catch her breath as she finished her dance with an elegant landing on a chair next to Harri at the kitchen table. 'Oh, it is *so* much better than that!'

Harri surveyed her carefully. 'How do you mean?'

Viv thrust the magazine at Harri. 'Our darling boy *only* made the front cover!'

'What? How? I mean, it's just a column inside . . .'

'Not any more!' Viv was in serious danger of exploding in an effervescent shower of stars. 'They've made him into a *feature*!'

Hands slightly shaking, Harri released the magazine from Viv's maniacal clutches and read the main headline: 'FREE TO A GOOD HOME SPECIAL: Our hottest candidate yet!'

'That's . . . that's not possible . . .' she stuttered. 'When I spoke to Chloë she said the column wasn't doing well at all . . . I – I don't believe it . . .'

'Believe it, sister,' Viv replied, sounding like a gruff supporting cast member from *Cagney and Lacey*. All that was missing was a gun sling and a bad seventies suit . . . She whipped the offensive publication from Harri's hands and flipped through it until she found the page. 'Look at that!'

The formerly innocuous 'Free to a Good Home' column was now a double-spread, glossy feature, a picture of Alex gracing most of the right-hand page. And, as if that wasn't bad enough, the worst thing – the *very* worst thing – was a quote from Harri herself, glowing accusingly at her in vivid red letters:

Alex is gorgeous, talented and caring.
Any girl would be lucky to call him hers.
Harri Langton, Alex's best friend

'That's *such* a sweet thing to say, darling,' Viv gushed, clamping a hand on Harri's arm. 'Al will be so flattered.'

Panic was threatening to remove Harri's capability of rational thought or physical movement. 'But I didn't say that,' she protested, doubt gnawing at the edge of her assertion. 'At least, I don't *think* I said that . . .'

'Well, you must have said it, darling, or else why would they print it?'

Viv's blind acceptance of journalistic integrity was touching, if completely unfounded, especially in the light of Harri's conversation with Chloë regarding the feature. *The feature is dying on its sweet arse here . . . your friend Alex is the first decent candidate we've had in two years . . .* Judging by the article's considerable promotion in *Juste Moi* it appeared that Chloë was at least safe from demotion to 'Celeb Gossip' for the time being.

'He's going to kill me,' Harri moaned, imagining the look on Alex's face when he saw the article and the damning evidence of her involvement in garish red letters.

Viv tutted. 'Stop being so melodramatic, Harriet! He is not going to kill you. He is going to *thank* you when all those lovely ladies start to reply. Trust me, I'm his mother. Nobody understands Alex like I do.'

Harri mentally activated everything crossable and hoped that, for once, Viv was right.

The week passed by in a blur as Harri tried to comprehend the new upgraded status of Alex's 'Free to a Good Home' article. After the initial shock of seeing the feature so prominent in the magazine, her confidence began to bounce back. After all, what was the worst that could happen? Even if Alex did find out and was annoyed at first, surely if Harri had managed to find him the woman of his dreams as a result then that would be enough to make him forgive her. Besides, by the end of the week Harri had something else to occupy her thoughts – namely, an unexpected argument with Rob on Friday evening.

Knowing he was unlikely to be home until after seven that night, Harri decided to surprise her boyfriend by making dinner for him. He seemed to be working so much lately that she thought he deserved a treat. She spent a good hour cleaning the kitchen and preparing the meal, creating a selection of Spanish tapas for a starter, with a main course of lemon, thyme and garlic roast chicken with butternut squash wedges and Mediterranean roasted vegetables – a little more adventurous than Rob would normally choose (being a firmly English eater, suspicious of anything 'foreign') but still safely recognisable for him to take the risk.

At seven-thirty, just as Harri was beginning to wonder what could be keeping Rob, her mobile rang.

'Hey, Red.' Rob's voice sounded weary.

'Hey you. What time will you be home?'

There was a long pause. 'I won't. Not until Monday night.'

Harri's eyes drifted over the dining table with its two perfectly prepared place settings, candles and open wine bottle. 'Oh.'

'That's what I was ringing to tell you. Kingston Corp found a glitch in our proposal and we had to travel up straight away to try to save the deal. I know I should've called you earlier, but it's been manic here since I arrived.'

Harri felt her heart plummeting. 'I wish you'd called me, Rob. I made dinner.'

There was a long sigh at the other end of the line. 'No, Red! Oh baby, I'm sorry. I had no idea.'

'It's fine, I understand.'

'No, you've every right to be upset. But I honestly had no choice but to come here.'

Moving to the table, Harri began to clear away the cutlery. She could feel angry tears building but she was determined not to let them fall. 'I know you didn't. I'll just be glad when you can finally tie up this Preston thing and get your life back. It seems a bit unfair that you're always the one who has to go dashing up the M6 every time your company hits a problem.'

The weariness increased in his voice but his answer was gentle. 'We've had this discussion before and it leads us nowhere, does it? I'm really sorry I didn't ring you and I feel bad that you went to all that trouble for me, but I'm here now and there's not much more I can do about it, is there?'

Harri hated it when things between her and Rob were tense. They had never been the kind of couple to bicker much in the past, but since the Preston job appeared in their lives it was as if a brooding tension was never far away from their conversations. Of course, she didn't blame Rob – he was just doing what his bosses asked him to. But Harri could feel considerable resentment growing within her at the company which demanded his absence from her so often.

'Well, maybe if you had a different job . . .' she began, instantly kicking herself for saying it.

Too late. Rob's irritation buzzed against her ear. 'Oh like *that's* going to happen with the way the job market is at the moment! You *know* how important this job is, Red – not just for me but for both of us.'

'I didn't mean it like that. I just think you deserve more than TGP give you. That's all I'm saying.'

'Oh, like you get from SLIT, you mean?'

Harri felt her hackles rising. 'That's completely different and you know it.'

'How? How is it different? George has had you doing more or less the same job since you started. I've worked my way up at TGP and now I'm head of a sales team with four people under me. That brings responsibility. Which means having to work away from home when they need me.'

'What about when *I* need you, Rob?' Tears stung Harri's eyes as the frustration of the past few months broke free. 'I know you have to work but ever since this Preston job appeared it's like I've been relegated to second place. And I'm sick of you working away at weekends. I'm sorry, but it's the truth . . .'

Rob groaned. 'Come on, Red, please . . .'

'No. I'm not going to apologise for how I feel. I wanted to spend this weekend with my boyfriend, not be twiddling my thumbs at home. And yes, you should've called me. Because then perhaps I wouldn't have wasted my time this evening.'

'What do you want me to do, eh? Quit my job? Come home? I've said I'm sorry, and yes, I would much rather be spending this weekend with my girlfriend than be holed up in some crappy office in Preston. But I can't change the situation and to be honest I don't want to fight about this. I think I'd better go.'

'Fine.' Harri ended the call and threw her mobile onto the table with a loud cry of frustration.

An hour later, curled up on her sofa with Ron Howard lying expansively across her lap, Harri had calmed down sufficiently to call a truce. Reaching for her mobile, she sent Rob a text:

I'm sorry. Call me when you get this. H xx

After staring at the mobile screen for a long time, Harri came to the depressing conclusion that Rob wasn't ready yet to accept her apology. Well fine, let him stew for a bit. In the meantime, she knew she had to do something, go somewhere – anywhere – to stop herself brooding over the argument. Who was likely to be around at ten o'clock on a Friday evening? Scrolling through the names on her mobile's address book, she considered the possibilities:

Auntie Rosemary? No, she would be at her Knit'n'Natter group with friends she had met in antenatal classes when she was expecting Rosie and James, and had kept in contact with ever since. They took it in turns to meet at one another's houses and put the world to rights over dry sherry, old movies and the brightly coloured knitting projects they never actually looked at as their needles clicked away.

Stella – now there was an idea. She'd mentioned earlier that Stefan was in Milan for the weekend so she would be at a loose end. Harri dialled the number and waited.

'Hello?'

'Hey, Stel, it's me. Just – er – Rob's busy so I'm free, if you wanted to do something?'

There was a muffled sound that bore a remarkable

resemblance to a male laugh and Stella muttered something away from the phone. 'Hey, hon, sorry, I . . . Something came up . . .' Another stifled laugh, this time matched by Stella's own. 'Call you tomorrow, OK?'

Before Harri could answer, the call ended. *Fantastic.* Returning to her address book screen, Harri continued the search.

Viv? Harri stared at her number and took a deep breath. Viv would want to know *why* Harri wasn't with Rob this evening. Which would, undoubtedly, entail her having to endure an endless commentary from Viv about Rob's job. After all the upset she'd already experienced tonight, was she really ready to put herself in the Vivienne Brannan firing line of animosity? She shook her head and looked over at Ron Howard, who had jealously claimed ownership of the TV remote control by sitting on it.

'What do you reckon, Ron, hmm? Face the wrath of Viv or sit here stewing over Rob?'

Ron Howard simply rolled over on his back and demanded a tummy tickle. Harri obliged, her thoughts cloudy and disorganised as she ruffled the thick, white fur on his substantial belly.

The only other option was Alex. After all, he'd called on her in a romantic emergency more than enough times in the past to warrant returning the favour.

'He-llo.'

'Hey, Al, it's Harri.'

'Hey.'

'Just wondering if you're up to anything tonight?'

'That's great.'

'Right . . . I was thinking maybe a film, or grab a pizza, or . . .'

'I see.'

What on earth was he playing at? 'Al, are you OK?'

'Ha! That's right, you've reached my answerphone. And you thought it was me all along! Gutted! So, hey, leave a message and I'll get back to you as soon as I can. Or *will* I?' A loud beep sounded, followed by Harri's own sigh of frustration.

'Hey, Al, it's me. Just wondering if you're busy, which, clearly, you are. *Very* amusing message there. Hilarious. Catch you later, moron.'

Groaning, she tossed the phone to the other end of the sofa and wandered through to the kitchen to make a cup of tea. Then she walked back into the living room and over to the large stack of DVDs in the corner. Discounting the romantic comedies – *You've Got Mail*, *Sleepless in Seattle*, *Because I Said So*, et al. – she reached the travel-related selection. She needed to escape, wrench her mind from Stone Yardley for a few hours to regain her focus. Running her hand across the glossy spines of the cases, the world was, quite literally, at her fingertips: Thailand, Fiji, New England, Norway, Venice . . . She paused, her hand hovering over the title, the thud of her heart loud in her ears. No, not Venice. Not tonight. It was too precious to be sullied by any lingering thoughts of the argument. Finally, she settled on *Dan Beagle's Guide to India*, snuggling down under a blanket on the sofa before hitting Play. Ron Howard curled himself over her feet as the famous adventurer, photographer and TV presenter's face appeared on screen.

'Hi, I'm Dan Beagle. For the next two hours, I want you to accompany me on a journey of discovery through this uniquely beautiful country. Welcome to my Indian Odyssey . . .'

A stab of loneliness jabbing inside, Harri smiled at her hero. 'Thank you, Dan.'

CHAPTER EIGHT

You've Got Mail . . .

The door opens and Stella's kitten heels click-clack onto the grubby magnolia tiles of the toilet floor. Harri holds her breath and wills her heartbeat to quieten in her ears, afraid that it might be loud enough for Stella to hear it echoing around the grey-green toilet walls.

'Listen, Harri. I didn't mean any harm by what I said, you know. I just wanted to be *honest*. Let's face it: enough people here were bound by their dishonesty until tonight . . . Look, I know you're upset, OK? I just never meant to hurt you. Dan and I – well, we're going to move back here as soon as the royalties for his book come through. So I'll be around again – just like old times, hey? Come out, would you? *Please*, Harri?'

Go away, Stella.

'We can make this all OK, I know we can, if you just come out now?'

Harri shakes her head silently.

There is a long sigh from the other side of the cubicle door. 'Well, for what it's worth, I know I did the right thing. There. I've said it. I never meant to hurt you or embarrass you; for that I'm really sorry. But I won't apologise for telling the truth. I can't, you see. Absolute truth is the only pure thing we have in this life; to deny its place is to deny life itself – that's what

87

Lama Rhabten taught me . . . But I suppose you don't need to hear that now. Look, here's my new mobile number . . .'

A white envelope is pushed timidly under the door to Harri's cubicle. 'Just call me when you're ready to talk, yeah?'

Harri waits until Stella has gone before she stoops to pick up the envelope.

When Harri had first agreed to Viv's Big Idea, she hadn't really considered how she was going to break the news to Alex. But now, with the 'Free to a Good Home' article making *Juste Moi*'s cover, the issue of how to tell him suddenly became a sticky subject. The easiest option was to tell him straight away, endure whatever initial reaction he might have and then just carry on. But the more Harri considered this, the trickier it seemed to be. Perhaps if Alex didn't find out about it and Harri was able to arrange some dates from any replies to the feature then all might be well . . . On the other hand, in a place as small and gossip-fuelled as Stone Yardley, how likely was it that nobody else would see the article and show him the magazine?

For a week, Harri waited, anticipating the moment when Alex found out. But nothing happened: Alex was just his usual, jovial self whenever he called or texted her.

After a fortnight, she began to relax a little. Maybe Viv represented *Juste Moi*'s entire readership in Stone Yardley - after all, she had to subscribe to receive it. Or maybe Chloë's worst fears had been proved founded and, following an unprecedented lack of response from the readership, she had been forced back into the prison otherwise known as 'Celeb Gossip' . . .

A little over a week after the argument, Rob finally sent a text:

I hate it when we fight. How about dinner at
mine 2nite at 7ish? Rx

It was clear from the moment Harri arrived at Rob's house
that evening that the argument had been forgotten. Everything
about her boyfriend seemed back to normal and she welcomed
the return of the Rob she loved so much.

'Things will be better soon, I promise,' he murmured into
her hair that night as she snuggled up to him. 'Once the Preston
job is sorted it'll be back to me and you.'

The following Saturday morning, Harri got up early to give
her cottage a much-needed clean. She was just scrubbing the bath
(dreaming about wandering around Venice's streets) when an
excited knocking at her front door broke her reverie. She opened
it to find Freddie Mills looking like he had just won the lottery,
brandishing a large grey post sack. 'London! Delivery from!' he
exclaimed, sounding for all the world like a Black Country Yoda.

Harri looked at her postman, then down at the sack. 'Are
you sure?'

Freddie nodded vigorously, a rebellious strand of hair
breaking free from his careful comb-over and flailing about
high above his head, like a waving antenna in the breeze. 'I
have an *official* delivery chit and everything! London deliveries
to our little village . . .' He shook his head in awestruck wonder
and handed her a clipboard and pen. 'Sign here, chick.'

Harri accepted the clipboard gingerly as if it were an incen-
diary device and checked the details:

TO: Harriet Langton, Two Trees Cottage,
Waterfall Lane, Stone Yardley, West Midlands.
SENDER: *Juste Moi* magazine, London W4

Stunned by this unexpected delivery, Harri signed the form and handed it back to Freddie, who grabbed the postbag and swung it heavily inside the hallway.

'Thanks. See you, Freddie.'

'No probs, Miss Langton. You just stay there and I'll bring the others in from the van.'

Shock rooted Harri to the doorstep. 'The *others*?'

But Freddie had already skipped down the path to his red Royal Mail van, and was flinging open the back doors with great gusto. When he reappeared, he was proudly pushing a red trolley back up the uneven path to Harri's door, laden with three more sacks. Harri watched dumbly as he carefully wheeled the trolley over the threshold and into her lounge, sending Ron Howard scuttling under the coffee table in fright.

'I'll just dump 'em in here, OK?' he said, shaking Harri's hand as he retreated to the doorstep. 'So much mail from London – well, I'll be. Thank you for making this poor old sod's day, Miss Langton! Ta-rar!' And with that, he was gone.

Harri stumbled back into her living room as Ron Howard slowly emerged from his hiding place. Hardly daring to look, she opened the first bag. It fell forward as she did so, its contents spilling out across the carpet, and Ron Howard sprang onto the sofa to save himself from being engulfed by the tidal wave of letters. Harri bent to pick up a handful and saw, with mounting dread, that each envelope bore the same five terrible words: 'Free to a Good Home'.

This was a nightmare: Alex was officially a hit with the desperate readership of *Juste Moi* – and now Harri must uphold the second part of her bargain with Viv: to find a girl for Alex from the vast selection of candidates.

It was going to be *hell* . . .

* * *

Getting too excited is perhaps not the best idea when you're in your fifties with sky-high blood pressure and under strict doctor's orders to avoid stress. But Viv was not likely to let some jumped-up locum's opinion intervene at a time like *this*. Harri eyed her friend with concern as she bounced around the living room like a three-year-old on Haribo overload.

'So . . . many . . . letters!' she gasped, plunging her hands into the nearest postbag and throwing envelopes into the air like a lottery winner revelling in wads of banknotes.

'Viv, calm down!'

'Calm down? How on earth do you expect me to do that, Harri? I mean, *look* at this! All these beautiful, intelligent young women eager to meet my lovely son! It's wonderful!' She clapped her hands together.

'*Look* at what you've done, Harri!'

Harri ignored her sinking feeling. 'Shouldn't that be *we*, Viv?'

Viv dismissed this with a flamboyant wave of her hand. 'Ooh, that's just details.'

Harri eyed her suspiciously. 'You are planning on helping me go through all of these, aren't you?'

Viv picked up a pale pink envelope and inspected the handwriting. 'Of course I am, darling! I'm a tad busy this week, but after that I'm all yours.'

'Right, well, I'll wait until you're free and then we'll start.'

Staring at her, Viv dropped the envelope back into the postbag. 'Harri, this is my son's future happiness we're dealing with – we can't delay it any longer. He's waited long enough, don't you think? So you just make a start and as soon as the Summer Fair planning committee stuff is sorted I'll be there to help.'

Harri folded her arms. 'I am not doing this all by myself, Viv.

This was *your* bright idea, remember? I don't mind making a start but you'd better be around to help with the lion's share – planning committee or no planning committee. Right?'

'Absolutely, darling. You have my word on it. I'll only be absent from duty for a week and then it's Team Harri and Viv all the way. In the meantime, you have my moral support, dear. And all the apple pie you can eat.'

By Tuesday evening, when Auntie Rosemary came to visit, the postbags were still sitting unopened underneath the window. Ron Howard, most offended by their presence, had gone off in a huff and was now curled up in the washing basket in the kitchen. There was no use Harri trying to hide the bags before her aunt walked in; the cottage was almost too small for its furniture already, without accommodating four enormous sacks.

'What, in the name of all that's good, are those?' Rosemary asked.

Harri groaned and shut the front door, following her aunt inside. 'It's a long story. Cup of tea?'

Rosemary bent down to inspect the sacks as Harri walked into the kitchen. '"Free to a Good Home"? What's this all about?'

'It's nothing, really. Just something I agreed to help with,' Harri replied, hoping that her breezy tone would appease Rosemary's curiosity.

It didn't, of course. 'Wait a minute – *Juste Moi* magazine? The only person I know around here who reads that tripe is—'

Harri pulled a face and dropped two teabags into the pot. 'Fancy a biscuit?' she interjected weakly. 'I think I've got some bourbons in the cupboard.'

Rosemary appeared in the kitchen doorway, face stern

and arms folded. 'What has Vivienne Brannan got you into this time?'

The kettle reached boiling point with a noisy whistling fanfare and Harri was glad of the moment it gave her to formulate her reply. 'It's just a project she's got. A daft idea, really. I only said I'd help her to stop her nagging.' She placed the teapot, mugs and milk jug on an old rose-printed tray that had been her mum's. 'Would you grab the biscuit tin, please?'

Rosemary followed her niece back into the living room. 'Hmm. If I know Viv, this is probably going to entail you doing a lot of work and her getting off scot-free.'

Harri poured the tea. 'To be honest, I wish I'd never agreed to the stupid idea in the first place. I should have realised that Viv would try to wriggle her way out of helping. But I have her word this time that she'll pull her weight, so I intend to hold her to it.'

'Well, I suppose you know what you're doing.' Auntie Rosemary placed a concerned hand on Harri's arm. 'But just be careful, OK? Viv's ideas usually end in disaster and I don't want you being caught up in the middle of another one.'

Harri smiled at her aunt. 'I'll be fine, honest. She's just thinking of Al, that's all.'

'What's all this got to do with Alex?'

There really was no point concealing the truth from Rosemary. Harri took a deep breath and told her aunt about Viv's Big Idea. Rosemary listened for a long time, her steady expression masking her true opinion, although Harri could guess what it was. When Harri had told her everything, Rosemary shrugged.

'I thought that woman couldn't surprise me any more but I was wrong. That has got to be the most ridiculous idea I have ever heard. Honestly, I swear she never grew out of her teenage phase. Your poor mother was always bailing her out of daft situations. Well, no matter. What concerns me is *you*, Harriet. I just don't want you losing a friend over this.'

Neither do I, thought Harri. 'I'll be careful, Auntie Ro, honestly. With any luck all the replies will be from complete psychos and Viv will give up the idea.'

Rosemary's nut-brown eyes narrowed. 'You don't believe that any more than I do,' she observed. 'You may be setting yourself up for a fall, that's all I'm saying.'

'So the police said they weren't going to investigate the unexplained lights over Innersley any more because of lack of evidence,' Tom was saying as Harri arrived at work next day.

Nus and George were anything but the rapt audience he was obviously hoping for, but he appeared undaunted.

'I mean, *seriously*, what does that say to you?'

Nus inspected her immaculate nails with an air of boredom. 'That you need to get a life?'

Tom let out a groan and turned to his boss. 'Aw, c'mon. George?'

George stifled a yawn and slid his ample backside off Harri's desk, pulling up the sagging waistband of his trousers as he did so. Harri stifled a giggle, recalling a comment Stella had made about him last week: *Forty-three with a beer gut to die for and he's still single? Shockers!*

'Thomas, a busy travel professional such as myself has no time for indulging in idle tittle-tattle. I suggest you turn your overfertile imagination to the task of coming up with irresistible offers on our Summer Coach Spectacular, all right?'

Tom's frame flopped resignedly. 'I can't believe there's a blatant government conspiracy going on right underneath our noses and *none* of you is even remotely interested.' He grabbed an empty brochure box and plodded into the stockroom.

Harri smiled at Nus. 'What's all that about?'

Nus leaned down to retrieve her mobile from her bag. 'UFOs above Innersley, apparently.' She started to text, her acrylic nails squeaking on the keypad as she did so.

George's flushed face appeared in the doorway to his office. 'Harriet, do you have a minute?'

'Sure,' she replied, standing up.

'And bring us a coffee while you're at it, eh, chick?'

'Ooh, tea, please,' Nus said, without looking up from her phone.

'Hot choc for me.' Tom's voice floated in from the depths of the stockroom.

Groaning, Harri collected everyone's mugs from the office and made her way to SLIT's ridiculously small kitchen. In truth, the title 'kitchen' was incredibly generous for what the room actually was; calling it a cupboard with a stainless-steel sink squeezed into one corner would be more accurate. The green vinyl covering the floor looked like it hadn't been cleaned in years and stuck to the soles of her shoes as Harri manoeuvred her way around the boxes of brochures that were haphazardly stacked by the entrance. A few brave shafts of light managed to break through the grey grime covering the tiny safety glass window as the old water boiler shuddered and bumped into life. Trying not to inhale the strong smell of mouldy plastic, Harri filled the mugs with hot water and balanced them on a 'wood-effect' tray that had once passed for mahogany (but now resembled grey-brown peeling chipboard) along with tea-bags, coffee jar, hot chocolate canister, slightly damp sugar bag and spoons, carefully navigating the boxes to emerge back into the office. Having worked at SLIT for as long as she had, she'd quickly learned that the safest way to prepare drinks was at her own desk rather than braving the kitchen's cramped confines.

Drinks duly delivered to Nus and Tom, she took her own mug and George's into his cramped office at the back of the shop.

'Ah, Harriet. Shut the door, would you?'

Harri did so, then sat down on the brown tweed chair that, like the office's owner, had seen decidedly better days.

'Right. I've got this – um – *situation* happening at the moment that's a little, well, *delicate*, and I need your help to fix it.'

Nightmarish thoughts raced through Harri's mind. 'Oh?'

'You see, the thing is, I'm up to my eyes in it right now, what with the planning required to make sure SLIT offers its customers the best in national *vacationing* and, to be totally frank, I've got piles . . . *big* ones . . .'

Harri shot to her feet. 'George, there are some things I don't need to know.'

George looked at her, mystified, his already flushed features then turning a pinker shade of puce as realisation dawned. 'Oh, no! No! I mean piles of *work* to do this week!'

The relief Harri felt was immense. However much she liked her boss, there were certain areas she just wasn't ready to enter with him. Relaxing, she resumed her seat. 'Sorry, George.'

George pulled an off-white handkerchief from his shirt pocket and dabbed his forehead. 'I should think so too. As if I would share something like that with a member of my own staff . . .'

'Absolutely. So, you were saying?'

'What? Oh, yes. Well, you see, there's this woman and she won't leave me alone.'

'Ooh, George, driving the ladies wild again, are you?'

'No I am not. At least, not *this* woman. The fact is, she's been bombarding me with phone calls for the past two weeks about some crazy business venture she's starting and I think she might be getting a little – um . . .' he leaned forward confidentially, '. . . *obsessed*, if you know what I mean.'

Harri resisted the urge to smile. 'I see. So why do you want my help?'

George pushed a dog-eared sticky note across his desk to her. 'Go and see her, would you? Her number's on there.'

'But I thought you said we were busy, George?'

'I said *I'm* busy,' he snapped, grabbing a handful of papers from his desk and shuffling them ineptly to emphasise his point. 'But I can spare *you*. I've told her to expect a call from my assistant manager.'

Harri surveyed him suspiciously. 'Assistant manager? Since when?'

'You've been here almost as long as I have,' George replied huffily. 'It was only a matter of time.' He took a long sip of coffee.

Sensing an opportunity, Harri shook her head. 'Nope, sorry, George. Not without a significant raise in my salary.'

George spluttered and wiped his mouth. 'Pardon?'

Harri smiled benevolently at her boss. 'You know what a raise is, don't you, George? Obviously taking on such a role would be a major step in my career – I would need to see more money to reflect the greater responsibility such a role would bring. Consider it an indicator of your greater trust in me.'

She kept her stare firmly fixed on her boss, who was now turning a rather interesting shade of lilac.

'Well, I . . . I . . .'

Harri looked at her watch. 'Going to have to hurry you, I'm afraid. *Very* busy day out there for me, you know.'

'Fine! We'll increase your salary . . .'

'By how much?'

'Eh?'

'Well, it's a competitive market out there, George. I might not accept.'

George was beginning to resemble a shoddily attired soon-to-be-active volcano. 'Are you taking the *michael*? Fine. Name your terms.'

'Fifteen per cent. Effective immediately.'

'What?'

'Or we can just keep it like it is. I'm sure that lady will calm down once you've had a *nice long chat* . . .'

George gripped the edge of his desk, eyes wild with panic. 'All right! Fifteen per cent it is.'

Harri rose serenely and opened the door. 'George, that's so thoughtful of you. Thank you.'

As she stepped out of the office, she heard his strangled voice call out behind her. '. . . but there's likely to be a *lot* more work for you now.'

'I wouldn't expect anything less,' Harri called over her shoulder, settling back at her desk, hardly believing her own audacity.

'What was all that about?' Nus asked, as Tom appeared beside her, the pair of them looking like wide-eyed bushbabies.

Harri picked up the phone and started to dial the number scibbled on the sticky note in George's untidy handwriting. 'Nothing. George's got woman trouble, that's all . . . Hello? Is that Emily Williams? Hi, it's Harri Langton, assistant manager at Sun Lovers International Travel . . .'

The look on Nus and Tom's faces was a picture.

'I'm just calling about the . . . er, yes, of course I'd be happy to visit you . . . erm, great, so what time would you . . . ? Oh, right, half an hour would be fine. OK . . .'

The call clicked on the other end of the line and Harri stared at the receiver. 'Bye then.'

Tom folded his arms as Nus stood up. '*Assistant manager?* Since when?'

Harri grabbed her bag and grinned at them as she passed. 'Can't explain now, I've got to head out. See you later!'

To say that the lady on the other end of the phone had been enthusiastic would be like saying Nureyev wasn't bad at dancing. Harri couldn't help but grin as she drove through the high-hedged lanes towards Emily's home. Poor George. After years of encountering disinterest from the good ladies of Stone Yardley – with the possible exception of his mother – someone as forthright as Emily must have scared him half to death.

'My place is a little hard to find,' Emily had gushed during the call. 'Head for Little Swinford and then just before you get to the grass triangle where the road splits towards Greenwell, you take a left down the farm track. It's a bit bumpy but it should be OK.'

Harri's ageing Fiat Punto bounced wildly along the dirt and gravel track before it passed through an opening in the hedge and headed steeply downhill. A small cluster of farm buildings nestled between two rounded hills came into view. Harri caught her breath; the place was stunning. An old tithe barn stood crookedly next to some whitewashed outbuildings, with the main farmhouse to the right. An elegant red-brick building, it was surrounded by a riot of cottage-garden flowers – delphiniums, poppies, Sweet Williams and lavender, with pale pink roses curling haphazardly around the green front door. As Harri parked and stepped out, she was almost knocked back into the car by a large black and white collie that bounded out of the house to greet her, closely followed by a tall, dark-haired lady dressed in a pale pink jumper, her faded jeans tucked hurriedly into her daffodil-patterned wellies.

'Fly! Fly, come here, you daft mutt!' she laughed as she approached. 'He's harmless, just a little too welcoming I'm afraid. You are OK with dogs, aren't you?'

Harri regained her balance and patted the overexcited dog as it head-butted her knees. 'Yes, I'm fine. He's a lovely dog.'

'Runt of the litter, that one, would you believe?' Emily shook her head and extended her hand. 'You must be Harri. I'm Emily, in case you hadn't guessed.'

Harri shook her hand. 'Nice to meet you. This place is amazing.'

Emily beamed brightly. 'Welcome to Greenwell Hill Farm. Sixteenth century, most of it. Until some horrible Victorian got a bit carried away with the farmhouse – those chimneys are ridiculous.'

Harri looked up to see four very ornate twisted chimneys rising up from the farmhouse roof. 'Wow.'

'Hmm, I know. I wanted to take them down but my hubby adores the things. No accounting for taste, obviously. Anyway, come in, the kettle's on.'

The warmth of the kitchen enveloped them like a cosy blanket as Harri and Emily entered. It was a study in shabby chic: faded pink gingham curtains hung at the large sash window, looking out to the rolling fields beyond; blue and white striped crockery was stacked haphazardly by the large white Belfast sink; bunches of dried lavender, rosemary and sage hung from the edges of the old whitewashed wood cupboards above the well-worn oak worktops; a freshly baked loaf was positioned invitingly on a breadboard, alongside a crackle-glazed butter dish and half-empty jar of home-made jam, while freshly picked flowers had been casually arranged in an old enamel jug on the old pine kitchen table.

Fly padded into the kitchen, claws clicking on the slate floor tiles and tail wagging wildly, headed over to Harri and flopped down across her feet.

'Fly! I'm sorry, Harri. He's got a thing for warming visitors' feet, I'm afraid,' Emily smiled ruefully as she filled a kettle and placed it on the stove. 'I think it's his way of making people stay.'

Harri leaned down to ruffle the soft fur on Fly's stomach. 'I don't mind, really. I have a cat so I'm not used to such an enthusiastic welcome.'

'We've got three of those too,' Emily smiled, 'but they seem to spend most of their time in the barn.'

After the kettle had come to its shrill whistling boil and the 'brown Betty' teapot was filled and covered with a hand-knitted bobble-topped tea-cosy, Emily joined Harri at the table.

Harri pulled out a notebook and pen. 'So, tell me about your business venture then.'

Emily visibly sparkled and grasped her blue-striped mug with both hands. 'Well, I've had this idea and, I have to admit, it's completely nuts, but I just can't seem to get it out of my mind, no matter how hard I try, you know?'

'Breathe, Emily!' Harri laughed. 'I'm here for a while.'

Emily flushed and shook her head. 'I'm sorry. It's just that I have all this . . . *stuff* . . . buzzing around in my head and I haven't really spoken to anyone except my hubby about it.'

She took a deep breath and sat back in her chair. 'Right, it's like this: I work in the bank in Stone Yardley, in Market Street – you know, the one between Chiltern's Ironmongers and the barbers? Well, I've worked there for ten years, since I came back from university, and it's OK, I mean, it pays the bills. But the job – it just feels like a strait-jacket, you know? The thing is, a while ago I started to have an idea for my own business, using the farm as a base. It won't go away; it's all I think about. And I know it's a crazy plan – I mean, Stu and I are both working and we only just manage to keep this place running, so the thought of going self-employed and risking all of this is so scary. It's still just an idea at the moment. Nobody knows at work or anything. I'm just looking at possibilities.'

'So what sort of thing do you want to do here?' Harri asked, taking a sip of strong tea.

'Craft weekends, writing retreats, art holidays, things like that,' Emily beamed. 'I did art and ceramics at uni and I have a couple of friends who are artists. My sister's a writer, so she said she'd be happy to help. Stu's really into photography and he has lots of walks around the fields here that he could take people out on. So, between us all I think we could come up with quite a varied programme.'

'Would you be providing accommodation here, too?'

'I'm not sure. I mean, we could turn the barn into a bunk-house, I suppose, or maybe work with some of the pubs and B&Bs in the villages near here. In the long term we'd like to convert some of the outbuildings, but that's a long way off. I just think it would be a great thing to offer to people perhaps from Birmingham or Worcester to begin with – you know, a fun break not too far from home? Eventually I could see people coming from all over the place. I mean, we're not far from the

M6 and there are so many gorgeous places nearby that we could take people to.'

'That's a brilliant idea. How can you see the travel agency helping, then?'

Emily picked up the teapot and topped up their mugs. 'Just help us to promote it initially, then maybe eventually take charge of bookings, and we'll give you commission on sales.'

Harri chewed her pen as she consulted the notes she'd been making. She could feel excitement rising within her: Emily's enthusiasm was infectious and even though she knew there would be a lot of work ahead to get the business off the ground, Harri was filled with admiration for the lady staring expectantly at her at the other side of the farmhouse table. 'I can't see any reason why this wouldn't work, to be honest with you,' she said after a while. 'I think your idea could turn into a lucrative business.'

The look of relief on Emily's face was immense.

'Really? I mean, please don't feel you have to say that just because you're here. If it's completely unworkable, I'd rather find out now before I start committing our finances.'

'Don't worry, I won't feel pressured. Besides, it won't be my decision at the end of the day. George will need to approve everything before we go ahead.'

Emily's smile faded. 'Oh. I don't think I've made a very good impression on your boss. He was really short with me on the phone this morning.'

Harri giggled. 'He's always short with people.'

'He is?'

'Yes, about five foot six usually. Sorry, it's a bit of an in-joke at SLIT. We reckon he's always trying to prove a point with everyone because he's, well, *overcompensating*?'

Emily brightened. 'Oh, I see.'

'He's harmless, honestly. He just can't cope with women who actually want to talk to him. Anyway, I can't see him objecting to your plans – especially if I say I'll take responsibility for it. Anything that brings in money without the need for him to do any work is bound to be a hit.'

'Would you really be prepared to do that?'

Harri smiled. 'Absolutely. I think it's a wonderful idea. I'm a bit envious, actually.'

'How come?'

'Well, you being prepared to give up your job and go for it with this business. It's inspirational. So I'd like to help.'

A strange smile passed across Emily's face. 'I'm so pleased to have met you, Harri. I think we're going to get on really well. Look, I've got a Victoria sponge in the pantry – don't suppose you fancy helping me eat it? That is, if you don't have something you have to get back for?'

Harri thought about the four sacks of *Juste Moi* letters lying menacingly in wait for her at home and grinned back. 'Nothing that can't wait. Cake sounds like a great idea.'

There are some people it takes a lifetime to get to know and others you understand in an instant. For Harri, Emily was most definitely in the latter category. What was meant to be a short, business-related conversation metamorphosed into a six-hour chat, happily winding its way through afternoon tea and on to a hearty pork and leek casserole dinner surrounded by the farm's assorted pets – Freeman, Hardy and Willis, the cats; Fly, and Jemima, a rescued duck that liked to snuggle in one corner of the dog bed in the kitchen. Emily's husband, Stu, came home around seven, much to the delight of Fly, who dashed around his ankles until his master bent down to stroke his back.

Harri watched the mayhem from over the top of her mug, enjoying the sense of peace it gave her. It had been a long time since she had felt part of a busy household, its warmth and noise pervading her being, catching her up in the casual luxury of everyday life. The last few years with her parents had been cruelly robbed of this carefree atmosphere – every quiet conversation carefully constructed to avoid the inevitable questions, every decision dictated by the demands of the disease slowly destroying her family. Whilst there was always humour in the house – her parents were adamant that being terminally ill didn't negate the need for laughter – a leaden sense of reality hung heavily around the room, silently reminding the family of what lay ahead. Harri didn't just lose her parents, she lost all the day-to-day, inconsequential things that most families experience without even noticing: kitchen sink conversations, arguments over whose turn it was to take the bins out or what programme to watch on television – insignificant exchanges that oiled each day and kept daily life rumbling on.

As Harri listened to the conversation flowing between Emily and Stu, she wondered if she would ever be part of that kind of effortless relationship again. There were moments with Rob where glimpses of it would appear, but if they were together all the time, would those moments naturally lengthen into a way of life? Pushing the thought aside, Harri checked her watch and smiled at the happy couple.

'I should really get going. I hadn't realised how late it was.'

'Blimey, sorry, we've kept you really late, haven't we?' Stu placed his arm around his wife. 'We don't get visitors very often and it's good to be able to share our business idea with someone other than ourselves or the animals. Us and our crazy dreams, eh?'

'They're not crazy,' Harri replied. 'I honestly think you've got the potential for a great business. It's just important to get all the details sorted before you both commit to it, that's all. I'll get you a list of all the local B&Bs and have a chat with them regarding block bookings. It's possible they'll be interested in a discount if you can guarantee a certain number of guests at a time. You need to think about logistics – like how many people you're going to have on each course, how you're going to feed everyone, transport to and from accommodation, costs involved and how to work all that into a tariff that will cover everything, without leaving you out of pocket or pricing yourself out of the market.'

'You can come again,' Stu said, exchanging a look with Emily, 'and not just for the business advice, either.'

'Glad to be of service,' Harri smiled as she rose to leave. 'Besides, with food as good as yours, it's my pleasure.'

When Harri walked up to her front door that evening, the clouds had cleared to reveal a full moon that lit the path as brightly as a streetlamp. Clicking her key into the lock she paused to look up past the cottage's blue-brick gable to the stars spreading out across the night sky. A memory of her mum flashed into her mind – back when Harri was a little girl and her family was as carefree as everyone else. At bedtime one night, Harri and her mother had pulled open the curtains in her bedroom to say good night to the moon (a family tradition for as long as she could remember) and Harri had noticed the twinkling stars in the indigo sky.

'I love the stars, Mummy.'

'Well, you know what they are, don't you, darling? Those are the nightlights of the angels. They put them on at night to remind us that they're there. All the people we love who have died don't ever forget us. They just put nightlights on to show us that they're watching and waiting for us. So even if we feel alone or scared, we can see the sparkly lights in the sky and know we're not on our own after all.'

It was a silly notion, typical of the tales her mum was so skilled at spinning: each ray of sunlight was someone in heaven opening a window; rainbows were what happened when angels knocked over paint pots in their art class; thunder was just God moving the piano when He was vacuuming the heavenly carpets. Yet there was something so comforting in these whimsical stories that made Harri immediately take them to heart.

She let out a long sigh, watching her moonlit breath rise into the night air.

'Thanks for the nightlights, Mum. Give my love to Dad and Gran. I miss you all . . .'

The night's chill shivered through her and, suddenly self-conscious, she quickly opened the cottage door and stepped inside.

CHAPTER NINE

The Big 'F'

The flickering strip light finally gives up the ghost and splutters off, throwing a third of the room into dinginess. Harri sniffs and looks around for toilet paper to blow her nose. True to form, the roll on the cistern is empty, save for half a sheet. On closer inspection, Harri discovers that the remaining remnant is the crackly medicated variety of toilet paper, wryly christened by Stella as 'scratch and sniff'.

Despite the panic still gripping her insides, Harri finds herself smiling.

'. . . And one, two, three, four . . . come on now, keep working, everybody!'

Stella leaned over to Harri. '*How* many sacks did you say there were?'

Harri grimaced. 'Four. Enormous ones.'

'You're kidding me!'

'. . . Good, people! Now, into your side lunges, stretch out wide . . .'

'I am *not* kidding.'

'So have you read them all, yet?'

'. . . two, three, four . . . stretch even more if you can . . .'

'No, I haven't.'

Stella gawped at her. 'Well, don't you think you need to maybe *start*?'

'. . . *Really* focus on your abs now and keep your chin nice and high . . .'

'I guess I had better start on them soon – if for nothing else than to get my living room back. If those sacks stay there any longer I think Ron will abandon me. I was waiting for Viv to help, seeing as it was *her* idea for *her* son.'

'. . . Keeping those stomach muscles taut, remember, concentrate on your core . . .'

'You could always help me, if you like? There's bound to be some completely weird ones in there . . .'

'. . . That's great! One more, people, *really* push hard . . .'

'Er, *no*, thank you. This mess is completely yours, hon.'

'. . . and now onto the other side, stretch it out . . .'

'Thanks for the support, Stel.'

'You're welcome. My *life*, what is she doing now?'

'. . . lifting the leg ninety degrees to the body and *hold* . . .'

'That's impossible, surely?'

Stella pulled a face. 'Stuff *that* . . . Fancy some more ice cream?' She clicked the remote control and the DVD froze, leaving the fitness trainer holding her impossible pose a lot longer than even she would recommend.

Harri giggled. 'Only you could enjoy watching fitness DVDs in the company of Ben & Jerry.'

Stella scooped three generous spoonfuls of chocolate ice cream into Harri's bowl and handed it back to her. 'Trust me, we're burning calories while we're doing this.'

'We are?'

'Absolutely. I read it in a magazine. If we watch a fitness

DVD and really concentrate on it, we end up burning the same amount of calories as we would if we were actually doing the exercises. Science *fact.*'

'And if we watch it whilst eating incredibly calorific snacks?'

Stella grinned. 'It's just carbohydrate loading. All the major athletes do it. Got to make sure we can go the distance, haven't we?'

'Stel, you are dreadful.'

'Maybe,' she answered mid-mouthful, 'but you have to admit, it's a great way to spend a Thursday evening. So when are you going to start reading the letters?'

'Tomorrow night. I'll start after work.'

Stella frowned. 'Aren't you seeing Rob tomorrow night?'

'He's in Preston all weekend.'

'Again? Flippin' Nora, Harri, that guy is more elusive than the Scarlet Pimpernel. If you were dating Lord Lucan you'd see him more often.'

'It's just this flipping Preston contract that his company are so intent on winning. Rob was really upset about this weekend – he called me from work at lunchtime today and it took me nearly twenty minutes to calm him down. Turns out he'd planned a surprise weekend away for us in the Cotswolds and he was going to spring it on me tomorrow evening after work. Then his boss told him he was needed in Preston.' She sighed and stabbed at the ice cream in her bowl. 'I hate to see him so bogged down with work and the worst thing is there's nothing I can do about it.'

Stella gave a sympathetic smile. 'That must be tough for the two of you. But at least he seems to be trying to make it up to you with all these gifts and surprises you keep getting. That's a good man in my book! So –' she gave Harri a playful jab in the ribs, 'all weekend with the Sacks of Desperation then, eh?'

Harri pulled a face. 'Hmm, lucky me.'

'Seriously, H, I reckon you should just drop them off at Al's and tell him they're a gift from the Gods of Dubious Dates.'

Harri laughed. 'Maybe I should.' Her thoughts switched to an issue she'd been mulling over that day. 'Actually, Stel, there's something I've been meaning to ask you about.'

A dark look passed across Stella's perfect features and she crossed her arms.

'Oh?'

Harri took a deep breath. It wasn't that her best friend never did anything for her, but it had to be said that Stella liked to see significant evidence of the benefits of a situation before agreeing. 'Well,' she began, as brightly as she could, 'you know that travel writer I like, Dan Beagle?'

'The cute guy with the daft name? Yes, I know him.'

'He's doing a seminar to mark the launch of his new book in Oxford next month. It's a Saturday evening and I know Rob doesn't want to go. The thing is, I don't want to look like a complete hypocrite after making such an issue with him about us spending more time together. I know he'll be fine about me doing something without him on a Saturday, it's just that I'd feel better about it if I wasn't going by myself.'

'So you want me to come with you?'

'Would you? We could make a day of it – a bit of a girly day out – maybe do some shopping and have lunch and then go to the Dan Beagle thing in the evening. I might even persuade Rob to go and see some of his old football team mates, seeing as he hasn't really seen that much of them lately.'

Stella thought for a moment, then clapped her hands. 'I've got a better idea. How about we make it a weekend away?'

Harri beamed. 'Now *that* is a fantastic idea! What did you have in mind?'

Stella's growing excitement was impossible to conceal. 'There's this amazing day spa in Oxford that was featured in *Red* magazine this month – it looks awesome and I really want to try it out. So why not travel down on the Friday night, stay in a hotel and then spend the Saturday at the spa before sexy Dan's talk? Then we could do some shopping on Sunday before we get back. It'll be my treat, OK?'

'Stel, that sounds *amazing*! But I can't ask you to pay for it all.'

Stella shrugged. 'Well, I feel bad that I haven't managed to take you abroad yet like I keep saying I'm going to, so this is my way of making it up to you. Besides, I'm interested to see if Mr Beagle is as fit in real life as he is in the pictures in those books of yours.'

Dan Beagle represented everything Harri longed to be: adventurer, traveller, photographer, daredevil. He seemed to think nothing of heading off into uncharted territory for months on end, with only his camera for company. In a few short years, this young explorer had won the acclaim of the world's press and the respect of his peers, redefining travel writing with his multi-award-winning books. What Harri loved the most about his work was the way he maintained his wide-eyed wonder at every new environment he discovered, whether it was virgin rainforest, inhospitable desert or treacherous frozen wasteland. Unlike the pale imitators who appeared in his wake, Dan seemed to understand and nurture an innate sense of childlike thrill at discovering new places in his world.

In her wildest dreams, Harri believed she was capable of this type of travel – never taking a step for granted as she boldly advanced into the unknown. From the comfort of her cottage, she immersed herself in Dan's words, letting him take her by the hand to lead her into countless magical places. As she soaked in every detail, it was as if he understood the traveller imprisoned within her, the free spirit straining against her cautiousness, bidding her to break out: *Welcome to my world, Harri. Come with me . . .*

Though she would never admit it to Stella, Harri harboured a hope that maybe, just maybe, Dan would look out into the seminar audience and see her sitting there. Instantly, he would stop talking, put his notes down on the lectern, step off the stage and walk towards her, bathed in the silver glow of a spotlight that charted his course down the hall. Reaching the end of her row, he would point straight at her.

'You.'

Harri would look around her, heart beating wildly, before bringing her wondering eyes back to his. He would smile and hold out his hand. 'Yes, you, Harri. I want you to come with me.'

'When?'

'Right now.'

And she would rise, all eyes in the place fixed on her. His large, warm hand would gently take hers and they would stride purposefully out of the hall and into the great, wide world . . .

It wasn't a love thing; not necessarily. Yes, Dan was undeniably good-looking, with rugged features, sun-bleached hair and sea-green eyes, but it was more than that for Harri. What she longed for was to travel the world with someone who understood her completely.

'Everybody needs a soul mate,' Mrs Bincham observed next day, nodding sagely as she doled out squares of what appeared to be meringue-covered flapjack to the bemused staff of SLIT. 'I mean, take me and my Geoff. I was working the tea round at Land Oak Steelworks and it was his first day. He complimented my Melting Moments and that was it – I just knew we were meant to be. Forty-three years later and we'm still as strong as ever. "Eth," he says to me, "when I met you I met my match. There ay none like you, pet." And he's right. Like I said before, Harriet – once that Big F's got you in its sights, there ay nothing you can do but go with the flow, if you know what I mean. *Tsk!* Go on, Thomas, it won't kill you.'

Tom paled and swallowed hard. 'Right, Mrs B. Um, thanks.' He eyed the flapjack slice cautiously then took a large bite.

'There now, see? Wasn't as much of a trauma as you thought, eh?'

'Mmmwwfffhhh . . .' Tom replied, his expression undulating between pleased, confused and disgusted.

Harri giggled as she watched Mrs Bincham trundle away with her notorious Tupperware. 'Enjoying your Lemon Meringue Flapjack, Tom?'

He swallowed and shuddered. 'It was a taste sensation. I think I need a lie down.'

George rushed in, white-faced and visibly shaking. 'Can you keep *that woman* and her ungodly concoctions away from me, please? The last time I ate something from that blasted box of hers I ended up on the Rennies for a week.'

'She means well, George,' Harri smiled as the front door opened and Nusrin appeared.

'Is she still here?' Nusrin whispered. George, Tom and Harri nodded and Nusrin pulled a face. 'Right, if she asks, I can't eat anything from Tupperware boxes, OK?'

George frowned. 'Why not?'

Nus smirked as she sat back at her desk. 'It's against my religion.'

'Why didn't I think of that?' Tom moaned.

'I don't think saying your gran's a Methodist counts,' Harri replied, checking her watch. 'Right, I'm going to go for lunch, if that's OK?'

George dismissed her with what he imagined to be an authoritative hand gesture. 'Off you go, Harriet.' Then he ruined the illusion of superiority by adding, 'Don't suppose you could take Mrs B with you?'

Harri grabbed her bag and headed for the door. 'Ooh, sorry, George. I think she's still got a bit of cleaning left to do. See you in an hour.'

George's groan followed her all the way out to the High Street.

Stone Yardley was a town, by rights, yet almost all of its residents still referred to it as 'the village'. Essentially two long streets forming a cross, the main shopping area had managed to retain the air of a friendly market town, even though the more recent additions of housing developments had extended it far beyond its original sixteenth-century plan. Despite the development of Berryhall – one of Europe's largest out-of-town shopping centres – only five miles up the road, most of the businesses in High Street and Market Street were still proudly trading thirty or forty years after their establishment. Local people jealously guarded their town and it was largely down to them that Stone Yardley remained a popular local shopping venue.

Harri, like so many of Stone Yardley's residents, had a great affection for her hometown. Whilst there were undeniably prettier places nearby – not least just over the neighbouring borders of Shropshire and Staffordshire – there was something homely and welcoming about its streets that set it apart from the faceless malls of Berryhall. There was a strong community spirit, meaning that it was often impossible to walk Stone Yardley's streets without bumping into several people you knew.

115

Today was no exception. As Harri left SLIT she met Lucy Allan, an old friend from school, Dave Simpson, who used to be one of her dad's old cricket buddies, and Mrs Gertrude Walker, the indomitable octogenarian Chairwoman of Stone Yardley's WI.

'Ah, Harriet,' she boomed, clasping a tweed-sleeved hand on Harri's arm with surprising strength for someone of her considerable years, 'I wonder if you've given any more thought to our invitation to come and address the ladies?'

'I'd love to,' Harri answered carefully, 'but I'm not sure what kind of travel would interest your members.' She had visions of her presentation being reduced to a glorified advert for STD coaches.

Gertrude's eyes narrowed slightly and a wry smile began to play across her thin lips. 'What kind of travel do you *think* the ladies would be interested to hear about?'

Harri felt a slow blush creeping across her cheeks. There were times when being a redhead with porcelain-pale skin was a distinct disadvantage . . . 'Um, well, British travel . . . erm . . . perhaps by coach?'

Gertrude threw her head back and guffawed so loudly that people walking past were stopped in their tracks. 'My dear, you have a very clichéd view of what Stone Yardley WI is all about! Believe me, the *last* thing our members want to hear about is having to be squeezed into luxury cattle trucks and herded about the countryside like a bunch of geriatrics. Some of us may appear old and frail but – take my word for it – many of our members have spent more time abroad during their retirement than they have spent in this village. I, for example, holidayed last in Malaysia, whilst Isobel Hannigan has just returned from a four-week safari in the Masai Mara.'

Harri was aware that her jaw was making a valiant bid for

the pavement, but this revelation had frozen her to the spot. 'Oh . . .'

'So, I was thinking you could perhaps talk to us about the latest trend for adventure travel,' Gertrude continued, 'if you think we could bear the excitement, that is?'

'I . . . er . . . yes, certainly . . .'

'Excellent! Well, I shall put together a list of possible dates and ping them over to you. You are on email, are you not?'

Harri suppressed a grin as she rummaged in her handbag. 'Yes, I am. Here's my card.'

'Wonderful. Actually, come to think of it, I don't suppose you're on Facebook, are you?'

'Yes, I am.'

'Excellent! I'll look you up this evening. Email is *so* last year, don't you think?'

Harri was still giggling to herself when she reached Lavender's, Stone Yardley's family bakers. As usual, the lunch queue stretched almost out of the door, so she patiently joined the back of it, enjoying the warm June sun on her back as she checked her mobile for messages.

Three texts were awaiting her attention. The first was from Auntie Rosemary, who still hadn't mastered the art of changing case in her texts, meaning that all her messages gave the impression of someone shouting angrily at you.

HI HARRIET ARE YOU COPING WITH THE LETTERS HOPE SO. TEA AT MINE IF YOU NEED A BREAK ANYTIME. REMEMBER GRANDMA DILLONS BDAY ON MONDAY. LUV AUNTIE R XX

From the text it appeared that Auntie Rosemary must be allergic to any punctuation that wasn't a full stop. 'Oh, I do

117

love you, Auntie Ro,' Harri murmured, flicking to the second text, which turned out to be from Rob:

Hey Red ☺
Missing you tons this week. Preston is a nightmare as usual. Will be all yours on Monday night tho – can't wait baby
R x

Harri felt a surge of excitement. The thought of spending Monday night with Rob was wonderful, especially after all the time he had spent away recently.

The last message was from a number she didn't recognise. It was only when she opened it that a leaden sense of reality thudded through her, stealing her sunny mood:

Hi Harri, hope you don't mind me texting you but thought this was quicker than mail or email. Just wondered how you're getting on with the replies for Alex? Obviously I know there's a lot of them so no pressure, but it's been a week and my editor's getting a tad jumpy. Any chance you could set up first date a.s.a.p and let us know? Doesn't have to be a keeper, just needs to happen sooner rather than later. Hope you're well. Chloe x

Groaning, Harri deleted the text and threw her phone into her bag. This was the last thing she needed to hear. Perhaps naïvely, she had assumed that after the feature in *Juste Moi* and receiving the mountain of replies, the ordeal would be over as far as Chloë and her overzealous editor were concerned.

As she reached the counter Harri surveyed the golden

pastries, sausage rolls, pies and toasted cheese and ham slices all lined up on the hot, glass shelves, and suddenly realised her appetite had vanished. Ordering some sausage rolls that she knew would ultimately end up easing Tom's gastric pain after the onslaught of Mrs Bincham's creation, she paid and went out into the bright sun of the High Street. Walking quickly past Wātea, she ducked down the narrow passageway that led to Reindeer Court, a small courtyard filled with boutique shops. Unlike the stalwart businesses on High Street and Market Street, the shops in Reindeer Court regularly changed hands – it was almost as if businesses came and went under the cover of darkness, hidden from Stone Yardley's eyes.

The changing face of the small courtyard fascinated Harri.

At present, Reindeer Court offered two dress shops – one stocking cheap but cheerful copies of designer clothes that celebs *du jour* were sporting, the other a kooky dress exchange that had surprised everyone by remaining in business for three years and now held the honour of being the longest-serving business in the courtyard; Beadazzled, a bead shop, open for only six months but already much loved by Stone Yardley's teenage goth contingent (which was considerably larger than Harri had realised); a hospice charity shop filled with aged china, battered furniture and an impressive selection of much loved if slightly tatty shoes arranged in its window; and, at the end of the courtyard, a tiny, yet immaculate kitchen equipment shop.

Harri pushed open the green-painted door of Somethin' Cookin' and an old-fashioned brass bell heralded her arrival. It never ceased to amaze her just how many weird and wonderful kitchen gadgets were squeezed into the space. Bunches of herbs hung from pan racks suspended from the ceiling; wicker baskets lined the floors containing everything from china blackbird pie funnels to steel apple slicers and wind-up egg timers; whilst

Shaker-style fabric aprons and brightly coloured oven gloves were draped on hooks at the end of the pine shelving units that held untold treasures, all of which were guaranteed to make your kitchen look like Nigella's.

As Harri approached the beechwood counter, Viv appeared from the minuscule stockroom that also served as a staffroom, cloakroom and kitchen.

'Harri *darling*! What a surprise! Are you on lunch? How long have you got, sweetheart? Long enough for a cup of tea, surely? I'll put the kettle on . . . One tick!'

She disappeared again, before Harri could answer. After a few moments, Harri heard the sound of a kettle boiling, and a puff of steam came into the shop, closely followed by a flushed Viv brandishing a stripy tray laden with two mugs, a sugar bowl, large hand-painted teapot and a biscuit jar.

No matter where she was or what she was doing, Viv always managed to look like a *Country Life* cliché – as if she should be accompanied by the caption: 'Viv likes nothing better than pottering about on her verdant allotment after another successful day of trading at her bespoke kitchen store . . .'

'I've got about half an hour,' Harri said, in a brave attempt to answer at least one of Viv's barrage of questions. Not that Viv was listening, of course.

'Have a biscuit – go on! They're fresh out of the Aga this morning.'

Harri took a bite of the deliciously sweet syrupy cookie and shook her head. 'You made these this morning?'

Viv shrugged. 'The chickens were up early and so was I. Besides, I couldn't get back to sleep after I'd fed them, so I thought why not do a spot of baking? Don't look so surprised, Harri, it's not like there's any great difficulty involved in making Golden Syrup Oaties.'

'Only you could think of baking as an early morning activity, Viv.'

Viv poured tea into two Denby mugs. 'Farmer's daughter, remember? It's bred into you.'

'So, how's business today?' Harri asked, taking one of the mugs and inhaling its inviting aroma.

'Slow. But then Fridays usually are. I think it's the hangover from the old half-day closing days. Stone Yardlians don't move very quickly with the times.'

Harri sipped her tea. 'Tell me about it. I swear, some of our customers at SLIT would probably prefer it if we still offered holidays by hansom cab. Although I did just meet an octogenarian with a taste for adventure travel.'

'Who on earth was that?'

'Mrs Walker from the WI.'

'That woman is *fierce*, Harri; you watch her. So, how are you getting on with all those lovely "Free to a Good Home" replies, eh?'

Harri felt her heart plummeting again, and took a large gulp of tea. 'I haven't started yet. I was waiting for you, remember?'

Viv's mug banged down on the wood counter as incredulousness painted her face. 'What do you mean, "haven't started yet"? This is *important*, Harri – no, more than that – it's *vital* to the future happiness of my beautiful son and, can I remind you, your absolute best male friend in the whole wide world? This is an emergency, Harri! Time is of the essence! When are you going to begin sorting them?'

Realising that Viv was unlikely to offer help any time soon – and recalling Chloë's thinly veiled panic in her text – Harri surrendered to the inevitable. 'I'll start tonight.'

* * *

Unusually for a Friday afternoon in the salubrious surroundings of SLIT, time seemed to pass at lightning speed. Harri tried to make every moment last, to put off the inevitability of the task ahead of her, but despite her best efforts, five thirty arrived like an irate customer, demanding her attention.

'You off anywhere nice tonight?' she asked Tom, hoping he would delay her with his usual long-winded descriptions of the various pub routes he and his equally spotty mates were planning to cover.

But instead he went red and mumbled, 'Mmmffh . . . gtta-date . . .' before dashing out of the door.

Harri smiled hopefully at Nusrin, but she was mid-text and merely lifted an elegant hand in reply as she followed Tom out.

George appeared from his office, tie loosely hanging to one side and middle shirt button open, revealing a completely unwarranted glimpse of grey-white vest beneath. 'Off you go then, Harriet.'

'Don't you want me to lock up, George?' Panic was setting in. What was *wrong* with everyone today? Why choose this Friday to break the habits of a lifetime? George was usually long gone by now muttering something unconvincing about mountains of paperwork to do at home (the George Duffield code for 'going for a pint at The Fleece', the rowdiest of Stone Yardley's three pubs).

'Nah, you're fine. Dave and the boys are meeting me here at seven, so there's no point in going home. We're heading for the bright lights of Birmingham tonight, on the prowl for lovely ladies!' He brandished a blue and white striped plastic bag that could have only come from Jackson's Chippy. 'Got my gladrags in here, you see.' He tapped the side of his nose and nodded sagely. 'Preparation, Harriet. That's what executive managers like myself are highly skilled in.'

Resignedly, Harri picked up her bag. 'Right, well, I'll leave you to it. Have a nice weekend.'

'That's if I can remember any of it,' George called after her, swinging his hips in an alarmingly energetic impression of a rotund, balding forty-something strutting his funky stuff on the dancefloor. 'When George Duffield parties, he parties like a pro!'

Harri smiled weakly and walked out, sincerely hoping that the 'lovely ladies' of the West Midlands would think better of going out tonight . . .

She made a deliberate detour to Stone Yardley's Co-op, hoping that the tiny supermarket would live up to its Friday evening reputation and have only one of its four tills open to cater for the long queue of customers snaking angrily round its cramped aisles. Of course, this wasn't the case: the Co-op was practically empty, with two cashiers patiently waiting to serve her. The supermarket had, quite clearly, received the same memo from the desk of The Big F as everyone else in Stone Yardley.

To all concerned:
You are strongly requested to act in highly improbable ways in order to allow Ms Harriet Langton to return home without delay. All usual time-wasting behaviour is strictly forbidden. Any attempt to ignore this advice will be treated as a breach of contract and will incur the severest penalty.
Please note that The Big F is on the case. Thank you.

Ron Howard greeted Harri like a long-lost friend, offering a less-than-convincing performance of a poor, starving beastie as he followed her into the house, miaowing plaintively. Harri

123

propped her bags of shopping on the kitchen worktop and reached up to grab a tin of cat food.

'Very good, Ron. Don't give up the day job, fatty.'

Seeing as nobody else in Stone Yardley was willing to help her delay the inevitable, she would just have to do it herself. She made a large mug of tea and took it upstairs, where she ran a warm, deep bubble bath, complete with candles. Pulling the small CD player from her bedroom as far as its flex would allow, she propped open the creaky wooden bathroom door with a travel book so she could hear the soothing tones of Newton Faulkner drifting in as she sank down amidst rose-scented bubbles.

Almost an hour later, she reluctantly climbed out. Dressing in her brushed-cotton tartan pyjama bottoms, one of Rob's faded T-shirts (that, wonderfully, still bore traces of his musky aftershave, even after a wash) and her oversized white fluffy towelling robe, she pulled on a pair of vivid pink and white bed-socks (so lovingly knitted by Grandma Dillon's decidedly shaky hands for her, last Christmas) and headed downstairs.

As soon as she reached the living-room doorway, the post-bags came into view, like four hulking shadowy gunslingers facing her at high noon. *Come on, punkette, make our day . . .*

'OK, it's time,' she said out loud, making Ron Howard's ample backside twitch in surprise. 'Let's do this!'

CHAPTER TEN

I Never Normally Do This, but . . .

Harri wishes she had worn a watch this evening: in the last-minute rush to get ready, she had forgotten to put it back on after her shower. She has a vague recollection of it lying on the duvet amidst her hastily removed T-shirt and jeans as she struggled into her dress and heels. Looking down at the band of white skin on her left wrist, she notices how much she has caught the sun in recent weeks. She smiles slightly. Stella has always told her that redheads don't tan: so she must have been surprised when she saw Harri tonight. But then, not as surprised as everyone else was . . .

She wonders how long she has been in the grey-green confines of her self-appointed sanctuary. It feels like hours, but she can still make out the distant echoes of voices in the hall, so it can't be that late – although it's definitely too late for salvaging the one friendship she values most. Way too late for that to ever be right again. *Idiot*, she scolds herself, as she rubs the watch strap mark self-consciously and feels another wave of emotion beginning to break over her.

Hi!
    First of all, let me say that I never normally do this. But I saw your photo and couldn't help myself . . .

Harri groaned and looked at the clock on the mantelpiece through bleary eyes. It was 9.30 a.m. and she had spent most of the previous night opening letters from *Juste Moi* hopefuls. She had drifted off on the sofa around four a.m., grabbing a precious few hours of sleep, before waking at seven and dragging her concrete-heavy limbs upstairs for a shower in a half-hearted attempt to wake up. A large cafetière of extra-strength coffee now sat on her table amidst the various piles of replies: Contenders, Possibles, Contingencies and Not Likelies. So far, the latter was the largest by a considerable margin – presently consisting of around a hundred letters and one rather large ginger cat. Harri shook her head at the sight of Ron Howard snoring happily amidst the rejects. At least someone was happy to be in that pile.

'There's obviously no creativity when it comes to "Free to a Good Home" replies,' she said to herself. 'I mean, almost every letter I've trawled through starts like this one.' She held out the offending missive like a barrister proffering damning evidence. Ron Howard opened one eye and flicked his left ear. 'I never normally do this . . .' – yeah, right – 'I couldn't help myself . . .' – I bet you couldn't – 'when I saw you, I knew you were the kind of guy I've been searching for . . .' – *purrrlease* – 'I've enclosed a photo, so you can see I'm not some desperate woman . . .' She turned the handwritten page over to view the photograph stapled to the other side and instantly pulled a face. 'Oh, my *life* – I don't need shocks like that when I've hardly slept.'

She yawned and stretched her arms above her head to try to remove the stiffness in her neck. This was *not* how she had envisaged spending her weekend. She gazed wistfully at the bulky brown padded envelope lying unopened next to a vase of yellow roses Auntie Rosemary had given her earlier in the week.

A new travel guide she had ordered online lay inside it – *Hidden Venice* – the latest insider guide to the city she longed to visit more than anywhere else in the world. It was waiting patiently for her to discover its manifold delights, something she had planned to indulge in all weekend, now relegated by the stacks of letters still to open.

Leaving the paper-strewn sofa, she walked over to the window and gently lifted the envelope from its resting place beside the roses. Her heart rate began to increase as she carefully opened the flap, reaching inside to pull the glossy-covered volume from its packaging. As the cover photo of Venice by night met her eyes, her breath caught in the back of her throat. She had seen this image a thousand times over the years, yet it never failed to send thrills racing right through her. Dorsoduro – even the name was enough to transport her to the place her heart most desired . . . Lights from the gondola piers and colonnaded balconies of elegant *palazzi* were reflected in the indigo-black waters of the Grand Canal, red and gold vertical trails rippling beneath the softly illuminated domes of the church of Santa Maria della Salute. It was at once familiar and strangely alien to Harri – her mother had bought her a postcard of this exact scene when she was at primary school for a class project and Harri had stashed it in her underwear drawer, only bringing it out when her mother had long forgotten its existence. From that moment on, it had taken pride of place beside her bed – first Blu-Tacked to the red and green poppy-covered wallpaper in her childhood bedroom, and later in a gilt-edged frame that had been a gift from her grandma when Harri was in her teens. 'Here, put that dog-eared Venice postcard of yours in this, sweetie,' Grandma had smiled, her sun-brown skin wrinkling at the corners of her ice-blue eyes as Harri threw her arms around her.

The faded, sticky-tape-repaired postcard still remained by her bed in its gilded frame now. It was the last thing she looked at before she closed her eyes and the first image she woke to see.

Venice claimed the largest shelf space by far in Harri's travel book collection – with everything from travel guides, maps and first-hand accounts of living there, to cookbooks of Venetian cuisine and novels set amidst its majestic buildings and canals. Whenever a travel programme promised reports from Venice, Harri watched it avidly; whenever one of her friends visited the city, Harri was the first visitor upon their return, eager to hear every detail and view every photograph.

As time went on and more people learned of Harri's long-distance love affair with the city, they brought her souvenirs whenever they visited Venice. Now she had a secret hoard of Venetian treasure – everything from kitsch snowglobes with Venice landmarks inside and tiny plastic gondolas, to local newspapers, a Venetian mask and guidebooks from the Basilica San Marco, the Palazzo Ducale and the Museo Diocesano d'Arte Sacra. Contained within a battered-looking printer paper box and hidden carefully under her bed, this was Harri's private joy – something she hadn't even shared with Rob.

Stella had been to the city several times, accompanied by someone a little wealthier and a little less in love with her than the previous companion each time. She had even visited Venice for a hen weekend with a gaggle of alcohol-fuelled female friends and once said she could see herself 'popping there for a weekend alone'. Harri could think of nothing worse: for her, Venice was the ultimate city of love. Being there with someone you didn't love or, worse still, being there on your own, seemed like the most tragic scenario. When she visited Venice, she promised herself time and again, she would walk there hand in hand with the love of her life.

She stroked the cover of *Hidden Venice* again and sighed. Looking back to the sacks and letter-covered coffee table, her heart sank and she put her book aside and returned to the task in hand.

Two hours later, Harri took a break. She was just about to make herself a sandwich when someone knocked at her door. *What if it's Alex?* Panicking, she grabbed handfuls of letters, stuffing them behind cushions on the sofa and into the wicker basket beside her armchair. Dragging the sacks into the kitchen, she opened the broom-cupboard door and heaved them inside. The knock came again, echoing through the cottage, as Harri shooed Ron Howard from his bed of rejects and, at a loss for how to disguise the piles of letters already sorted, she grabbed a blue and white gingham tablecloth from the ironing board and threw it over the table, placing the vase of yellow roses in the middle. With a final check to make sure no offending items were on view, she straightened her jumper and made her way to the front door.

'What on earth were you doing in there, Harri?' Auntie Rosemary beamed, standing on the porch step, holding a large polka-dot cake tin in both hands.

'Nothing.' Harri tried her best to look nonchalant, but knew her deeply flushed cheeks were giving the game away.

'Going through those dreadful letters, were you? Don't look at me like that, Harri. I've known you all your life, remember. You've never been adept at lying – I can read you like a book. Now, can I come in?'

Smiling at her aunt, Harri bowed and motioned for her to enter.

When she stepped into the living room, Rosemary took one look at the coffee table and chuckled. 'Ooh, nicely done, Harriet. The old "stuff-and-stash" technique, eh?'

'When did you get so clever, eh?'

Rosemary sat down on the sofa and reached behind the cushion to grab a handful of crumpled papers. 'You forget that I am the mother of your cousin James. The things he stashed under his bed when he was at home would make your hair curl even more than it already does, trust me.'

'I'll put the kettle on.'

'Excellent idea. So, how's it all going?'

Harri grimaced as she poured hot water into the teapot, warming it like her mum used to do. 'Slowly. Let's just say that the Not Likely pile is growing at an alarming rate.'

'You poor sweetie. Well, it's a good thing I came round, then.'

By the time she returned to the living room with the tea tray, Ron Howard had smugly staked his claim on Rosemary's lap. 'I see you have a friend.'

Rosemary patted his ginger and white head. 'Ah, yes, I seem to have found my calling in life – at least as far as Ron's concerned. Now, look in that tin, won't you? I brought supplies!'

Harri pushed the tray onto the least lumpy side of the coffee table, before opening the large tin and squealing with delight. 'Your famous Lemon Drizzle Cake – with white chocolate buttons on the top! Oh, Auntie Rosemary, you're such a star!'

'I'm glad you approve, darling. Now, go and get a knife and some plates and then we can get started.'

'Get started on what?'

Rosemary smiled. 'You didn't think I'd let you do this all on your own, did you? Perish the thought, sweetheart! If you're

going to spend your whole weekend shifting through these –'
she paused to look at one of the crumpled pages in her hand
– '*dreadfully* constructed letters, then you'll need some
company. That's if you don't mind?'

Harri smiled as relief flooded through her weary frame. 'I
don't mind at all.'

The selection of replies, it had to be said, improved in ingenuity
as Harri and Rosemary progressed through the first sack. One
of Rosemary's personal favourites was one from a lady now
known affectionately as the Cat Lady.

> *. . . As the saying goes, 'love me, love my cats'! If we're going
> to meet, which I have a good feeling we will, it's important
> that you meet my two babies – of the feline variety, that
> is! Firstly, there's Monty – we call him this because he has
> a fondness for digging up the flowerbeds, like the curly-
> haired bloke who used to do* Gardener's World. *I have to
> say that our Monty is a little over-amorous at times, but
> as long as you don't have brown trousers, your leg should
> be safe from his advances! Then, there's Mrs Snuffles, who
> likes nothing better than sleeping in the dirty washing
> basket. Seriously, the smellier the better, as far as she's
> concerned. So if you happen to like getting sweaty, she'll
> adore you . . .*

'I don't know what's worse – Monty the randy tom or Mrs
Snuffles snuggling up to your sweaty unmentionables,' she
laughed.

Harri was particularly impressed by a sender she named the
Job Application Lady.

Alex

<u>Re:</u> Juste Moi *feature*

Having seen the 'Free to a Good Home' article in Juste Moi *magazine (Issue 105, page 46), I am writing to apply for consideration.*

Further to my CV (enclosed), please consider the following additional information in support of my application:

<u>What I can offer:</u>

- *Loyalty*
- *Financial independence – I run my own successful PR consultancy*
- *Considerable circle of friends – many with connections*
- *Acceptance of partner's flaws*
- *Conciliatory nature*
- *Excellent time management*
- *Sense of humour and intelligence*

<u>My expectations:</u>

- *A partner who meets my required lifestyle demands*
- *A non-confrontational nature*
- *Faithfulness – I cannot stress this enough*
- *A willingness to put my needs first whenever possible*
- *An appreciation of fine wines would be viewed as a considerable benefit . . .*

'I've never thought of dating as being like applying for a job before,' Rosemary said.

Harri smiled. 'Perhaps this is where Alex has been going wrong. He should just post up a card at the Job Centre and collect CVs instead. Much more civilised than all that "having to meet people" rigmarole.'

'It would certainly be better than you having to sort through this bilge. Honestly, most of these replies are written in that awful text-speak. Don't they teach girls correct English grammar these days?'

'Apparently not. Blimey, do you realise we've cleared one sack already?'

Auntie Rosemary frowned. 'Are you sure that one's empty?'

Harri upturned the sack and shook it. A single fuchsia-pink envelope fluttered out and landed on the wool rug at her feet, closely followed by a strong waft of musky perfume, which made both Harri and her aunt balk as the scent snatched the breath from the back of their throats. It was the kind of perfume that ladies of a certain age love giving as Christmas presents to their unsuspecting great-nieces. Even Ron Howard, who was usually able to withstand the most strenuous efforts to evict him from his chosen warm spot, jumped up in horror from Auntie Rosemary's lap, scampering out of the living room and up the stairs.

'What, in the name of all that's gracious, is *that*?'

Harri bent down and picked up the offending item by one corner. 'I have a funny feeling that this one might be destined for the Not Likelies.'

Rosemary pulled a face and stood up. 'I think it might be destined for the bin. The *outside* bin. What a terrible smell! I'm going to the kitchen for some fresh air. Coffee?'

'Love one.' Harri surveyed the pink envelope with its large, loopy handwriting and couldn't help but be intrigued. Taking a deep breath, she ripped open the envelope and took out the equally strong-scented and vivid-hued letter.

Hey Alex

What's a man like you doing in this Free to a Good Home thing?

I saw you there and I thought you looked like my kind of guy. I mean, you're successful, tall and really fit, so what's not to love, right?

I think we have loads in common. You have your own business and I love spending money. You're well fit and I know I look good. I like a man who will treat me right and it sounds like you want a woman you can take care of.

Interests? Well, travel, but none of that backpacking stuff, which is my worst nightmare. It's got to be five-star all the way or I'm not even stepping into the airport. My appearance means a lot to me, so I make sure I invest in my looks. I like to be tanned and my nails are my pride and joy. Had my boobs done recently and, let me say, you won't have any complaints in that arena. I'm blonde, five foot ten inches and a size eight. I love shopping, expensive shoes and perfumes. (This one was made in Paris for me by a French businessman who begged me to date him for three years. I didn't.) I hate cooking but love five-star restaurants. Hate films with subtitles and don't do talking for hours – action is what counts, know what I mean?

I know you're going to want to meet me. My number's at the top of the letter and my photo's on the back. Call me – soon.

Chelsea Buckden

A wry grin spreading across her face, Harri looked at the photo, which was fastened to the letter with a silver, sparkly paper clip, and guffawed so loudly that Auntie Rosemary appeared in the doorway. The thought of how horrified Alex would be when faced with this orange-tinged, platinum-blonde-haired plastic Jordan wannabe made tears roll down her cheeks.

One thing Alex was always more than happy to rant about was what he called 'plastic salon junkies'. 'Why in the world would any sane male choose to date a fake, plastic stick insect with more silicone than skin, who is more orange than an Oompa Loompa? You can't have any kind of meaningful inter-change with someone who can't move their face. Honestly, you'd be better off dating a Barbie doll – at least you can chuck her in a cupboard when you get bored of her . . .'

Harri's sides were aching as she struggled to catch her breath. 'Alex and the fantastic plastic Chelsea – now *there's* a match I'd like to see.'

'Harriet Langton, stop being so cruel. You're doing this to *help* your friend, remember?'

'I know, I know, I'm just joking, Auntie Ro. Look, I'm dumping Chelsea on the Not Likely pile.'

'Good, well, make sure you dump her right at the bottom of that pile, please. I don't think my poor nostrils can take much more of that dreadful stench.'

From the beginning, Harri never imagined that trawling through Alex's fan mail would be fun; yet as the hours passed, she found herself relishing the unexpected time spent with her aunt. As they made steady progress through the second sack and headed towards the third, she was filled with a comforting sense of peace and belonging that she hadn't experienced for such a long time. Her mind drifted back to another living room, twenty years before, where the laughter warming its walls was that of her parents, long before cancer appeared.

Dad was a natural comedian – a serial practical joker and purveyor of an arsenal of devastatingly funny one-liners – and all sources of hilarity in the Langton household could be traced back to him. Mum, on the other hand, was the straight-woman in the outfit: 'The Ernie to my Eric, the Corbett to my Barker,' Dad used to say. Whilst her dad's witticisms would reduce everyone within earshot to giggling wrecks, Harri's mum's face remained unmoved – which made the joke even funnier. Occasionally, she would crack, grabbing her husband and kissing the bald patch on the top of his head as he wrapped his arms around her. 'I love you, you nutter!'

When someone you love dies, the things you miss are often surprising. In Harri's most private moments, her parents' laughter was the one sound she longed to hear again; memories of the silliest conversations would cause sharp slivers of pain to stab at her heart. One of the most memorable was a running joke that started whilst driving home from a Cornish summer holiday in Looe. Dad had decided to take a detour through Bodmin, but they ended up stuck behind a bin lorry driving through the narrow high street and because cars were double-parked along the length of the road, they were forced to stop every time a large, gruff-faced bin man jumped out to throw rubbish sacks into the wagon's waiting jaws.

As usual, Dad started it. 'We're stuck behind a bin lorry in Bodmin.'

Mum smiled. 'We're stuck behind a bin lorry with a big bin man in Bodmin.'

'We're stuck behind a bin lorry, with a big burly bin man in Bodmin.'

Dad started to giggle. It never ceased to amaze Harri how

such a tiny, elfin sound could come out of such a tall, broad-shouldered man like her dad. 'We're stuck behind a bin lorry, with a big, burly bin man with a big, black, bin bag in Bodmin . . .'

And so it continued for the next hour. By the time they arrived at Grandma and Grandpa Langton's cottage on the edge of Dartmoor, the three of them were helpless with laughter. Dad practically fell out of the car, Harri emerged clutching her sides and Mum had lost every last vestige of her famous composure. The look of complete confusion on Grandma Langton's face at the sight of her guffawing, gasping family is something Harri would never forget.

Now, sitting next to her aunt, Harri felt a glimmer of that feeling again: safety, familiarity, humour. A bittersweet shiver ran through her.

Auntie Rosemary turned to look at her. 'Are you all right?'

Harri swallowed the lump in her throat and smiled back. 'I'm fine.'

By eight o'clock that evening, only half a sack remained. Harri had caught her aunt surreptitiously glancing at the clock on the mantelpiece several times during the past hour and decided to make the decision for her.

'Hey, it's late. I'd better let you go.'

Rosemary made a valiant effort to hide her relief. 'But you still have some left to sort through. I can't just leave you.'

'Yes, you can. Look, you've been an amazing help and I really, really appreciate everything you've done. But you need a weekend too and I'm more than capable of dealing with these.'

'Well, if you're sure . . .'

Harri wrapped her arms around her aunt. 'Completely sure.

Thank you so much – it's been really lovely to spend the day with you.'

'It's been fun, hasn't it?' Rosemary's cheeks flushed and she reached up to cup Harri's face with both hands. 'No, more than that, it's been *wonderful*. I don't get the chance to spend Saturday afternoons with my own little girl now she's so far away.'

'You miss Rosie a lot, don't you?'

'Yes, very much so. Even though it's been seven years since she left for America. So it's lovely to spend time with my niece.'

'Aw, thanks, Auntie Ro. It's been ages since I had a family day too. Mum and I didn't get many days like this.'

Tears sparkled at the corners of Auntie Rosemary's dark eyes. 'Niamh would have been so very proud of you, my darling. You remind me of her more and more, you know.'

They walked slowly to the front door and Auntie Rosemary stepped out onto the porch step, then turned back. 'Just promise me that you won't waste a single day, Harriet. For your mother. For me?'

Harri smiled. 'I'll try not to.' She watched her aunt leave and then closed the door. As if by magic, Ron Howard appeared at her feet and started to rub around her ankles, purring lovingly. 'Creep,' she smiled down at him. 'You only love me because I feed you.'

By ten p.m., the lack of sleep was beginning to take its toll. Harri's eye sockets ached and her stomach felt like someone had placed a heavy weight inside it. She filed the last letter in the Possible pile and sank back into the sofa as Ron Howard rolled on his back, waiting to be tickled. 'That's me done, Ron.' She ruffled the soft white fur on his belly as she looked at the completed piles of letters on the coffee table. To her surprise, the Contenders pile was looking quite healthy – at least thirty letters had made the grade. Leaning forward, she took the top letter and blinked a couple of times to focus her weary eyes on its contents.

Hi Alex,

I'm Annie. I'm twenty-nine and actually looking forward to thirty, odd though it sounds. I work as an office administrator for my friend's design business and one day I'd like to run my own bookshop, preferably somewhere near the sea.

I tried to think of a ton of clever things to say, but in the end I reckoned it was better to just be myself. There's no point pretending to be someone I'm not – it only ever causes problems. So, this is me. I'm a great listener, I love meeting new people and I enjoy great conversation – preferably over excellent coffee, but I have been known to settle for bog-standard instant if the company's good enough! I'd just like to meet someone interesting, someone who's seen a bit of this world and isn't obsessed by life in a small town.

Anyway, I've enclosed a photo, so see what you think. Hope to hear from you soon.

Annie Brookes

Harri smiled at the photo of the pretty blonde with pale blue eyes. 'Well, congratulations, Annie Brookes. It looks like you're about to meet my mate Alex.'

The next morning, Harri woke early and enjoyed a leisurely breakfast before feeding Ron Howard, grabbing her bag and keys and stepping out into the warm June morning. As she closed the gate, she saw Mrs Littleton, her octogenarian next-door neighbour, who was balancing on an incredibly rickety-looking wooden stepladder in her garden, a rusty pair of shears in hand, attacking a large privet hedge with alarming vigour. Even on the top step she barely reached five foot tall and was truly a sight to behold, dressed in baggy light blue velour tracksuit bottoms tucked into her white sports socks, tartan bobbled slippers and an oversized white T-shirt with the legend 'I Am The Stig' emblazoned across it.

'Morning, Mrs L!'

'Ooh, morning, chick! Forgive me, I've not got my Sunday best on today.'

'That's fine. Are you OK?'

Mrs Littleton pulled a tissue out of the waistband of her tracksuit bottoms and wiped her brow. 'Never better. It's just this blasted privet – it's been blocking my view for too long. So I'm showing it who's boss.'

Harri smiled. If this was how her neighbour dealt with troublesome shrubbery, it was no wonder her eighty-seven-year-old husband always looked so worried. In all the time Harri had lived in Two Trees Cottage, she had never seen Stan Littleton look anything but pale and nervous, following his bustling wife around the shops or trailing behind her as she marched purposefully along Stone Yardley's streets. She remembered Merv quipping once that, 'Imelda Littleton may look small and frail but she's got balls of steel.'

'How's Stan?'

Mrs L gave her false teeth a disapproving suck and shook her head. 'He says he's sickening for something. Reckons he caught a cold at the market last Wednesday.'

'Oh, I'm sorry to hear that. Give him my regards, won't you?'

Mrs L nodded. 'I will. Even though it's just a bad attack of the "don't-want-tos" in my opinion. We're meant to be going to Ethel Bincham's for afternoon tea today and he's trying to get out of it. But I told him, "Stan," I said to him, "we've been invited, so we're going!"' She swung the shears and angrily lopped off an offending branch of privet.

Harri stifled a giggle: if the choice was between enduring the dubious culinary delights of Mrs Bincham at her most creative, and staying at home feigning the flu, she was definitely with Stan on that one. The memory of Lemon Meringue Flapjacks was still firmly lodged in her mind. One cake was bad enough; the thought of afternoon tea was enough to put you off your food for *months*.

She was still smiling about the plight of poor Mr Littleton when she climbed the stile from the field opposite her house and walked up the gravel path to St Mary's. The quietly elegant red sandstone building was surrounded by cedar trees, its large stained-glass windows catching the morning sunlight. Its tall spire rose magnificently towards the heavens as the beautiful sound of bells filled the air – although in reality this sound was not from Stone Yardley's enthusiastic campanologists, but rather a looped track from a BBC sound effects CD played through speakers in the bell tower: a much safer option as any attempt to ring the church bells could end in the tower collapsing.

Harri paused to take in the view. Closing her eyes, she pictured herself as a small girl, running up the pathway to catch up with her parents on the way to church. At the sound of her footsteps on the gravel, Dad would spin round with a huge smile and scoop her up into his arms, swinging her round and round in circles whilst Mum protested: 'Put her down, Mick, you'll make her dizzy!' So Dad would obediently oblige, winking at Harri when Mum wasn't looking, and Harri would hold both their hands and walk in through the large wooden doors. Even now, a tiny part of her still expected to turn and find them there, waiting to accompany her into church, despite the fact that Harri knew their graves lay side by side at the western side of St Mary's, where the afternoon sun warmed the earth. Harri rarely visited the graves – only to replace the flowers when Auntie Rosemary was away. Mum and Dad weren't in the graves – she remembered her mother explaining that when people die, 'all that's left is the empty packet: all the good bits go to heaven and are more alive than they ever were on earth.' Harri liked to think that Mum and Dad were jumping about somewhere right now – indulging in tickle-fights like they used to do, making up ridiculous word-play games that would go on for hours, or just giggling like a pair of lovesick teenagers as they watched their daughter bumbling through her life on earth. She hoped they would like what they saw . . .

'Harri! Woo-hoo!' Her reverie was shattered by the noisy arrival of Viv, arm-in-arm with Merv.

'Greetings, fair maiden,' Merv boomed, giving a flamboyant bow. 'How *doeth* thee on such a fine summer's morn?'

'Pack it in, Mervyn,' Viv giggled, playfully punching his arm and hurting him more than she had intended. 'Ignore him, Harri. He has some ridiculous notion that the Stone Yardley Players are going to cast him as Shylock in their next Shakespeare-in-the-Park production.'

'Thinking of giving the Bard a run for his money, eh?' Harri asked.

Merv's collection of chins fell. 'Mock all you like, ladies, but I'll have you know that Cynthia Eccles was more than impressed with my audition piece on Friday.'

Viv pulled a face. 'Cynthia Eccles is more interested in auditioning you on the casting couch than she is for any of their productions. Honestly, since she got divorced she's been like

142

a flipping rabbit on heat. Anything remotely male isn't safe from her advances.' She poked an accusing finger into Merv's ample stomach. 'So watch out, mister. Or else.'

Merv turned a whiter shade of beige and suddenly bore a startling resemblance to Stan Littleton. 'Yes, dear.'

Viv hooked her arm through Harri's. 'Sit by us, sweetie, and then you can fill me in on all the news with those *lovely* letters.'

The morning service was busy as usual, filled with the jovial chatter of Stone Yardley's finest as warm sunlight fell in multi-coloured trails through the stained-glass windows to the paved floor below. A gaggle of children scampered from their parents' grasp and ran up and down the aisle giggling loudly, almost knocking over Pete, the young curate, as he made his way to the front of the church.

'Blimey, it's like Le Mans in here this morning,' he joked with a broad smile. Conversations ceased as a rumble of laughter rolled across the congregation and the service began.

It was all Harri could do to fend off Viv's urgent whispers throughout the sermon, which served only to intensify her curiosity. By the time the final hymn finished and the blessing was spoken, Viv was so wound up she was in danger of drilling down into the ground like a Laura Ashley-attired Black & Decker.

'*SO?*' she demanded, grabbing Harri's sleeve. 'How are you getting on?'

'All sorted.'

Viv's plum-painted lips fell open. 'Wait – you've been through all the letters? I *told* you I was going to help with those. Really, darling, you shouldn't have done it all alone.'

'I didn't. Auntie Rosemary helped me.'

Viv's face fell. 'Oh.'

'Don't worry, I told her not to give you too hard a time.

Anyway, I'm contacting the first lucky lady this afternoon,' Harri replied breezily.

If Viv's eyes had opened any wider, her eyeballs could conceivably have popped out and rolled down the aisle. 'Name? Age? Details?'

Harri stood up. 'Annie Brookes. She's twenty-nine and works as an office administrator. She's blonde, pale blue eyes and I'd say she's quite pretty.'

Viv's smile lit up the whole pew. 'Ooh, well, she sounds lovely!'

'More to the point, she seems relatively sane – and, trust me, that's the most enviable quality we could hope for with the general standard of replies.'

'Surely there were a lot of Possibles, though?'

'Thirty-two, to be exact. And over three hundred Not Likelies.'

'You're kidding.'

'Anyway, the good thing is that Annie Brookes seems to be the nicest of all of them,' Harri continued, hoping that she sounded confident in this fact.

Viv wasn't listening. A wistful expression wafted across her features as her train of thought whisked her away to a town called Improbable. 'Annie Brookes . . . what a sweet name. She sounds like a *lovely* young lady – and how *odd* that her initials are exactly the same as Alex's! Annie and Alex *Brannan*,' she giggled, clamping a hand to her breastbone like an overexcited silent movie heroine. 'Perfect!'

Merv pulled a face and shook his head. 'You won't get any sense out of her for days now, you realise.'

'Hmm, I know. Looks like *you're* in for a lovely week, then,' Harri smiled.

Merv's shoulders slumped as he made a slovenly exit from the church.

'They could be perfect with the same initials – like Abba!'

Viv breathed, as Harri took her arm and escorted her out into the sunny afternoon.

'The couples in Abba got divorced.'

'Ah, but Alex and Annie won't be like them,' Viv smiled, 'because they'll be truly in love! I just know they will! Oh, this is going to work like a *dream*!'

Harri groaned. No pressure, then . . .

'Hello?'

'Hi – can I speak to Annie Brookes, please?'

'Speaking.'

'Oh, hello, I'm calling about your reply to the "Free to a Good Home" column in *Juste Moi*.'

There was a pause at the other end of the line, followed by an audibly nervous sigh. 'Right . . .'

'OK, this is going to sound a bit odd, but I've been sorting through the replies and was very impressed by your letter.'

Silence.

This was not the response Harri had anticipated. 'So – um – I was wondering if you're still interested in meeting Alex Brannan?'

Annie sounded uncertain when she answered. 'I kind of thought I'd be hearing from Alex . . . Are you from the magazine?'

Mentally kicking herself, Harri realised she hadn't given her name. 'I'm so sorry, forgive me. I'm Harri Langton – I nominated Alex for the column.'

There was a tangible sense of relief from the other end of the line. 'Oh, right, the girl from the article. You said all that nice stuff about him.'

Harri pulled a face at the receiver. 'That's right, I did. So, would you like to meet Alex?'

'Yes, definitely.'

'OK. I need to meet you before he does, if that's OK?'

'Er, sure, that's fine. Whereabouts are you?'

'Stone Yardley – how about you?'

'I'm in Ellingsgate, so not far. I could do tomorrow – it's my half-day, so I'm free anytime from two thirty.'

Harri's head was spinning but she managed to claim sufficient control over her thoughts to answer. 'Great. How about I meet you at three thirty in the Land Oak, just at the end of the High Street?'

'Cool. I'll see you then.'

Ending the call, Harri let out a long groan and flopped back into her sofa, spooking Ron Howard, who leaped off and hid under the table, peering up at her with yellow-green eyes. 'Why, Ron? Why do I let myself in for this stuff?'

Ron Howard scowled at her and turned his back.

'Great. Well, thanks for your support.' Shaking her head, she found a number on her mobile and placed another call.

'He-ello.' Alex's familiar greeting made her smile despite her mood.

'Al, it's Harri.'

'Harriet! How wonderful to hear from you. I thought you'd finally taken my advice and gone travelling – or, more realistically, been abducted by aliens. Where have you *been* all week?'

Harri rubbed her eyes and stared at the ceiling. 'Sorry, I've just been snowed under. I was meaning to come to see you.'

His laugh tickled her ear. 'Yeah, right, whatever. I know how you operate, you fair-weather friend. Just pick me up when you want me and throw me away when you don't.' He feigned a pitiful sniff. 'But that's – fine, you know. I can take rejection . . .'

Ooh, if only you knew, Brannan. 'OK, I get it. I'm the worst friend in history. How can I ever make it up to you?'

'How about coffee in, say, half an hour? I can head over to yours—'

'No!' Harri said, a little too loudly and far too quickly. Struggling to back up, she attempted a breezy laugh. 'The cottage is a mess. I'll come to you.'

'Whatever, Captain Freakout. See you in a bit.'

In true Great British summer style, the bright sunlight that had been present all day had given way to murky grey clouds and a wind had sprung up from nowhere, robbing the day of its warmth. Harri shivered as she walked across the playing fields on the way to the High Street. Passing the goalposts, where two young lads were engrossed in a manic battle of 'keepy-uppy', she was instantly reminded of Rob.

Until the beginning of this year – when his precious job had rudely assumed centre stage in his attention – Rob's Saturday afternoon football matches had been a staple of Harri's life. A star striker for Dynamo Stone Yardley (a serious amateur squad in the local pub league), Rob was a first-choice player, called on for most of the team's games – something Harri was unbelievably proud of even though she had no interest in football. Consequently, Harri had become very familiar with the soggy sidelines at King Edward VI playing fields. Standing with the other players' wives and girlfriends, she had witnessed countless matches and even one local cup victory when DSY thrashed the beefy boys from Red Lion United two years ago.

Despite the fact that the football pitch was more often than not freezing, damp or just downright inhospitable, some of Harri's happiest moments were spent here, cheering Rob's nifty footwork, booing when the ref's decision went against them and catching up on the latest shenanigans from the assembled significant others of the team. In truth, the gossip factor was the most enjoyable aspect – not least because it afforded Harri a sense of family that she so craved. But also the twists and turns of DSY's love lives were more sensational than any soap-opera plotline. During her time as a DSY 'WAG', Harri had witnessed several affairs, more than one revenge-hungry bunny-boiler ex, and a very nasty incident that began with a disagreement over a woman, was followed by a hastily wielded football boot and resulted in a brief excursion to A&E. Still, at least it kept the local paper, *Stone Yardley Chronicle*, in suitably salubrious stories – a blessing considering the vast majority of its column inches were given over to adverts for double-glazing and car dealers.

Even though these days Rob was more interested in chasing promotion in Preston than scoring goals for DSY, the rest of the team still held him in high regard, meeting up with him whenever they could. Harri often went along, enjoying the opportunity to meet up with Rob's mates and their partners.

'Do you realise that you and Rob are one of our most successful couples?' Cathy Simpkiss had remarked, only last week. 'I mean, you guys have been together a good couple of years longer than anyone else. Dave and I have managed three years, but it's been tough, I don't mind admitting it. What's your secret?'

Proud to have her and Rob's relationship recognised like this, Harri smiled. 'We just love being together,' she replied. 'And even though Rob's away a lot with work at the moment, he still makes the effort to spend time with me whenever he can. I think we've come to the point where we're secure enough in our relationship to cope with being apart. I completely trust him and I know he trusts me, too.'

Cathy shook her head in awe and clamped a perfectly manicured hand on Harri's arm. 'That's just – *awesome*,' she breathed. 'So all you need now is for him to, you know, pop the Big Question, and then you'll be home and dry!'

Reaching the gates at the town end of the playing fields, Harri pulled a face. It didn't seem right to talk about relationships in terms of a race, but in a way Cathy was right. Certainly as far as the collected girlfriends of DSY were concerned, it was all about getting down the aisle as quickly as possible, preferably for the financial stability. Harri wasn't entirely convinced by this relationship ambition, but she could understand the need to pursue a strong commitment – especially after seven years.

But then, with Rob's frequent mentions of 'the future' lately, maybe the 'Big Question' wasn't really that far away now . . . As she walked through the small cluster of houses on Park Street, she remembered his text from Friday and felt a ray of hope warming her heart. Tomorrow night it's just me and him, she reminded herself.

The last few customers were leaving Wātea as Harri arrived. Alex looked more than a little stressed as he turned the Open sign to Closed and bolted the door behind her.

'Honestly, H, what part of "We close at four p.m." don't they understand? I actually pulled down the blind on the door half an hour ago and two ladies walked in. They wouldn't leave until I'd served them tea and cake.'

'Well, that's the price you pay for being popular,' Harri smiled. 'Want a hand clearing up?'

Alex handed her a broom. 'You're an angel, Langton.'

'Not so much of an angel, actually. I was hoping to trade my services for one of your famous hazelnut hot chocolates.'

'Right, I see. With whipped cream, I suppose?'

Harri nodded. 'And chopped nuts.'

Alex folded his arms, a wry smile on his lips. 'Anything else?'

'A little drizzle of that caramel syrup would be nice too.'

'Blimey, you drive a hard bargain.'

'Absolutely.' Harri rolled up her sleeves and started sweeping.

Half an hour later, the coffee lounge was cleaned, swept and mopped. Alex joined Harri at the table nearest the window and handed her a large duck-egg-blue mug filled with hot chocolate and cream.

'I just happened to have two slices of apple pie left over,' he grinned, pushing a plate over to her. 'I thought you might fancy more calories to add to the thousand you've already got there.'

Harri beamed. 'You know me so well.'

Alex shook his head. 'It never ceases to amaze me how you eat as much as you do without becoming the size of a small planet.'

She took a large bite of pie. 'Excellent metabolism, you know.'

Outside, the High Street was emptying as Stone Yardley's shopkeepers closed up and headed home. The breeze had strengthened to a brisk wind and sharp splats of rain began to fall against the window.

'So much for the great British summer, huh?' Alex said, stirring the mountain of cream atop his mug into the hot chocolate beneath. 'Mind you, it has its benefits. Sales of hot chocolate have rocketed this week.'

'Excellent.' It was time to put Operation *Juste Moi* into action. Harri took a deep breath. 'So, are you doing anything particular tomorrow evening?'

Alex frowned. 'Monday night? No, nothing once I finish up here. Why?'

Harri smiled. 'Because there's someone I'd like you to meet.'

'Really? Who?'

'Just an old friend from college. We met up again a while ago and I think you two have a lot in common.'

Alex leaned forward. 'Details?'

'Her name is Annie, she's twenty-nine, blonde, blue eyes and she's really nice.'

'That's hardly details, H.'

'Well, I can't tell you everything, can I? I mean I need to leave some things for you to find out for yourself. Bit of mystery and all that.' Harri hoped with all her might that Alex would buy it. To her surprise, he did, his face lighting up at the prospect.

'Hmm, you're right. Excellent work, my good friend.'

Harri raised her mug. 'Pleased to be of service.'

'So, Great Matchmaking Maestro, what's the plan?'

'I'm meeting up with her tomorrow, so how about I bring her here and then you two can see how you get on?'

Alex's eyes twinkled above the cream mountain in his mug. 'It's a date!'

'Afternoon off? On a Monday?' Judging by his shocked expression, Harri finally claiming her long overdue time off was tantamount to asking for the moon on a stick.

'Yes, George. We're not very busy today and Tom and Nus can more than cope if we get a rush.'

George rubbed his forehead and leaned back in his chair, which gave an alarming creak as he did so. 'Well, I'm not sure, Harriet. It's very late notice, after all. And now you're *assistant manager*, there's a certain standard you should uphold for the other members of staff.'

Harri folded her arms and surveyed her boss sternly. 'You

151

mean like the excellent example *you* set your staff when you finish early for the day to "work at home"? I wasn't aware you lived at The Fleece now.'

George flushed. 'I have no idea what you are referring to, Harriet.'

'That's funny, then, because I saw Rena Davenport only last week and she said that you two often share a drink when she's working her afternoon shift in there. I'll go and tell Nus and Tom, shall I?'

George squirmed in his seat. 'You know, I really think you should look after yourself more, Harriet,' he said as authoritatively as he could, even though his voice was more of a squeak when it came out. 'Why don't you take the afternoon off?'

Harri feigned surprise. 'Really? Oh George, that's so sweet of you. I could just hug you!'

Her boss shrank back like a cockroach from the light, a look of pure terror on his face. 'That – that won't be necessary, thank you very much. Public displays of affection are not part of your contract, you know.'

'Right.' She took a respectful step back and watched her portly employer visibly relax. 'Thanks, George.'

'You're welcome. Just don't give me shocks like that on a regular basis, OK? With my angina it could be fatal.'

At three thirty, Harri pushed open the dark wood and stained-glass doors to enter the cosy lounge of the Land Oak. She quickly surveyed the interior but saw only three older men and a woman who was trying (and failing) to pass for forty, her shockingly dyed red hair clashing wildly with the bright fuchsia-pink lipstick painted well over the edges of her lips. With no sign of Annie, Harri ordered a coffee from the bar and found a seat at a plush banquette in one of the pub's bay windows. She checked her watch and tried to calm the waltzing butterflies in her stomach. *What am I doing?* she asked herself for the umpteenth time that afternoon.

She was just about to give the whole thing up as a bad job when the lounge door opened and a pretty young woman entered. Harri stood up and waved as the girl thankfully headed over.

'Annie? I'm Harri.'

'Hi. I'm so sorry I'm late. I got caught behind a tractor on the A449 and couldn't overtake for miles.'

'That's no problem. Would you like a drink?'

'Just an orange juice, thanks.'

When Harri returned from the bar, Annie pulled out a rolled copy of *Juste Moi*, laying it carefully on the polished dark wood table.

'I read this again this morning.' Annie smiled nervously. 'You make him sound really nice.'

'He is. He's a nice guy. I think you'll like him.'

'Are you kidding? Of course I'll like him! I mean, look . . .' she pointed at Alex's photo grinning up from the curled-edged page, '. . . he's *gorgeous*!'

'Hmm.' Harri took a large gulp of coffee.

Annie looked around. 'So – um – where is he?'

'Oh, don't worry, you'll meet him later.'

'Right. Forgive me, I kind of thought we were meeting him here?'

'No, you're going to meet him at Wātea, his café. A bit later. I just needed to have a chat with you first, that's all.'

'Wow, you're taking this whole matchmaking thing seriously, aren't you?'

Harri sighed. 'You have no idea.'

*   *   *

153

By the time Harri and Annie arrived at Wātea, it was nearly five o'clock. Rush-hour traffic was building in the High Street and teenagers in school uniforms were gathered around the low-walled planters in front of Reindeer Court, trying their best to look surly and disenchanted with the world around them.

At Harri's request, Annie had left the copy of *Juste Moi* in her car and had been sworn to secrecy over the article. 'It's probably best we don't tell him. He'd only get embarrassed.'

Alex's brown eyes lit up as soon as they entered, wiping his hands on his denim apron and running a cursory hand through his mussed-up sandy-brown hair. Harri couldn't help but notice that he had made much more of an effort today than would normally be seen on a Monday. His dark blue T-shirt accentuated the toned muscles in his chest and somehow made his tanned skin glow even more than usual. His baggy jeans looked new, although his red Converse trainers were the usual suspects, and his ever-present Maori bead necklace had been joined by a silver St Christopher (a present from an unnamed female friend, somewhere between Thailand and Indonesia).

'Hey, Harri,' he beamed, walking over to meet them. As he reached her side, Harri caught a waft of newly applied aftershave. Blimey, he really was making an effort . . .

'Hey, Al. I'd like you to meet Annie.'

Annie's eyes twinkled as she extended her hand to meet Alex's. 'Hi, it's great to meet you. Harri's told me *so* much about you.'

'She has?' Alex shot Harri a glance and turned the merest shade pinker. 'I'm afraid she hasn't told me much about you.'

Annie gave Harri a mock frown and playfully punched her arm. 'That's dreadful. Some friend you are.' She winked and Harri couldn't help feeling she was trying a little too hard to play the 'old friend from college' role that they'd agreed in the pub earlier. 'So,' she linked an arm through his, leading him towards the counter, 'I guess you'll have to probe me for information, then.'

Alex looked over his shoulder and mouthed, 'Thank you!' as they walked away.

'My work here is done,' Harri mumbled to herself, feeling relief flooding every inch of her body as she walked out of Wātea into the fresh air. Looking at her watch, she quickened her pace and headed home. She had the infinitely more exciting prospect of her evening with Rob to look forward to. The thought of his devastating smile and his strong arms around her put an extra spring in her step. This was going to be one special evening.

At seven thirty, Harri drove into October Crescent and parked her car on the short drive in front of Rob's house. The sun was beginning to dip behind the early evening clouds, gilding everything in rich golden light. Even Rob's boxy eighties detached house looked halfway decent – no mean feat, considering its tiny dark windows, grey bricks, and uninspiring porch, which always struck Harri as a bit of a half-hearted architectural afterthought, an attempt to make the building look homely. Whilst she absolutely loved Rob, she was certain that she would never possess the same feelings about his house.

Rob opened the door before she reached for the doorbell, a tea towel slung casually over one shoulder, looking more handsome than ever. 'Hey, beautiful. I've been waiting for you.'

Harri leaned in for a long, slow kiss. 'I like the sound of that.'

'Mmm, well, if you're impressed by the welcome then wait till you see what's inside,' he winked, making Harri's stomach flutter. He laced his warm fingers through hers and drew her inside.

Jamie Cullum was crooning seductively from the speakers as Harri walked into the living room, and the whole house was filled with the delicious, spicy aroma of cooking. Harri caught her breath as she saw the table, immaculately laid out with candles, Rob's best wine glasses, white linen tablecloth and red napkins. The lights had been dimmed and the total effect was stunning.

Rob's arms encircled Harri's waist from behind as he drew her close and gently kissed her neck, his breath hot on her skin. 'You like?' he whispered in her ear.

'I – yes, I like a lot. Thank you.' She reached up and stroked the back of his neck. 'You've gone to a lot of trouble for me tonight.'

'Well, I promised I was going to make it up to you so I wanted to do it properly. Man, you smell amazing.' He spun her round and kissed her. It felt so good to be in his arms again – and it was now, losing herself in his kiss, that Harri realised how much she'd missed him.

After a while, he pulled back to look at her. 'You look great, Red,' he smiled, his eyes drinking in every detail. Harri felt her heart skip. The jade-green dress that Stella had persuaded her to buy a few months back had finally been brought out of the wardrobe and she had to admit that it complemented her auburn hair perfectly. Whilst it felt a little odd to be dressing up just for dinner at Rob's, she thanked heaven now that she could see his reaction.

'Well, you know, I thought I'd make an effort. This place looks amazing, honey. You didn't have to go to all this fuss for me.'

Rob grinned and headed into the kitchen. Harri followed. 'Yes, I did. It's been rubbish being away so much during the past couple of months and I wanted you all to myself. Besides, we might just be celebrating.'

Harri felt a thrill of anticipation sparkle through her. 'How come?'

Rob stirred a pan, replaced the lid and opened a bottle of wine. 'I'll tell you later. First we need to enjoy this meal that, I have to say, is going to be rather fantastic.'

Harri followed him to the living room, where he pulled out a chair for her at the dining table like a waiter in an expensive restaurant and carefully laid a napkin across her lap. Then, pouring two glasses of wine, he handed one to her.

'What are we drinking to?' she asked, his actions thrilling her.

'To the future,' he answered, 'to *our* future.'

The meal was stunning, especially considering Rob's frequent protests that he didn't enjoy cooking. The beef and red wine stew was perfectly cooked, flavoured with garlic and ginger, followed by a rich chocolate mousse with crispy sugar biscuits. Harri managed to finish it all, despite the growing excitement buzzing inside her.

Rob stood to take the empty plates back to the kitchen and Harri joined him. As the filter machine percolated coffee, Rob pulled Harri to him and kissed her again.

'You know that I love you, don't you?'

'Of course I do.'

'And I hate being away from you.' He stroked her face softly. 'When I'm on my own in the hotel room in Preston all I can think about is being close to you. Like this . . .' He drew her even closer. 'It's the thought of holding you in my arms again that keeps me going. And the thought of one day – soon – never having to leave you again.'

Rob's eyes shone with so much love as they held hers and Harri felt a renewed rush of love for him. He looked happy, more relaxed than she had seen him in a long time, gazing at her with so much peace in his expression.

Ask me, she willed him. *This is the perfect moment* . . .

He opened his mouth to speak, but was interrupted by the shrill tone of *The A-Team* theme tune from his mobile.

Not wanting the moment to end, Harri squeezed his arm. 'Ignore it.'

Rob was clearly torn and for a moment the ringtone continued, a rude intruder on their private moment. Then, smiling apologetically, he reached into his jeans pocket and answered his phone.

Harri looked away, ignoring the thud of disappointment within.

'Hi mate. Look, this isn't a good time . . .' He stroked Harri's hair to summon her attention and mouthed 'I love you' as the caller's voice muttered indeterminably from the handset. 'Yeah, well, it'll have to wait until tomorrow, OK? Because I have far more important things to do tonight than solve your problems, that's why.' Pulling Harri against his hips, he began to sway with a wicked expression on his face, and it was all Harri could do not to giggle out loud at the sheer audacity of the situation. Whatever would Rob's boss think if he could see *exactly* what the important things preventing him from talking about work tonight were? 'Fine. I'll look forward to that then.' He ended the call and, laughing, launched into his best Patrick-Swayze-in-*Dirty-Dancing* impression, burying his face in her neck and murmuring 'Oh baby,' as they moved around the kitchen.

'I can't believe you were doing that with your boss on the phone,' Harri giggled when Rob finally let go.

'It wasn't my boss,' Rob replied, moving to the filter machine and pouring two mugs of coffee. 'It was one of my team. I've told them not to ring me at home but somehow the message never seems to get through their thick skulls.' He handed her a mug. 'They've had enough of my time this weekend as it is.

Whatever the issue is, it will still be there in the morning. You, on the other hand, need my attention right now.'

Returning to the living room, they sat down on Rob's black leather sofa. Harri took a deep breath and turned to him. 'So, about what you were saying earlier: what might we be celebrating?'

He winked at her. 'Only that it looks like the Preston contract is almost wrapped up. So you might just have to deal with more evenings like this, if that's OK?' Something in Harri's expression must have betrayed her true feelings because Rob's smile faded. 'That *is* OK, isn't it, Red?'

'Yes – of course. That's wonderful.' Harri looked away, embarrassed at her mistake. How could she have thought Rob was going to propose tonight?

'What else did you think I was going to . . .' Rob's voice trailed away as realisation dawned. 'Wait – no – you didn't think . . . ?'

'I'm sorry, baby. It was a daft idea.' She lifted her head. 'Ignore me.'

Shocked, Rob stared back at Harri, then wrapped his arms around her. 'No, no, don't be silly. It's my fault – what else would you have thought after the meal and everything?' He gave a long sigh into her hair. 'Red, I will ask you – you know I will. Just not yet, that's all. And I wouldn't propose in my living room, for heaven's sake. I'm going to do it properly – at the right time, you know?'

Harri could hear his heart beating quickly against her ear and she half-wondered if passion or panic was fuelling his pulse. 'It's fine,' she said, pulling back to look at him. 'I love you.'

Later, when they lay snuggled together on the sofa, Harri smiled against his chest. *This* was the Rob she loved and believed in. When they were together like this, his hands tracing winding trails up her spine and his breath hot against her cheek, *anything* was possible. Rob lifted her chin and kissed her deeply, his mouth lazily claiming hers, and Harri let the moment sweep her away. As they kissed, she imagined them entwined together under a blanket, a gondolier navigating them through dusky canals under gorgeous bridges as the lights of Venice floated by overhead and rippled in the waters beneath them . . .

'I love you, Rob,' she said again, as the kiss ended.

Rob looked deep into her eyes. 'I know you do.'

CHAPTER ELEVEN

If Only You Knew . . .

It's amazing the memories that go through your mind when you're stuck in a confined space. One minute Harri is seven years old again, sitting on the high yellow stool in Grandma Langton's kitchen, helping her to make gingerbread men; the next, she is walking hand in hand through the park with her father; then she is sitting in SLIT, advising Mr and Mrs Carter on suitable hotels in Ambleside for their next coach trip.

Looking up at the skylight she can see that the rain has ceased for the time being. She wonders whether it will be raining again when she leaves. The thought of moving from the ladies' out into the waiting world fills her with icy dread. One thing's for certain: she's not ready to emerge from her sanctuary just yet . . .

The thing that Harri loved more than anything else as a little girl was baking with her grandmother. Whilst she knew even then that her cooking skills were never going to set the world on fire (although she came close recently with an overenthusiastic attempt at flambéed chicken), she relished the hours spent in Grandma Langton's kitchen. Throughout her formative years, she learned to make scones, biscuits, shortbread, flapjacks, and even Christmas pudding – a feat that was highly lauded by her parents. But the most important feature of these baking adventures was the advice her grandmother always bestowed – on everything from friendships, dreams and ambitions, to housework, shopping and life in general. No matter what the subject, Grandma Langton had a handy pearl of wisdom to share.

On one occasion, a school friend had turned on Harri just before she had set off to Devon with her parents and when they arrived at her grandparents' house, her distress was still raw. After pacifying her granddaughter with a glass of warm milk and a home-made butterfly bun, Grandma Langton had taken her by the hand and led her into the kitchen, where enticing aromas of roasting lamb filled her nostrils and soothed her aching heart.

'Harriet, I've lived a good deal longer than you have and I can tell you this: in life friends will come and go. Some last for a moment, others for a lifetime. The only way we find out who our true friends are is when we look back to see who's been walking with us the longest. For now, all you can do is to make sure *you* are the best friend you can be to those that will have you. If someone walks away, let them. There will be someone else along quicker than you think. The best friends might take a while to find, but when you do, hang on to them.'

In later years, several people proved to be the true friends that Grandma Langton had talked about for Harri. One of them was Viv. When Stella, Rob and Auntie Rosemary moaned at Harri for getting mixed up in the mess Vivienne Brannan's whims often caused, Harri held her tongue. Deep down, she had a very good reason for indulging Alex's mother. Viv was her mother, Niamh's, best friend. They met at art college in their late teens and had remained close ever since. When Alex's father walked out on the family, Harri's mum rallied round Viv, helping her to rebuild her life and emerge stronger than ever – so when first Michael Langton and then Niamh were diagnosed with cancer, Viv returned the favour. As Niamh lay in hospital, drifting in and out of consciousness, Viv promised to take care of Harri – and was good to her word. In the years that followed, Harri found Viv to be someone who, beneath the fuss and fluster, cared for her as much as she did for her own son. So, the dice were cast – and nothing could change that.

A week after Alex had unwittingly entertained his first 'Free to a Good Home' date, Harri arrived at Viv's house for dinner. Viv was still fussing around the steaming copper pans on the Aga, so she thrust a large glass of red wine into Harri's hand and urged her to go and sit outside while the meal was cooking.

'Go, go, go,' she demanded, flapping a checked tea towel at Harri as if she was an annoying bluebottle fly. 'I'll be out in a tick.'

'Whatever you say, Delia,' Harri grinned, walking towards the conservatory.

'Oy,' Viv frowned, waving a wooden spoon chastisingly, 'don't take the name of Delia in vain. That woman is a *saint*.'

Laughing, Harri headed outside and settled down on one of Viv's expensive wooden garden chairs to soak in the view across the fields towards the river beyond. It was a beautiful evening – warm and clear with a light breeze that caused the tall stems of bamboo in Viv's back garden to gently rustle. Harri took in a deep lungful of fresh air and wriggled down in the teak garden seat. After all the craziness of the past few weeks, things finally appeared to be settling down again. Alex was well on the way to finding the (albeit heavily contrived) love of his life, and things with Rob were wonderfully relaxed.

'Right, food should be ready in half an hour,' Viv announced as she emerged from the conservatory, wiping her hands on her apron before grabbing her own glass of wine. 'What a thoroughly gorgeous evening. Don't you just love this time of year?'

'It is beautiful,' Harri agreed. 'Makes you feel like everything is well with the world.'

Viv eyed her with more than a hint of suspicion. 'You're awfully chirpy this evening.'

Smiling benevolently, Harri raised her glass. 'Yes, I am.'

'Anything I should know about?'

'Not really. Things are really good with Rob and it looks like Preston's days are numbered.'

Viv lifted her wine glass in a toast. 'I'll drink to that. Maybe *then* he'll get his backside into gear and make an honest woman of you, eh?'

'Perhaps he will – and then you can stop going on about it.'

'Ah, but you know me, I'll always find something to "mother" you on. So,' she leaned forward eagerly, 'ask me, then.'

'Ask you about what?'

'About Alex.'

Harri had to admit that her interest had suddenly shot up several hundred notches. Apart from a couple of vaguely happy text messages, she hadn't heard from or spoken to her best friend since he met the lovely Annie. 'How did the date go?'

'Try *dates*,' Viv beamed. 'As in *several*!'

'Wow. So what has he said?'

Viv raised her eyes to the pinkening clouds lazily drifting overhead. 'Well, you know Alex. Vague in the extreme when it comes to me. All I know is that they met for drinks and then dinner. Twice. Other than that, the details have been sketchy, to say the least. I expect he'll be much more likely to talk to you, though.'

'Perhaps, but I haven't actually seen him since he met Annie.'

'Hmm, I gathered that. That's why he's coming for dinner tonight.'

'What?'

'Well, I thought with you here he might be more willing to – you know – *elucidate* slightly.'

Irritated, Harri put her glass down on the table and stared at Viv. 'So this is why you were so adamant that I come over?'

Viv's attempt at shock certainly wouldn't have won any BAFTAs. 'No! Absolutely not! I just . . .' she looked decidedly sheepish, '. . . OK, I'm sorry, darling. It's just that he refuses to talk to me about it and it's been a *whole week*! I've been like a grasshopper on a barbecue and my son is being an utter beast about the whole thing. I promise I asked you first, Harri. Honestly.'

Harri couldn't hide her amusement. 'Viv, you're dreadful.'

Viv sighed and looked down at her feet despondently. 'I know I am. I'm sorry. I just thought, with you here and Alex having no plans for the evening, it was, well, the perfect opportunity to encourage some conversation—'

Just then, the doorbell rang and Viv's contrition vaporised as she jumped up, clapping her hands. 'Excellent! There he is!'

Harri watched her dash back into the house and shook her head. Only Viv could turn a pleasant summer's evening meal into a military-style coup.

A moment later, Viv reappeared with Alex ambling casually behind her, a box of chocolates in his hand. He beamed widely when he saw Harri.

'Wotcha, H. I didn't realise Mum had roped you in for backup.' He bent down to give her a hug.

165

'Neither did I, until about thirty seconds ago,' Harri smiled, hugging him back.

Viv whisked the chocolates from his hands and pushed him into the chair next to Harri. 'Right, well, help yourself to a drink, Al. I've got to go and check on the meal. I'm sure you two have *lots* to talk about!'

Alex poured a glass of wine. 'My mother is about as subtle as a demolition ball.'

'She's excited about your love life, that's all. I think it's sweet.'

'Well, I'm glad someone's excited about it.' Harri was suddenly aware of the sparkle retreating from his eyes. She knew this look only too well.

'Oh, Al, what's happened?'

He flicked a greenfly off the chair arm and gave her a resigned smile. 'Oh, I dunno, H. Annie was really nice. You were right: we had loads in common, she was interesting, we had great conversations . . .'

'But?'

He sighed. 'There was something missing.'

Harri frowned. 'Like what?'

He shrugged. 'I have no idea. The magic wasn't there, I guess.'

'That's never stopped you before.'

Alex laughed and playfully punched her arm. 'Harsh. But true. Anyway, I said the whole "thanks, but no thanks" speech and that was that. She didn't seem all that surprised, to be honest.'

'Ah.' Harri called to mind the promising pile of Contenders waiting patiently on her coffee table. 'Well, I may have a few more suggestions.'

Alex's sparkle made a welcome comeback. 'Really? Who?'

'Well, there's Erin.'

'OK. Details?'

Panicking, Harri racked her brain for the contents of the second letter in the Contenders pile.

Dear Alex,

I'm going to start by being completely unoriginal and say that this isn't something I usually do. Clichéd, I know, but I'd like you to know that anyway. And, of course, that I'm not some sad, desperate woman feeling her biological clock ticking furiously. I just liked the look of you and thought, what the heck?

So, about me. I'm thirty, five foot nine inches tall with a good figure. I have dark brown hair and green eyes (don't worry, it's not as scary as it sounds) and I'm the Events Manager at Hillford Hall. I love live music and I sing with my brother's band – you might have seen us around, Loose Covers? We do a lot of cheesy eighties and nineties covers, but we're pretty good and we seem to get a lot of repeat bookings, so I suppose we're moderately successful. Just a bit of fun, really.

Anyway, I think we might get on and I'm willing to give it a shot if you are. If you're interested, call me. The number's at the bottom of this letter.

Erin Donnelly

'She sounds great,' Alex nodded appreciatively. 'So when am I meeting her?'

Harri drove her beloved car onto the long, expansive gravel drive leading to Hillford Hall and instantly felt out of place as she parked amidst the Jaguars, Bentleys, Mercedes and Aston Martins languishing luxuriously by the immaculately manicured hedges that bordered the car park. It wasn't the first time she'd visited the sprawling, red sandstone Georgian mansion – Harri made several visits each year to meet with Philip Lombard, the hotel's charismatic Aussie manager, to arrange special event accommodation packages – but every time she arrived, she couldn't help but be overawed by the majesty of the place.

Philip was talking to a pretty young receptionist when Harri entered and he smiled broadly when he saw her.

'Harri, what a great surprise. I wasn't expecting to see you till next month.' He walked over and kissed her on both cheeks. Harri returned the favour, noticing his expensive aftershave and impeccable suit as she did so. No wonder the suave forty-something was considered one of the most eligible bachelors in the area.

'Don't worry, Phil. I'm actually here to see Erin.'

'Ah, excellent. I was wanting the two of you to meet, actually. Erin and I have big plans for the events programme next year and we really want to increase our weekend packages. I'd appreciate your input and I'd be happy for SLIT to handle the lion's share of bookings.'

'Excellent. Well, if you email me the details I'll liaise with Erin and we'll put something together.'

'Wonderful.' A mischievous smile played on his lips. 'Are you sure I can't spirit you away from George to work here? I could really use your expertise, you know.'

'It's tempting, Phil, and I'll bear it in mind, I promise. I'm just not ready to leave the world behind me yet, you know? Not even for this magnificent place.'

Phil laughed. 'OK, well, you can't blame a guy for trying. Erin's in the Blessenden Suite – second floor, follow the signs to the East Wing.'

Everything about Hillford Hall whispered understated

luxury. Once a country seat of the Earl of Dudley, the stunning mansion sat in thirty acres of landscaped parkland, complete with a silver expanse of lake at its front. There was an other-worldliness about this place; when Harri was here she could easily imagine herself on a historic estate somewhere in France, Italy or Austria.

The Hall's state rooms were once the envy of many in élite society: a hundred and fifty years ago, countless extravagant parties and soirées took place here as the Earl and his family threw ever more elaborate social events to impress the great and good of the country. Nowadays, the majority of the Hall's guests were rich businesspeople, wedding parties and the occasional visiting celebrity, especially when Hillford hosted one of its famous outdoor concerts.

Harri followed the signs along the thickly carpeted hallway until she reached a set of large polished oak doors with shiny brass handles. Taking a deep breath, she entered.

Named in honour of Lady Blessenden, wife of an eminent lord, and a notorious socialite who scandalised 1920s society with her many affairs, the Blessenden Suite was every bit as opulent as its namesake had been. Two enormous glittering crystal chandeliers hung from the intricately moulded plaster ceiling, while a huge carved four-poster bed assumed pride of place, draped with gold brocade curtains and crisp Egyptian cotton bed linen.

Standing by the bed, a tall, immaculately attired young woman with glossy mahogany hair looked entirely at home in her impressive surroundings. Glancing up from her clipboard, she flashed a friendly smile at Harri.

'Hi. Can I help?'

Harri approached and extended her hand. 'Hi, I'm Harri. We spoke on the phone earlier.'

Erin flushed slightly and quickly shook Harri's hand. 'Great to meet you. Thanks for coming so quickly.'

'You're welcome. Phil – er – Mr Lombard said he wants us to work together on Hillford's concert packages for next year.'

Erin nodded. 'Yes, absolutely. While you're here remind me to arrange a date for that. But now,' she linked her arm through Harri's, 'let's head to my office so we can discuss your very gorgeous friend.'

One thing was certain about Erin Donnelly: she was a very self-assured woman. Where Annie had been endearingly shy, Erin was refreshingly honest, unafraid of her own opinions, yet still exceedingly open to other people's. She was bright, articulate and interesting – not to mention the owner of looks that were likely to bring about serious whiplash injuries for admiring males in her vicinity. Alex was bound to be bowled over.

'So, let me get this straight: I'm someone you met through work?' Erin repeated, obviously a long way from being convinced that this cover story was going to work.

Harri ignored the insistent butterflies in her stomach and managed a smile. 'Yes, that's right. And it's not exactly a lie, seeing as we're going to be working together soon anyway.'

'Sounds to me like you're trying to convince yourself,' Erin noted wryly.

Blimey, is it that obvious? Harri pushed away the mounting panic within her and attempted a nonchalant smile. 'No, not at all. It's just that I think Al will react better if he thinks we already know each other, you know?'

Erin smiled. 'Fine. So when am I meeting him?'

Next day, Stella made an unexpected appearance at SLIT. Harri was thrilled to see her. It had been the kind of day where lunchtime takes forever to arrive, then passes in the blink of an eye, and the assembled staff of the travel agency were desperately in need of something to break the monotony of what was looking like being a long afternoon.

'Great to see you, Stella,' Nus beamed. 'So, what's the gossip?'

Coming from the famously underwhelmed Nus, this welcome was tantamount to a red carpet reception and twenty-one-gun salute.

'Thanks, Nus,' Stella replied uncertainly. 'Not much goss, I'm afraid, except that I've booked Harri and me into a day spa the weekend after next.'

'Stel, that's fantastic! I mentioned it to Rob and he's fine with it, so we can go.'

Stella tucked a perfectly straightened strand of blonde hair behind one ear as she gave Harri a stern look. 'It's *fine* for us to go anyway, whatever your boyfriend says.'

Tom groaned. 'Oh, man, a spa? I can't think of anything worse.'

'Good job you're not going, then,' Nus scowled at him. 'Which spa are you going to?'

'La Mer.' Stella's eyes lit up and she began gabbling excitedly about the luxurious treatments and the list of celebs that reportedly frequented the establishment. '. . . I mean, actresses from *Emmerdale* and *Hollyoaks* have been to La Mer, so it must be, you know, top notch! I got us on a two-for-one deal too, so I was mightily chuffed with that.'

'You're going to La Mer? Oh my *life*, that's like the most amazing place,' Nus said, becoming more animated than Harri had seen her in months. 'They have, like, fifty treatments and it's awesome! There's this floral steam room, like a sauna but with aromatherapy oils – it's meant to be amazing for your skin. We had their brochure last month when Mrs Harris was booking her mother's sixtieth birthday surprise, remember?'

Harri thought back and remembered the commotion La Mer's brochure had caused. Nus had spent every lunch break for two weeks engrossed in its glossy pages and nearly ended up in fisticuffs with Mrs Harris when she wanted to take it home. Even George had been spotted sneaking a look at the exclusive delights when he thought nobody was looking.

'Blimey, Stel, is this going to be expensive?'

Stella dismissed this with a flick of her hair. 'Stop panicking, H. It's all taken care of. *Julian's* paying.' She looked at her watch and began to leave. 'Right, I've got to go. I'll call you later, yeah?'

Harri followed her to the door. 'Hang on a minute, who's Julian?'

'Oh, he's just a guy,' she smiled, and walked out onto the High Street with Harri in tow.

'What do you mean, "just a guy"? What happened to Stefan?'

Stella shook her head. 'We're over. It's cool.'

'But I thought he was going to be the walk-in closet of your dreams?'

'Yes, well, he wasn't.'

'And Julian is?'

Stella folded her arms defensively. 'He might be, he might not. But he's a generous guy who just happens to know the owner of La Mer. So when I told him about me and you needing a day spa he was only too willing to oblige. Happy?'

Harri laughed. 'Perfectly. Speak to you later, then?'

Stella's phone began playing 'Lady Marmalade' somewhere in her oversized bag and she stared at the screen before answering the call. 'I have to take this, OK? Speak later, then. Julian! Hello, *you* . . .'

Harri watched her friend walking away. Another day, another prospective millionaire . . . It must be so easy for someone like

Stella, she mused, with a seemingly endless supply of well-heeled guys waiting to indulge her every whim. She must have dated fifteen men in the past year and yet Harri had never seen her hurt or upset when a relationship ended. Stella just seemed to shrug it off and move on to the next willing suitor. Sometimes, Harri wished she could be more like her best friend – less affected by the world around her, less concerned by others' opinions of her. Maybe then she could have some stamps in her passport . . .

'If you're planning on standing out there all day, the least you can do is give these out,' George barked in her ear, making Harri jump. He thrust some badly printed leaflets into her hand.

'What are these?'

George's face had disdain written all over it. 'Leaflets, Harriet. You know, bits of paper you give people to show them what we do?'

Harri sighed. 'Can't we send Tom out, George? I was supposed to be working on the Hillford Hall proposal this afternoon.'

Her boss ran a hand through his imaginary thick, flowing hair. 'That can wait.' He prodded the leaflets with a chubby finger. '*These* can't.'

It was frustrating, but at least this menial task would kill an hour or so. 'Fine. I'll take them around the local shops and try to get some displayed.'

'Excellent!' George exclaimed, slapping Harri on the back so hard that she was nearly propelled across the busy road. 'Off you go, then, *assistant manager* of ours.'

The High Street was busy today as Harri reluctantly started her leaflet drop. Several mums were chatting by the entrance to the Co-op, their children suspiciously observing each other from the comfort of their buggies. One of the ladies waved Harri over as she neared them.

'Not waitressing today?' she smiled.

Harri laughed. 'No, I only do that as a hobby. Doing my real job today.' She handed over a leaflet and the other mothers gathered round to read it.

'Twenty per cent off? That's pretty good.'

'I've been on at Will for ages about a holiday. Maybe we should pop in.'

'Feel free to,' Harri replied, surprised at this unexpectedly enthusiastic reaction. 'We have some fantastic family holidays at the moment.'

Harri continued down the street. A frantic Jack Russell on an extendable lead dashed past her, dragging a tiny elderly lady along in its wake. Harri stepped aside to let them pass before walking into Stone Yardley's post office and newsagent's.

Doreen Perry looked up from a stack of newspapers and smiled. She had been postmistress for as long as Harri could remember and, remarkably, seemed to have resisted the passage of time. Amply-bosomed yet diminutive in stature, she had a deep love of hand-knitted cardigans. But most remarkable by far was Doreen's hair, which had always remained in the same beehive style. The sheer height of it was a feat in itself and added significantly to her presence; the colour had progressed from peroxide blonde in the seventies to purpley-red in the eighties, jet black in the nineties, and was now a shade she lovingly termed 'Cilla Red' after her favourite TV personality.

'Afternoon, missy,' she smiled, stepping down from the raised platform behind the counter and instantly losing about ten inches from her height. 'How's everything going?'

'Good, thanks, Doreen. George has me delivering leaflets, I'm afraid.'

Doreen tutted and shook her head, the beehive barely following suit. 'That *man*. Thinks he's Stone Yardley's answer to Donald Trump or something – only without the hair, eh?' she chuckled. It was a sound that brought back a thousand memories of Harri's childhood visits to the post office: of idly lingering by the stationery displays looking at pencil cases, novelty erasers and crayon pens with interchangeable colours, while Doreen chatted to Mum.

'Right, I s'pose you'd like me to put one of those things up, eh?'

'Would that be OK?'

'Sure, give it here,' Doreen replied, taking a leaflet. 'I'll stick it in the window. And you tell that boss of yours that he's five weeks overdue paying his paper bill.'

Harri grinned. 'I'll make sure I pass it on.'

The sun had broken free from its leaden cloud prison as Harri stepped outside and heard her name being called. Turning, she saw Emily Williams hurrying towards her, dressed in her bank uniform.

'Harri! Hey! I was just on my way to see you.'

'Hi, Emily. How's everything going?'

'Good,' Emily replied breathlessly. 'Great, actually. I contacted those hotels and B&Bs you found for me and six of them have agreed to do special weekend rates.'

'Wow, that's fantastic! Well done.'

'Thanks. Although I'm starting to wonder if the whole thing might just be a bit too huge a step for us. I mean, Stu and I have only just got everything settled with money and so on – the last thing I want to do is to jeopardise our financial security.'

'Hmm, if I were you I'd be thinking exactly the same thing,' Harri admitted. Except, of course, she probably wouldn't have

175

even reached that stage in her thinking, having talked herself out of it long before. 'But I think it comes down to following your heart. If you and Stu truly believe in this then you should go for it.'

Emily's expression lit up like the bright sunlight surrounding them. 'You think so?'

'Absolutely. Actually, I've got some contacts with a taxi company in Ellingsgate – they might be able to offer you some sort of deal on transfers between the accommodation and the farm.'

'I hadn't even thought about that. You're brilliant!' Emily flung her arms around Harri, taking her completely by surprise. 'Ooh, thank you! I'm so glad I ran into you today!'

Walking back to SLIT, an unexpected heaviness claimed Harri's insides. Maybe it was seeing someone willing to chase their dream – or maybe it was just the thought of the two and a half hours of utter tediousness that lay ahead of her. Firmly discounting the former, Harri picked up her pace to return to work.

'Come to mine for dinner this Wednesday,' Alex said. 'I need to pick your brains.'

Harri stroked a purring Ron Howard and smiled into her mobile phone. 'Good luck with that, then. Should take you all of – oh – five minutes.'

'You are a comedy genius, H. You need to warn me when you're going to unleash your hilarity on me like that. Anyway, say yes.'

'I'm not sure what Rob's doing yet.'

'Please, H. I have a fantastic new recipe for clam chowder and I can tell you all about the time I was working in New Orleans during Mardi Gras . . .'

It was too tempting to refuse. 'OK, fine, what time?'

'Eight-ish. And bring something for pud.'

'I'll do that. See you Wednesday.' Harri ended the call and tickled Ron Howard's ear, which flicked appreciatively. 'Right, then. Better call Rob.'

Rob's voice was warm and ever so slightly husky when he answered. 'Hey, gorgeous. This is an unexpected pleasure.'

'Well, the last thing I want to ever be is predictable.' Harri felt a frisson of delight tingle through her.

His laugh was impossibly charming. 'I wouldn't dream of accusing you of that, Red. So, what can I do for you?'

'Al's invited me for dinner on Wednesday night. I think there's some crisis in his life that he needs my help with.'

'Good job he has you to sort him out then, hey?'

'You don't mind if I go? I mean, if you've got something planned . . .'

'Not at all. Go and have fun with your mate. Looks like I'll be doing late ones all this week, anyway.' A phone started to ring on his end of the line. 'And there's another dimwit who needs my help. I'd better go, lovely lady. I'll call you later.'

Snuggled up in her cosy cottage with a very appreciative feline draped magnificently across her lap, Harri allowed herself a moment to revel in how good life felt right now. She had a boyfriend who not only was supportive but also downright sexy; her career finally seemed to be taking shape at SLIT with her new assistant manager role, the forthcoming Hillford Hall concert packages and the potential of Emily's new business to consider; even Alex's prospective love life looked rosy.

Harri loved the fact that Rob respected her right to have her own friends – even if his obvious respect for Alex and pleasant civility whenever they met didn't quite extend to

Alex's old university mates – especially during the Sunday night pub quiz at the Star and Highwayman pub. Rob took exception to the world that Alex's friends represented: middle-class, university educated and moderately successful. Their 'years-out' before entering the workplace and apparent lack of career drive were alien to Rob who, like all of *his* friends, had reached their current occupational positions through hard work and dedication, only to find themselves working under managers who appeared to receive 'golden-ticket' promotions by virtue of the fact that they had a degree.

That said, most of the rivalry between the two camps was good-natured, blokey banter that highly amused both sides, usually taking the form of mildly offensive team names for the pub quiz: 'We're Not Boffins', 'All Degree No Trousers', 'All Mouth No Degree', 'Too Clever To Work', 'Dead-End Jobs Aren't Us' – and so on, *ad infinitum*. They were all as bad as each other, in Harri's opinion, but the light-hearted name-calling had nevertheless become somewhat of a highlight every Sunday night at the pub.

On Wednesday evening, after an hour of general chat over dinner, Harri decided to cut to the chase. 'What did you want to talk to me about, then?'

Alex's smile faded and he grabbed their empty plates. 'I'll just put these in the kitchen. Do you want more coffee?'

'No, I'm fine thanks. Is everything OK?'

Alex's carefree laugh was completely unconvincing. 'Of course. If you want to move to the sofa I'll be right with you.'

Harri settled down in the ample confines of Alex's oversized sofa, tucking her legs up underneath herself and feeling completely at home. She adored their conversations: the opportunity to discuss the world with someone who completely

178

understood her fascination with it. Alex had a million conversations beginning, 'When I was in . . .' – so unlike anyone else in Stone Yardley.

'When I was in Tokyo working at the Hilton . . . When I was in Vietnam . . . I remember this amazing thing that happened when I was in Ecuador . . .'

This evening had been no exception. Over richly steaming bowls of creamy clam chowder and yellow cornbread, Alex had told Harri about the New Orleans Mardi Gras, bringing vivid-hued images dancing into her mind – jumping brass bands, drums, laughter and crowds of brightly attired people swaying through the city streets.

'I tell you, H, it was amazing. Noise like you wouldn't believe, and it seems like everyone in the city is out dancing. I was working in the kitchen of this hotel and Carlos, the head chef, gave me the evening off so I could go. He was like, "Get out there, boy! The music is waitin' for ya!" It's crazy! Everyone's so friendly and you just get swept along with the parade. I ended up at this tiny restaurant with a girl I met in the crowd. I think she was relieved to meet a fellow Brit in the middle of all the madness. She was travelling across the States and had decided to go for a slap-up meal on her last night in the city. Poor girl, she'd spent ages getting ready, hair and make-up all done and her best dress she'd brought from home, and then they gave her this huge, white plastic bib to wear while she was eating the meal. She was mortified! Mind you, we ended up laughing about it.'

'Did you keep in touch with her?'

Alex pulled a face. 'Nah. Of course not. When you're travelling it's better not to get into relationships. Everyone's heading in different directions: it doesn't make for a firm foundation, you know?'

Harri smiled. 'So what was different about the girl you came home for?'

A familiar sadness claimed Alex's eyes. 'She was heading home. And so, it turned out, was I.'

Harri didn't ask Alex about Nina very often. She knew most of the story already – not just from Alex himself but also from Viv, whose take on the whole thing was a lot less charitable than her son's. After nine and a half years of travelling the world, Alex met Nina in a bar in New York – and everything changed. She had been travelling for a year and was spending her final month in Manhattan before coming back to the UK to start a restaurant in Bristol with her brother. It was love at first sight for both of them and, after three weeks of inseparability, Alex made the decision to return to England with her. They opened the restaurant, moved in together and Alex proposed (much to his mother's delight). A month before the wedding, Alex came back to the flat they shared to find Nina in bed with his best friend, Tim. Incensed, he moved out and ended up staying with his friends Sandie and Brendan in Somerset for a few months. While he was there, Brendan found the advert for the auction of the Welcome Tea Rooms and encouraged Alex to bid for it. And the rest, as they say, is history.

Most people would have sworn off relationships after an experience like that, but for Alex it had the opposite effect. After years of non-commitment, being in a loving, seemingly settled relationship brought about a sea change in his thinking, making the security it afforded him something he craved to feel again. Hence the past three years of searching for someone to claim his heart as Nina had done – and the countless heartaches encountered along the way. Not that anyone but Harri knew this, of course. As far as anyone in Stone Yardley was concerned, Alex was the jovial, laid-back guy who owned Wātea, with surfer-style good looks and not a care in the world.

'Budge up, chuck!' Alex had arrived back from the kitchen with a plate of ratafias and flopped down on the sofa next to Harri. 'Try one of these.'

Harri took a bite of the crisp, dome-shaped biscuit and the most intense sweet, almond flavour filled her mouth. 'Wow, that's amazing.'

'My good friend Luca, who I met in Adelaide, gave me the recipe. Pretty good, huh?'

She nodded and answered crumbily, 'Fantastic.'

Alex's laugh was loud and warm. 'Such a refined dinner guest. You must come back again. Now, I need to ask you something.'

'OK.'

'Right. Um . . .' He took a breath and his chocolate-brown eyes made a wide sweep of the living room. 'It's about your friends.'

Harri frowned. 'Which ones?'

'Well, Annie and Erin. Actually, more Erin to be honest.'

'OK, what about her?'

Alex brushed some crumbs from his shirt and turned squarely to face Harri. 'How much do you know about her, exactly?'

This was a question Harri had not prepared herself for. Should she tell Alex the truth about his two 'Free to a Good Home' dates or perpetuate the stories he had already heard? Suddenly, face to face with her best friend, the prospect of shattering the illusion she had so carefully constructed seemed too difficult to dismantle. Surely the opportunity would present itself further down the line, wouldn't it? There and then, Harri made a decision: Alex didn't need to know the truth until he

181

found someone who might become permanent. It would be *so* much easier to tell him then. 'I told you, we met through work.'

Alex wasn't pacified by this. 'Yes, I know,' he answered, dismissively, 'but how much do you *actually* know about her?'

Seeing the trust in his eyes for her and the obvious battle within him, Harri relented slightly. There was no point in making the lie any bigger than it already was. 'I have to be honest, Al. I only know what I've told you. Erin's the events manager at Hillford Hall and she sings in her brother's covers band in her spare time. She likes Mexican and Thai food, hates prawns and her favourite film is *Magnolia*. Other than that, I don't know any more. Why do you ask?'

Alex gave the back of his neck a self-conscious rub. 'Oh, I dunno, H. She seems nice – I mean, *really* nice – but I just feel like there's something she's not telling me.'

'Maybe that's just you being paranoid.'

He laughed. 'Yeah, maybe. Sorry, H. I must seem really ungrateful.'

'About what?'

'Well, you've set me up with two very lovely women and all I can do is find fault with them.'

Ignoring the stab of guilt inside, Harri smiled and patted his hand. 'Isn't that what dating's about, Al? You try out lots of different people to find what you like.'

'So before Rob, did you date much?'

The question took Harri completely by surprise. 'I – er – not that much, really. I went out with a guy in my last year of school for about eight months but it didn't go anywhere. Then I had a few dates here and there but nothing serious until I met Rob.'

Alex nodded and looked down at his feet. 'Right.'

Unsure of how to take this reaction, Harri added: 'Not that I've ever felt short-changed by my lack of dating experience, mind you. Everybody's different, Al. Are you seeing Erin again?'

'I don't think so.' He looked up at her again. 'I'm sorry, H. I don't deserve everything you're doing for me.'

Harri made her best attempt at a smile. *Oh, Alex, if only you knew . . .*

CHAPTER TWELVE

Come Away With Me . . .

There are stains on the grubby ceiling tiles as Harri looks up past the flickering strip lights. She is instantly reminded of something Dad used to say when she was little: 'You can make shapes and faces out of everything, if you just look hard enough.'

Consequently, one of their favourite games when Harri was growing up was 'Finding Faces' – smiling faces in tree trunks; funny faces in the concrete slabs of the patio; a spooky-looking ghost-shape in the woodchip wallpaper in their downstairs loo; and dragons, castles and cartoon characters in the clouds above them as they walked on Dartmoor's hills behind Grandma Langton's house. Dad loved doing 'mirror pictures' with Harri – making strange and wonderful shapes by folding paper over poster paint splodges. Later in life Harri learned that psychologists used these for conducting mental assessments. This always made her smile, wondering what an eminent professional might have made of Dad's creations.

Looking at the array of stains across the ceiling, Harri pushes the familiar stab of sadness away and begins to make a mental note of the shapes: butterfly, castle, old man, wine glass . . .

* * *

Stella met Harri from work the following Friday and proudly produced two spa passes from her surprisingly authentic-looking Chanel bag.

'These, my good friend, are our passports to day-long luxury.'

An audacious thrill zipped through Harri. 'This is going to be such a great weekend, I know it!'

Stella linked an arm through Harri's as they walked down the High Street. 'Just think, H: a whole day of amazing treatments and relaxation, then a whole day of shopping. Utter bliss – well, apart from the boring bit tomorrow night, of course.'

'Which just happens to be the main reason for this trip, can I remind you?'

Stella snorted. 'Yeah, well, I'm only going to that because your Dan bloke's a hottie.'

My Dan. Harri giggled and felt her cheeks turning pink. *If only.* Still, the thought of an entire evening in the presence of the man who held the key to her dreams was fantastic – and enough of a reward to quiet her concern about not being with Rob for a whole weekend when he was at home. Of course, Rob had been fine about her spending the weekend away. He'd even arranged a long overdue game of five-a-side with his former Dynamo Stone Yardley teammates, followed by a lazy afternoon (and evening too, no doubt) in the Star and Highwayman.

'Go,' he'd urged her, amused at her reluctance to leave. 'It's about time the tables were turned on me. I'm actually looking forward to being the one pining at home for a change.'

'So, are you packed?' Stella asked.

'Yep. Did it last night.'

Stella stopped dead, yanking Harri back like she was on a

bungee rope. '*Last night!* My life, Harri, I can't believe you left it so late! My case has been packed *for a week*. Planning, H. It's essential for a trip like this.'

An hour later, they were speeding down the M40 in Stella's baby blue Nissan Figaro. Christina Aguilera was blasting from the impressive sound system and Stella was singing along loudly. Harri leaned back in the comfortable seat and let herself relax. This was by far the most spontaneous thing she had done since posting the fateful *Juste Moi* letter months ago – and this time nothing was going to go wrong. Maybe, she thought to herself, a weekend abroad could be the next step. And then . . . who knows what I might find the courage to do? 'Baby steps,' her mother always used to say, 'take baby steps and then you'll be amazed by what you can achieve.'

The sun was just sinking below the horizon when the lights of Oxford came into view. It was all Harri could do not to whoop out loud as they drove through the impossibly gorgeous streets, and even Stella turned down the music to take in the view.

Stanton Lodge was a gorgeous Regency building of honey-yellow Cotswold stone, surrounded by a small hedged garden. Stella parked and they carried their cases to the large, dark blue front door surrounded by wisteria blooms. Harri pressed the brass doorbell and a short, immaculately dressed woman opened the door.

'Hello, ladies. Come in, come in!' She ushered them along a brightly lit hallway, painted in a calming palette of creams and soft, grassy greens, towards a mahogany desk, where a young man in a dark blue suit smiled to greet them. 'Leo, these ladies are staying with us tonight. Will you check them in and then help them with their bags?'

'Yes, Mrs Hammond.'

'Excellent. I'll let you settle in and then if you would like some tea I'll be in the drawing room, just over there.'

'That would be great, thank you,' Stella replied, clearly loving the attention and the luxurious surroundings.

Leo carried their cases up to their second-floor room. Harri caught her breath as she walked inside – the room was easily as big as the whole of the downstairs of Two Trees Cottage. Two double beds were covered in luxurious linen and matching curtains hung gracefully from the large picture window. The cream carpet sank beneath their feet and ran through into the generous en suite bathroom, complete with slipper bath and an extra-large shower cubicle. Thick, white towels were draped over the heated rail and a basket of Crabtree & Evelyn toiletries had been placed on the glass shelf above the washbasin.

Stella waited until Leo had left the room before letting out a loud shriek and flinging herself on the nearest bed. 'How fab is this, eh?'

Harri sat down on the other double and gently stroked the brocade counterpane. 'It's wonderful, Stel. It must've cost a fortune.'

'Correction: it *did* cost Julian a fortune!'

'Stel, I feel awful about that.'

'*Pah*, don't. He can afford it. He said I was worth every penny,' she grinned.

Harri didn't dare to think what that little statement implied about her friend.

Half an hour later, Harri and Stella were enjoying tea and generous slices of rich, home-made coffee and walnut cake in the Lodge's elegant drawing room. Mrs Hammond refilled their bone-china cups and smiled at her guests.

'Would you like some more cake?'

Stella accepted, having wolfed her first slice down, but Harri politely declined, still enjoying every morsel as if she needed to capture and savour every moment of the weekend.

'So, what have you planned during your stay, ladies?'

'We're going to La Mer tomorrow and then a book launch in the evening.'

Mrs Hammond leaned forward with interest. 'A book launch? How splendid! Which author?'

'Dan Beagle – the travel writer. He's a bit of a hero of mine,' Harri replied.

A wide smile lit up Mrs Hammond's perfectly made-up face. 'Daniel! Oh, how wonderful!'

Harri's pulse rate shot up. 'You know him?'

'Yes, I know him very well. You see, I was a teacher in my former life and Daniel Beagle was one of my best students.'

'That's amazing. What subject did you teach?' Harri asked, on the edge of her seat with excitement.

Mrs Hammond's laugh was like a twittering soprano. '*Everything*, my dear! I was his very first teacher at primary school – but even at that young age, I knew he was destined for greatness. I've followed his progress with great interest.'

'Do you ever see him?' Harri's question carried a slight sliver of hope.

'Heavens, no. Haven't seen him in years. Mind you, my friend still sends his mother Christmas cards.'

'Oh.'

'Well, there you go, H,' Stella laughed, once they were back up in their room, 'you now have a great excuse to start a conversation with the Beaglemeister. "I know your first teacher"– you have to admit, it's an original chat-up line.'

Harri ignored her friend's amusement and hid behind Dan's latest book.

That night, after a sumptuous dinner, Harri snuggled down

in the impossibly comfortable bed, luxuriating in the sensation of cool Egyptian cotton against her skin. Resting her head on soft, peach-scented duck-feather pillows, she closed her eyes and drifted into a dream.

She had just arrived at an airport in some far-flung destination, the hot tropical air shocking her body as she descended the steps from the aircraft onto the baking tarmac, shielding her eyes from the bright sunlight. An overwhelming sense of euphoria claimed her entire being: this was it – she'd finally conquered her fears and travelled across the world to arrive here. Everything around her was new and unfamiliar – accents, languages, smells, sights and sounds launched a dizzying assault on her senses. After collecting her case, she walked through into Arrivals, watching as her fellow travellers were claimed by waiting families, welcomed with tears and smiles. A sudden cold shot of panic hit her stomach as, scanning the faces of strangers clamouring around, she realised nobody was waiting for her. Struck by a blow of complete loneliness, she pushed her way through the happy bodies until she emerged on the other side, looking back at their unrestrained glee with aching eyes. Why had she come all this way just to feel as lonely as she did in her little cottage in Stone Yardley? Resignation sapping every ounce of strength from her body, she started to walk back towards the check-in desks. At that moment, a figure appeared in the sliding airport terminal doors, sprinting towards her, his features thrown into shadow by the sunlight behind him.

'Wait!' he shouted. 'Please, Harri, wait for me!'

Squinting against the sun, Harri watched the approaching man until he reached her side, sea-green eyes wild with emotion as his strong arms pulled her close to his body.

'I thought you weren't coming. I thought I was going to be

all alone,' Harri sobbed against his chest as his hands traced tiny circles across her shoulders.

'I'm here now, Harri. You're with me and you're safe – and that's all that matters. The world is ours for the taking. You'll never be lonely again.'

Lifting her head, Harri stared into the shining depths of Dan's eyes as his soft lips enveloped hers, her body shaking as their embrace intensified. Breaking the kiss, Dan buried his head in her neck, his breath hot against her ear.

'Harri . . . oh, Harri . . .'

'Mmm . . . Dan . . .'

'*Harri!* Wake up, you saddo.'

The dream dissolved like Alka-Seltzer in water as Harri came crashing back to reality, opening her eyes to see Stella's amused expression inches from her face. 'Nice dream?'

'I – er – I . . .' Harri stammered, frantically trying to get her bearings.

Stella threw her head back and laughed loudly. 'You were *so* dreaming about Dan Beagle!'

A burning flush dashed across Harri's cheeks. 'No, I wasn't.'

'Liar. You were talking in your sleep, hon.' She slapped the back of her hand to her forehead like Sarah Bernhardt on a lime-lit stage. '"Oh, Dan, Dan, kiss me, Dan!"'

Thoroughly embarrassed, Harri turned away. 'Get lost.'

'Aw, come on, H, it's sweet.'

'Stop mocking me and do something useful – put the kettle on,' Harri retorted, battling the ample cosiness of her bed to lift her leaden frame up to a seated position.

Stella held her hands up in surrender. 'OK, sorry. You have to admit, though, it's a lovely thing to have a dream like that. All I dreamed about last night were fluffy towels and expensive carpets.'

As she turned her back to fiddle with the tiny travel kettle in the corner of the room, Harri had to smile. Dreaming about lavish home furnishings in celebrity houses was probably the ultimate turn-on for her friend.

Stella brought back two cups of tea and sat on Harri's bed. 'Didn't mean to mock, H. I honestly thought it was sweet.'

'It's just a silly dream, that's all,' Harri replied, sipping her tea.

'Hey, it's cool, honestly.' Stella reached across and squeezed Harri's hand. 'You're allowed to have dreams, you know. We're here for a fantastic weekend and nothing's going to spoil it, OK? We are going to have the most phenomenal English breakfast, and then we are going to be pampered, buffed, massaged and polished to within an inch of our lives. And then, my nutty friend, we are going to go and lust after that hunky explorer of yours for *hours* tonight. And tomorrow, we shop. So drink your tea, get your little sleepy bum out of bed and let's do this!'

When Harri was little, bathtime was her favourite time of the day. It wasn't just the chance to play with the yellow rubber duck in the bathwater that made the experience so magical – it was the feeling of being completely safe and afterwards, sitting on Mum's lap swathed in a huge, yellow bath towel, having her hair towelled dry.

This memory returned in comforting splendour as she lay back on a beech-wood recliner in an enormous white, fluffy towelling robe in the luxurious surroundings of La Mer. Despite her amusement at Stella's near-obsessional fascination with the day spa, Harri had to admit that it was stunning. Every detail had been carefully considered and no expense had been spared to create a sanctuary of peace and relaxation. Subdued

191

lighting, heated floors, sumptuous pools and soothing music added to the exclusive ambience and the treatments were more indulgent than Harri had ever experienced.

After a Sea Salt Buff, she was relaxing with a tropical fruit smoothie, enjoying the tingle of her glowing skin, waiting for Stella to return from her Hot Stone Massage, when a woman in her mid-forties padded past and paused to bestow a glowing smile.

'*Heaven*, isn't it?' she breathed.

Harri nodded. 'It's really nice.'

The woman extended a freshly manicured hand. 'I'm Sonia. This your first time?'

'Yes. My friend brought me.'

Sonia giggled and sat down on the recliner next to Harri. 'It's my ninth time here. Just can't seem to keep away. My – erm – *friend* brought me too, only he's at a business meeting for most of today. Dreadful shame that he can't be here to enjoy it, but so generous of him to let me experience it for him, don't you think?'

Smiling politely, Harri took a long sip of smoothie to stifle her mirth. Sonia smoothed down one of the flaps of her towelling robe, looking like an overly pampered cat that had unexpectedly acquired a large amount of cream.

'Makes all the hassle worthwhile, I suppose . . .' The definite pause was obviously Harri's cue to enquire further, but, in a rare moment of selfishness, Harri declined the invitation. After a couple of awkward seconds, Sonia decided to press on regardless. 'He's married, you see. Brings me with him on his . . . shall we call them *business* trips? Wife has no idea, by all accounts. She's so bound up in being a mother to his kids that she can't see how *unfulfilled* he is, poor lamb . . .'

Any remaining sliver of post-massage glow that Harri had

192

enjoyed now disintegrated as a well of discomfort rose inside her. The absolute last thing she wanted today was to be treated to the brazen honesty of a woman she'd barely met. 'Right, well, I—'

'You see, the thing is,' Sonia gushed, leaning forward so far that Harri received an unwanted glimpse of over-tanned cleavage, 'when your drive is as strong as his, only someone without the distractions of family can match it, if you know what I mean? And I'm telling you, what they say about a woman in her forties is *so true* . . .'

A strange, strangled cry broke the peaceful ambience of the spa and Harri suddenly realised it was coming from her own throat. She was just about to make her excuses and beat a hasty retreat when, to her boundless relief, Stella appeared beside her.

'I'm back and, can I just say, my therapist was a miracle-worker!'

'Well, I should be getting along.' Sonia rose and smiled insincerely at Stella as she passed. 'Need to make sure every inch is fully glowing for *later* . . .'

Harri ignored the nausea in the pit of her stomach and smiled weakly. 'Yes, well, um, good luck with that.'

Amused, Stella claimed the adjacent recliner. 'Who on earth was that?'

Harri pulled a face. 'Somebody's mistress, apparently. Honestly, Stel, she was so *brazen* about it.'

'Welcome to the world of the rich and irresponsible,' Stella grinned. 'My massage therapist was just telling me some of the stories she hears here. Terrible stuff!'

'Hmm, well, I've heard more than enough to last me a lifetime,' Harri shuddered.

'Hold that thought.' Stella's eyes followed a tall, dark-haired

193

man in a La Mer uniform as he passed them and disappeared into a treatment room. 'I think he's doing my next therapy – gorgeous! I *knew* I'd love this place!'

At five thirty, Harri and Stella reluctantly left La Mer and caught a taxi back to their hotel to get ready for their literary evening at Lady Margaret Hall.

Lady Margaret Hall was the grandest setting for Dan's launch evening. The approach alone to one of Oxford's most beautiful colleges was enough to strike awe into its visitors: perfectly manicured grounds elegantly embraced its statuesque buildings, where knowledge and learning had been revered for over a hundred and thirty years. As Harri and Stella approached the entrance, a sense of hope and possibility seemed to ooze forth from the impressive red brick and York stone building.

For some reason, Stella had decided to wear her Jimmy Choo eBay copy shoes with impossibly high heels, which were great when you just had to sit looking chic at a party, but useless if you had to walk any distance. Of course, even wobbling like a small child in Mummy's shoes, Stella still managed to look like she'd stepped straight out of a high-fashion magazine: her blonde hair pulled back into a sleek, high ponytail, a simple black shift dress complementing her enviable figure and every detail of her appearance carefully planned to impress.

'Would you slow down?'

Harri waited for her to catch up. 'Whatever possessed you to wear those shoes?'

'I *wanted* to make an effort for you, actually, seeing as this is supposed to be our girly weekend away. Besides, I love my Choos.'

'Even if they're not real?'

Stella looked offended. 'They're real to me. Anyway, if Julian turns out to be the keeper I think he might be, the next pair *will* be real.'

Harri laughed. 'Let's keep our fingers crossed for Julian, then.'

'You're only mocking because you're jealous.'

'I am not. Unlike *you*, I'm looking for reliability and long-term commitment in a relationship, not a bottomless bank account.'

'Oooh, pardon me for having such inferior hopes for my love life,' Stella mocked. 'Maybe I should get Julian to take me *camping*.'

'Ha-ha.' Harri decided to ask her friend the question she'd been grappling with since they left their hotel. 'Seriously, though, do I look OK?'

'Yeah, you look great. You always do. That's the annoying thing: I have to plan to look this good, but you just turn up looking amazing – and you don't even realise.'

Unbeknownst to Stella, Harri had been secretly planning her outfit for tonight for the past three weeks and yet, even as they were getting ready earlier today, she was unsure about her choice of an aubergine sleeveless dress with a cropped black shrug. 'I'm just worried I look a bit too – you know – *overdressed*.'

Stella's laugh ricocheted around the elegant buildings. 'Only you could look stunning and worry about it.'

Harri stared down at the diamanté decoration on her black flats. 'I just . . . it doesn't matter.'

'Sweets, you look gorgeous, OK? Dan will love it.'

'I didn't do it for Dan.'

Stella's arm slipped round Harri's shoulder as they headed for the lights of the Hall. 'Yes, you did. But that's fine. Come on, let's get inside. I feel like I'm walking on bleeding stumps here.'

The place was already abuzz with excited conversation when Harri and Stella entered the oak-panelled room, lit by delicate glass lamps suspended in threes from the white moulded plaster ceiling. Rich tapestries and fine portraits of the college founders adorned the walls, and the polished parquet flooring caught the light. A lectern had been placed on a small platform at one end of the room and around seventy red velvet chairs were arranged facing it. Several people had already claimed the first few rows, proudly guarding their vantage points for the evening ahead.

Stella bustled her way through a seated group of fifty-somethings to claim two seats a third of the way down the room. Far more pink than anybody should rightfully blush, Harri followed her best friend, apologising profusely to the people they had barged past.

'We could have just walked around the edge of the room to get here,' she growled at Stella as she sat down, juggling her bag and coat.

'No, we couldn't. That shop window for Botox over there was eyeing up these seats,' Stella replied, not-so-subtly indicating a heavily made-up woman with an immovable expression two rows behind them. 'I couldn't take the risk.'

'Stel, you're dreadful.'

'No, H, I'm not. Actually, I was thinking of you.'

Harri raised an eyebrow. 'You were?'

Opening her compact mirror and refreshing her lipgloss, Stella nodded. 'Absolutely. Look over there.' She tipped the end of her gloss bottle in the direction of the stage.

Harri turned to see Dan Beagle himself strolling casually through the doorway and onto the platform, laughing with the event organiser and sound technician less than twenty feet away from her.

'Oh . . . my . . . *life* . . .' she breathed, as her heart rate doubled.

'Exactly. That's why these seats are so good: not too far away so you can't behold the beauty of the man, yet not too close to feel like he's sitting on your lap. Although . . .' she grinned, a wicked glint in her eye, 'maybe that wouldn't be such a bad thing after all. The man is *stunning*.'

'He is.' Harri had decided beforehand that she wasn't going to be affected by the sight of her hero, yet now she found herself degenerating into a blushing, breathless teenager, incapable of rational thought or speech. What on earth was wrong with her? Dan Beagle was causing her entire being to tingle – something she hadn't felt in a long time.

'You're going *so* red,' Stella teased, her laugh echoing around the hallowed walls. '*Ow!* There's no need to kick me!'

'Just *shush*,' Harri whispered through gritted teeth. 'I'm well aware of the colour I'm turning, thank you very much.'

Stella folded her arms and surveyed Harri with unbridled amusement.

A tall woman with raven hair, swept up at an impossible angle, stepped in front of the stage and smiled expectantly. The audience fell silent immediately, eager for the evening to begin. Harri leaned back and took a deep breath.

'Good evening, ladies and gentlemen. My name is Gabriella Rovira, Head of Events, and it is my very great pleasure to welcome you all here to the breathtaking surroundings of Lady Margaret Hall for an evening that promises to be fascinating. I know that many of you have travelled some distance to be here tonight and I would like to thank you for doing so; however, I think I can safely say that no one here has travelled *quite* as far as our guest speaker.' A ripple of polite laughter traversed the room. 'Tonight's speaker became an adventurer at the tender age of fifteen, accompanying his father on a trip to the rainforests of Bolivia; since then, he has made more than two hundred voyages across the world, chronicling his epic journeys through a series of award-winning books, photographic exhibitions and, of course, his television programmes. May I have your heartiest applause, please, as I invite the BAFTA award-winning, *Sunday Times* bestselling author, presenter, photographer and – most of all – *traveller* to the stage: Dan Beagle!'

'She wants him in the *worst* way, doesn't she?' Stella giggled under her breath.

'Sssh! There he is!'

'Oh *brother* . . .'

Harri ignored Stella's sarcasm as Dan stepped onto the stage, holding up his hands to halt the applause. 'Thank you, Gabriella. I have to admit, halfway through that introduction I was wondering who the better qualified guy was that you had lined up to speak instead of me tonight!'

The audience laughed much louder than the joke deserved and Harri was instantly reminded of Stella in their first year of secondary school, following Jason Harding – star rugby player and the first object of her affections – around the edges of the school playing field, laughing uncomfortably loud whenever he made even the lamest of jokes. Get a grip, Harri, she chided herself. You're not here to drool like a lovesick teenager. You're here to be inspired . . .

As Dan spoke, images from around the world flashed up on the large screen behind him. Each one sent shivers of delight racing down Harri's spine as her eyes drank in every detail. Sunlight streaming through dense Brazilian rainforest

198

canopies, throwing spotlights of pure gold onto the forest floor hundreds of feet below; the broad smiles and inquisitive eyes of Patagonian village children as they stared down the camera lens; nomadic tribeswomen, swathed in thick woven blankets against the biting winds of the Mongolian plains; the barren, desolate landscape of a dried-up lake bed in the outback of Australia, its surface cracked by the scorching sun and peppered with the skeletal frames of weather-beaten trees; a bustling street market somewhere in sub-Saharan Africa, alive with movement and colour so vivid that Harri could almost hear its clamorous din ringing in her head. Hearing the words directly from the man himself brought these places to life even more than his books did. His passion, emotion and near reverence for the world he had spent so many years exploring seemed to effuse from every pore of his being, drawing the audience to the edge of their seats as he recounted tale after tale of his adventures.

For a brief moment, Harri wrenched her eyes away to check Stella's reaction. Expecting Stella to be inspecting her nails with a bored look, Harri was amazed to see her best friend's attention completely caught by the man on the stage. In fact, Harri couldn't remember ever seeing her quite so enthralled.

Half an hour into Dan's talk, a slide flashed up on the screen that sent murmurs of approval fluttering around the audience: 'DO YOU HAVE THE GOLDEN TICKET?'

Harri felt her pulse rate increase and the audience around her leaned forward as one person.

'Now, I realise this is slightly corny in such elegant surroundings,' Dan smiled, 'but I thought it would be good to have a bit of fun tonight. I've hidden a golden ticket in an envelope underneath one of your chairs. The person who finds it will win a special, leather-bound signed edition of my new book,

Wilderness Roads. There are only two of these in the world and one of them is mine. So, go on then, have a look!'

The Hall was shaken by the excited commotion of seventy chairs scraping back and one hundred and forty knees hitting the polished parquet as the audience members strained to look under their chairs. Harri and Stella followed suit, squeezing down between the rows of giggling people.

'Aw, it's not here,' Stella grinned, sitting back on her chair and resuming her observation of Dan.

Please let it be me, just this once, Harri pleaded silently, reaching underneath her chair. To her astonishment, her fingers closed around paper. Quickly, carefully, she pulled and it came away from the seat base in her hands.

Stella looked down at Harri and her expression instantly changed. Jumping up, she shouted, 'Here! It's here!'

Harri stumbled to her feet, the room around her beginning to spin, and held the envelope aloft to the disappointment of most of the audience and the kind congratulations of those nearest to her. Dan looked over and a strange expression claimed his features. Almost in slow motion, he left the stage holding the book and began to make his way down the room. Suddenly, it was as if the room, the people and the world around them melted away: it was just Dan and Harri, his eyes transfixed as he moved towards her. *Just like in her dream.* Harri was only aware of his eyes, green as the waters lapping the Indian Ocean beach pictured behind him, his look of pure astonishment and the insistent beat of her own heart. Finally, he arrived at her side and she held out the envelope to him as his fingers lightly brushed hers to accept it.

But something was horribly wrong. Dan's expression was real, his touch was silken on her skin, but his eyes weren't claiming hers. Following his gaze, Harri's stomach jerked into

200

a twisted knot as she saw Stella staring back at Dan, an expression identical to his on her face. For what felt like an eternity, all three remained where they stood – a cruel triangle of fascination, rapture and crushing loss. Dan handed the book to Harri without taking his eyes from Stella and murmured, 'Come and see me afterwards and I'll sign it for you.'

Stella nodded and Dan slowly stepped back, an unspoken understanding that Harri was denied access to passing between them, before he gathered himself together and returned to the stage.

Harri sank back into her chair, feeling as if her heart had been ripped from her chest and stamped into the floor by the one person she thought would cherish it. Swallowing her tears, she stared at the floor as Dan resumed his talk. She didn't look at Stella: she couldn't. Not after the look she had witnessed passing between her and Dan. It was too much to bear.

The evening passed in a pain-edged blur, Harri desperately trying to hold it together and focus on the beautiful photographs appearing behind Dan. Finally, as the audience spontaneously rose to their feet to applaud him, Harri grabbed her coat and bag and hurried out of the Hall into the coolness of the alabaster-pillared lobby. Tears streaming down her face, she fled the building, running into the darkened grounds. It was a clear night and stars flickered like tiny pinpricks of light in the celestial indigo miles above her. Looking up, Harri wished she could disappear. This was all wrong. It shouldn't have happened like this. While she knew she had been crazy to entertain thoughts of going off on adventures with Dan, she couldn't stop the feelings of hurt and betrayal from bombarding her mind.

Angry at her own reaction, she slumped against a stone

sundial and tried to corral her emotions. The *one thing* she secretly guarded as hers and hers alone – the raw beauty of Dan's world and her dream to be invited inside it – had been snatched away from her hands tonight. He meant *nothing* to Stella – no more than another handsome guy in possession of a small fortune – so why had such priceless treasure been cast wilfully at her feet? As much as Harri loved her best friend, right now she wasn't sure she could even be in the same town as her, let alone the same room.

It wasn't that she was angry at Dan being bowled over by Stella. After all, she was gorgeous and any man would have been insane for not noticing it. And it wasn't that Harri wanted Dan to fall in love with her, either. That would plainly be ridiculous – she was in love with Rob and couldn't imagine being with anyone else. What hurt the most was that Dan represented the confident traveller she longed to be, so his disinterest in her removed another excuse from the well-rehearsed arsenal she relied on to justify not travelling alone. When the all-too-familiar loneliness ventured from the shadows in her life, it was Dan's words, Dan's voice and the images he captured that had kept her company through the long, empty nights. Dan was *hers* – someone she looked up to, aspired to be like and whose work she respected.

Harri swallowed hard and dug in her handbag for a tissue. Wiping her eyes, she inhaled deeply, filling her aching lungs afresh and feeling the stormy seas within her beginning to quell. Willing her heart to quieten down, she managed to salvage the tattered remnants of her common sense.

She was just beginning to feel calmer when she saw Stella carefully stepping in her ridiculously high heels across the dark, dewy grass, carrying Dan's book. Taking another breath, Harri turned to face her friend.

'Hey.'

'Hey yourself. Are you OK? I looked round and you'd gone.'

'I – um – I just needed some fresh air, that's all.'

Stella's blue eyes narrowed. 'Yeah, right, except that isn't what this is about, is it?'

Harri forced a smile, ignoring the pulse of her heart against her chest. 'It is. Honestly. Just all a bit much, winning the book, you know?'

'That would be this book that you completely forgot?' She handed it to Harri, who hugged it close.

'Like I said, I was a little overwhelmed.'

Stella's expression brightened. 'Oh, that's OK then. I was worried you might have been upset about Dan and me. I mean, you must have seen the way he looked at me? I'm still shaking, H! I've never had a reaction to a guy like that before. Look, I actually have goose bumps! You know, if he asked me to go off with him right now I'd just grab my bag and go.'

Feeling like she had been punched in the stomach, Harri hoped the involuntary rush of air from her mouth sounded enough like a laugh to pacify Stella. 'It seems to have been an exciting evening all round.'

'Too right.' Stella's eyes were alive, sparkling as bright as the stars above her head. 'So, er, I suppose we'd better get back in there and get this signed for you then, eh?'

Steeling herself, Harri nodded.

Harri wasn't jealous of the way Dan's eyes never left her best friend's as he signed her book that evening, or the way his hand lingered softly on Stella's arm as they chatted for what seemed like hours, to the exclusion of everyone else. But Harri still resented the fact that up until this evening Dan had merely been a source of amusement to Stella, who had mockingly referred to him as 'your hunky travel guy', poking fun at what she called Harri's 'schoolgirl crush'.

That night, as she lay in her hotel room bed, she waited until she could hear Stella's breathing pattern become deepened by sleep before allowing her tears, which been threatening to break forth all evening, to pour down her cheeks, carrying her broken dreams with them as they soaked her linen pillowcase.

Stella was uncharacteristically quiet on the drive home next day. In fact, she had been like this since breakfast that morning – even while they were shopping, which was strange, seeing as spending money was usually Stella's *raison d'être*. Harri sat in the passenger seat and willed the miles to pass more quickly.

'How amazing was our illicit weekend then, eh?' Stella's question brought Harri sharply back to reality.

'Yeah. Great.'

'I mean, who would've thought a boring talk on expeditions in a dusty old building could turn out to be so fascinating?'

'Hmm.'

'And Dan signed your book! How cool was that! You see, I told you it was worth going to see him.'

No, you didn't, Harri thought, watching fields, trees and motorway asphalt rushing past the window.

There was a pause as Stella fiddled with the radio until she found a station playing thudding dance music. Harri closed her eyes and willed the tension headache banging away inside her head to leave.

'So, go on then. Ask me.'

'Ask you what?'

'Come on, I know you're dying to know what Dan and I were talking about last night.'

Harri swallowed hard and desperately tried to think of another topic to change the subject. Frustratingly, nothing came.

Not that it mattered to Stella. 'He's *amazing*, Harri! I mean, you know me, I've met my fair share of different blokes in the past, but he's something else. And those eyes! Seriously, it's years since I went giggly over a chap, but I'm a flippin' mess today. And he's been texting me all morning – seriously, H, he's so sweet!'

Please stop. Just stop now, Harri pleaded silently, half-entertaining the idea of opening the car door and escaping via a high-speed stunt roll across the hard shoulder of the M40. 'What time do you think we'll be back?'

'What? Oh – er – I don't know, about four-ish?'

'Cool. I'd better text Rob and let him know.' Harri reached into her bag and busied herself with her mobile phone.

Stella continued her eulogy for a few more minutes, until Harri's obvious snub finally registered. 'OK, what's the problem?'

'There's no problem,' Harri answered curtly, not looking up from her phone.

'Don't give me that. You've been arsey with me all morning.'

'I'm surprised you noticed.'

'What's *that* supposed to mean?'

'Nothing.'

Stella slowed the car a little. 'Come on, Harri. If you've something to say to me then just say it.'

Harri looked up, her blood beginning to boil. '*Fine*. I will, then. You weren't supposed to fall for Dan, OK? All you care about is how much money he has, when he is so much more than just a healthy bank balance! You can have your pick of men – like Julian, for example. Remember him? The guy who paid for this whole weekend? Out of all the men in the world, why pick the one that I like?'

The Figaro swerved slightly as Stella turned to stare open-mouthed at Harri. Gripping the steering wheel, her eyes returned to the road as she shook her head slowly. 'I can't believe you just said that.'

Neither could Harri. But there was no going back. 'It's just like you have everything you want, Stella. Amazing looks, guys at your beck and call, holidays whenever you want . . . The one thing I've always had is Dan.'

'In your *head*,' Stella retorted, 'and that's only the image of him you've concocted. Until tonight you'd never met him, so how can you make out like I've stolen him from you?'

'Dan means nothing to you. All you've ever done is poke fun at him.'

'No, I haven't! I've always said he was fit . . .'

'Oh, like that's all he is – another piece of meat for you to lust over until you find the next one? He's been the butt of so many jokes you've made, Stella! Even when we were sat in that hall last night, you were still mocking me for liking him so much.'

Stella slammed her fist on the steering wheel. 'Would you listen to yourself? You're acting like a spoiled child over this – and blaming me for something I haven't done. He's not yours, Harri! You don't have the monopoly on Dan Beagle. And there were seventy other people "lusting over" him last night. Am I supposed to apologise to them, too?'

'It isn't him, it's what he represents,' Harri returned. 'I have images, thoughts, dreams of the world – *up here*,' she tapped her forehead. 'And I know I'm going to sound like a lovesick groupie, but I wanted him to ask me to travel with him. That was *my* dream.'

'Don't be ridiculous, Harri! Like that was ever going to happen.'

'But it *is* happening. For *you* . . .' Harri's voice cracked and she stopped.

Silence filled the car's interior as both friends processed the facts their argument had revealed. After a while, Stella spoke, a marked difference in her demeanour. 'I'm sorry. I didn't know you felt that way.'

Harri's head flopped back against the headrest and she closed her eyes. 'Well, you do now.'

The bright click-click of the indicator broke the atmosphere in the car as they turned off the motorway and drove along the A-road through fields and countryside towards Stone Yardley. Despite her sense of justice at letting out her true feelings, Harri's conscience began to prickle into life the nearer they came to home. This wasn't Stella's fault and neither was it Dan's. They were clearly attracted to one another, and who could blame them? Certainly not Harri, even though the events of last night still held her heart in their grasp.

She was just about to speak when Stella beat her to it. 'Look, the last thing I wanted was to upset you, H. You're my best friend, for crying out loud. The truth is, I have no idea what happened last night – I just know that this feels different to the other guys. And I'm sorry, but I can't let this opportunity pass me by. I don't want us to fall out, but I have to see where this could go.'

Harri nodded. 'I know. And you should – Dan's amazing. He could be really good for you.'

Stella's eyes flicked across to Harri. 'You think?'

'I know.'

'Thanks, H. That means a lot.' Relief spread across her face. 'By the way, what you said about me having whatever I wanted?

It's not like that at all. I have fleeting relationships that never really seem to go anywhere. And the holidays only happen when someone else is paying for me. I *don't* have everything. You do. You have a brilliant boyfriend, who is still there for you after seven years. I've never had anyone love me and want to stay with me as long as that. You guys are going to get married, have kids, grow old together – the whole shebang. I'm lucky if I can keep the same boyfriend for longer than a month. That's why I have to try this out with Dan – because I think he might have the potential to be *my* Rob.'

They had turned into Waterfall Lane and were almost at her home. Harri waited until Stella had pulled up outside the cottage before giving her a hug. 'I'm sorry, Stel. Go for it with Dan.'

Stella hugged her back. 'Thank you. And thanks for an awesome weekend.'

Harri watched Stella speed away, a cloud of dust rising from the road as she did so. Her best friend's words rang out in her mind:

I don't have everything. You do . . . You have Rob . . .

Feeling a rush of peace, Harri made a call on her mobile as she walked up the path to Two Trees Cottage. 'Hey fantastic boyfriend of mine – I'm home!'

That night, Harri thought a lot about the events of the weekend. Seeing Dan's reaction to her best friend had hurt her, unquestionably. But while the unfairness of it still smarted, the experience began to assume a deeper significance. Dan's world was compellingly beautiful and would always be something Harri returned to – but it was ultimately untouchable. Stella's words had really hit home: what mattered was what Harri had, right here in Stone Yardley. Rob, her job at SLIT,

Stella, Auntie Rosemary, Alex and Viv – people she loved and who loved her back. And as far as her dream of travelling was concerned, Dan Beagle wasn't responsible for showing Harri the world. It was up to her to see it for herself.

The next morning at SLIT George had decided to utilise visual aids for the benefit of his weekly 'motivational chat' and was struggling to erect a shiny new whiteboard.

'Erm, do you need some help with that?' Tom offered.

'No, thank you very much, Thomas,' George replied with a great deal more fluster in his voice than he had intended. 'Everything's under control here.'

Tom checked his watch and shrugged helplessly at Harri, who stepped forward to assist. George, red-faced and shiny-headed, allowed his assistant manager to complete the task for him.

'There,' Harri said, handing George the pack of whiteboard pens from the desk beside her.

'Thank you, Harriet.'

'Right, well, today I want to talk to you about STDs.' He ignored Nusrin's snigger and carried on. 'Somers Travel Direct has been a proud supplier of SLIT for years and it's always been our intention to work closely with them. As you well know, luxury coach tours are by far our biggest seller and we want to continue that tradition.'

Nus groaned and grabbed a tube of expensive hand cream from her desk, busying herself with the important task of keeping her elegant fingers moisturised.

George punched his pudgy hands onto his hips and jutted his chin forward. 'Problem, Nusrin?'

Nus looked up at him, eyes as innocent as a small puppy's. 'No, boss.'

'Good. So, this week we need to pull out all the stops to sell those lovely coach tours, OK?'

'Why?' Tom asked, peering at George through particularly lank curls this morning.

'Sorry?'

'Why do we need to push coach tours, seeing as they're what we sell the most of anyway?'

Harri resisted the urge to smile, her inner amusement at the volcano-on-the-edge that was her boss trying to stay positive in the face of increasing ridicule, lifting her heavy mood.

'*Because*, Thomas, STD have generously offered to increase our commission on each sale to thirty per cent, provided we sell four more coach tours each week. This is an opportunity for all of us to get behind our brand-new initiative . . .' He turned and began to write squeakily on the whiteboard, the letters large and veering at a steep angle from left to right. Then, swinging back round, he gestured magnificently towards the two wonky words on the board: '. . . OPARATION SELLMORE!'

'You've spelled it wrong,' Nus offered, shooting a wry look in Harri's direction. 'Operation has an "e" after the "p", not an "a"'

George's neck flushed and he reached for his handkerchief to wipe his forehead. 'And well done to you, Nusrin, for passing my hidden spelling test. You weren't expecting me to sneak one of *those* in now, were you? See, that's why I am the owner of the most successful travel business in Stone Yardley and why, only last week, I was personally asked by the Mayor of Brindley to be the Secretary of the local Chamber of Commerce.' He paused for his staff to soak in the news of his prestigious appointment.

'Don't secretaries have to be able to spell?' Tom asked.

George's smile faded. 'Mock all you want, Thomas, but I don't see you attempting to better yourself.'

'So, you're saying we have a new target for coach tour sales?' Harri interjected as the front door opened to reveal Auntie Rosemary carrying a huge bouquet of flowers and a very odd expression. 'Would you excuse me?'

'Go ahead,' George replied, his eyes switching straight back to Tom and Nus. 'You see, that's the kind of enthusiasm that's going to make the difference here . . .'

Auntie Rosemary was patiently waiting by the brochure rack when Harri walked over. 'Sorry to interrupt you when you're in the middle of a meeting,' Rosemary whispered, 'but I didn't think you'd want to wait to receive these.' She handed Harri the bouquet.

'Wow, they're gorgeous, Auntie R! Thank you so much.'

Auntie Rosemary smiled broadly. 'I think you should read the card, Harriet.'

Harri looked between the bronze arum lilies, burnt orange chrysanthemums, dark green foliage and gold gerberas to find the card, clipped to a wooden stick with a heart-shaped peg. Opening its tiny envelope, she read the message in her aunt's loopy handwriting:

Missed you this weekend, Red. Thought you might like these. Can't do this evening – work stuff again (boo) but promise to make it up to you on Friday.
   Rob xx

Harri felt a whoosh of joy shake her like the backdraught from a speeding lorry as she read Rob's message. 'Wow, I can't believe it! When did he order them?'

'His secretary called this morning. Apparently he was very specific about the wording.'

'Thank you so much for bringing them round,' Harri said, squeezing her aunt's arm. 'They've really cheered me up.'

'You're welcome, my darling. Well, you have a lovely day and I'll call you later on in the week.'

As Rosemary left, Tom and Nus hurried over to enthuse about the surprise bouquet with Harri, leaving George gesticulating impotently by the wonky whiteboard.

At lunchtime, Harri went to Wātea to grab a sandwich. Alex was stacking thickly cut, gooey squares of chocolate brownie on the glass-dome-covered cake stands and waved to her with the pair of silver tongs in his hand as she walked in.

'Hey, H. How was Oxford?'

'Gorgeous. The spa was amazing.'

Alex pulled a face. 'Ugh, not my idea of a day out to be slathered in expensive crud and pummelled to within an inch of your life, but each to their own.'

'Well, I enjoyed it,' Harri smiled ruefully.

'And when all's said and done, that's what matters. What can I get you?'

Harri looked up at the large chalkboard behind Alex's head to read the tempting options available to her. 'Oh, blimey, I don't know. My head's a shed today. What would you recommend?'

Alex observed her carefully. 'The brie and pancetta's hard to beat if you don't mind waiting for me to toast it for you. Tough night?'

'You could say that.'

'Hmm. How about I get us both a coffee and you can tell me all about it?'

'I'd love to, but I really should be getting back. George is on a charm offensive with STD coaches and Tom and Nus are threatening to resign. I daren't leave them alone with each other for too long.'

'Right you are then. That boyfriend of yours hasn't upset you, has he?'

'No he hasn't.' She felt pride swelling inside her. 'Actually, he just sent me the most amazing bouquet of flowers.'

'Excellent, that's what we like to hear. So your love life's sorted, but what about mine? When am I meeting your next friend?'

'I have three for you to choose from, actually,' Harri replied, the morning's surprise giving her a shot of boldness she maybe should have checked before firing back at him.

Alex chuckled and his brown eyes sparkled. 'Why not set up dates with all of them and I'll decide from there?'

Harri nodded. 'Absolutely. Leave it to me.'

CHAPTER THIRTEEN

So Many Girls, So Little Time . . .

Harri can feel her toes beginning to lose their feeling as the coolness of the ladies' creeps further into her bones. She stamps her feet on the magnolia floor tiles, hearing the sound of her heels echoing around the walls, as empty as the cavernous hole in her own heart.

I should have said something. For the past hour she has been trying her best to ignore the insistent voice of her conscience, but now it pushes its way to centre stage in her mind. *I shouldn't have just run.*

After all, running away had created the problem in the first place . . .

There is a lot to be said for organisational skills, and Harri's aptitude for organisation was flawless. From her very first class at primary school, her abilities were noted and utilised by almost every teacher in each successive year. Often, Harri wished that she could have been blessed with something more exciting: like Angela Hartley who, from the age of about twelve, was known for her beautiful singing voice in school productions and church events; or Liam Richardson, whose razor-sharp wit marked him out as a popular comedian and eventually paved the way for his moderately successful career on the stand-up circuit; or Fiona Dart, who had hearts breaking all over Stone Yardley as soon as she hit her teens, with her periwinkle-blue eyes, porcelain skin and thick, lustrous black hair. Still, at least Harri's gift was always going to be *useful*.

But even Harri's considerable aptitude for organisation was struggling now. Trying to juggle work, Rob (whose work schedule was especially erratic this week) *and* arrange to vet three new dates for Alex was turning out to be a much more complicated proposition than she had bargained for. Not least because of the tricky problem of thinking up plausible stories to explain how she knew each of the 'Free to a Good Home' applicants.

'So I'm a friend of a friend?' the tall, blonde woman sitting opposite her asked.

'Yes.'

'Which friend?'

Harri smiled as best she could. 'It doesn't matter. Make a name up – Alex won't bother to ask.'

'But what if he does? I've got to say, Harri, this whole thing doesn't sit easy with me. I mean, if Alex turns out to be the love of my life then how am I going to feel knowing that I lied to him right at the start of our relationship?'

Blimey, thought Harri, and I thought I was a forward-planner. 'OK, let's think of something else, Becky. How about we got chatting last year when you came into the travel agency to book your holiday?'

Becky considered this for a moment, twisting the stem of her wine glass as she did so. 'That would be easier to do, I think. So when am I meeting him?'

Harri pulled out a small notebook from her bag and flicked the pages until she found the list that seemed to be running her life this week. 'Today's Tuesday, so you'll be meeting him tomorrow evening, if that's good for you?'

'Or I could do tonight?' Becky's eagerness was impossible to conceal.

'No, not tonight,' Harri replied quickly. 'He's busy tonight.'

'Alex, I'd like you to meet Lucy. Lucy, this is Alex.'

Alex looked down at the diminutive brunette standing before him and smiled broadly. 'Great to meet you, Lucy.'

Lucy shook his hand. 'I've heard so much about you,' she rushed, letting out a laugh that sounded like a donkey on helium.

Startled, Alex stared at Harri, who smiled reassuringly and shrugged. Leaving them chatting, she beat a hasty retreat from the Star and Highwayman, checking her list again in the car park. '7.15 p.m. Charlotte Manning, Asda café, Lornal.'

Her head was buzzing with everything she needed to do as she drove the seven miles from Stone Yardley towards the larger town of Lornal. The scenery began to change from fields to houses and on into the industrial heart of the Black Country, once the cradle of the Industrial Revolution. The road rose to skirt the edges of what Harri learned in school had been a volcano in prehistoric times, past houses, the large new hospital and the shiny new office complexes rising from the ashes of the old steelworks. Turning past the gleaming steel and glass constructions, Harri headed for the twenty-four-hour superstore nestled between office buildings, shopping outlets and restaurant franchises.

Having parked in the enormous car park, Harri hurriedly made her way to the café. As she entered the bustling space she pulled a photo from her bag and scanned the customers for the elegant face smiling up at her. An eclectic selection of people populated the busy cafeteria: mums struggling to squeeze overstuffed pushchairs into the small space between cream vinyl tables and white plastic swivel chairs bolted to the floor; elderly couples tucking into fish, chips and peas, still wrapped up in overcoats and hats despite the warm summer evening; two off-duty store security guards reading decidedly dog-eared copies of the *Sun* and the *Mirror* over the remnants of their all-day breakfasts; a group of sniggering teenage girls pointing at a very embarrassed teenage boy at the next table, who looked like he was willing the laminate pine-effect flooring beneath his feet to gape open and swallow him whole; and a young couple dressed in office clothes, holding hands across the table as they sipped frothy cappuccinos from oversized white cups.

Finally, the lady from the photograph came into view. She was sitting by the window, managing to appear both completely out of place in her designer suit yet utterly at home with her easy smile. She uncurled her long fingers from the stem of her tall latte glass and waved to Harri. One thing was certain: her photograph did her no justice whatsoever – she was stunningly beautiful. Her long, ebony hair was pulled back into an efficient ponytail and the single row of pearls she wore at her neck shone against her coffee-hued complexion. Alex's dropping jaw was going to cause serious damage to Wātea's stylish slate floor when he met this lady . . .

'Hi, Charlotte, sorry I'm late.'

'No problem. The office was crazy so I only just got here myself. I took the liberty of buying you a coffee – hope that's OK?'

Harri sat down and grasped the proffered mug gratefully. 'Thank you so much. You have no idea how lovely this is. I don't think I've stopped all day.'

'You're a travel agent, right?'

'Yes, although today I found myself wondering if any of our customers actually realise they can travel more than a couple of hundred miles.'

Charlotte's dark chocolate eyes sparkled. 'Sounds like fun. Mind you, I'd kill for a holiday right now. But the way my schedule's looking, I'll be lucky to even get a skiing trip in this year. Maybe I should come in to see you about booking something for next year?'

'You're welcome any time. I'm sorry, what is it you do again?'

Charlotte smiled over the top of her latte glass. 'Barrister. Just qualified.'

'Wow. That's amazing.'

'Thanks. It's taken a long time to get there but I'm glad I made the effort. So tell me about Alex.'

Charlotte listened intently while Harri repeated the details of her best friend, a speech that already felt like an aged script in her head.

'Great. And I'm meeting him Thursday?'

Harri nodded. 'Yes. Now there's just one more thing I need to mention. It's about how we know each other . . .'

When Harri arrived home later that evening she was exhausted. It had taken longer than she'd bargained for to convince Charlotte to adopt the 'how we know each other' story she'd hastily concocted on the drive to Lornal. Even now, she wasn't entirely sure that she could trust the beautiful barrister to stick to the story. Still, at least it was one more thing to tick off the List of Doom, which meant one less thing to demand her attention this week.

She flopped down on the sofa and glared at the piles of letters still claiming squatters' rights on her coffee table.

Never again. Next time, I'll say no and buy a new travel book instead, she told herself. That's more than enough adventure for me, thank you very much.

After grabbing one of her woefully underused Nigella cookbooks and toying with the idea of swanning into the kitchen and rustling up a 'divine little supper', she quickly abandoned the idea and called Stone Yardley's only Chinese takeaway instead.

Twenty minutes later, a knock summoned Harri to her front door. Taking her purse from her bag, she skilfully avoided Ron Howard's ginger and white striped tail that was unhelpfully laid across her route and opened the door.

'Hi,' she said without looking up, rummaging in her purse for the right money.

'You don't need to give me any money, you know.'

Harri's head jerked up sharply. 'Stella?'

'You were expecting someone else?'

'I'm waiting for a takeaway. Sorry, come in.'

Stella followed her into the cottage, an odd expression on her face. Harri went to put the kettle on and it was only when she returned that she realised Stella was carrying a huge rucksack.

'I can't stay, sorry,' she said, and Harri noticed her friend was wringing her hands slowly – one of the rare glimpses of vulnerability that she ever displayed.

'Is everything OK?'

Stella's laugh was nervous and excited at the same time. 'It's happening, Harri! I can't believe it!'

'What? What's happening?'

Stella took a deep breath and sat quickly on the edge of the sofa.

'I've only gone and packed my job in, H! I did it this

morning: walked straight in and put my resignation letter into Greasy Garner's hands. Honestly, you should've seen his expression! I thought he was going to have a coronary on the spot!'

Harri sank slowly onto the seat next to her. 'Stel, are you sure about this? What are you going to do? I mean, how are you going to pay your rent?'

Stella's eyes were wild with emotion. 'I'm not. I moved out this afternoon. Didn't get my deposit back, of course, but it doesn't matter.'

Harri shook her head, the revelations refusing to make sense. 'But it does matter! What are you going to do for money? Where are you going to live . . . ?' she tailed off as her eyes moved to the bulky rucksack.

Stella caught Harri's expression and threw her head back with an almighty guffaw. 'Don't panic, you muppet, I'm not moving in with you! I mean, don't take this the wrong way, H, I love you heaps and everything, but we'd murder each other before the first week was up!'

Secretly relieved by this, Harri asked, 'So, where are you going?'

'I'm following my heart – can you believe I just said that? I mean, that's the kind of thing that Alex would say and now I'm actually coming out with the same rubbish. Crazy, eh?'

Harri placed a concerned hand on Stella's arm. 'Seriously, Stel, you're worrying me now. Have you honestly thought all this through?'

'No, not really. I'm just going with the flow – and for the first time in my life I actually know what I want. And it's not shoes or clothes or the latest designer handbag.' She gripped Harri's hand. 'It's Dan!'

'I – I don't understand . . .'

'Dan called me last night and asked me to go away with him. We're going to Tibet – can you believe it?'

Harri opened her mouth to speak, but words failed to materialise.

'He said, "Come away with me, Stella. Let me show you the world." How *sweet* was that! So I just said yes. I mean, who could refuse an offer like that?'

I couldn't, Harri conceded silently, pushing the lump in her throat away with a hard swallow. Stella was going to live out the dream Harri had harboured for years: to be so close yet so far to it coming true was heartbreaking. 'When are you leaving?'

Stella patted the rucksack. 'Right now. The taxi's outside, I've got all my savings with me and my flight's booked. I'm meeting Dan at Birmingham Airport in two hours. It's happening, Harri. This is it!'

Questions pushed, jostled and tumbled over each other in Harri's mind. 'But how long are you . . . ? When are you coming back?'

'I have no idea. I don't know if I'm ever coming back. But I'll be in touch, I promise. I'll try to call you when I land, OK?'

Tears were filling Harri's eyes as Stella hugged her tightly. 'Just be careful,' she managed to say before emotion stole her voice completely.

'I will. He loves me, H. He says his world isn't complete unless I'm in it. And I think I might be in love with him too. You take care of yourself, OK?'

Harri nodded as a car horn blared impatiently outside. 'You should probably go.'

Stella wiped her eyes and stood up. Swinging the rucksack heavily onto her shoulder, she turned and began to walk slowly to the front door. The sight of her lugging the enormous pack would have been comical if Harri's heart had not been shattering into a million shards at that precise moment.

Stella opened the door to reveal a startled Chinese man on the doorstep, hand still raised mid-knock.

'Delivery for Langton?' he stammered.

Harri quickly gathered her emotions and nodded. 'Yes, thanks.'

Stella dug in the pocket of her jeans and handed the delivery man a fistful of notes and change. 'This one's on me, H. Keep the change,' she smiled as he thrust the white, plastic carrier bag into her hands and scurried back down the path. The taxi horn beeped again.

'Right. Here I go – wish me luck?'

Harri hugged Stella for the last time. 'You won't need it with Dan. Have a fantastic time.'

Stella squeezed Harri's shoulder and started to walk away. When she reached the garden gate, she turned back, the street-light overhead bathing her frame in a soft white glow. 'Be happy, H.'

Harri forced herself to smile. 'I will.'

Harri watched the red rear lights of the taxi moving along Waterfall Lane until they disappeared out of view. Alone at last, she finally allowed the crushing weight of hurt to crash over her, sinking to the cool stone of the doorstep in the open doorway. Ron Howard appeared and curled himself around her, pushing his head against her shoulder and resting his paws on her arm. Harri stroked the soft fur of his head as his features blurred into a white and ginger haze through her tears.

How can this be happening? Harri felt more alone than she had in years. Inevitably, memories of the months following her mother's death flooded her mind and she was back where she started – a lost soul on the steps of Two Trees Cottage, with only the insistent attentions of a ginger and white kitten for company.

Harri couldn't tell how long she remained there, gazing up at the orange-hued clouds building in the inky blackness overhead, but after a while she felt the tears subsiding and shakily rose to her feet. Picking up the takeaway bag that had been discarded when she fell, Harri slowly shut out the still night and walked slowly towards the kitchen, oblivious to the overexcited mewings of Ron Howard as he dashed in affectionate circles round her legs.

Setting out the foil trays in a space cleared between the dreaded letters, Harri found her favourite DVD from the stack by the television and put it on. She needed to escape from the thoughts ricocheting around her brain. Settling back into her sofa with a bowl and chopsticks, a wave of calm began to lap over her bruised soul as the opening titles appeared on the screen: *The Beauty of Venice – a Venetian Guide to La Serenissima*.

'Hi, um, can I speak to Harri, please?'

Harri frowned as she tried to place the voice on the other end of the call. Lack of sleep, combined with the mental effort she'd had to exert this week, was making it hard for her to maintain any semblance of coherent thought. Playing an impromptu round of 'Name That Voice' was the last thing she needed today – especially seeing as George was officially on the warpath. It was ten o'clock on Thursday morning and he had already blasted the assembled staff of SLIT with no less than three separate rants.

'. . . and *don't* think I haven't noticed the amount of texting going on in this place,' George's voice boomed through from his office as Tom hid his laughter behind his *X-Files* mug and Nus rolled her eyes. 'It may have escaped your attention but this is not the Carphone Warehouse!'

Harri screwed up her aching eyes and tried to focus on the phone call. 'Sorry, yes, this is Harri.'

'OK, good. Hi, it's Becks. Sorry to ring you at work, but it's kind of an emergency.'

Becks? Becks who? Harri had been secretly hoping that the caller would inadvertently offer her some clue to their identity, but now all she could conclude was that Victoria Beckham had just happened to have phoned Sun Lovers International Travel.

She shook her head. There was no other option. 'Look, forgive me for being dim, but who is this?'

'Becks? Becky Yarnell – I met Alex last night.'

A large, shiny penny, like the ones Harri's dad used to save in an oversized Bell's whisky bottle, dropped in her mind, sending alternate ripples of relief and panic racing through her. 'Oh, of course. Sorry. I'm not quite with it today . . .'

'We might have a problem,' Becky rushed.

'Might we?' Harri couldn't help noticing the sudden thudding heartbeat in her ears.

'I just might have – *inadvertently* – um, let a little something slip last night?'

Oh brother. 'Like what?'

'It wasn't my fault, Harri. You have to believe me. It's just that he was so . . . *lovely*, you know? I mean, of course you do. You're the one who nominated him, after all . . .'

Harri shuddered. *Don't remind me.*

'. . . He was asking me to tell him about how I knew you and I tried, honestly. But I was there, gazing into those awesome brown eyes of his, and – I don't know – I got a bit muddled and . . .'

'Are you likely to be on the *work phone* for long, Harriet?' an incandescent George hissed right by Harri's ear, making her jump. 'Only I don't know about you, but I'd quite like to see some work done in here today.'

Harri placed her hand over the receiver and turned to glare at him. 'This is an emergency call, George. The caller called me, OK? And I don't know if you've noticed, but this travel agency is so deserted today that it makes the *Marie Celeste* look like Westfield shopping centre on the last Saturday before Christmas.'

George opened his mouth and shut it quickly, obviously thinking better of unleashing whatever vitriolic comeback he was about to choose. 'Right, well, just as long as it's at *their* expense . . .' He backed quickly away to the safety of his office.

'Sorry, Becky. You were saying?'

'I got confused. I couldn't remember whether I was a friend of a friend, or just a customer you got chatting to . . . So I said both. And then he asked me which friend and my mind went blank. So I said Justine. And he said, "Justine who?" – and I panicked. The only surname I could come up with was . . .'

Harri shut her eyes. 'Moore?'

Becky gasped. 'Yes! How did you know?'

'I'm a genius,' Harri groaned, secretly praying that the threadbare office chair on which she sat would miraculously sprout wings and whisk her away. 'So what did Alex say?'

'He didn't. But I could tell he didn't believe me. I don't think he wants to see me again, either, 'cos he did the whole "well, it was nice to meet you anyway" speech at the end of the evening and didn't offer to walk me home.'

'Ah.'

'Just thought you should know. I really am sorry.'

Harri let out a long sigh. 'It's fine. Thanks for telling me.'

'Mind if I say something?'

'Knock yourself out.'

'Alex doesn't strike me as the kind of guy who needs help to find someone.'

'Hmm, well, believe it or not he asked me to help him, so—'

'For what it's worth, I think it's wrong to lie to him. He seems to trust you a lot.'

Harri could feel her heart plummeting to her toes. 'Right. Er – thanks.'

'OK. Bye then.'

As Harri ended the call and dropped her forehead on the desk, Nus patted her shoulder and placed a mug of hot coffee beside her. 'Don't let the George flip get to you,' she grinned. 'Come on, Tom and I need your help to deal with all these thousands of customers.'

Harri lifted her head and managed a weak smile. 'Absolutely. Bring them on.'

The morning dragged by. The lack of footfall, coupled with an uncharacteristic efficiency within SLIT, meant that Harri had precious little to occupy her mind, inevitably allowing her anxiety to pace back and forth. By lunchtime, she could bear it no longer. It was time to face the music. If Alex had rumbled her plan, the best thing she could do was confront the situation head on.

Wātea was alive with lunchtime activity when Harri walked in. A wide cross-section of Stone Yardley residents were noisily enjoying their lunch – teenagers, elderly couples, middle-aged ladies from Viv's bridge club and several businessmen taking advantage of the coffee lounge's free Wi-Fi, their netbooks and papers strewn across the bar that looked out onto the High Street.

Alex was weaving his way through the packed diners, holding two plates of bruschetta and salad high over his head, a white tea towel slung hastily over one shoulder and two sets of knives and forks tightly wrapped in serviettes poking out from the back pocket of his jeans. Watching him expertly navigating the chairs, baby buggies and bags pushed thoughtlessly into his path, Harri mused that he could probably do this journey with his eyes closed.

Harri moved slowly towards the counter, keeping her eyes on him, as Alex reached his destination – a perfectly attired older lady and her much younger female companion on the far side of the room. Both ladies' faces lit up as he spoke to them. Alex's ability to make everyone feel at home was something Harri marvelled at: no matter how rushed off his feet he was, he always found time to make his customers feel like they were the only people in Wātea. The perfect host.

Just then, he looked over and his eyes met hers. Harri felt fear creeping around the edges of her stomach as he left the ladies and began to pick his way back towards her. Was he stressed, or just caught in the busyness of the lunchtime rush – or was it anger she saw in his expression? She couldn't tell. As he reached the counter, he summoned the attention of the plump, forty-something lady with shockingly peroxide blonde hair, who was busy reloading and attaching an espresso arm of the coffee machine.

'Bren – are you OK to hold the fort for five minutes?'

Brenda nodded, her round face flushed from the machine's steam. 'Just don't be away for ages, yeah? The bank lot'll be in any minute.'

'Cool, thanks.' Alex turned to Harri. 'Let's go up to the flat.'

Harri followed him through into the work kitchen behind the counter and up the winding staircase into the coolness of his living room. Bright sunshine streamed in through the large windows, a light breeze making the long voile curtains billow out like sails.

Nervously, she looked at her watch. 'I – I haven't got long, Al. George is having one of his "bad days" and I need to make sure he doesn't offend the others too much.'

'Right . . .' Alex seemed distracted, moving absent-mindedly round his kitchen, tidying crockery from the sink drainer away in cupboards, switching the kettle on, then off again.

Harri took a deep breath. 'Look, Al, there's something I need to—'

'Do you think I'm paranoid?' Alex blurted out suddenly.

'What?'

His eyes were full of concern as he faced her. 'Seriously, do you?'

'Paranoid about what?'

'Something's been bugging me since I met your mate Justine's friend yesterday. I'm starting to think there's something wrong with me.'

Harri's mouth had suddenly become dry. She swallowed hard. 'Don't be daft.'

'I mean it, H. You've introduced me to all these lovely, completely normal women and I should just be enjoying the experience. But all I can think of – and it's been the same with every one of them so far – is that they're hiding something from me.'

'Like what?'

Alex leaned heavily against the kitchen worktop and raised his eyes to the ceiling. 'I have no idea. It's just like their stories are – I don't know – missing something. I mean, that girl from yesterday . . .'

'Becky.'

'Yeah, that's the one. We were getting along great and then I asked her how she knew you and she just went *weird* on me. I've gone over and over it in my head and I can't rationalise

228

it at all. It was almost as if she was *guilty* about something, you know? But there was no reason why she should be guilty about anything. And then, about an hour ago, it all made sense.'

'Ah. Well, I need to explain why—'

Shaking his head incredulously, Alex shrugged. 'I'm projecting memories of Nina onto them.'

'Sorry?'

'I worked it out, Harri. I'm *expecting* them to be hiding something. Maybe it's because I didn't see it coming with Nina that I'm so defensive now.'

Her relief at not being found out was tempered by a sudden surge of compassion for Alex. 'Al, honey, it's not that at all. You're just meeting a lot of new people in one go: you're bound to be a little cautious.'

'You think? Honestly, H, it's been niggling me all morning. I don't want to end up some lonely, old emotional cripple.'

Harri had to laugh at this. 'Now you *are* being daft. You're fine. Maybe three dates in a week wasn't such a brilliant idea.'

The merest hint of a smile returned to his expression. 'Hmm, maybe it was a bit ambitious. Still, one more date tonight and then you've kindly given me the weekend off.'

'True. Charlotte's lovely, though. I have a good feeling about her.' She looked at the clock above the kitchen counter. 'Blimey, I ought to get back. Are you feeling a bit better about this?'

'Much, thanks.'

They returned to the coffee shop and Harri gave Alex a hug before saying goodbye to Brenda and walking to the door. Her hand was just reaching to push it open when it swung in towards her and a middle-aged lady wearing a bright pink beret let out a yelp of surprise.

'Ooh! Sorry, Harriet, didn't see you there!'

'That's all right, Ivy. How's business today?'

'Busy, I expect. It's my day off, so I've left our Sid and that idiotic apprentice of his holding the fort. We've got five MOTs booked in. Still, not my problem. So . . .' she gave Harri's arm a playful jab with her elbow, '. . . here to check on Stone Yardley's famous *Alex*, eh?'

Mystified, Harri nodded blankly, reasoning that Ivy Evans must be the latest in a long line of female Stone Yardley residents to join the unofficial Alex Brannan Fan Club. 'And I'm late for work, so I'd better get back.'

'Ooh, don't let me keep you then,' Ivy grinned.

'Harri! I'm sorry, was there something you wanted?' Alex called.

For the briefest of moments, Harri's conscience prickled into life, Becky's words echoing inside: *It's wrong to lie to him . . . He seems to trust you a lot . . .* Shaking the thought quickly away, Harri called back, 'No, just thought I'd pop in.'

Alex raised his hand in thanks as Harri began to leave. 'Job's a good 'un, then. Hello, Ivy. Lovely to see you this warm Thursday.'

'No, Alex, it's nice to see *you* . . .'

The afternoon passed quietly. George was nowhere to be seen: he had excused himself at two o'clock in order to 'go and see a potential client' and didn't return.

At five thirty, as Harri waved goodbye to her colleagues, she was interrupted by her mobile buzzing in her bag.

'Can you stop in at Wātea on your way home?' Alex asked.

'Sure, but I can't stay. I'm cooking Rob's tea tonight.'

'No problem. It'll only take a minute. Let yourself in – I'm just clearing up in the kitchen.'

Five minutes later, Harri pushed open Wātea's door. 'Hi,' she called out, walking past the tables stacked with chairs, the smell of disinfectant from the recently mopped floor filling her nostrils. But in the doorway to the work kitchen, she froze.

Instead of finding Alex busily wiping down the stainless-steel work surfaces as she'd expected, she came face to face with him leaning against the sink, a curling copy of *Juste Moi* open in his hands.

'"Alex is thirty-three, six feet tall, with sandy brown hair and dark brown eyes. He loves travel, long conversations and old films, but his passion is food, evident in the successful coffee lounge he owns. Having spent ten years of his life travelling the world, he is more than ready to settle down with the right young lady . . ."'

'Alex, I—'

'Wait, please. I haven't finished. "Best friend Harri Langton was only too happy to recommend him to *Juste Moi* readers. 'Alex is gorgeous, talented and caring. Any girl would be lucky to call him hers. I count myself incredibly blessed to be his friend.' Could *you* be the girl of our globetrotting guy's dreams? Get in touch!" *Fascinating* article, don't you think?'

'I – it's . . .'

Alex's eyes were full of accusation when they met hers. He held up the magazine and pointed to the front cover. 'And I'm presuming this is your friend *Justine Moore*'s magazine, right? Justine Moore, for heaven's sake . . . Seriously, I don't know what's worse, Harri – you lying to me in the first place or your woeful lack of imagination when making up back stories for these women.'

'OK, look, let me explain . . .'

Alex tossed the magazine to one side and folded his arms. 'Go right ahead. I'm looking forward to this.'

'It wasn't my idea. I just . . . got talked into it. I *was* going to tell you . . .'

'Tell me *what*, exactly? That you'd decided to tell the whole of the UK about how crap I am at dating? That you thought it would be a fantastic wheeze to stick me up for public auction? An auction in some crazed meat market dreamed up by a stupid magazine for people who think Alan Titchmarsh is edgy? Or what, were you thinking that national humiliation was just what I needed to get me back on track with my love life?'

'But you asked for my help,' Harri protested.

Alex threw his hands in the air. 'Yes, Harri, I asked for your help to meet women. But I kind of thought they would be women you *actually knew*, not some random girls you picked from a list.'

'I – it wasn't like that, Alex.'

'Really? So tell me how it was then, Harri. Come on, I'm curious: at what point did this ridiculous plan seem like a good idea to you?'

It was time to tell the truth. Becky had been right – he deserved to know. 'It was your mum's idea,' she said quietly, wishing she couldn't see the sense of betrayal in his expression. 'She asked me to help because she thought I would be able to choose the right girls for you. You have to believe me, I didn't want to get involved and I've been dreading this moment since that damn magazine came out. I ended up spending a whole weekend sorting through all the replies and I hated every moment of it, OK? I've really regretted saying I'd help Viv with this.'

'I should've guessed that Mum would have had something to do with it,' he replied, scuffing at the black and white kitchen floor tiles with the toe of his red Converse boots. 'Crazy woman. I could well understand her thinking up a scheme like that, but *you* . . .' He shook his head. 'I'm sorry, I'm finding this all a bit much to take in. I thought we were friends.'

'We *are* friends, Alex.'

'Friends don't lie to each other, H. Friends don't do something as – as – flippin' *dumb* as this. I thought you understood me. Now it appears you don't know me at all.'

'Oh, Alex, don't say that.' Harri watched helplessly as Alex passed her and walked slowly up the stairs, leaving her alone and devastated in Wātea's kitchen. Heart thumping, she tried to work out what to do next. Should she follow him or leave? There was something in the way he had looked at her just now that she had never seen before – hurt, disappointment, disbelief. Deep down, she knew she had to resolve the situation. She was not going to lose Alex over this. He was too good a friend let go.

Harri walked purposefully up the stairs to his flat. When she reached the living room he was sitting on the sofa, staring blankly at the television, his features illuminated by its flickering blue light.

Harri wiped her eyes and took a deep breath. 'I know you probably don't want to hear it, but I want to apologise. I'm sorry I didn't tell you and I'm sorry I ever got involved. Just don't be too hard on your mum, OK? I know she goes overboard with things but, beneath it all, she loves you to bits and she doesn't want you to get hurt.'

Alex gave a weary sigh and looked at her. 'A *magazine*, Harri . . .'

'Yeah, one that nobody except your mum and Ivy Evans reads.'

'Do you know how much of a gossip Ivy Evans is? I mean, if this gets back to the lads I'll be a laughing stock.'

'I don't think you will. Especially seeing as you had so many replies – and at least fifty of them were half-decent women.'

A small smile began to dance along his lips. 'How many replies were there?'

'Over eight hundred. It took me hours to read through them all.'

'You read them all?'

'Yes. Well, Auntie Rosemary helped me.'

He laughed. 'And where was my mother in all of this?'

Harri felt the tension easing between them and took a step closer. 'Um, she was . . . things came up, you know.'

'Figures.' His eyes searched her out. 'Who did you do it for, then? For my mum? For the magazine? Or for me?'

'I just wanted to make sure that the people you met were worthy of you, that's all.'

He stared at her for a long time, an odd expression playing across his face. Just when Harri was wondering if she should say something to break the uncomfortable scrutiny, he spoke. 'What are you like, eh? Come here.' He patted the sofa next to him and Harri sat down. He nudged her and the mischief magically reappeared in his eyes. 'You are a nutter, Harri Langton.'

'I know.'

Alex chuckled and wrapped his arms around her. 'My crazy friend,' he smiled into her hair. 'I'm sorry I freaked out, mate. It was just a bit of a shock.'

Harri hugged him back, relieved by his words. 'That's OK. You were entitled to be upset.' Breaking the hug, she looked up at the welcome sight of his broad smile. 'We're still friends, right?'

'Well, it was touch and go for a bit there, you know. And you owe me big time.'

'Oh, here we go.'

'Yes – for mental anguish caused by Justine Moore and her friends.'

'All of whom, you said yourself, were perfectly lovely.'

'Well, yes, but . . .'

'So actually, forgetting the conspiratorial nature of the plan – and the national humiliation thing – it wasn't exactly an unpleasant experience for you, was it?'

Alex smiled ruefully. 'I can't believe you're trying to win this argument, Langton, after all you've done.'

'Admit it, Brannan, I have *great* taste in women.'

Alex's laugh was loud and welcome. 'You know, you really should get a T-shirt with that on. Fine, yes, OK, your choice wasn't half bad.'

'I thank you.'

'But, that said, I still think I should demand some recompense from you for the mental cruelty I've endured.'

Uh-oh. Harri had seen that look in his eyes before and it could only mean trouble. Come to think of it, it was almost a carbon copy of the one Viv displayed before she proposed her Big Idea. 'Like what?'

'Keep going.'

Harri could hardly believe her ears. 'Pardon me?'

'Well, now I know why the women I've met so far were acting so strange, I'm not worried about meeting the others. And I have to admit, you picked some stunners.'

Indignation pumping through her, Harri shook her head violently. 'No. Absolutely not.'

Alex laughed. 'I don't think you have the right to refuse, given your recent deception.'

'Yes, I have. I've done more than enough to help your love life.'

'Er, *that's* debatable, Harri. I think it's the least you can do to make amends.'

'No way, Al! Do you know how much of my life has been taken over by arranging those dates for you? There's not a hope in hell of you persuading me to do this again.'

He reached out and grabbed her hand. 'I'm not asking you to meet them and all of that stuff. Just call them up, see if they sound half sane and then give them my number. Think of it as excellent event management experience.' His eyes became still as he added softly, 'I really would appreciate the help, H. Please?'

Harri stared at him. 'I suppose I could do that,' she conceded.

'Excellent. Consider yourself forgiven, then. Now, you better get going to see that boyfriend of yours and I need to make myself look irresistible for – um – thingy . . .'

'Charlotte.'

'That's her. See, H? We make a great team. I think this could really work.'

Harri nodded. 'I think you might be right.'

CHAPTER FOURTEEN

Business as Usual . . .

The door to the ladies' opens and a pair of heels click in. Self-consciously, Harri lowers her breathing, as if in doing so she will somehow blend into the fixtures and fittings of the toilet cubicle and disappear altogether.

'Harriet, are you still in here?' Viv calls softly.

Harri doesn't answer.

Viv waits for a moment. There is a creak and a thump as the pneumatic door hinge shuts and Harri listens carefully, unsure whether Viv has left or not.

A gentle knock on the cubicle door confirms her worst fears: Viv isn't likely to be halted by silence. 'Oh, Harri, what a mess. That friend of yours shouldn't have come tonight. I don't know why Alex invited her. All that rubbish about "truth and justice" . . . I mean, what on earth would that young woman know about either of those words? But you don't need to hear that, I suppose. Are you OK? Harriet?'

It's obvious that Viv won't be satisfied until she gets an answer. Harri shivers. 'I'm fine.' Her voice is small and resigned – it almost doesn't sound like hers.

There is a scraping sound as Viv drags the old, orange plastic chair by the washbasins to the cubicle door and sits down. 'Well, if you aren't coming out, I'm going to stay with you for a bit. You shouldn't be on your own after . . . well, after an experience like *that*.'

Harri's groan is silent in the cubicle but deafening in her head.

Stella didn't call when her plane landed. Neither did she call for the next few weeks – and as July ended and then August gave way to September, Harri's disappointment began to ebb a little. After all, it made sense: Stella was off touring a remote part of the world with the man she loved, so why on earth would she remember to get in touch? Still, the hurt remained that Stella was embarking on Harri's dream adventure without her.

Only when the last week of September arrived did Harri finally bring herself to revisit one of Dan's books.

'I'm surprised you're still reading that,' Rob said, appearing from her kitchen carrying a large pizza box and a bottle of Dr Pepper, 'considering that the chap stole your best friend.'

'I think he might just be what Stella needs,' Harri replied. 'And I still admire his work.'

Rob planked a kiss on the top of Harri's head. 'See, that's what I love about you, you've so forgiving.'

Harri grimaced. 'I didn't say I'd forgiven him yet. I just like his books.'

'Fair enough.' Rob opened the box and they helped themselves to large slices of hot pizza, the stringy cheese wrapping greasily round their fingers.

'So I was thinking,' Rob said between mouthfuls, 'how about I take you away somewhere for Christmas this year?'

This took Harri completely by surprise and she stared at him. 'Really?'

He laughed. 'Yes, really. Don't look so shocked, Red! I just thought, you know, I've been away so much this year and you deserve a treat for putting up with me.'

Harri nudged him. 'Well, I can't argue with that!'

'*So*, what do you think?'

'I think it's a wonderful idea. I'd love to. Where were you thinking of going?'

A sparkle appeared in Rob's eyes. 'Funny you should mention that because . . .' He pulled a folded brochure from his back pocket and put it in Harri's lap.

Harri grabbed a piece of kitchen roll to wipe her fingers, gazing in wonder at the turreted, pink-hued granite castle sitting within immaculately manicured gardens and reflected in an ornamental lake. 'Inverguthrie Castle,' she read, heart racing now. 'Scotland?'

'Yeah. A friend told me about it and said it was pretty special. It's near Oban and the scenery is amazing round there – it's near a campsite Nick and I went to with Dad a couple of times when we were kids.'

Harri slowly turned the brochure pages, drinking in the details. Of all the gifts he'd given her this year this one was the most special. Inverguthrie Castle was more than a treat: it was the kind of place where memorable moments happened . . . Heart racing, she dared to entertain the possibility of what *else* Rob might surprise her with while they were there . . . 'This is amazing, baby. Thank you so much!'

'So, it's OK if I book it?'

Harri threw her arms around him. 'Yes! Absolutely, yes!'

Rob ruffled her hair. 'Good job I booked it already then, isn't it?'

Snuggled against his chest, euphoria lighting up every atom

of her being like a billion stars twinkling inside, Harri was thrilled to hear his heart beating as fast as hers. This was it: it was finally happening.

'Scotland? For Christmas?' Viv repeated, her face a picture of disbelief.

'Yes,' Harri smiled, picking a blade of field grass from the overgrown verge as they walked towards Stone Yardley's allotments. It was a surprisingly warm Monday evening and clouds of swirling midges rose from the road before them.

'Well, I'll be. And you're *sure* he's actually booked it?'

'That's what he said.' Harri was enjoying this. She'd already told Alex, Tom, Nus and Auntie Rosemary the news, but it was Viv she was most looking forward to telling. Seeing her so surprised by Rob's revelation was pure, unadulterated joy.

Viv batted away a swarm of midges with an irritation perhaps not wholly directed at them. '*Blasted* things,' she growled. 'Why is it the minute we get any decent weather they come and ruin it for everyone? They'll be all over the allotment, you'll see. If they get in the sloe gin, Merv'll be impossible all evening.'

'Viv, calm down,' Harri giggled. 'Merv's a lot bigger than them. I'm sure he'll cope.'

'Yes, well, they're still annoying,' Viv muttered, flapping her hand melodramatically in front of her face.

The lane turned a sharp left and a bright, golden shaft of low early evening sunlight made Harri and Viv shield their eyes as they rounded the corner. Casting a cursory glance at her friend, Harri patted Viv's shoulder. 'Is everything OK?'

Viv scowled. 'Well, it would be if my son had deigned to forgive me yet.'

'Ah.'

240

'I mean, he's perfectly pleasant to me most of the time, but whenever I make any observation about his life he becomes the most beastly individual.'

'Well, you have to admit, Viv, he has the right to a bit of payback.'

Viv gave an exasperated groan and folded her arms. 'Sure, a little bit of revenge is perfectly justified, but *two months*? Besides, he can't say it wasn't worth it in the end, can he? Look at all the beautiful women you've put him in touch with recently.'

This was true. Since Ivy Evans had unwittingly rumbled Viv's Big Idea, Harri had spoken to no less than twenty women and passed on fifteen numbers to Alex. The five that didn't make the grade included one who admitted sending a photo she'd found on the internet, three who had quite clearly lied about their ages and one who had such a mono-tone voice that she sounded like a robot with a personality bypass.

As for Alex, he seemed completely satisfied with the current state of affairs. A couple of dates a week with ladies that were obviously interested in him were certainly good for his ego, if not ultimately likely to bring him any closer to finding The One.

'He's certainly working his way through the Contenders,' Harri said, watching a peacock butterfly flutter up in front of her. 'If he carries on discounting them we'll be on to the Possibles soon.' Harri found herself increasingly mystified at the women he ruled out. The beautiful barrister from Lornal – who Harri would have laid odds on being perfect for Alex – lasted less than a week, and all he could say to justify her dismissal was that she was 'a little scary'.

'There just *has* to be a suitable girlfriend in all those replies,'

Viv moaned. 'He's too picky for his own good. I just wish he wouldn't keep doing the "I was betrayed by my mother" routine with that mocking smirk of his.' She tutted, loudly. 'Just like his father in that respect, although mercilessly not in any other way.'

Stepping over a weather-worn wooden stile, they began to cross the strip of field grass that separated the allotments from the road. Featherlike, gold-edged clouds ambled lazily across the deepening blue sky as Viv and Harri approached runner bean poles, staked chrysanthemums and cane tepees filled with the last throes of sweet peas. Viv unlocked a large iron gate with her allotment key – the ownership of which she was incredibly proud, especially considering the waiting list for these small pieces of Stone Yardley – and they walked down along the narrow. gravel path, passing row upon row of lovingly tended strips until they reached the middle plot.

A group of people were sitting on a haphazard collection of chairs at the far end of the allotment in front of a large, double-fronted green and blue painted shed. The seating arrangements ranged from scuffed, wooden chairs to gaudy linen deck chairs and a couple of shabby-looking sunloungers. At the centre of them all was Merv, sitting magnificently in a moth-eaten Dralon armchair like a fifty-something ragamuffin king holding court in his verdant kingdom.

'Ah! And thus the lovely ladies approach!' he boomed as the assembled gardeners turned and called out their welcomes.

'Mervyn, have you gone and started without us?' Viv feigned offence.

'He's been leading us astray,' laughed a tall, broad man with a beard that could hide several species of wildlife with ease. 'We wanted to wait for you, of course.'

'I've no doubt, Bill,' Viv replied, giving him a hug.

A middle-aged lady with wild, greying frizzy hair smiled. 'Proper persuasive, he is!'

'Too persuasive for his own good, Elsie, trust me. So, what are we on tonight then?'

'Elderberry wine!' chorused the group, raising their glasses in a noisy toast and laughing raucously.

Viv shot a weary look at Harri. 'Well, it looks like we arrived just in time. I trust the bar is open?'

Merv sprang out of his chair with a sprightliness only ever witnessed when alcohol was mentioned and opened the stable door of the shed. Above the door was a sign, painted in bright, yellow letters on a black background: 'THE ROSE & SLUG'.

'Now, what libation can I tempt you with tonight, dearest?' Merv called from the lit interior of the shed.

'Have we any sloe gin?'

Merv's multi-chinned face appeared in the doorway. '*Have* we any sloe gin? What a preposterous question! *Of course* we have, woman! Alf furnished us with more supplies only this afternoon.'

A short, wiry man wearing a khaki polo shirt and jeans that looked as if they hadn't seen a washing machine for years raised a swarthy brown hand. 'Guilty as charged, m'lud.'

'Sloe gin for my beloved!' Merv handed Viv a White Horse whisky glass filled with glistening purple spirit. 'And for the fair Lady Harriet?'

Harri walked carefully around the chairs to peer in through the pine-scented doorway. This was Viv and Mervyn's pride and joy: the real reason they 'popped to the allotment' most evenings and weekends. Far from being the humble wooden shed it first appeared to be, the Rose & Slug was, in fact, a pint-sized fully functioning pub, complete with beer pulls, optics, towelling beer mats and even a polished oak bar, made from an old beam Merv had rescued from a reclamation timber yard in Ellingsgate. Over the years, the hostelry had assumed many guises, from the Anderson shelter left over from the war, which was rusting on the plot in the late seventies when Viv first took tenancy, to the rickety but well-loved potting shed that served faithfully from 1986 to 2002, when it was finally retired. The current construction, a surprise Christmas gift from Merv, was palatial by comparison with the former buildings. Through the decades the selection of alcohol on offer had widened considerably too: Elsie and Norm's home-made wine in the Anderson shelter; Bill's lethal home-brew beer in the potting shed; and now, Alf's sloe gin, the ubiquitous wine, whisky blends and beer from the local Latham's craft brewery (Bill's infamous brewing skills now thankfully retired).

Harri chose to play it safe with a glass of Viv's home-made lemonade, and settled down on a dusty, blue canvas director's chair. The jovial conversation lapped her ears as she inhaled the fragrant evening air. She loved it here; as with so many aspects of Stone Yardley, this was a place laden with friendly ghosts from her childhood.

When Viv was first granted the allotment, Harri's parents had helped her to clear the unkempt wreck of weeds and rubble – a mammoth task, considering the diminutive size of the plot, which took several weeks to complete. That first summer, Harri spent many evenings during the holidays playing amongst the newly planted beds with her cousins, James and Rosie, as Auntie Rosemary, Mum, Dad and Viv chatted, weeded and dug over the soil. At the time unremarkable, these moments were precious to her now; endless, carefree hours of childhood that would all too soon be tamed and constrained by the cold shadow of illness.

As she sipped her lemonade, she remembered the thrill of eating tea outdoors – jacket potatoes cooked in tin foil nestled in the embers of the rusted tin incinerator bin and slices of pork pie and sticky flapjack brought in old Quality Street and Roses tins by Viv – young Harri swinging her legs on the red and blue checked fold-up chair, sucking up lemonade through two green stripey straws. Sitting here now, Harri realised that Alex must also have been at those *al fresco* events but, being a few years older than her (a gap of gargantuan proportions at the time), he just blended into the gang of 'the big boys' whose rough games always ended up being banished to the strip of field beyond the allotment gate by his flustered mother.

'Entering the S of the Y comp this year then, Merv?' Elsie asked, her face flushing from one too many glasses of her elderberry wine.

Merv scowled and pulled a face. 'Nah. Can't be bothered to go through that rigmarole again, to be honest with you. Flamin' nightmare from start to finish, it was.'

'Shame,' Bill piped up. 'I was rather hoping for a repeat performance of Councillor Pollock's renaming ceremony!' He let out a huge guffaw, his ample beer belly jiggling up and down.

'It was an honest mistake,' Merv protested, a wicked twinkle in his eyes as the rest of the allotment holders broke into helpless laughter.

There were certain moments in Stone Yardley history that had become almost mythical, and Merv's presentation of his winner's rosette and certificate in the regional finals of the Shed of the Year competition had quickly passed into these hallowed ranks. Almost one hundred people had gathered at the allotments for the occasion, and the Rose & Slug was

245

bedecked in Laura Ashley fabric bunting created by Viv (ever the *Country Living* devotee). Stone Yardley's Conservative town councillor, Bert Pollock, had been tasked with delivering Merv's prize – a job he clearly considered beneath him, judging by his haughty expression, yet, owing to the impending council elections and the presence of a photographer and journalist from the *Stone Yardley Chronicle*, unfortunately necessary. Unbeknown to the local politician, Merv had spent almost the entire previous night highly amused by a slip of the tongue he had made after consuming a particularly large quantity of Elsie's blackberry wine, where he mistakenly swapped the first letters of Councillor Pollock's name, thus christening him 'Pert Bollock', to the utter hilarity of the allotment gang. On his big day, slightly nervous about speaking in front of the unexpectedly large crowd, he tripped over his words and, with all the aplomb of a Shakespearean actor, eloquently thanked 'Councillor Pert' for his prize. Realising his mistake, he began guffawing uncontrollably as a chorus of 'Bollock!' from the allotment holders finished what he had started.

'I don't think the local Tories are likely to be knocking on your door during their next recruitment drive,' Alf grinned toothlessly.

'I'll drink to that!' Bill raised his glass and the Rose & Slug's regulars joined in the toast.

Viv pulled up an old wicker armchair by Harri's side, her glass considerably fuller than before. 'So has Al said anything to you about his dates?'

'Not really. He just texts me "Next!" whenever he wants another number.'

'Ooh, that son of mine,' sighed Viv. 'No wonder I have so many grey hairs.'

246

'Look, I'm having dinner at his on Wednesday night, so I'll see what I can find out for you.'

Viv instantly brightened. 'That would be fantastic, darling!'

'. . . Honestly, H, the markets in Port Louise are something else. The colours are phenomenal, you know – piles of spices, freshly picked fruit like mangoes, papaya and pineapples, and bolts of exquisitely hand-printed fabrics where every pattern tells a story. And the *smells* are amazing! Not just cinnamon, ginger and turmeric, but all round the edges of the market there are these little food stalls selling chapattis, deep-fried prawns and noodles.'

Harri took a mouthful of rich Beef Daube, tasting the bay, rosemary, thyme and garlic swirling together across her palate. She looked at the photo of Alex standing with a smiling stall-holder by a stack of woven baskets in the middle of a busy market. 'Mauritius,' she said, her mind alive with images of turquoise seas lapping against palm-fringed white sandy beaches, fields of sugar cane and the full moon rising behind volcanic mountains.

'I had some of my happiest times there, you know,' Alex said wistfully. 'I spent three weeks there and then two weeks in the Seychelles. There was quite a difference between the two. But I have to admit that Mauritius got my vote in the end. I just loved the mix of cultures – Chinese, Creole and Indian, all living and working together.'

'It sounds wonderful.' Harri decided that now was the best time to broach the subject of his recent dates. 'So, how are you doing with the "Free to a Good Home" ladies?'

Alex picked up his empty plate and took it into the kitchen. 'Fine. I think.' He unscrewed a stove-top espresso pot and began to fill it with water. 'Coffee?'

'Thanks. What do you mean, you "think"?'

'Well, they're all much of a muchness, you know? All beautiful, all interesting – the dates are fun and I'm enjoying myself.'

'But none of them is worth taking any further?'

Alex's eyes narrowed. 'My mother put you up to this, didn't she?'

Harri knew that her innocent expression was about as convincing as a politician's apology. 'I was just interested, that's all.'

'Hmm. Don't give up the day job. Espionage doesn't suit you.'

'So we keep going?'

Alex nodded. 'Definitely. Business as usual, O Wise Matchmaker.'

'Hardly a matchmaker, Al. Not if my recent success rate is anything to go by.'

'Well, maybe the next date you recommend will change my life, eh? And talking of life-changing occurrences,' he grinned, taking two espresso cups from a cupboard, 'what's the latest on romantic Scotland?'

'Rob's sorted it all.'

The espresso pot began to steam and bubble loudly. 'That's good then.'

'It is,' Harri said happily.

Alex brought the coffee cups over to the lounge area and Harri joined him on the sofa. 'I'm really pleased he's making an effort for you, H. It's about time.'

'Absolutely.'

'And you're not bothered that he organised it without asking you?'

Harri frowned. 'No. Should I be?'

Suddenly looking uncertain, he rubbed the back of his neck. 'I don't want to put a dampener on things, it's just that Rob confuses me. How come he knows how much you want to travel yet it's always him making the decisions about where you go together? Surely you're the expert?'

This was unexpected, and unwelcome, especially considering how much Rob was doing for her. She could feel her hackles rising. 'But it *should* come from him, shouldn't it? It means so much more to not be the one organising everything in our relationship.'

'But why?'

'Because it means he's doing something he *wants* to do and not something he feels obliged to.'

'So what about what *you* want?' He lowered his voice and stared straight into her eyes. 'What about Venice?'

This was too far, even for Alex. Harri stiffened. 'What about it?'

'You are besotted with the place. Mum says you have it on your screensaver at work. And Rosemary told me about that old postcard you have—'

Incensed, Harri rose to her feet, instantly feeling stupid for doing so. 'Nobody is meant to know about that!'

'Look, H, relax, OK? She only told me because she thought I might have been there and could tell you more about it.'

'And when exactly were you talking to my aunt?'

'Yesterday, actually. She came into Wātea for lunch. She just cares about you, mate.'

Harri crossed her arms. 'Well, I'm fine. *We're* fine. And Scotland is wonderful.'

'H, sit down. I'm sorry.'

Though part of her wanted to walk out right there and then, Harri knew she was overreacting and the sensible side of her compelled her to stay. Slowly, she resumed her seat. 'I'm sorry, but you should give Rob a break. He's doing so much for me – for both of us. And I'm proud of him.'

Just then, the door phone buzzed. Alex rose and patted her knee as he did so. 'Then that's all that matters.'

Harri watched him walk over to the phone, willing the unease in her stomach to leave. Why were Viv and Auntie Rosemary talking about her behind her back, and to Alex of all people? It didn't make sense.

'Hey, Jack! I'll come down.' Alex turned to Harri. 'Jack's at the door. Dating emergency – he's making dinner for a girl he's seeing but he forgot dessert. Good job I have a banoffee pie in the fridge downstairs, eh?'

He disappeared down the stairs and Harri took the empty espresso cups into the kitchen. She had just made a start on loading the dishwasher when Alex called up, 'Harri, could you bring the cardboard box by the coffee table down here, please?'

'OK.' She found the large box where he said it would be and headed downstairs.

Jack and Alex were standing in the work kitchen when she arrived. Harri liked Jack Stevens immensely, even though he was one of the worst culprits amongst Alex's mates for winding Rob's friends up. A graphic designer with crazy, spiked hair and a wicked sense of humour, Jack was effortlessly unique in everything from his eclectic fashion sense and ever-changing hair colour (tonight, white-blond) to the much-loved, Union Jack roofed, classic Mini Cooper he drove, which, his mates often quipped, he cared more about than any of the constant stream of women he dated.

'Hey, Harri,' Jack smiled, his dark blue eyes full of mischief as usual. 'Wasn't expecting to see you here.'

'Hi, Jack.' She handed him the box. 'I only come for the food and travel stories.'

'Research, eh?'

'You could say that.'

'Cool. Hey, thanks for taking this in for me, man. Don't know what it is with Parcelforce and my address. The two just don't seem to be mutually compatible.'

'No worries,' Alex smiled. 'Can't have Mabel going without rear brake cylinders and circlips now, can we? Thanks, H.'

'You're welcome.' Sensing that further 'bloke conversation' was imminent, Harri excused herself and headed back upstairs. After putting the dishwasher on, she checked her mobile for messages. A text from Rob flashed up on the screen:

Hope the travel dinner is ok. Preston emergency so off there early 2moro. Shud be back Sat but not sure. Sorry Red. R xx

Harri stared at the words, emotion welling up in her throat. There had been noticeably less mention of Preston or Rob's job during the past couple of months and she had begun to entertain the hope that its importance might be waning. Her vulnerability still keen after the recent exchange with Alex, the last thing she needed was the re-emergence of Rob's obsession with work. With Alex still happily chatting downstairs, she decided to cut the evening short and go home to a long soak in the bath, followed by a classic old movie romance to lose herself in.

Gathering her things together, she started to make her way down the winding staircase, but the mention of her name made her stop halfway.

'Harri looks well,' Jack was saying.

'Does she?'

'She always does, man. You two certainly looked cosy tonight.'

Harri put a hand over her mouth to muffle her giggle. Typical Jack, stirring as usual. He was an *impossible* wind-up merchant at the best of times and loved ribbing Alex the most.

She heard Alex laugh. 'We did not.'

'Come on, Al. You mean to tell me you've never looked at H and considered it? That red hair of hers, not to mention those eyes . . . Amy Adams *in your flat* . . .'

Harri rolled her eyes. Not *that* one again.

'She's just a mate, Jack. You know that.'

'Uh-huh . . . Still, beats me why you're bothering with all those dates when you have something like *that* for dinner.'

'Mate, be serious.'

Jack's laugh rang around the tiled walls of the work kitchen. 'You are too easy to wind up, man! Your face!'

'Very funny, Mr Comedy Genius. Harri's a really good friend and yeah, she's attractive, but she's *so* not my type. I mean, look at her – she spends her whole life sorting out other people's holidays but she's never been out of the country, as far as I know. Whoever heard of a travel agent that's never travelled anywhere? I mean, she comes here to learn about the world she's too scared to experience for herself. Trust me, I'm just taking pity on her, that's all.'

Jack laughed again. 'Harsh. So you're doing your bit for charity, huh?'

'Yeah – yeah, exactly.'

Hidden in the shadow of the stairwell, Harri felt her legs shaking as her pulse rate shot up. Of all the people in Stone Yardley that could have made this observation about her life, Alex was the last one she'd expected. To hear him mocking her – with such apparent ease – sent daggers flying at her heart. *How could he say that?*

'Well, I still think you're protesting too much. Right, I'd better get back – my date will think I've abandoned her. Thanks for the pie, Al. You might just have saved my life.'

Harri heard the back door open and Alex saying goodbye. Panicking, she quickly ran back upstairs, grabbed a film magazine on the sofa and flicked quickly through it, just as Alex walked back in.

'Sorry about that,' he said, his face a little flushed – although it was anyone's guess whether this was due to the run up the stairs or the exchange of words he had just shared with Jack. 'You know Jack, always taking the mick.'

'Hmm.' Harri was struggling to hold back her anger and hurt, but wasn't about to let Alex see that. She was pretty sure that he would deny it if confronted and, besides, if that was what he really thought of her she didn't want him pretending otherwise just because he had been found out. She just needed to leave – quickly. 'Anyway, I've got quite a bit of stuff to do at home, so I think I'll make a move.'

Alex was a little taken aback by this. 'Really? Are you sure? I thought we could check out that new travel show I recorded last week.'

'Tempting, but no.' *Wouldn't want to put you to any trouble, Alex.* 'But let me know if it's worth watching, OK?'

'Right – um – cool.' He was watching her carefully as she stood and walked past him towards the stairs. 'I'll – see you out then.'

They walked downstairs and through the kitchen, into the darkened coffee lounge. Harri could hear Alex breathing behind her and her desire to be out of his presence intensified. She watched while he unbolted the door and turned to smile at him. 'Thanks for dinner.'

He stepped forward hesitantly and they shared an awkward half-hug. 'So, you'll let me have the next number tomorrow? Business as usual and all that?'

Harri nodded as a thought appeared in her mind, sparkling dangerously. 'Certainly will. 'Night then.'

Released at last, she walked quickly away from Wātea, aware that Alex was watching her leave. Tears already forming in her eyes, she rounded the corner to Stone Yardley's small car park, got into her car and shut the door, just in time for the flood to begin. Tears falling, she rested her arms on the steering wheel and dropped her forehead against them, feeling the car swaying slightly as sobs rocked her body. *How dare he say something like that?* And the casual way he had written her off. She had never thought of him as two-faced before, yet this revelation had presented an Alex she didn't know. Suddenly it seemed as if the people she cared most about were deserting her in one way or another: first Stella, then Rob and now Alex. Was it true that he thought of her only as some pathetic charity case? It was too much, especially considering all she had done for him. It just wasn't *fair*. Wiping her face with her coat sleeve, she started the engine and pulled out of the car park. As she drove through the darkening streets, her hurt began to metamorphose into something entirely different: an anger more scathing than any she had felt before, fuelling a new desire inside her. Revenge. The darkly compulsive thought in her mind was now formulating into a plan with frightening alacrity. All the way home it grew, making more and more sense the nearer she drove to her cottage and, by the time she reached her front door, it was fully formed.

Pausing to stroke a very pleasantly surprised Ron Howard as he wound around her legs, she kneeled down and retrieved a box file from underneath the coffee table. Looking at the white sticker on the front, she opened the file and smiled as she took out an overly scented letter.

'Well, hello Not Likelies,' she said. 'My friend Alex needs a date to remember, so tonight's your lucky night. And the winner is . . .' she held it up in front of her like a golden envelope at the Oscars, the prospect of revenge now intoxicating in its appeal, '. . . Miss Chelsea Buckden.'

CHAPTER FIFTEEN

The Date From Hell . . .

'Harri, you *have* to let up on yourself. None of this is your fault.'

'Evidently your son doesn't agree.'

Viv sighs, its echo cold and metallic as it reverberates around the toilet. 'He's understandably upset by what happened tonight. He just needs some time to calm down.'

Forgive me if I don't believe you, Harri thinks to herself. I saw the way he looked at me.

'It's that friend of yours who's to blame,' Viv continues, oblivious to Harri's opinion. 'Silly, *silly* girl. Of course, she won't have any idea of what she's done. Didn't hang around long enough to find out. Probably the best decision she's made all night.'

Harri gazes up at the pool of water gathering at one end of the skylight. 'Has Stella gone?'

'Yes. Yes, she has.' Though Harri can't see her face, she can guess what Viv's expression will be.

But what about Alex? Harri looks up at the grimy ceiling as a fresh onslaught of emotion grips her throat.

Chelsea Buckden was every inch the antithesis of what Alex was looking for when Harri met her the next day in the small Caffè Nero franchise behind the bus depot in Lornal. Breaking from her usual method of calling to vet Alex's possible dates, Harri was keen to do this particular interview in person. After all, it was the *least* she could do, given the circumstances . . .

The none-too-subtle tones of Chelsea's 'Free to a Good Home' reply rang in Harri's ears, making the prospect of her revenge even more delicious.

. . . I think we have loads in common. You have your own business and I love spending money. You're well fit and I know I look good. I like a man who will treat me right and it sounds like you want a woman you can take care of . . .

Chelsea's ironed-flat, brassy blonde hair was moulded into a high beehive and hairsprayed to within an inch of its life; thick, tangerine foundation clung heavily to her face, whilst almost black eyeshadow, false lashes and more liquid eyeliner than most women would use in a month made her eyes look as if she either hadn't slept for a fortnight or was auditioning to be a panda at London Zoo. Her bulging, almost perfectly spherical breasts looked so removed from the rest of her chest that it gave the impression she could walk away from them at any time, and her too-short (in all directions) body-con dress left absolutely nothing to the imagination. There was no denying the fact: when it came to flaunting her sexuality Chelsea Buckden was the kind of woman blessed with all the demureness of an Exocet missile.

She gave a disinterested yawn and inspected her too-long acrylic nails as Harri approached.

'Hi,' Harri smiled, extending her hand which, unsurprisingly, wasn't accepted.

'You'd better get coffee,' Chelsea replied. 'That irate guy behind the counter's been giving me grief.'

A little taken aback, Harri nodded. 'Sure, erm, what would you like?'

Chelsea chewed her gum and looked Harri up and down contemptuously. Picking up her baby-pink phone, her eyes moved away to the screen. 'Soy latte, extra shot, extra hot. Large.'

'She with you?' asked the stocky bloke behind the counter, tending to Harri's order.

'You could say that. I'm meeting her for a friend.'

'Too scared to show up, was he? I would be. She makes Jodie Marsh look virginal.'

Harri smiled and sorted through the change in her purse. 'Can I take a couple of those chocolate muffins as well, please?'

'No problem. That's five ninety, please.'

Harri handed over her money. 'Thanks.'

Stocky Bloke grinned. 'You're welcome. Just promise me you won't take make-up tips from that *thing*, OK?'

'I think I'm safe on that score, thank you!'

Chelsea was texting when Harri rejoined her at the table, her nails making squeaky clicks as they hit the keys. Ending her acrylic communication, she tossed the phone carelessly onto the table, where it spun across the polished wood. 'This Alex – he's fit, yeah?'

'Well, you saw his photo, so—'

'And he's loaded?'

Harri frowned. 'I, er, don't know if I'd say that, exactly.'

Chelsea leaned forward, her silicone enhancements bobbing across the table top and almost toppling her muffin in the process. 'But he has his own coffee shop, right? So I mean, he must be raking it in.'

Stocky Bloke, who had begun to clear the table next to them,

258

sniggered. 'Yeah, chick, all closet millionaires, us coffee-shop owners.'

'Er – nobody asked you,' retorted Chelsea, giving him a look that could have withered steel. Turning back to Harri, she raised an overplucked, pencilled eyebrow. 'So when am I meeting him?'

Harri reached in her bag for her diary. 'Let me just check. Is tomorrow night any good for you?'

'Can't do. I don't finish work till six and then me and the girls are hitting the town.'

'Oh, right. Birmingham?'

Chelsea shot a disdainful look at Harri. '*No*. Wolverhampton.'

'Ah, sorry. My mistake.'

'Yeah, well, no offence, but I'm guessing it's been a while since you went out. Only the chavs and desperados go to Broad Street now.'

It was all Harri could do not to burst out laughing. This was turning out better than she'd hoped. Alex was in for the nightmare date of his life. 'OK, how about next Monday evening? It's only for a drink, anyway, to begin with.'

A filthy smirk snaked its way over Chelsea's collagen-pumped lips. 'Yeah, well, I think you'll find it won't stop at one *drink*. When it comes to me, men always get more than they bargained for, know what I mean?'

Harri took a large gulp of coffee to hide her smile.

Driving home half an hour later, Harri was thrilled at the prospect of Alex's comeuppance, even if the small, sensible part of her mind refused to be convinced. Still, she told herself, as revenge went, it was relatively tame: true, it would probably be the most excruciating hour of his life, but that was all. After all, what was the worst that could happen?

* * *

259

Despite Rob being frustratingly AWOL and Alex's conversation with Jack still sitting uncomfortably in her mind, Harri didn't have long to mull over everything, as Friday afternoon was unusually busy for SLIT – at one point the customers even creating a queue (something akin to the arrival of a rare comet as far as the staff were concerned).

'If this goes on, we'll have to get more chairs!' George exclaimed excitedly as he dashed past Harri's desk with an armful of brochures.

Tom leaned back and smirked at Harri. 'If this goes on, we should ask for more money.'

'I reckon your pay rise is going to fund the new chairs,' Nus called over. 'Dream on, Tombo.'

Tom pulled a face and returned to helping Mr and Mrs Talbot choose their coach tour.

'I'm looking for a family holiday, somewhere child-friendly, for next June,' said the young woman with the small child on her lap, sitting opposite Harri. 'I notice you have some offers in the window. We want to take Jacob here on his first trip. We've been saving since he was born and think it's the right time to book something.'

Harri smiled and made a mental note of the family holidays SLIT currently had on offer, bearing in mind the usual desired locations for their customers: Cornwall, Devon, Pembrokeshire . . . 'Great. So did you have anywhere particular in mind?'

'Somewhere hot – Spain or Greece?'

This was such a shock to Harri that she found herself doing a double take. 'S-sorry, did you say you're looking for a holiday *abroad*?'

A strange expression passed across her customer's face. 'Yes – that's not a problem, is it?'

Aware she was now staring at the lady as if she were seeing a mirage, Harri checked herself and grabbed a handful of brochures. 'No, no, of course not, it's just . . . Never mind. Right, well, we have a great selection here . . .'

An hour later, most of the customers had left and Tom, Nus, Harri and George were gathered in the centre of the shop, recovering from the rush with well-earned mugs of tea.

'In-cred-ible.' George shook his red shiny head, his face flushed from the afternoon's excitement. 'I can't remember a day like it.'

'Oh, but you haven't heard the best of it,' said Tom. 'Harri sold a holiday abroad.'

This revelation was met with utter disbelief by George and Nus. 'No!'

'Yes, indeedy. Tell them, H.'

Harri nodded. 'Two weeks. Crete.'

George blew out a whistle. 'Well, I never. An extraordinary day all round then.'

The phone on Harri's desk interrupted their conversation and Harri wheeled her chair over to answer it.

'Hi, Harri? It's Emily. Sorry to ring you at work, but something amazing just happened.'

'Must be the day for it,' Harri replied.

'Sorry?'

'Nothing. What's up?'

'I quit!'

Following the shock of the foreign holiday sale today, Harri found herself struggling to comprehend this news. 'What? When?'

'Just now! I walked into my boss's office and handed in my resignation. Can you believe it?'

'Well, I . . . no, I can't. Are you – how are you feeling?'

Emily giggled nervously and Harri could hear her breathing quickly. 'I'm shaking! I'll be OK – I think. I just wanted to thank you.'

'What for?'

Harri could almost feel the glow emitting from Emily's effervescent glee. 'For what you said about being spontaneous.'

'I said I couldn't do it—'

'No, I don't mean that! I mean what you said about your friend doing it.'

A thud of realisation hit Harri's stomach. She closed her eyes. 'Alex.' She remembered mentioning his story over dinner at the farm in summer.

'Yes, Alex. I need to meet this man and thank him – his story was just an inspiration. Next time you come over you must bring him!'

'Right, well, I'm not sure he'd be up for the—'

'Anyway, I've got to go. I need to tell Stu. He owes me a tenner, actually: he bet me last night that I wouldn't go through with it! I'll call you next week and we'll arrange to meet up, OK? Bye!'

Harri slowly replaced the receiver and stared hard at the phone. This was turning out to be a very strange day indeed . . .

Walking into the green-scented coolness of Eadern Blooms later that day felt like stepping into an oasis of pure calm. The familiar yellow tiles, white-painted walls and swathes of glorious flowers soothed Harri's eyes and wrapped their loveliness around her heart like a warm jumper on a snowy day. So many things seemed to have happened this week to push her out of her comfort zone: Rob's sudden change from attentive to distracted by the re-emergence of the Preston job; the continuing absence of Stella; Alex's conversation with Jack and her resulting plot with the nightmare known as Chelsea Buckden; even Emily's sudden spontaneity this afternoon – what Harri needed more than anything right now was someone to listen to her.

Auntie Rosemary was putting the finishing touches to a large basket arrangement, wrapping lengths of baby-pink ribbon around its handle and stapling an elaborate florist's bow at the front. Harri loved watching her aunt work – the effortlessness with which she created amazing displays; stripping stems, curling ribbon and working her magic on blooms and foliage. Harri often wondered whether her aunt found comfort in bringing joy to so many people. Rosemary certainly seemed to be at her most peaceful when up to her eyes in greenery and multi-coloured flowers – and, knowing the problems she had contended with over the years: her husband leaving her with two small children to provide for – Harri could only assume that the cheery florist's shop had been a source of strength and hope for her aunt.

'Harri, sweetheart!' Auntie Rosemary exclaimed when she looked up from her work. 'What a wonderful surprise! It's lovely to see you. Do you want to pop the kettle on and I'll just finish this? Barnie's coming to take it any minute.'

Like the rest of the shop, Eadern Blooms' small kitchen was light, welcoming and homely: faded flowery tiles by the small yellow sink; Auntie Rosemary's home-made bunting (which sometimes made an appearance in the front at Easter) hanging happily around the tiny window; the collection of mismatched mugs jumbled together by the kettle; teaspoons stacked haphazardly in an old lidless teapot; the patchwork tea cosy that had been there for as long as Harri could remember and that once served as a makeshift crown when she was playing princesses with her cousin Rosie.

Harri looked through the steam at the small cork notice-board covered with a hotchpotch of photographs. There was a black-and-white image of Rosemary as a young woman, strikingly good-looking with her closely cropped, almost black hair and long, lithe limbs, posing with an ice-cream cornet and a pretty smile on holiday in Bridlington. A slightly creased colour photo featured a heavily pregnant Rosemary with a surly-looking toddler on her lap (Harri's cousin James only discovered the power of charm many years later). And right in the middle, amidst weddings, christenings and funerals, flower shows, carnivals and birthdays, was a photo that caused Harri's heart to beat furiously: Mum and Dad, looking happy and healthy, with Harri as a young child, all auburn curls and carefree smile. The sense of family that she missed so much was there in glorious Kodacolor for all to see. It was a permanent testament to something that had once been so vital, living, real.

Swept away by a tidal flow of nostalgia and longing, Harri reached out and stroked the fading gloss of the image, wiping away the condensation from the kettle steam as hot tears welled in her eyes. The rattling sound of Auntie Rosemary walking through the rainbow-coloured bead curtain from the shop brought her sharply back to the present.

'How are you getting on, sweetheart?'

Wiping her eyes quickly, Harri poured boiling water from the kettle into the old, bright yellow teapot and stirred it. 'Almost done. Just drowned the teabags.'

Rosemary squeezed Harri's arm. 'It always tickled me when your mum said that.'

'I know.' Harri's eyes drifted back to the photographs and her aunt caught it immediately.

'I still find it hard believing they're gone,' she said, her gentle voice suddenly small and vulnerable. 'You know, even this afternoon, a lady walked past the window and I could have *sworn* it was your mum. All these years and I still expect her to walk in through the door . . .' She sniffed, pulled an embroidered handkerchief from the sleeve of her cardigan and wiped her nose. 'Right then, let's find some spare smiles from the cupboard and put them on, shall we? Can't have us all mournful at the start of a weekend.'

Ten minutes later, sitting on the high, pine stools behind the counter, Auntie Rosemary opened a pack of French Fancies and passed it to Harri. 'You see? A good auntie never forgets her niece's favourite cakes.'

No matter how far away from her childhood the years took her, one glimpse at the brown-, pink- and yellow-iced cakes in their white, pleated cases brought the same childish thrill shimmering through Harri. Selecting her favourite (the pink one, of course), she inhaled its sugary, sweet aroma as she took a bite. 'Thank you,' she mumbled stickily, laughing at her own reaction to the fondant treats.

'You're welcome, my darling.' Auntie Rosemary's smile faded slightly. 'Actually, I was meaning to tell you something that I – I'm not altogether proud of.'

'Wait, let me guess: you have a secret crush on Jeremy Clarkson?'

'Certainly *not*. I cannot abide the man – arrogant and self-opinionated. Such a shame, when his mother was the one who invented those lovely Paddington Bear toys.'

'She did? Wow. Um, OK then: you wore crazy flares in the seventies?'

Rosemary raised her eyes heavenwards. 'Darling, *everyone* wore crazy flares in the seventies.'

Harri laughed. 'I know. I've seen photographic evidence of

Mum and Dad. Oh! I've got it! You're the latest recruit to the Birmingham mafia that Tom at work is always going on about?'

'Harriet Langton, stop it. I'm trying to confess something here.'

'Sorry, Auntie Ro. Confess away.'

Her aunt took a deep breath. 'I told Alex about your Venice postcard.'

In all the madness of the past couple of days, Harri had forgotten Alex's revelation about his conversation with Auntie Rosemary. While at the time she had been annoyed by her aunt's uncharacteristic gossiping, today Harri couldn't find it within herself to bear a grudge – especially in light of Rosemary's contrite expression.

'I know. Don't worry, I'm not going to relieve you of your auntie duties.'

'Oh, Harri, I really am sorry. We were talking about all the places he'd visited so I thought how lovely it would be if he'd been to Venice and could tell you all about it. But he hadn't been and – and since then I've felt so awful, betraying your confidence like that.'

The mention of Alex sent a swell of nausea undulating inside Harri. 'It's fine, honestly.'

'I'm so glad, sweetheart. He really is a smashing young man. I just hope all these young ladies you're setting him up with are worthy.'

Harri stuffed the last of her French Fancy in her mouth and chewed quickly, trying her best to ignore the wagging finger of her conscience. 'So how's your week been?'

Auntie Rosemary picked up the teapot to top up their mugs. 'Busy. As ever. There seems to be an inordinate amount of weddings this month. I reckon we've done twice the amount of bouquets and buttonholes than we did in July – and that's supposed to be when everyone gets married. In fact, this weekend is the first for about six weeks when the girls and I haven't had a church to dress. Mind you, I still have to deliver three sets of bridal party flowers in the morning, so I've not been let off the hook completely. Well, Barnie and I have to deliver them. Speaking of which,' she pulled up her cardigan sleeve to look at her watch, 'he should have been here half an hour ago. What on earth can be keeping him?'

'Maybe it's the traffic. George was saying there's temporary lights on Lidgate Hill.'

Auntie Rosemary winced. 'Ooh, nasty. Well, if he's caught in that, heaven knows when he'll get here . . .'

Just then, the door flew open and a flustered-looking man dressed in a dark blue polo shirt and jeans bustled into the shop. Barnie Davies was the owner of quite the most splendidly lustrous white hair in Stone Yardley. In fact, so flowing and full were his locks that he had been nicknamed 'L'Oréal' by the regulars at the Land Oak, who delighted in quipping, 'Because you're worth it!' whenever they handed him a pint.

He held up his hands as he approached the counter. 'I know, I know! Traffic was *horrendous*, Rosemary – backed up from the other side of Ellingsgate. Why on earth the council decided Friday rush hour was the best time to dig up the road is beyond me.' He stopped and smiled a twinkly-eyed greeting. 'Hello, Harri. Glad you're here: she's less likely to throttle me if you're in the room.'

Auntie Rosemary tutted and winked at Harri. 'The man is impossible. I'm afraid this basket's got to go out, Barnie. It's for an eightieth birthday party at the village hall tonight and I promised it would be there before seven.'

Barnie feigned frustration and jabbed his fists on his hips,

267

making his ample belly bobble over the top of his jeans. 'You are a slave driver, Rosemary Duncan.'

'And *you* are lucky to have a job here, remember?' Rosemary replied, flushing a little as an irresistible smile danced across her lips.

'Competition was stiff for this job, you know,' Barnie grinned at Harri. 'Apparently at the interview it was between me and a spotty, seventeen-year-old, six-stone weakling. Personally, I think it was my suave and debonair demeanour that won her over in the end.'

'I still have his number. I could call him right now . . .'

'All right, I get the hint!' He picked up the basket arrangement and turned to leave. 'Don't let her phone anyone, Harri!'

'You have my word. Nice to see you, Barnie.' Harri watched her aunt carefully as Barnie left the shop. 'He's a lovely man, isn't he?'

'Hmm? Yes, yes, I suppose he is.'

'There's no "suppose" about it! He likes you – and I think the feeling might just be mutual.'

Horrified, Auntie Rosemary stared at her. 'I – I – absolutely *not*! Barnie is an employee and a good friend.'

'Oh, come off it, Auntie Ro, there was more chemistry between you two just now than in a mad professor's lab!'

Rosemary's hand shot up to the back of her hair, a subtle defence mechanism Harri had learned to spot over the years. 'He's a good man. But there's nothing like . . . *that* going on.'

'I think you'd both like it if there was, though. He's not married, is he?'

'No, but . . .'

Harri picked up a chocolate-iced French Fancy and slowly peeled off the white cake case. 'Well, then . . .'

Now definitely in full flush, Auntie Rosemary crossed her

arms. 'I am going to change the subject, Harriet, because I'm guessing there's a reason you decided to come and see me today.'

Harri's mirth extinguished quicker than a lit match in an ice bucket. It occurred to her that, while she was aware of her need to chat with her aunt, she hadn't really thought through exactly *what* she wanted to talk about. In lieu of anything resembling a plan, she just decided to start somewhere in the midst of the mess, hoping that the rest would form an orderly queue behind it. So, she began with the Alex and Jack conversation and, inevitably, ended up with the vision in Lycra known as Chelsea Buckden.

'. . . Honestly, Auntie Ro, you have to see her to believe it. And that scent that she'd smothered her letter in? She *reeks* of it! She's everything awful that she wrote in her letter and more.'

Auntie Rosemary dunked a HobNob in her tea, her expression grave. 'I must say, sweetheart, I'm surprised at you.'

Harri's face fell. 'Why?'

'This isn't like you to be planning revenge. This isn't who you are.'

'But I told you what Alex said . . .'

Dismissing this with a wave of her hand, Rosemary fixed Harri with a stern look. 'That doesn't matter. The point is, you overheard a conversation you weren't supposed to hear . . .'

'Exactly!'

'Wait – let me finish, Harriet. You heard *part* of a conversation, with no clue as to its context. It's highly likely you misunderstood what Alex meant.'

'He called me a charity case! He mocked the fact that I haven't travelled. How, *exactly*, could I have missed the meaning of that?'

'Well, I admit it doesn't sound very nice.'

'Nice? It's the most horrible, hurtful thing anyone's ever said to me! And he's meant to be my friend, Auntie Ro. Besides, me setting him up with Chelsea will just make him squirm a bit.' Harri let out a sigh of exasperation. 'Anyway, it's all arranged now. There's nothing I can do about it.'

'Fair enough. Personally, I think you should just confront him about what you heard.'

'He'd only deny it. If that's the way he really feels about me I don't want him to pretend otherwise.'

Auntie Rosemary tutted. 'Oh, don't be ridiculous, Harriet. That young man thinks the world of you – it's blatantly obvious. My guess is that his friend put him on the spot so he simply resorted to the classic male tactic of joking his way out of the conversation.'

'Auntie Ro, you didn't hear what he said.'

'You're right. I didn't,' Auntie Rosemary replied, picking up the empty mugs to return them to the kitchen. 'All the same, I think it's a daft thing to lose a friendship over.'

As Rosemary disappeared through the bead curtain, Harri stared through the steamed-up windows at the darkening sky over Stone Yardley. Whatever her aunt said, Harri knew that setting Alex up with Chelsea was a mild comeback compared with how much he had upset her. Besides, after his date from hell she would probably find someone nice to take away some of the sting – and it would be back to business as usual for the 'Free to a Good Home' dates. Satisfied with her reasoning, Harri hopped off the stool and went to find her aunt.

To placate the tenaciously disapproving voice of her conscience, when she returned home that afternoon Harri threw herself into the task of finding Alex's 'date after Chelsea'. After an hour of sorting through the remaining letters in the contenders pile later that afternoon, Harri decided to take a break, grabbing her new *Hidden Venice* book to lose herself in its pages for a while.

There is a delicious, intoxicating otherworldliness about Venice that sweeps your heart into another realm, never to return . . . Walk her streets and you pass people going about their day: children running and laughing, safe from the threat of traffic in this carless realm; couples huddled cosily over coffee and zaletti in street cafés, or entwined on stone benches overlooking the canals. But you will find no such thing as an 'ordinary day' in this city of serenity. Turn around and discover an elaborately attired street performer, or a shop window filled with opulent splendour. Where else in the world would a confectioner display their wares nestled amidst rich swathes of velvet, exquisitely painted Venetian masks and dew-fresh roses—

The shrill ring of her phone brought her careering back to the damp autumn afternoon in her tiny cottage, and she hastily dug around underneath the letters and magazines strewn across the sofa to find it.

'Hello?'

'Hey, Red. How's my favourite travel agent?'

The sound of Rob's voice sent a shiver of delight through her. 'Hey, you. I didn't know if I'd hear from you today – how's Preston going?'

'Ah, not so good, I'm afraid.'

Harri could hear the disappointment in his voice and it made her want to hug him. Jovial voices were murmuring in the background and she thought she heard somebody call his name. 'Seems busy there.'

He laughed, the sound warming her ear. 'Yeah, we've been flat out. We're just – you know – taking a breather before we start again.'

'So I'm guessing you're there all weekend, then?'

'Yeah. I'm sorry, baby. I don't think I'll be home till Wednesday.'

Disappointment dropped like a medicine ball in her heart. 'Right. Well, just try not to work too hard, OK?'

'Will do. And, hey, just keep thinking about that Scottish castle at Christmas, yeah? You know you're my favourite girl, right?'

Harri stared out of the front window to the damp fields shrouded in grey autumnal mist. 'Of course I do. You take care and text me when you get home.' A thought occurred to her. 'How come you didn't call me on my mobile?'

Rob's answer was singularly damning in its simplicity. 'I knew you'd be at home.'

As Harri hung up she sighed and looked over at Ron Howard, who was hinting he might just be sociable if she gave him a cat treat. 'Great, Ron. So I'm not only on my own this weekend but thoroughly predictable as well.'

It was going to be a long weekend.

On Monday morning, Alex called Harri at work to run over the details of his date for the evening.

'So, what's she like?' he asked.

Harri stifled a grin. 'Different. She's unlike anyone you've met before.'

'Unique, huh? Excellent. And her name is . . . ?'

'Chelsea.'

'Right. Haven't dated a Chelsea before, so this should be interesting.'

Oh yes, Harri thought to herself, it will definitely be interesting, Alex.

That evening, Harri was surprised to find that she had developed butterflies about the possible events unfolding at the Star and Highwayman. Odd, she thought. She decided that distraction was the best course of action: the last thing she wanted was to start obsessing over what might be happening. When tidying her house didn't succeed in removing the frustrating fluttering within, she drove over to Rob's house to pick up his post, then slowly drove home.

The traffic lights turned red as she reached the crossroads where High Street met Market Street, bringing her car to a standstill outside Wātea. Casting a glance at the darkened windows of the coffee shop and the flat above, her curiosity grew. Alex had said earlier that he would only be able to spend an hour with Chelsea, due to the fact that he had an early delivery in the morning. So why wasn't he home yet? Perhaps he had gone to see Jack, or Steve, or one of his other mates, after his terrible date . . . Or maybe Chelsea had imprisoned him in her acrylic-taloned clutches and it was impossible for him to escape . . . Worse still, the experience may have been so awful that he was now wandering the streets of Stone Yardley, a wild-eyed, gibbering wreck . . .

The sharp honk of a car horn behind her made Harri realise that the lights had changed to green and she quickly drove off, smiling at her own melodramatics.

Next morning, Harri could bear the suspense no longer. She decided to call in at Wātea before work and face Alex. After such a dreadful date, he was bound to have plenty to say to her – good or bad – so this, Harri concluded, as the coffee shop came into view through the heavy rain that had been pummelling Stone Yardley since the early hours, was the sensible option.

The red and white delivery van from Hickson & Butler was just pulling away when Harri arrived, revealing Alex hastily stacking boxes on the pavement. He looked up but didn't smile when he saw her.

'Hi, Al.'

'Hey, do me a favour and grab these, would you? I need to get them out of the rain.'

Harri accepted three boxes from his outstretched hands and followed him into the coffee lounge. She could feel anticipation tingling through her as she watched him placing boxes in the storeroom, the muscles in his broad back flexing beneath his rain-splattered pale blue T-shirt. She waited in the doorway to the work kitchen with the boxes in her arms, trying to gauge his mood from the hunch of his shoulders. Finally, he turned back and relieved her of them.

'I'm glad you came,' Alex said, after a long time. 'We need to talk.'

He's mad, thought Harri. She flashed a bright smile at him. 'The date was a mistake, wasn't it?'

He closed the storeroom door and turned to face her – and for the first time she could see a vulnerability in his expression that she wasn't expecting. 'What do you mean?'

'Well, at the time I thought Chelsea would be different for you. But I have to admit, last night I realised I'd made a *terrible* mistake. I'm just so sorry that I realised too late to stop it.' She could feel a rush of satisfaction as she saw the confusion on his face. *And now you know how you made me feel, Alex* . . . 'But I'll find someone really nice for your next date, I promise.'

His eyes fell away. 'There's no point . . .'

This was more fun than she'd imagined. 'Oh, come on, Al. Was the date really that bad? I'm sure the next one will be amazing.'

Slowly, he lifted his head, his chocolate eyes meeting hers. 'No, Harri,' he said softly. 'There really *is* no point . . . because I'm in love.'

'*What?*'

An enormous smile appeared on his face. 'Completely, utterly, totally in love!'

Shock robbed her mouth of words, leaving her gawping.

'I *know*! Mad or what! She's amazing, H – and it's just like you said: she's unlike anyone I've ever met before. Everything about her fascinates me. I couldn't stop staring at her all night.' His eyes searched her face. 'Well, come on – say something!'

'You – you can't be serious?'

'I can and I am. I love her.'

'But – but she's not your type!'

'Type *schmype*, H! I know it isn't logical, but then when was love ever ruled by logic? I'm telling you, she's the one I've been looking for. And I have *you* to thank for it!' He gathered Harri up in an enthusiastic bear hug, holding on to her for longer than she expected. Unable to break free, she remained helpless with her face pressed against his chest, his thumping heart beating furiously by her ear.

Her thoughts raced at high speed as she tried to make sense of what Alex was saying. Surely he couldn't be serious? Everything about Chelsea screamed against every quality Alex had said he wanted in a woman: she was only interested in Alex's bank balance and couldn't care less about the man behind it, his hopes, his dreams or his character.

Or maybe – Harri's mind made a handbrake turn as another explanation took to the floor for a spin – maybe he'd rumbled her plan to set him up with the worst possible date and all this was merely an elaborate double bluff to place the joke firmly on her. Alex the joker, getting his own back on her for the date to end all dates.

'OK, very funny. You win.'

Alex broke the hug and stared at her. 'I win what?'

Harri shook her head. 'You know, you really had me going for a moment there. Very clever.'

'H, what are you talking about?'

'You got me back – for setting you up with a terrible date. And I almost believed you. But come on, I mean, *seriously*, you were never going to fall in love with someone like Chelsea, were you?'

Alex was looking at Harri like she had just accused him of murder. His smile was gone, his face frozen in disbelief. Suddenly, Harri's shiny new theory began to shatter into a million fragments.

'I'm not joking, H. You didn't set me up with a terrible date. I'm in *love*. And it's all your fault.'

CHAPTER SIXTEEN

Anyone but Her . . .

It is becoming scarily clear that Viv has no intention of leaving anytime soon.

'Are you cold in there? You must be cold in there – it's freezing.'

Harri shivers. 'I'm fine.'

'Well, anyway, you might need this.'

A plum-coloured pashmina flops over the top of the door to Harri's cubicle. She takes it gratefully and wraps it around her shoulders. 'Thank you, Viv.'

'You're welcome. Have you eaten?'

'I'm not hungry.'

'No, well, neither would I be if I was sitting in a toilet cubicle. Won't you come out, darling? You being in here isn't doing anyone any good.'

Harri's head is beginning to pound. She rests her elbows on her lap and massages her temples with slow, circular movements. 'I'm not ready. Not yet.'

'But most people have gone now, Harriet. And those that are left probably didn't even notice you leave.'

'Viv, *everyone* saw me leave, remember? They all watched the humiliating spectacle right before all hell broke loose.'

'That's as maybe, but the fact remains you can't stay in there indefinitely.'

She's right, of course. Harri knows she has inadvertently backed herself into a corner by her choice of sanctuary and she wishes she had just walked out of the village hall instead. But she wasn't thinking clearly: all that mattered was getting away from the pitying eyes of Stone Yardley's finest. If *only* she'd never confided in Stella . . .

From: stellababy@danbeagle.co.uk
To: armchairtraveller@gmail.com
Subject: Surprise!

Hey sweets

Yes it's me! A little later than planned, but then you know me, always fashionably late for everything. Well, I was. Now I'm travelling with Dan and his kamikaze camera crew who think six a.m. is a lie-in, I can't remember the last time I was late for anything.

Anyhow, how on earth are you? Still vetting women for Alex? I really hope not, for your sake, but I have a feeling it's still going on, knowing you. Don't suppose his mum's helping much either.

Things here are phenomenal! Dan is just amazing, but then I guess you knew that already. We've been travelling for a couple of months, filming his new series, so that's why it's taken me so long to find somewhere with a halfway decent internet connection. We're here in Kathmandu for at least the next three weeks and fully online, so email me back with all the goss, OK? I'm loving what I'm learning here, but I

could do with a bit of light relief from Stone
Yardley ☺
Email me!
Luvya tons
Stel xxx

Harri read and reread the email. She had convinced herself by
now that she was unlikely to hear from Stella. While the granite
lump of hurt still refused to budge inside her at Stella's sudden
departure, Harri found herself needing to confide in someone
so, unusually for Stella, her timing couldn't have been more
perfect.

It was early November and any hopes Harri had entertained
of Alex becoming tired of Chelsea had faded into obscurity.
It was worse than she could ever have imagined: her spur-of-
the-moment decision had led to a relationship that threatened
to steal her best friend away forever.

Chelsea was *everywhere*, making her orange-hued presence
felt in all areas of Alex's life – her influence seeping in like
an insipid flood, silently intoxicating him and imperceptibly
moving him away from everyone else. He seemed to spend
every available minute with his new girlfriend, much to the
frustration of his mates. Even his once regular attendance
at the Star and Highwayman's Sunday night pub quiz began
to wane. He started to dress differently, his vintage T-shirts,
faded jeans and hoodies began to disappear in favour of a
smarter, if less original GAP and French Connection wardrobe. In an effort to involve Chelsea with his business he
had let her change the décor, so some of his travel photographs had been removed in favour of contrived IKEA 'art'.
He was every inch the man in love and clearly very happy,

but to Harri it seemed as if his identity was slowly being eroded away.

Unfortunately for Harri, Alex and Chelsea's splendid isolation from his friends didn't extend to her. Quite the opposite, in fact: Alex's thankfulness at her introducing him to Chelsea knew no bounds, so he was constantly looking for opportunities to invite her to spend time with them. Worst of all, he happily informed Harri that Chelsea *liked* her and tried to encourage the friendship of 'my two favourite ladies'.

Chelsea *liked* her. The phrase made Harri shudder whenever she heard it. She had nothing in common with the woman and found very little endearing about her, yet she couldn't bring herself to be rude to Chelsea. After all, she was Alex's girlfriend now and, whatever she might think, Harri wanted to support her best friend.

As far as Chelsea was concerned, however, the situation was slightly different from the picture she presented to Alex. When Harri was in the room it was an opportunity for Chelsea to compete – to make sure that Alex could see how superior she was to any other woman. No matter what Harri talked about, Chelsea could top it. Whatever Harri had done, Chelsea had done it better; whatever Harri had experienced, Chelsea had experienced it ten times more. In fact, it was quickly getting to the stage where Harri was choosing increasingly random topics of conversation just to see what Chelsea would come up with to challenge them. Of course, Alex couldn't see it. Alex couldn't see anything other than the woman who had stolen his heart.

Harri ended up confiding in Emily about it all, after a chance remark led to a full-blown conversation.

Since Emily had handed in her resignation, the wheels had been put in motion for establishing her new holiday business and she had enlisted Harri's help with the mountain of tasks she faced. In return, she had offered meals at her lovely farmhouse home – something Harri was glad to accept, especially as Wednesday evening at Alex's had turned into cringe-worthy Chelsea worship sessions. It was during dinner at Emily's house, a couple of weeks before Stella made contact, that the topic of Chelsea had come up.

'I popped into Wātea yesterday,' Emily said, bringing a freshly brewed pot of coffee to the large, pine kitchen table as Fly padded around her feet. 'It's changed a bit in there recently, hasn't it?'

Harri grimaced. 'Yes, it has. But then so has Alex.'

Emily's dark green eyes saw more than Harri had intended. 'Really? How come?'

Normally, Harri would have laughed the question off, or changed the subject, but she found the opportunity to discuss the situation too inviting to decline. Emily listened intently, stroking Fly's head as it rested on her knee, and when Harri had finished she reached across to place her hand on Harri's arm.

'Poor you. That's a toughie, for sure.'

Harri sipped her coffee. 'The worst thing is, I just feel so hypocritical. I don't like Chelsea and I especially don't like how Al is changing, but I care about him and I don't want him to feel like he can't share that part of his life with me.'

'Isn't there any way you can tell him how you feel?' Emily asked, passing a plate of home-made white chocolate and walnut cookies to Harri.

'No, because then I'd have to admit why I introduced him to Chelsea in the first place. If he knew the truth it would end our friendship for good.'

'Well, for what it's worth, I admire you for sticking in there. She sounds absolutely horrendous.'

281

It was nice to have someone who understood, but Emily's reassuring words did little to quell the storm inside. So when Stella's email arrived, it seemed a gift too good to ignore. In her lunchbreak, checking that George, Tom and Nus weren't looking, she quickly typed a reply.

From: armchairtraveller@gmail.com
To: stellababy@danbeagle.co.uk
Subject: RE: Surprise!

Hi Stel

It was SO good to hear from you! How are you doing? Are you coping without your straighteners and hairdryer? You have no idea how jealous I am of you actually getting to see that big, wide world.

Things here are OK, some surprises but mostly Stone Yardley hasn't changed. Oh, except we now have a Country & Western-themed club, can you believe it? the Cross Hotel has had a revamp and it's now the Nashville Crossing! It's still full of sixteen-year-olds pretending to be eighteen, and forty-something guys pretending to be twenty-one, of course, but now they can do it to the strains of Billy Ray Cyrus and Rascal Flatts . . . Barmy, but it could only happen in Stone Yardley!

I'm really glad you emailed me – I need your advice. I made a stupid mistake and now everything is such a mess. Alex has a new girlfriend and it's all my fault. I set him up with her to get my own back after I heard him telling Jack that the only reason he invites me round for food is to take pity on me. She was meant to be the worst possible date but he's gone and fallen in love with the woman! Seriously, Stel, she's the kind of bimbo, Z-list celeb clone that you used to laugh at when we went to clubs in Birmingham. Her heroine is Katie Price and she's only interested in dim boyfriends with big bank balances. I hate it, but more than that, I hate myself for ever starting this whole thing. If I had just confronted him then I could have saved myself so much grief.

Don't get me wrong: this isn't because Al's going out with someone. Let's face it, I wouldn't have put myself through all the hassle of those magazine replies if I didn't want him to have a girlfriend. I just wish it could have been anyone but her. Anyone. What should I do? I don't know if you have an answer – I don't even know if there is an answer – I just need your advice.

Sorry to lay this on you, but you did ask!

Email me soon

H xx

Already feeling lighter for having shared her thoughts, Harri hit Send and relaxed back in her chair. Stella would know what to do – and even if she didn't, she would definitely have an opinion. All Harri had to do now was wait.

Mrs Bincham was all of a fluster when she arrived at SLIT the next day. It took Tom, Nus and Harri the best part of five minutes to get any kind of sense out of her. Finally, after much cajoling and a hastily prepared mug of strong tea, she regained the power of almost rational speech.

'My Geoff's proposed!'

Tom, Nus and Harri exchanged glances.

'Erm – but aren't you married already?' Nus asked.

'What on earth do you take me for, Nusrin? I'm a respectable woman!'

'Mrs B, I don't think Nus was implying that you and Geoff—'

'And none of your twopenneth either, Thomas!'

'Ethel, calm down,' Harri soothed. 'Now tell us what happened.'

Mrs B dabbed at her brow with a yellow duster. 'This morning, over breakfast, Geoff looked up from his *OK!* magazine and says, "Eth, I think it's about time we renewed our wedding vows. What's good enough for these celebrities is good enough for us. So how's about it, our bab?" Well, you could've knocked me down with a feather when I heard that!'

'So what did you say?'

'I didn't say nothing, Nusrin. I just got out of there as fast as these old legs could take me. I'm an old woman now – he shouldn't be giving me shocks like that at my age!'

'I think it's a lovely idea, Mrs B,' Harri reassured her. 'It means he still loves you and wants to tell the world.'

Mrs Bincham fixed Harri with a hard stare. 'That's as maybe, but I think it's got more to do with him being so celebrity obsessed. I blame those blasted magazines he buys, I do. Next thing you know, Geoff'll be asking me to have one of them boob jobs!'

They all had to look away at this point, hiding their laughter from Ethel's attention.

'What on earth's going on?' George was standing in the open doorway from the street, macintosh half off his shoulders as if he was about to perform a middle-aged, chubby striptease.

'It's fine, George. Ethel's just had a bit of a shock this morning,' Tom replied, patting Mrs B's hand protectively.

For once, real compassion made a brief glimpse on George's flushed face. 'Oh dear, are you . . . is everything OK?'

Ethel waved a hand dismissively. 'Nothing for you to worry about, Mr Duffield. I'll be fine in a jiff.'

'Geoff's proposed – again,' said Nus, clearly loving this Wednesday morning drama.

'He has? What did you say?'

'Oh, for pity's sake, I haven't said *anything* yet. I was too much of a dither.'

George placed his sodden raincoat on the coatstand by the door and approached Ethel. Kneeling down (not an easy task for someone of his considerable girth), he gently took her hand between both of his. 'Ethel. How long have I known you and Geoff?'

Mrs B was mystified by this question. 'Years, I s'pose.'

'And in all that time, I've hardly ever known the two of you to fight – bicker a little, maybe, but nothing worthy of note.'

'Right . . .'

'Geoff's a good man, Ethel. He loves you and he's stuck by you all these years, hasn't he?'

'Mostly. Of course, he had that wobble when he turned forty, but we don't mention that nowadays.'

'What wobble?' Tom enquired, only to be shushed by Harri.

'So all he wants to do is to show everyone how proud he is to be your husband,' George continued, much to the surprise of the staff gathered around him. 'One little chance to say to everyone, "This is my wife and I love her." Now, you wouldn't want to deny him that opportunity, would you?' He shook his head encouragingly.

Baffled, Ethel slowly shook her head along with him. 'No, but I—'

'I think you should go home now and tell him you accept,' George smiled.

'But, the cleaning . . .'

Raising his eyes to heaven, George's smile tightened slightly. 'Don't you worry about the cleaning. I'm sure we can manage without you for one day.'

'We manage without you most days . . . *ow*!' Tom yelped as Nusrin's elbow made sharp contact with his ribs.

'You're right!' Mrs B stood shakily to her feet and Harri helped her into her coat. 'Thank you, Mr Duffield.' She patted the top of his head as she walked out.

Amazed by the spectacle they had just witnessed, Nus, Tom and Harri gawped at George, who was wobbling slightly in his kneeling position.

'Wow, George, you old romantic you,' Harri grinned. 'Didn't realise you had it in you.'

'I don't. I just couldn't face an entire morning of her moping around doing no cleaning,' George barked back. 'Now quit mickey-taking and help me up, will you? I think my back's gone . . .'

Rob was not impressed by Geoff Bincham's early morning proposal, although the thought of the old man reading *OK!* with his full English did amuse him.

'I never had old man Bincham down as a celebrity junkie,' he laughed, twisting spaghetti onto his fork. 'He's such a gruff old beggar whenever I see him.'

'You've never forgiven him for sending you off in that under-sixteens cup match, have you?'

'Well, I reckon his eyesight was going even then. He was a rubbish referee. So when's this all taking place?'

'Just before Christmas.' Harri took a sip of wine and watched the candle flickering on the restaurant table between them. 'I think it's romantic.'

She looked around at the other diners in the small Italian restaurant. It was unusual for Rob to suggest they ate out, even at weekends, let alone on a Wednesday night. So when he had texted her that afternoon to tell her he had booked a table at Violetta's, she was delighted.

She looked back at him and thought again how handsome he looked. He certainly seemed to be making an effort after the brief Preston blip in September – in fact, he had barely even mentioned work for the best part of a month. It couldn't have happened at a better time: all the frustration she was feeling with the Alex–Chelsea situation had demanded so much of her thoughts recently that she needed things with Rob to be on an even keel. She gazed into his eyes, the thrill of their unexpected closeness bubbling up inside her. 'Anyway, don't you go pretending you're a love cynic, Rob Southwood. After all, you're the one who booked a break at an impossibly romantic Scottish castle for us.'

Rob gave an overdramatic sigh and rolled his eyes. 'You've rumbled me. I confess, I am a closet romantic.' He lowered his voice, 'But keep it quiet. I'm just not ready to come out in public with it yet, OK?'

Harri giggled. 'Don't worry, your secret's safe with me.'

News of the Binchams' marriage vow renewal spread around Stone Yardley like wildfire. Geoff Bincham had been very specific about what he wanted. 'We need one of them celebrity weddings with all the trimmings. Only the best for me and my Eth.' Rising to the challenge, the people of Stone Yardley rallied round: Auntie Rosemary offered to provide flowers, Viv used her powers of persuasion (and, rumour had it, a rather splendid three-layer chocolate cake) to secure Stone Yardley Village Hall at short notice, and Harri was volunteered to enlist the help of Alex for catering purposes. Harri strongly suspected that this had been Viv's idea as a way of cajoling her son into taking part, but she agreed anyway. At least it would give her a rare opportunity to spend some time with him sans Chelsea.

By Friday of that week, the weather had turned decidedly wintry. Graphite-grey clouds shrouded Stone Yardley in stubborn dankness, while incessant rain, driven by blustering wind, pummelled its streets and inhabitants. George, who had proclaimed to his bemused staff that he was suffering from Seasonal Affective Disorder and insisted on ensconcing himself in his office gazing at a daylight simulation lamp, had made the decision to close at three o'clock. Unsurprisingly, nobody tried to dissuade him – in fact, Tom and Nus had switched off their computers and grabbed their coats before George had even finished talking. After checking that her boss was feeling well enough to lock up by himself, Harri left and battled her way down the High Street with her umbrella bending under the force of the wind and rain until she reached Wātea.

Delicious aromas of coffee and the comforting warmth of Wātea's interior wrapped around her senses like a giant hug as she entered, leaving the stormy street and weather-beaten shoppers behind. The coffee lounge was half full with customers obviously taking their time to put off having to step outside again.

Alex was wiping down the counter and didn't notice Harri's

arrival. She approached and knocked her fist on the vintage wood.

'Knock, knock?'

Alex's head jerked up and he smiled. 'Hey, stranger! What brings you to my establishment this early on a Friday?'

'Oh, you know, the wind blew me in.'

Genuine pleasure lit up Alex's face. 'Terrible when the weather does that to you, eh?'

Enjoying the glimpse of the Alex she had been missing so much, Harri grinned back. 'Dreadful. So, any chance of a coffee?'

Alex folded his arms and took a sharp intake of breath. 'I'm afraid that's only possible if it accompanies a seriously large slab of chocolate fudge cake.'

Harri shrugged. 'Then I have no choice.'

'Cool. Pick a table and I'll bring it over.'

Harri chose a table by one of the few remaining photographs from Alex's travels (him pointing at a Route 66 sign next to the most enormous American sedan she had ever seen), peeled off her coat and unwound the scarf Auntie Rosemary had made for her at the Knit 'n' Natter group last year, draping them both on the back of her chair. Smoothing down the auburn curls that had blown free from her ponytail during her blustery trek here, she looked around the room, noting how much had changed since Chelsea had arrived on the scene. Gone were the treasures from Alex's adventures – the Masai blanket, African masks and Australian dream-time art; the stacks of travel magazines in wicker baskets by the sides of sofas had been replaced with month-old editions of glossy women's magazines and the kind of celebrity gossip rags that Geoff Bincham would have been in seventh heaven with. It was as if the brave, free spirit of Wātea had been subdued behind the bars of somebody else's opinion – and Harri couldn't ignore her sadness at its unwelcome incarceration.

'Your obscenely calorific confection, ma'am,' Alex said, pushing a large slab of moist, dark cake layered with thick, chocolate fudge frosting, sprinkled with pink sugar crystals. 'The sparkles are complimentary, by the way.'

'How fab are those! Where did they come from?'

Taking the seat opposite, Alex handed her a mug of coffee and took a sip from his own. 'Abigail Reece had her birthday party here after school yesterday.'

'Really? You hosted a kids' party?'

'Well, she came in with her mum and best friend from school, so I got Brenda to dash to the Co-op for candles and girly cake decorations.'

'Al, that's so sweet.'

He dismissed the comment, stealing a small corner of her cake with his teaspoon. 'Nah, it's just that I know it's been tough for them since Paul left. Plus, it's not every day you turn eight.'

'You big softie. I think that's really nice, though.'

'Well, thank you.'

They exchanged smiles, Harri loving the total absence of tension between them.

'I have a confession to make, actually.'

This sparked his interest and he leaned forward eagerly. 'You do? Ooh, this had better be a juicy revelation. It's been far too dull a day so far.'

'Sorry to disappoint. I'm here on the scrounge, I'm afraid.'

'Typical. Let me guess: my mother sent you?'

'No. Well, she might have unofficially had something to do with it, but that's just a suspicion on my part. Mr and Mrs Bincham are renewing their marriage vows next month and we're all clubbing together to throw a party for them at the Village Hall.'

'So you need food?'

Harri gave a sheepish smile. 'Bingo.'

Leaning back in his chair, Alex crossed his arms behind his head and appeared to be in deep thought. As he did so, Harri caught a glimpse of his carved Maori bead necklace, hidden well beneath the collar of his girlfriend-approved GAP T-shirt. The sight of it made her inexplicably happy – as if it were proof that not all of him had been Chelsea-ised yet. 'We-ell, I don't know, being so close to Christmas and everything . . .'

Harri's heart plummeted. 'Oh . . .'

A huge smirk broke free. 'You are so easy to wind up, H! Of course I'll do it. I think it's wonderful what they're doing. But there's one condition.'

'OK, what?'

'You help me. I don't mind giving my time for free but I can't ask Brenda or the other girls to do the same. Do we have a deal, Ms Langton?'

Harri shook his hand. 'Absolutely.'

That weekend, Stella replied to Harri's email.

From: stellababy@danbeagle.co.uk
To: armchairtraveller@gmail.com
Subject: Eek!
Blimey, when I asked for gossip I wasn't expecting anything nearly as interesting as that! Poor you, H!
First off, let me say what you're too nice to write: Al's woman sounds like a right old nightmare! I bet you want to scratch her eyes

out when she does that competing thing. Can't abide that myself, but then, thankfully, I'm not you. If I was in your shoes I'd probably have committed GBH by now . . . And what he said to Jack! If you ask me, he thoroughly deserves to end up with a nightmare girlfriend. (Actually, Dan said I need to learn to be more compassionate, so we're going to visit this old monk friend of his in Tibet soon. You never know, I might be all chilled and **chi** the next time I see you!)

One thing I would say, though (and I can only say this seeing as I'm thousands of miles away and therefore you can't punch me) – are you **sure** the reason you feel so strongly about Chelsea is that you're just looking out for Al? Only it strikes me that he's dated awful women before and none of them ever seemed to bother you like this one . . . I'm not suggesting anything, it's just an observation.

Things are good here, although I swear that if and when I get to heaven I'm going to have a good old chat with the Almighty about why he created mosquitoes. I mean, what purpose do they serve? Flipping, horrible, buzzy bitey things. Honestly, H, I've got so many bites I look like a pepperoni pizza. Good job Dan's smitten with me, that's all I can say, because it's **not** a pretty sight.

Email me back soon – this is more fun than I expected ☺

Stel xxx

Stella's words brought comfort and disquiet in equal proportions and they played on Harri's mind all weekend as she helped Rob to tidy his loft – one of those jobs that aren't much fun at the best of times, but are somehow tolerable with two people tackling it. As a reward for their dusty labours, Rob suggested they go to the Sunday night pub quiz. Harri, grateful for the distraction, agreed and, as Sunday night approached, she even caught herself looking forward to the chance of being immersed in meaningless trivia for a couple of hours.

The absolute last thing she was expecting to find when they walked into the Star and Highwayman was Alex sitting amidst his mates with Chelsea dangling off his lap. Judging by his friends' expressions, they didn't expect to witness this either. They sat in polite audience around Alex and Chelsea, their faces pulled into too-tight smiles as they did their best to sustain an air of normality. Rob's fingers gripped Harri's in a reflex action when he saw Alex – which made Harri feel secure. She was here with her boyfriend who was proud to walk into his local pub holding her hand; the boyfriend who, in little under a month from now, would be whisking her away to an impossibly romantic Scottish castle where they *just happened* to do weddings . . .

Rob's friends had already commandeered a table and, considering the sheer number of people seated round it, were either attempting a new world record for the largest pub team or else working on the theory that the more bodies present, the better their chances of winning the grand prize of five drinks vouchers. Cathy Simpkiss waved at Harri and beckoned her over to claim the two remaining seats amongst the throng, as Rob headed to the bar to order drinks.

'Harri! It's lovely to see you!' The others smiled and nodded their hellos.

293

'Hi, Cathy. Hey, everyone.'

Cathy nudged her. 'You and Roberto look pretty cosy this evening. Anything I should know about?'

Harri could feel her cheeks making a valiant bid to match her hair colour. 'No, we're just happy.'

'I reckon she's up the duff,' a broad guy in a well-filled rugby shirt piped up, his comment met with sniggers from the other men. 'She's glowing tonight!'

'I am *not*, Trev, thank you very much. It's just hot in here.'

'Talking about me again, are you?' Rob said as he sat beside her, placing his pint and her red wine on the varnished table and pocketing his change.

'I was just saying, Rob, you two look loved-up tonight,' said Cathy.

Rob's arm slipped around Harri's shoulders and she leaned into the embrace, delighted by the gesture. 'Well, we are. Actually,' he sipped his pint, 'I'm taking this lovely lady of mine to a castle in Scotland for Christmas.'

'Leaving her there for Nessie to play with, are you?' laughed Kelvin, the tallest of the group by a good five inches.

'No, actually. We're having a romantic Christmas break,' Rob replied, his fingers caressing Harri's arm as he did so.

Buoyed by this, Harri let the jibes and jovial laughter swirl about her ears as she looked around the packed pub lounge at the other teams. Without thinking, her gaze rested on Alex's table. Unsurprisingly, Chelsea was holding court – in her element, knowing all eyes were fixed on her as she sat forward provocatively on Alex's lap, twisting a lock of brassy blonde hair coyly around her painted fingernails while she spoke.

Feeling her irritation rising, Harri switched her attention to Alex and noted, to her surprise, that he wasn't in awe of Chelsea's performance. A broad smile was painted across his lips, but his body language told a different story. As Harri tried to get a better view of his expression, his eyes suddenly locked with hers and he mouthed 'Hi' before Harri, reddening again, looked away.

Rob's fingers moved a strand of hair away from her face as her gaze returned to him. 'You OK, Red?'

Shaking the question mark from her mind, Harri snuggled against him and smiled. 'Yes, I'm fine. I love you.'

Rob bent down and kissed her forehead. 'Yeah, I know.'

There was a metallic screech of electronic feedback, followed by a couple of loud thumps as Colin, the larger-than-life compere of the pub quiz, looking like a radio DJ from the eighties with his bleached blond-streaked mullet, thin moustache and shades-of-beige patterned shirt, brandished his microphone. 'OK, ladies and gentlemen. Welcome to the infamous, world-famous Star and Highwayman Pub Quiz of Ultimate Info-tainment. You'll find quiz sheets on your tables, plus exclusive biros provided at considerable cost for your quizzing pleasure tonight. Please make sure you hand these back in at the end of the quiz, though, because, as you know, there *is* a national shortage.'

The assembled quiz teams laughed politely, even though Colin's biro-shortage joke had been recycled more times than the average milk bottle.

'Eyes down, here we go for the first round . . .'

As the quiz progressed, Harri had to resist the urge to sneak a glance at Alex. To her knowledge, this was the first time he had been seen in public with Chelsea and, if his earlier expression was anything to go by, it might be proving to be more of a trial than he had anticipated.

'Capital of Colombia?' Trev repeated under his breath, as the team huddled around him.

'Isn't it something like Colombia City?' Cathy suggested.

'No, I don't think so.'

Kelvin frowned. 'For some reason I have Caracas in my mind.'

'That's Venezuela's capital. Colombia's is Bogota,' Harri answered, loving the proud expression on Rob's face as the rest of the team congratulated her.

'My secret weapon, aren't you, Red?'

In the middle of the anagram round – something Harri could never work out – she took the opportunity to head to the ladies', leaving Rob's team deep in deliberation. The toilet cubicle smelled of stale cigarettes and the tell-tale remnants of somebody's rebellion against the smoking ban were bobbing accusingly in the toilet bowl. As she emerged into the relative freshness of the washroom area, Harri was aware of the main door to the ladies' opening. Looking up from the washbasin, she came face to face with false eyelashes, fake tan and a stormy-looking orange-foundationed expression. Chelsea was *not* amused.

'Oh, hi, Chelsea. Enjoying the pub quiz?'

'What the hell are you playing at?'

Nice to meet you too, Chelsea. 'Sorry?'

'You know.'

Harri shook the excess water from her hands and walked over to the roller towel, yanking it down with perhaps a little more vigour than normal. 'I have no idea what you're on about.'

'Oh, yes, you do. Being all lovey-dovey with your boyfriend, answering all those questions and looking so smug, making Alex look at you all the time like he wishes he was on your team.'

Harri had to laugh at the preposterousness of this. '*Excuse me?* You obviously don't know your boyfriend as well as you

296

think you do, mate. He'd rather bum-walk on hot coals than join Rob's mates for a packet of peanuts, let alone a pub quiz. They wind him up, Chelsea, that's why he's staring them out. It's a ritual.'

Chelsea remained where she was, hands on hips, chewing her gum frantically. 'Yeah, well – it didn't look like that to me.'

Despite her steadily building anger at Chelsea's attitude, Harri kept a friendly smile firmly in place. 'Don't worry, Alex only has eyes for you.' She began to walk towards the door, but was stopped abruptly by Chelsea's surprisingly strong grip on her arm.

'And that's the way it's *always* going to be, right? Alex is mine now and he knows I'm the best there is for him. Sooner or later he's going to get tired of his geek friends – and sooner or later, he's going to get tired of *you*. I'm the most important thing in his life, yeah, so you just need to get over it and walk away.'

Harri's heartbeat pulsed deafeningly in her ears. 'What did you say?'

'You heard. Back off. The best thing you can do for Alex is to leave him alone. He doesn't need you whining in his ear about how tragic your life is and how you never get to travel anywhere. Oh, yeah, he told me that. It's so sad, Harri: you think he's being friendly, but really you're just someone he feels sorry for.'

'He said that, did he?'

'Yeah. He said you were a pathetic charity case and he was just taking pity on you 'cos your mum and dad snuffed it.'

That was the last straw. Burning hot anger and hurt bubbled up like molten lava deep inside her, and she felt her hands clenching into incensed fists. She had to get out of there – *quickly* – or else she might end up doing something she

297

regretted. Without another word, she flung open the door to the pub lounge and left a smirking Chelsea assuming centre stage in the ladies'.

For the rest of the night, she sat rigidly by Rob's side, unwilling to let anyone else see the offence and indignation searing through her like a raging firestorm. How *dare* she say that stuff – and, more to the point, how *dare* Alex say that about her, for the second time?

As she sat numbly in the passenger seat of Rob's car on the journey home, Harri came to an important conclusion: Alex was welcome to Chelsea; it was the last time she would let him get close to her.

CHAPTER SEVENTEEN

All I Want for Christmas . . .

Viv coughs and Harri hears the chair legs scuffing on the floor tiles as she shifts position.

'Viv, I'll be fine. You go – I just need a little more time.'

'Then I'll stay until you're ready.'

Squinting her eyes against the dull ache now throbbing its way around her eye sockets, Harri groans – out loud this time, hoping against hope that Viv will take the hint. 'Honestly, I don't need babysitting, Viv. I know you mean well and I really appreciate it, but I have to deal with this in my own way.'

'You're just like your mother,' Viv mutters, loud enough for her to hear.

'What?'

'I said, you're just like Niamh. *Stubborn.* As a donkey.'

'Don't you mean a mule?'

'No, Harriet, I mean a donkey. And don't be clever: I knew your mother a good many years longer than you did and I know about donkeys because my father kept them when I was little. Completely immovable when they want to be—'

Harri winces again. The headache is getting worse. 'Viv, do you have any paracetamol?'

Interrupted mid-flow, it takes Viv some time to back up. 'Well, I was just – er – paracetamol, did you say?'

'Or aspirin. Or pretty much anything as long as it's not ibuprofen.'

'Have you got a headache?'

'No, Viv, I'm thinking of topping myself with two tablets. *Of course*, I have a headache!'

Viv tuts, but Harri can hear her rummaging in her handbag. 'You've become so sarcastic since you came back. Here.'

A small packet of Panadol skids underneath the cubicle door, landing at Harri's feet. 'Thank you. Don't suppose you've got a bottle of water, have you?'

'What do you think I am – a minibar? Of course I haven't . . . Oh never mind,' the chair scrapes back, 'I'll go and see if I can find one. Stay where you are. And don't do anything stupid.'

Harri hangs her head. *It's too late for that . . .*

December blew into Stone Yardley with an icy intensity, stronger than even its older residents could remember witnessing before. First came the sharp frosts that added twenty minutes of windscreen scraping and spluttering engines to every car journey; a week later the whole area was shrouded in freezing fog, causing traffic to crawl at a snail's pace due to the shortened visibility; by the week before Christmas snow had claimed the roads and pavements, bringing cars, pedestrians and schools to a standstill.

Nevertheless, preparations for Ethel and Geoff Bincham's big day continued in earnest, contingencies being put in place daily as the arctic conditions prevailed. It was fortunate that Harri had asked Emily and Stu to help out, Stu being the proud owner of a bright red Massey Ferguson tractor complete with snow plough (which he had inherited from his father several years before).

'Even if we get ten-foot drifts, we'll get the Binchams to their party,' he'd joked, patting the back wheel of the tractor lovingly.

Since the pub quiz, Harri had found a plethora of plausible excuses for not spending time with Alex: she was getting more involved in setting up Emily and Stu's holiday business, or she had more work at SLIT, or she was spending time with Rob, who seemed to become more loving as the weeks went on. Alex didn't question any of these, but Harri suspected he had an opinion on it that she wasn't party to. Not that she cared, of course. Knowing that he had ridiculed her behind her back not once but *twice* was more painful than she would admit to anyone.

As the Binchams' celebration inched closer, Harri was aware that she would have to break the deadlock with Alex – albeit temporarily – in order to assist him with the catering. Dad had always impressed upon her the importance of keeping promises, no matter what, and it had consequently become a vital component of Harri's ongoing memorial to him. It was the reason she hadn't backed down from the 'Free to a Good Home' letters, helped Viv out of her many idiotic schemes and not broken her friendship with Stella when she got together with Dan. Like it or not, the fact remained that she had promised Alex she would help. And so it was that, with a heart heavier than a concrete overcoat, she trudged slowly across the snow-blanketed playing fields and past the church towards the town on the last Friday before Christmas. Snow was falling at an impressive rate: the large, feathery flakes that looked, as Mum used to put it, 'like they mean business' kissing her cold cheeks.

With SLIT closed due to the inclement weather, Harri had arranged to meet Alex at Wātea just after lunchtime to begin prepping dishes for the next day's celebration. Their phone conversation had been businesslike and to the point, with none of the usual banter. *What are we going to talk about?* Harri wondered, emerging onto the High Street. *What will we say to fill the hours?*

Only one brave couple was seated in Wātea, drinking hot chocolate with whipped cream and melting marshmallows, when Harri arrived.

'Aren't *you* a sight for sore eyes,' Brenda called from behind the counter as Harri took off her boots and changed into a pair of trainers. 'He's been like a bear with a migraine the last few weeks. How come we haven't seen you much lately?'

Harri was about to answer when Alex strode in from the kitchen, carrying a denim apron. 'She's been busy,' he said gruffly. 'Christmas and all that.'

Brenda caught the tension between them immediately. 'Righty-ho. Well, I'll hold the fort here and you guys get on with the stuff for tomorrow. I don't think we're likely to get a rush now, looking at the way that snow's coming down.'

Alex threw the apron at Harri and turned back to the kitchen. 'Yeah, well, call me if it gets too busy.'

Brenda raised an eyebrow at Harri, who quickly took off her coat, stashing it along with her bag and boots behind the counter. 'Good luck with Mr Mardy.'

Harri tied the apron around her waist. 'Thanks. I think I might need it.'

In all the time she had spent with Alex, Harri had never seen him like this. He spoke only to give her brief instructions – 'Chop those', 'Make this', 'Mix that' – and the remainder of the time he worked with head bowed, shoulders hunched, eye contact denied. Given Harri's reluctance to be here at all, that was just fine by her.

Brenda left at four o'clock, with no customers to serve and the snow building steadily on the pavement outside, and Harri was afforded a few minutes' respite from the stony silence when Alex left the kitchen to see his assistant manager to the door. Alone, she stared up at the strip lights and took a deep breath to steady her nerves. She was still angry at him, still reeling from his subtle betrayal, but to be in the same room with him totally devoid of any warmth was worse than not seeing him at all. Needing some noise to keep the silence at bay, she boiled the kettle, fetching two mugs and teabags from the storeroom.

'What's going on, Harri?' Alex demanded, striding back into the kitchen and facing her with eyes that laid her soul bare.

Exposed by his stare, Harri crossed her arms in front of her. 'I don't know what you mean.'

'This – *us*,' he stuttered. 'Why are you shutting me out?'

'I – I'm not . . .'

He stepped towards her, ready for a fight. 'Yes, you are. For weeks now. I can't deal with this, Harri; I don't understand it. I don't get why you've stopped calling, stopped visiting . . . It's like you've built this massive wall around yourself and I can't get in.'

So much of her wanted to deliver a devastating parting shot and leave, but at that moment Auntie Rosemary's words reverberated through her mind: *This isn't like you, Harri. This isn't who you are . . .*

'I just don't know how to be with you right now,' she answered slowly, every word considered before she spoke it. 'I'm not sure what to say, or what to believe . . .'

Alex's brow furrowed and Harri noticed how tired his eyes looked. 'What do you mean, what to believe? I'm not the one who's changed – I'm still the same.'

A weight crushed her throat, as if the air in the kitchen had suddenly become thicker than treacle, reducing her voice to a strained whisper. 'No you're not. You pity me.'

'What? No, Harri!'

She nodded slowly, unable to look at him now. 'Yes, you do. You were only spending time with me because you felt sorry for me.'

Alex shook his head, incredulity claiming his features. 'Where is all this coming from?'

Straightening up to bring her eyes level with his, Harri felt a shot of indignation firing down through her backbone. He was *not* going to make out this was all her imagination. Not now. 'I heard you, Alex. I heard you telling Jack you pitied me.'

His expression moved through disbelief and realisation to sheer horror and his voice cracked as he spoke. 'Hell, Harri, I—'

'Don't say you didn't mean it, OK? Say anything else, but don't deny what you said. I don't want you to lie to me because you feel embarrassed. It's better that I know the truth.'

'It *isn't* the truth.'

Harri's laugh was cold and hollow. 'Sure.'

'It's not!'

'You're forgetting, I *heard* you say it, Alex.'

'I know, I know that, but . . . but I was stupid. If I'd known you were listening—' He broke off when he saw her expression and pushed both hands up into his hair. 'Harri, you have to believe me: I didn't mean it. I don't pity you at all. Your friendship means the world to me, I – I'd never do anything to jeopardise that.'

She took a breath and released the second accusation. 'Then why did you tell Chelsea the same thing?'

His expression clouded. 'Chelsea?'

'She told me, a couple of weeks ago. Said you felt sorry for me because my parents died and I've had such a pathetically tragic life.'

'No, no, you've made a mistake, Harri. Chels wouldn't say that. I know she wouldn't.'

Harri began to quickly untie her apron, hurt and embarrassment making her hands clumsy. 'Whatever. I can't do this any more.'

Alex stepped forward and took hold of her shoulders. 'Stop – just *stop*, will you? This is ridiculous, Harri. I don't want to lose your friendship over this.' He paused, his dark eyes searching hers for any sign of forgiveness. 'OK, if you say she said that, then I believe you. I can't understand it and all I can think is that she's got her wires crossed somewhere. But I believe you, Harri.'

For a long time they remained, eyes locked, breathing like runners after a sprint, each one unsure of their next move. Stalemate. The closeness was disquieting, but Harri couldn't move.

A loud click from the kettle reaching the end of its boil made them both jump, breaking the tension between them. Alex's hand lowered as Harri's shoulders relaxed.

'I was making you tea,' she offered weakly.

'Good,' he replied, staring blankly at the kettle, then back at her. 'Why didn't you say anything about what I said to Jack?'

'Because I was hurt and angry. And I didn't want you to deny how you felt.'

'I honestly didn't mean that. I can't imagine not having you in my life. You're my closest friend and I depend on you more than I let on.'

'Then why say it? Twice?'

He stared at her. 'Jack was winding me up and I – I suppose

305

I just said something to shut him up. And Chels – well, I did tell her about your mum and dad, but I swear I never said I pitied you. Look, H, I can't excuse being an idiot, but I really am so sorry I hurt you.' He glanced back at the kettle. 'Will you be staying for a cuppa?'

Harri summoned the tiniest of smiles forward for duty. 'I guess I will.'

The ceasefire was uneasy and far from a full armistice, but it was sufficient to slacken the strain between them. They drank their tea slowly, Harri aware of a thousand thoughts trekking across Alex's brow. When she reached out to collect his empty mug, Alex caught her arm, gathering her up in his arms, not waiting for an invitation, and they hugged uncomfortably for several awkward moments, Alex prolonging it for much longer than Harri did.

By the time Harri left, she was feeling more positive. While it was clear that it would take more than a cup of tea and a faltering hug to repair the damage done over the last few months, it felt like a step in the right direction. Their friendship had survived its biggest test in years.

But unbeknown to both of them, a larger ordeal lay ahead.

Preparations for the Binchams' big day started early the next morning. When Harri arrived at the snow-covered church, Auntie Rosemary was already there, wobbling on the top step of her trusty stepladder as she attempted to fit a garland around the stone doorway.

'Auntie Rosemary, what on earth are you doing?'

'Won't be a tick, Harri. Be a dear: hold these, would you?' She passed down a handful of foliage sprigs and a pair of secateurs.

'How long have you been here?'

Rosemary tutted and straightened a pink ribbon bow near the middle of the garland. 'Ah, that's better. I'm sorry, my darling, what were you saying?'

Harri smiled. 'Nothing. So, what can I do?'

Rosemary carefully made her way back down the ladder and dug in her cardigan pocket for a shabby-looking folded envelope with writing on the back. 'Let's see . . . um . . . could you fit the end of pew arrangements for me? They just need hanging.'

'No problem.'

'Excellent.' She pulled a chewed biro from the messy bun at the back of her head and ticked another two items off her list. 'That's almost everything done. Not bad, considering I only arrived here at six this morning.'

'*Only?*'

They walked into the church together. 'Believe me, Harriet, six o'clock is practically a lie-in compared to some weddings I've worked on over the years. It used to drive your cousins mad when I got them up before the birds, dragging them out with me because I had wedding flowers to do.'

'Oh, I bet James loved that!' Harri laughed.

'Well, let's just say I wasn't his favourite person in the summer,' Rosemary replied, sitting down on a pew and rubbing her back. 'So is Rob coming tonight?'

'Yes. There wasn't any point asking him to help with the preparations today: he's useless at anything practical.'

Auntie Rosemary nodded, but her eyes had a strange look to them. 'You are happy, aren't you, darling?'

Harri hated this question. After all, what did it mean? Was it possible to be happy with every arena of your life, or was it more a case of getting the majority of it somewhere near happy and ignoring the rest? In many ways Harri loved her life – her

307

little cottage, her job (for all its annoyances and frustrations it was the best occupation in the world for her), Rob, her friends and her travel books . . . In that sense she was content. But the loneliness waiting for her whenever she was by herself, the queue of dreams still waiting unfulfilled – in these areas she was far from where she wanted to be. 'I'm good, thanks.'

'That's not what I asked.' Rosemary stood suddenly, her eyes drifting away up the aisle. 'I'll just be up by the pulpit if you need anything, all right?'

Surprised by her aunt's sudden shift in demeanour, Harri set to work.

From the church she went straight to the Binchams' house to deliver a small blue brooch that had been her mother's, for Ethel to wear. The house was a flurry of activity, with seemingly half the females of Stone Yardley crammed into the front room of the Edwardian blue-brick semi, whilst Geoff and several friends were in the process of being evicted down the stairs by Ethel's sister, Flo.

'. . . but shouldn't I wait with our Eth?' Geoff protested.

'You can see her at the church, Geoffrey, and that's the end of it. Now get your backside out of that door!' Flo demanded, bundling her brother-in-law and his entourage out into the porch with surprising force for a lady of her age. 'This is about the only time we's'll ask you to go down the pub, so you'd best make the most of it!'

In the middle of the front room, Mrs Bincham was standing shakily on a small footstool as the women fussed around her, the back of her cream dress hitched up on an ironing board while a red-faced relative ironed the hem with great enthusiasm. The room smelled of violets and lavender, and the faces of the Binchams' children and grandchildren smiled down from gilt frames clustered upon the mantelpiece.

'Stand still, our Eth,' the ironing lady boomed. 'We don't want you all creased up going down the aisle, do we?'

'But I'm going to have to sit down in the car,' Ethel protested, to no avail. Her face lit up when she saw Harri. 'Oh, Harriet, you're here.'

'You look lovely, Mrs B,' she smiled, handing her the brooch. 'Here's something borrowed and blue for you. It's old as well.'

Beaming, she accepted it. 'Oh, it's proper bostin', our kid. Proper bostin' . . .' She sniffed and caused a minor panic amongst the fussing female guests, who rushed up with hankies. Shooing them away, she smiled down at Harri. 'Mind you, I'm pretty much sorted for the something old – our Geoff'll do for that!'

It quickly became apparent that nothing was going to go to plan today. At ten o'clock Harri parked her car in the small car park at the Village Hall, having had to make three detours already: to pick up extra balloons from Clownaround, the party supplies shop in Ellingsgate; to collect a celebration cake that had been kindly donated by Sugarbuds cake shop; and, finally, when she was halfway to the Village Hall, a call from George had her turning the car round and heading back to SLIT to pick up a box of wine he had offered for the party that evening.

At least there had been no more snow. Instead, the pale winter sun shone brightly, causing the lying snow to sparkle like the Clarnico Mint Creams that Grandma Langton had always handed round at Christmas.

Alex was lifting catering crates from the boot of his car when Harri arrived.

'Hey, you. I thought you were aiming to be here an hour ago.'

Harri balanced the three cake boxes on the roof of her car as she shut the passenger door. 'Don't ask. I've somehow managed to clock up ten miles over a two-mile journey.'

'Some skill you have there. Need a hand with those?'

'Nope, I'm good. Lead the way, sir!'

As they unpacked boxes, set up tables, fixed balloons and streamers around the hall, their conversation flowed easily – much to Harri's relief after the turmoil of recent months. It was wonderful, and Harri dared to hope that it was a good sign for the future.

Viv breezed in at half-past two, apologising profusely for her tardiness and offering to help. True to form, she had arrived at the very moment everything was done, but – as she pointed out – it was the thought that counted, wasn't it? Still, at least she found one useful thing to do and, five minutes later, they stood in the middle of the hall drinking hot tea from an eclectic selection of mugs.

'I never had you down as a Stourbridge Town fan, Mum,' Alex said, pointing at her mug.

'I rather like their colours. I'm thinking of signing up for a season ticket, what do you think? Anyway, *you* can talk: apparently you feel like Chicken Tonight.'

'Why on earth would anyone have a mug with that on it?' Harri chuckled.

Alex laughed. 'Evidently they don't any more, seeing as it's here.'

'Well, I really don't know what to make of mine,' said Harri, turning her Hamlet Cigar mug round to reveal the legend 'For the man who thinks that little bit bigger'.

'I shudder to think,' Viv said, looking at her watch. 'Gracious me! Look at the time! We have to change and get over to St Mary's for four!'

Quickly, they finished their tea and donned hats, coats and gloves to head out into the chilly afternoon.

The saying goes that you're never too old to be in love: in Ethel and Geoff's case this was undeniably true. Forty-three years since he had complimented her Melting Moments, they appeared as smitten with each other as ever.

The packed congregation's excited chatter hushed as Etta James's sultry voice began to sing the opening lines of 'At Last', accompanied by sweeping strings. Harri gave Rob's warm hand beside her an involuntary squeeze as the sheer romance of the song and the occasion lifted her heart. Before the ceremony, Rob had arrived at the church fifteen minutes after Harri, surprising her by catching her hand and spinning her round for a very public kiss – much to the surprise of Alex and Viv, who she was standing with at the time. Viv smiled politely, but Alex looked away, an odd expression on his face.

The whole of the church smelled of winter roses, freesias and lilies. Auntie Rosemary had done the Binchams proud: every available flat surface had been adorned with flowers in hues of palest yellow, white, cream and lilac. Instead of Geoff waiting nervously alone by the altar, he had chosen to walk in with Ethel; and as the song swelled around the vaulted arches of the red sandstone church, in they came – Geoff proudly dressed in his best suit, escorting the love of his life down the aisle. She was wearing a white lace shrug over her cream dress, and a pale yellow rose was nestled amongst her newly set grey curls.

They made their way slowly past smiling friends and family – mainly because both of them had received new hips in the last eighteen months – but it all added to the effect, imbuing their entrance with a slow-motion quality. As the song neared its conclusion, they stopped by the chancel step and Pete, the curate, took his place in front of them.

'Welcome, everyone, to this very special day. I must say that you all scrub up pretty well for a Saturday – it's nice to see Stone Yardlians don't save their finery for a Sunday only.'

A rumble of laughter passed around the pews.

'And now to the best bit. Ethel and Geoff will renew the vows they made to each other over forty years ago, as a symbol of their continuing commitment to, and love for, one another. Shall we stand and pray . . .'

And so, surrounded by people who loved them, the Binchams stood and reaffirmed their promises to love, honour and cherish one another for the rest of their lives; tears welling in Geoff's eyes as he gazed at his wife, adding, 'You'm bostin' pet,' in a whisper at the end, to which Ethel replied, 'You ay too bad yerself,' in reply. It was a humbling experience to witness this tender exchange of promises between the Black Country couple.

'I think you should kiss your bride, Geoff,' Pete smiled.

'Too right!' Geoff replied, swooping Ethel into a Clark Gable-style clinch as the assembled guests broke into applause.

'Put me down, Geoffrey!' Ethel laughed, but her eyes were alive as she playfully reprimanded her husband. Watching the two of them now, so in love and so much a part of one another, Harri was certain that neither of them saw an old person smiling back. In their eyes they were the same young, beautiful dreamers whose hearts had connected over a tea trolley forty-three years ago.

'That was amazing,' Harri said, as she and Rob drove along wintry streets back to the Village Hall.

312

'Yeah,' he replied, gazing out of the window. 'Reckon that'll be us in forty-three years' time?'

Harri made a mental calculation to see how old she would be by then. It wasn't a comforting conclusion . . . 'That's if we can have the aisle widened for our Zimmer frames.'

'I'm sure that won't be a problem,' he laughed. 'Better put it in the diary then.'

To hear Rob considering their long-term future together was everything Harri had hoped for. Her thoughts immediately drifted to this Christmas. Spending such a magical time of year with the man she loved was a thrilling prospect, and part of her still found it hard to believe that it was going to be a reality in less than a week. Despite the tricky terrain of this year, they had emerged stronger than ever, and now their future seemed brighter than she could have dared hope for. He seemed ready to commit, if his constant hints over recent weeks were anything to go by. And, if that happened, maybe next year he would fulfil her heart's deepest desire and they would walk hand in hand through the Venetian splendour of the city of her dreams on their honeymoon.

Geoff Bincham was certainly true to his word when he said he wanted 'one of them celebrity weddings'. Two magnificent-looking thrones, which the Beckhams themselves would have been envious of, had been placed at the top table – although Ethel and Geoff had been warned sternly by Enid Weatherington of St Mary's Craft Guild not to lean back on them, 'because the papier-mâché won't cope with the weight'. The WI had supplied little satin bags embroidered with an intertwining E&G motif for the bridal favours, filled with gold chocolate dragees. Geoff had wanted to release doves when they arrived at their reception, but with doves being hard to come by in Stone Yardley, this had proved impossible. However, at the eleventh hour, Geoff's cousin

Alf had stepped into the breach: and so, at five p.m., floodlit by security lights and with their assembled guests around them, Ethel and Geoff hesitantly opened four long wicker baskets to release twenty racing pigeons in a cloud of feathers and beating wings from the car park of the Village Hall.

After speeches and toasts, the guests helped to move tables and chairs aside to make way for dancing. Unbeknown to Geoff and Ethel (who were bracing themselves for a night of dubious tracks from Disco Dave, Stone Yardley's resident DJ), Rod Norton from Stone Yardley High School had arranged for the area swing band to come and play, filling the small hall with the irresistible music of George Gershwin, Glenn Miller and Cole Porter.

Chelsea was conspicuous by her absence – having booked a weekend away with her girlfriends a month before – so Alex danced with his mother, and from her vantage point behind a table halfway down the hall, Harri understood a little more of Viv's all-encompassing desire to see her son happy. Twirling and laughing, her love for him beamed out like a Wallis-attired beacon. It made Harri smile, despite the ache in her heart, at the sight of the parental bond she missed so keenly at events such as this. Her parents would have been straight up on that dancefloor, twisting and bopping without a worry in the world.

Looking around, Harri was suddenly aware that Rob was no longer sitting by her side. She glanced over at the bar, but he wasn't there either; neither was he outside in the car park with his friends, sneaking a crafty cigarette. Harri was just about to hurry back inside when Rob appeared, strolling through the snow from behind the hall. He was hunched over his mobile, jacket collar turned up against the cold as he walked, and he stopped dead when he saw her.

'Hey,' he said, his voice slightly strained.

'I was wondering where you were. Is everything OK?' Harri asked, a sudden shot of caution lancing through her peace of mind.

It was almost as if he looked straight through her. 'I'm fine. Look, do you mind if we go now? I don't really feel like dancing and it's been a bit of a tough week.'

Mystified, Harri nodded. 'Um, yeah, OK. Let me get my coat and say goodbye to Geoff and Ethel.'

Rob turned to walk away. 'I'll be in the car.'

Her relaxed state shattered, she hurried quickly inside, collecting her coat and bag before approaching the Binchams, who were swaying jerkily to 'In the Mood'.

'Must you go?' Mrs B asked as she hugged her, disappointed. 'I've not seen you dance yet.'

'I'm sorry. I don't think Rob's feeling too good – he's been working really hard lately.' Picking her way carefully past the dancing guests, she headed for the door, but turned back when she heard someone call her name.

Alex jogged towards her. 'You off?'

''Fraid so. Rob wants to go home.'

'Loser. Why don't you drop him off and come back to boogie?' His dark eyes twinkled beneath the fairy lights.

'I can't, sorry. But it's been a wonderful day.'

'It has.' Alex's stare was a little too intense for comfort. 'Thanks for your help, H. I couldn't have done it without you.'

'You're welcome. Have a good night.'

'I will. Hey, I'm doing food for the Christmas Amble on Tuesday night. Fancy sous chef-ing again for me?'

'Sure, as long as I've done all my packing – we head off for Scotland on Wednesday morning.'

'Ah, yes. The great unexpected romantic break. Well, text me if you're able to help, yeah?'

315

'I will. G'night.'

He leaned forward and kissed her cheek. ''Night, Harri.'

Rob was silent for the entire journey back to his house, which only served to intensify Harri's sense of impending doom. When they walked into his hallway, he stopped and slowly faced her.

'You – er – might not want to stay tonight.'

'Don't be silly, I've got all my stuff with me and—'

'I can't do the Scotland trip.'

'S-sorry?'

It appeared that he couldn't bring himself to look her in the eye, shoving his hands into his corduroy jacket pockets and staring down at the beige carpet. 'Something's come up.'

Heart reeling, Harri placed her hands on her hips, staring at him in disbelief. 'What on earth could have come up over Christmas?'

'I'm really sorry, I know how much you were looking forward to it and it's the last thing I wanted to happen. But this is important, Red.'

This was not turning into the night she thought it would be. 'I should flippin' well hope so. I'd hate to be let down over something *trivial*.'

'See, I knew you'd act like this.'

It was too late for damage limitation. Harri's crushing disappointment and hurt were fuelling her anger. 'Act like what, exactly? Like someone who's been looking forward to something for weeks and has just been told it isn't happening? How long have you known about this – this *thing*?'

'Baby, I got the call only half an hour ago.'

'Who from?'

He groaned. 'It doesn't matter.'

'Well, I think it does. I'm curious to know who is so

316

important that they can command you to do something over Christmas.'

'It's *work*, OK?'

Hearing the 'w' word kicked her indignation up to another level entirely. 'It's *Christmas*, Rob. And you promised.'

At last, his eyes met hers and it was clear from his guilty stare that he knew exactly how much he was letting her down. 'Please, Red, you have to believe me. If it was any other job I'd tell them to get lost.'

Harri closed her eyes, her whole body shaking intensely now. 'Preston.'

His voice lowered. 'Yes, Preston. I thought we had it in the bag but there's been – um – a development.'

'What? Someone die? World War Three been declared?'

'My line manager's resigned. The bosses have cancelled everyone's leave for the next two weeks. I either work or I don't have a job to come back to in the New Year.'

Harri felt the flames of anger extinguishing slowly. 'They can't do that, can they?'

Rob shrugged. 'They can do whatever they like at the moment. Sales staff are ten a penny right now and everyone's competing for the same jobs. If I don't do this, there will be twenty other people willing to step into my place. You have to believe me, I was *vicious* with them when they phoned. If there was any way to avoid it, I would. My hands are tied – what can I do?'

'Well, it's not fair.'

He reached out and placed his hand on her shoulder. 'I know, baby. I'll make it up to you, I promise.'

Feeling her dream splintering, Harri looked away. When she spoke, her voice was the mousy, resigned version of herself that she hated so much. 'When do you have to go?'

He sighed. 'I'll catch a train in the morning and head straight up there.'

'But what about your Christmas present?'

'We'll have to do all that when I get back.'

She couldn't believe how quickly her time with Rob had been snatched away. The injustice of it all was too much to bear; it was as if all the promise of the past couple of months was being cruelly snuffed out. 'In two weeks?'

'Yes. I'm sorry, Red. I know how much this break meant to you.'

'To both of us,' the confident version of herself screamed out inside her head. 'Didn't it?'

For Harri, the remainder of the weekend passed in a soulless fog, the brave ship of hope that had sustained her now dashed and wrecked beyond repair. Rob's texts were apologetic but immaterial: the inescapable reality of his absence spoke volumes. So, once again, as countless times before, Harri carefully folded up her disappointment and packed it away with the remnants of dreams long dead.

On Tuesday, SLIT closed early to allow Tom, Nus, Harri and George time to get ready for one of the highlights of the town's calendar: the Christmas Amble.

Every year in Stone Yardley, the shops and businesses joined with the local Lions Club, Rotary Club and WI to host a late-night Christmas shopping event. This year's was Dickens-themed, and the locals had gone to town with authentic costumes, preposterous ladies' hats and bustling crinolines. Hot-chestnut stalls, Victorian games like shove ha'penny and bar skittles, a barrel organ and carol singers lined the streets as shoppers milled around, buying last-minute presents, cakes and treats for the impending festive season. Strings of coloured lights lit up the streets and candle lanterns burned in every shop window, bathing the whole of the High Street in a warm, multihued glow. Lavender's Bakery had even hired a snow machine, which enthusiastically festooned unsuspecting shoppers with white foam flakes from the flat above the shop as they passed by underneath. The Salvation Army band were playing Christmas carols with great gusto and, with the remnants of the previous week's snowfall still covering the pavements, the whole of the town centre was filled with a wonderfully Christmassy atmosphere.

Wātea was providing hot chocolate and slices of toasted fruit loaf with lashings of butter for the chilly shoppers' pleasure, with proceeds going to the local children's hospice. Alex was dressed in a long, dark grey tailcoat, a red muffler knotted at his neck, with a grey striped waistcoat and white shirt beneath. To complete the look, a brushed satin top hat was perched on his head, at a typically Alex-like jaunty angle. The sight of him made Harri smile – after all the darkness of the last couple of days it was wonderful to see a friendly face.

'Mistress Langton! How delightful to see you this festive night of nights!'

Harri managed to salvage a smile and wrapped Auntie Rosemary's borrowed crochet shawl tighter around her body.

'Show us the frock then,' Alex grinned.

Obediently, Harri did a little twirl, thanking heaven that Tom's sister was the wardrobe mistress for a semi-professional opera society and had brought in a selection of Victorian gowns that afternoon for her to try on. The periwinkle-blue dress complemented her eyes, while the cream shawl set off her red curls piled up and pinned at the back of her head. 'Will I do?'

'Absolutely. You look great, H. No, I mean it. The colour of that dress looks amazing with your hair . . .' He paused, a self-conscious smile lingering on his lips.

'Thanks,' Harri laughed awkwardly, and the moment was gone.

'Right – um – you take over buttering duties from me while I go and refill the chocolate pot, OK?'

She watched as he disappeared inside Wātea, a little unnerved by his unexpected reaction. Quickly dismissing it, she picked up the butter knife and began to work.

This year's Christmas Amble was one of the best attended, due in no small part to a concerted effort by shopkeepers and volunteers alike to spread the word. It even had its own Facebook page, set up by one of the High School pupils as part of a media studies project, and a group of students were shooting video footage to upload onto YouTube. The fusion of Dickensian nostalgia and twenty-first-century social media was a strangely amusing one and, despite her bruised heart, Harri had to smile.

Alex returned with a large vacuum flask of hot chocolate and together they set about serving the fast-growing queue. For the best part of two hours their activity barred any opportunity for conversation, except for the odd observation or fleeting joke. As the crowds began to thin and stalls closed, Alex nudged Harri.

'So – lookin' forward to a wee bit o' lovin' in the Highlands tomorrow, eh?'

Entirely without warning, Harri burst into tears. Shocked, Alex grabbed the cash box and ushered her inside the warmth of Wātea.

'Hey, hey, what's the matter?'

Surprised by the suddenness of her emotion, Harri was unable to speak, racked as she was by violent sobs. Alex, thrown from his comfort zone by the sight of his distraught friend, watched helplessly, stroking her arm with hesitant fingers. So there they stood, the buzz of the ultraviolet bug catcher the only intervening sound for several uncomfortable minutes. When her tears subsided, Harri wiped her eyes and blew out a long breath. 'Wow, I'm sorry. Don't ask me where that came from.'

'It must've come from somewhere,' Alex said carefully, his voice low and serious.

She could dismiss it, play it down or laugh it off – but, really, what was the point? Alex would find out sooner or later. So why hide it? Harri sighed. 'Rob cancelled our trip to Scotland.'

'He did *what*? When?'

'Saturday night. That's why we left early: his boss called him to say his Christmas leave had been postponed because the contract he's been working on had hit problems.'

It was clear what Alex made of this. 'And you believed him?'

'I had no reason not to. But that doesn't mean I've forgiven him. He let me down – *again* – just when I thought things were reaching an even keel.' Her eyes moved away from his, towards the illuminated street outside. 'If it's work then I guess I can't be mad at him . . . But the thing is, I'm getting tired of this constant lurching between famine and feast with him. One minute he's talking about growing old together and the next he's dropping me like a hot stone for some stupid work thing that's taken over his life.' She looked back at Alex's indeterminable expression – was it pity she saw? Shock? Indifference? 'I'd just like to be his priority for once, you know?'

'Mate, I'm sorry. You must feel terrible.'

'I'm fine.'

'No you're not. How long have I known you, eh? I've

never heard you speak like that about Rob. You're always defending him.'

'Well, I don't feel like doing that tonight. He doesn't deserve it.'

Alex clapped his hands. 'That's it! That's the *real you* coming out at last!'

'I've always been me.'

'Not when it comes to matters of Rob you haven't.'

Harri rested against a table. 'You're right. I'm not going to let him do this to me. All day I've been going over and over it in my mind and I just keep coming back to the same conclusion: maybe this relationship just isn't ever going to be what I hope it will.'

'You deserve more.'

'Yeah, I know.' She ran her hand along the periwinkle satin folds of her dress. 'I think I should probably go, if you don't mind. It's late and I'm really not very good company.'

'You're always good company,' Alex said warmly. 'You sure I can't tempt you to stay?'

Afraid that it might induce another bout of tears, Harri shook her head. 'Thanks, but I think I just need to go home.'

'Wait – let me drive you.'

Walking slowly to the door, Harri pulled it open and looked back at his tall Victorian-clothed figure, cast into shadow by the light behind the counter, like a period drama hero. 'I'll be fine. Sorry to subject you to all that.'

His smile was full of compassion as he saluted her with a little bow. 'All part of the service. Take care, you.'

Stepping out into the almost empty street, Harri filled her lungs with crisp December air and looked up at the inky black sky. A single star flickered brightly directly overhead, as if keeping watch.

'Thank you, Mum,' she whispered.

Walking slowly past weary shopkeepers dismantling their stalls and unwinding Christmas lights, Harri headed home, conflicting thoughts swirling endlessly like wild whirling dervishes, around and around in her mind.

With Rob gone, Auntie Rosemary safely on a train bound for Newcastle to spend Christmas with Grandma Dillon and everybody else busy with their own plans for the festive season, Harri was left with the task of sorting out her own Christmas. This was virgin territory for her: up until now, Harri had gone to Auntie Rosemary's on Christmas Day and to Rob's mum, Clarice's, home on Boxing Day. When Rosemary realised that Harri would be on her own she wanted to cancel her trip, but Harri was adamant that she should go as planned. Rob may have ruined Christmas for her, but there was no way he was going to spoil it for her aunt and grandmother as well.

Viv and Merv were going on a cruise around the Caribbean, much to Viv's chagrin: 'Three weeks stuck on a floating hotel with people we can't get away from isn't *my* idea of a relaxing holiday, Mervyn!' – and Alex was spending Christmas Day with Chelsea before driving down to Somerset to stay a few days with Sandie and Brendan. Although the thought of organising Christmas for herself wasn't exactly appealing, Harri decided firmly to make an effort.

The day before Christmas Eve, she drove into Stone Yardley to buy food and drop off Alex's present. Parking in the Co-op's packed car park, she was just walking towards the store entrance when she saw someone waving at her beside a battered-looking Land Rover.

'Hi, Harri! Merry Christmas!'

'Nice to see you, Emily. I'm glad I'm not the only person crazy enough to attempt the supermarket today.'

There was a bark from inside the Land Rover and Fly bounded up at the passenger window, licking it enthusiastically. Harri placed her hand against the cold glass. 'Hello, Fly.'

'I swear that dog gets more excited than a kid about Christmas,' Emily laughed.

'My cat will just be amazed that he gets me all to himself for two weeks.'

Emily frowned. 'But I thought you and Rob were—'

'He's had to work over Christmas,' Harri said quickly, not wanting to have a post mortem on her situation in the middle of the shoppers' car park, 'so I'm having a quiet one.'

'Don't do that, honey – come to us for Christmas.'

Taken aback, Harri held up her hands. 'No – no, you don't have to do that, Em. I'll be perfectly OK: I have Nigella and Delia to guide me through the rigours of Christmas dinner.'

Emily was having none of it. 'Nonsense. I insist! Stu went a bit OTT on the catering side, so we have enough food to feed all of Stone Yardley and half of Ellingsgate combined. Trust me, you'd be doing me a favour, helping to demolish my hubby's man-made grub mountain.'

Her suggestion brought a much-needed boost to Harri's heart and she found herself agreeing. 'Well, when you put it like that, how can I refuse?'

Christmas Day morning was icy and bright, a sharp frost the night before adorning every tree branch and gate post with an exquisite layer of white crystals. Donning her thick wool coat, long scarf and striped beanie hat, Harri made sure Ron Howard was fed and left him curled happily in the middle of a faux fur throw on the sofa. She went to pick up her mobile phone from the coffee table, but then thought better of it. Since the night of the Christmas Amble, Harri had become less willing to respond to Rob's messages and now at least five of them lay unopened in her phone inbox. Being bombarded by increasingly grovelling texts was the last thing she needed today. Collecting the bag of presents for her hosts, she stepped out into the still air and walked to her car. With Elbow's 'One Day Like This' playing on her stereo, she drove through the quiet roads under clotted cream skies.

As she passed through the small villages on the fringes of the Black Country's border, the decorated windows revealed fleeting snapshots of other people's Christmases: families gathering for a day that could prove to be restful or stressful; presents, food, too many repeats on TV . . . all playing out behind closed doors. In her car, she was an onlooker, granted a glance at what Christmas was for others. But this sensation was nothing new to Harri: this was how every Christmas felt to her. It was the one day of the year when being without family seemed the cruellest – not least because every programme, advert and film on television seemed to feature the clichéd image of complete families: mum, dad, two kids . . . Strangely enough, furniture store adverts were the worst for Harri. One sight of smiling family groups snuggling together (albeit on *horrendous* sofas) was enough to reduce her to a sobbing wreck from the start of December to New Year's Day. Consequently, she always felt one step removed from Christmas – and it was only when she drove down the long, steep track towards Emily and Stu's farm that she realised how apprehensive the thought of fitting herself into someone else's festivities was making her.

The farmhouse smelled amazing when she walked inside – roasting meat, freshly cut herbs, the spicy tang of cinnamon and ginger. It looked like the Williamses had bought the entire

325

contents of a Christmas tree light factory and hung them over every available banister, doorway, picture frame and shelf. Harri made a mental note not to stand still for too long today in case she too was draped with multicoloured lights.

Emily and Stu fussed around their houseguest, sitting her down on a shabbily chic upholstered armchair by the wood-burner, bringing her rose tea and home-made star-shaped cinnamon biscuits, and apologising profusely for Fly's over-enthusiastic attentions. Classic Christmas songs were drifting in from the radio in the kitchen while *It's a Wonderful Life* played on the sitting-room television. Harri let it all infuse through her, forgetting her previous trepidation and, blissfully, finally able to put Rob out of her mind.

The day turned out to be wonderful beyond what she could have anticipated, and Emily and Stu were the perfect hosts. Christmas dinner at three (accompanied by the obligatory message from Her Majesty, of course); home-made Christmas cake with slices of Red Leicester cheese in the warmth of the sitting room; good-natured competition over games of Who's in the Bag? and Trivial Pursuit, leading to relaxed, late evening conversation with coffee as Fly and the three cats took turns to claim squatter's rights on laps and feet.

When Harri arrived home in the early hours, she was glowing. Sleepy and content, she pulled the secret Venice box from its hiding place, climbed into bed and snuggled down under the bedclothes. One by one, she brought out her treas-ures – and even though she had gazed upon them a thousand times before, her heart was still thrilled at the sight until, at last, she drifted away into sleep.

Hey Red ☺ I know ur mad at me but I had no choice remember? Work is a nightmare. Nobody wants 2b here and my team r miserable. Only a few people I can talk to, rest r losers. BTW, where's good 4 holidays in Spain? Mel from my team wanted to know so I said I'd ask. Please call me, Red. This is getting stupid. R xx

By New Year's Eve, Harri had received fifteen such texts from Rob, each one progressively more desperate than the last. Not wanting to take the situation into the New Year, she finally phoned him at lunchtime. The call rang out for some time before he answered breathlessly.

'Sorry, baby, I was in the bathroom . . . Hi.'

'Hi.'

'So am I forgiven yet? I really am sorry, you know.'

Harri sighed. 'Yes, but only just.'

Rob's relief was audible. 'Thank you – I was worried you might never forgive me.'

'Well, I have, so . . . Just promise me you won't ever do that to me again, OK? Don't build up something for weeks and then drop me from a great height. You know how excited I was about that break – it was something we needed.'

'Babe, you know I had no choice . . .'

Harri could feel her nerves twitching. 'Are all your team there?'

There was a pause. 'Well, no, but . . .'

'Right. So who's missing?'

'Only a couple.' Rob sounded defensive. 'John Marshall couldn't because his wife's just had a baby, and Sue Gerard had already arranged for her mother to come out of sheltered housing to stay with her over Christmas.'

'Anyone else?'

'One or two refused . . . but . . .'

Harri stared out of her kitchen window. 'The point is that you could have said no, couldn't you?'

'Well, I . . .'

'So next time, you can do the same. That's all I'm saying.' She decided to change the subject to avoid further argument. 'Anyway, what are you doing for New Year?'

'Hitting the hotel bar, probably. I might not call later. I'm planning on getting very drunk.'

Great, thought Harri, first Christmas and now New Year without him. 'Right. Better say Happy New Year now, then.'

She heard him breathe out slowly. 'Happy New Year, baby. Next year will be better, I promise. Call you tomorrow night, yeah?'

Ending the call, Harri ruffled Ron Howard's fur. Purring appreciatively, he rolled onto his back, stretching all four paws out like a slow yoga posture. 'Just me and you then, eh, Ron? So what's it going to be – wild night out on the town? Firework display in the back garden?'

Ron opened his eyes and made a half-purr, half-miaow sound, as if to say, 'Why are you asking me? I'm a cat.' Pulling a face, Harri stood and wandered into the kitchen to put the kettle on.

Just then, a loud knock summoned her to the front door. She opened it and, to her surprise, found Alex.

She hugged him, glad to have company. 'Wow, I wasn't expecting to see you today! Come in – the kettle's on.'

'Ah, a woman after my own heart,' Alex chirped, following her into the living room. 'I'm out with Chels tonight at an obscenely expensive party, so I thought I'd pop in for the last bit of sanity I'm likely to enjoy this year.'

Harri sliced up a home-made Dundee cake (a present from Viv before she headed off for her 'cruise of doom') and took a slab of Double Gloucester cheese out of the fridge.

'Thought you might like a bit of cake with your tea.'

Alex chuckled. 'Absolutely. It's not like I haven't already eaten my own bodyweight in food over the past few days or anything. Is it my mum's?'

'The very same.'

'So what's the cheese for?'

Harri stared incredulously at him. 'To have with the cake, of course. Don't tell me you didn't know that?'

'You're having me on.'

'You mean with all the travelling you've done over the years, you've never had fruit cake and cheese before?'

'Never.'

Harri tutted and gave him a look of mock despair. 'Honestly, you know *nothing*. In Yorkshire it's practically written into the constitution.'

'I've never been to Yorkshire.'

'Well, that would be why you didn't know. Wow, you mean there's one place in the world I've been to, but you haven't?'

'It would appear so.'

Smiling, she handed him a slice of cake and a wedge of cheese. 'Trust me, it's worth it.'

Alex had to agree when he'd tasted the combination – and Harri was amused at how the tables had been turned: now she was the one with travel stories, introducing him to exotic new flavours . . .

After an hour of jocular conversation, Alex paused and looked at her. 'I've been meaning to say something, H, and I've been thinking about it all over Christmas.'

Subconsciously, Harri braced herself. 'Go on.'

He twisted on the sofa to face her squarely. 'I'm just so sorry that you heard me being a complete idiot with Jack. I would have reacted exactly the same if I'd been in your shoes – no, worse, probably. And Chelsea overreacted at the pub. She gets nervous around people she doesn't know, you see – it's a defence mechanism to talk about herself all the time. The thing is, H, I don't want you to feel blocked out now I'm with her. I know I've been guilty of "new relationship syndrome" lately – the guys gave me a right rollicking about it, believe me – so one of my New Year's resolutions is to spend more time with my friends and not be so insular.' He stopped and his chocolate stare widened. 'But one thing that won't change is Chelsea. I love her, Harri. I've never felt like this about anyone before – not even Nina. And I'd like you to be happy for me. I know you had your misgivings at first, but she's so much better with me now, you know. She's really starting to soften and I know she loves me. I think – hell, I know – she's the One.'

Something inside Harri sank like lead. 'Really? Wow . . . look, Al, the reason I started the whole *Juste Moi* thing was because I wanted you to be happy. If Chelsea is the one who does that, then it's fine by me.'

Alex hugged her. 'Thank you. You don't know what that means.'

Pressed against his chest, Harri silently disagreed. *I know: it means Chelsea is here to stay*. Heart thudding, she closed her eyes.

CHAPTER EIGHTEEN

Questions and Answers . . .

A bottle of water rolls under the door. Harri picks it up and takes a long swig to wash down the headache pills. There is silence as she drinks, but she is aware of Viv waiting patiently on the other side of the cubicle.

'Thanks.'

'You're welcome. Oh, why won't you come home with me, sweetheart? I can make up the bed in the guest room, you can get a good night's sleep and everything will look brighter in the morning.'

'I don't think it will. And I don't think I'd be very good company either.'

'For heaven's sake, Harriet, I'm not asking you for *company*,' Viv scoffs. 'I'm trying to be supportive. At some point you have to move out of there.'

Her words have far more resonance than she intended.

Preston eventually released Rob from its clutches halfway through the first week of January. He certainly seemed intent on making up to Harri: large bouquets of flowers arrived at SLIT at least twice a week, much to the delight of Nus (and utter disgust of Tom, who denounced the gesture as 'lame-central'); he made a point of taking her out every Friday night;

he even half-mentioned they could holiday abroad this year, although, sadly, there was no mention of Venice. Initially, Harri remained highly suspicious of his actions, believing that it was too good to last. But as January passed into February, his tenaciousness began to melt her heart.

'Well, I'll say one thing for your young man,' Auntie Rosemary said one Saturday lunchtime, as they sat on the high stools in Eadern Blooms, eating gigantic baguettes from Lavender's Bakery during Harri's lunchbreak, 'he's doing my business the power of good. All those bouquets have really helped to buck the January slump for us.'

Harri smiled and swung her legs from her stool like she used to do as a little girl. 'He still hasn't worked out that the flower orders he places online come through to you.'

'But aside from all these grand gestures, how is he with you?'

The tone of her question took Harri by surprise. 'Um, he's – good. Great, actually. He seems to be making a real effort with me.'

Auntie Rosemary's expression remained static. 'Well, as long as you're happy, that's all.'

Harri studied her aunt, perplexed at her lukewarm response to Rob's actions. Wasn't she the one who had always said Rob should be more demonstrative, take her out more, consider their future together? So how come this wasn't good enough, all of a sudden?

The question played on her mind all day until, at five thirty, when she was locking the shutters at SLIT, its monopoly on her thoughts was broken by the shrill ringing of her mobile.

'Hello?'

'Harri! There's an emergency – I need your help!'

'Emily? Whatever's happened? Are you OK?'

'I'm fine, but I might just have made the worst mistake of my life! Can you come over?'

Harri had already started to walk quickly towards the car park. 'I'm on my way—'

'Wait! There's one more thing: can you bring some old clothes to wear? And – I really don't know how to ask this, but – could you *find someone* to bring with you?'

Stopping dead in her tracks, Harri stared at her phone. 'Eh?'

An hour later, Harri's silver-grey Punto sped along the road out of Stone Yardley, hastily purloined mops, brooms, two buckets and a bag of cleaning products rattling and clanking noisily in the back.

'This is completely nuts. What on earth was she thinking?' Alex asked, placing a steadying hand surreptitiously on the passenger door handle.

Harri smiled. It always amused her that such a laid-back man in all other areas of his life could become so nervous when faced with the terrifying prospect of being a passenger in somebody else's car. They had only been travelling for ten minutes, yet already Harri had caught his foot stabbing at his invisible brake pedal in the footwell. It wasn't Harri's driving that was the problem, either: he reacted the same in any car.

'I think Emily just got carried away.'

'That's got to be the Understatement of the Year so far! Who advertises a craft weekend without having everything ready beforehand?'

'Evidently, Emily does.'

Alex spread his right hand out on his knee, as if to reassure Harri that he was calm, although the other hand was still gripping the handle. 'And how many people has she got coming?'

'Fifteen.' Harri indicated left at a T-junction, turning onto a narrower country lane. 'It could've been a total disaster for accommodation with it being Valentine's Weekend, but I called Barbara at Little Swinford Country Club and, thankfully, they've had a cancellation. Otherwise I don't know what she would have done.'

'So what are we clearing out, then?'

'One of the outbuildings that Stu's been renovating to use as a craft studio. It's got heat, light and electricity, but there's a load of junk that needs shifting and everything needs to be cleaned.'

Alex rubbed the back of his neck. 'And there was me thinking I'd got a relaxing blokey weekend while Chelsea is away. Fat chance.'

Harri smiled and reached over to squeeze his knee. 'Thanks so much for volunteering.'

'Yeah, whatever. Write it on my headstone.'

A last-minute thought was responsible for Alex now being seated in Harri's car, being driven towards Emily and Stu's farm in the dusky February light. Earlier dashing around trying to scrounge cleaning implements from the shops in the High Street and finding no brooms, Harri suddenly remembered that Alex had two in the storecupboard at Wātea.

'I need your brooms! It's an emergency.' Seeing Alex's concern, she quickly clarified. 'Well, no-one's died or anything, it's just that my friend's been really daft and I need to go and help her.'

This amused Alex. 'OK, I need to hear more.'

'I don't have time – I've got to grab some old clothes from home and get over there as soon as I can.'

'What about Rob? Is he not coming with you?'

Harri muffled a snigger. 'Rob is allergic to cleaning at the best of times, Al. The last thing he's going to want to spend his Saturday night doing is volunteering to do that. I've really got to go, sorry.'

Alex handed her the brooms and then stopped as a thought struck him. 'Wait there.'

'Al, I can't . . .' she protested, but it was too late: he had already dashed upstairs. After much banging of cupboard doors and heavy footsteps thumping around in the flat above, he reappeared dressed in a vintage T-shirt Harri hadn't seen him wear since he met Chelsea, old ripped jeans and his much-loved red Converse boots, which had been consigned to the back of his wardrobe in recent months.

'OK, ready,' he panted, grabbing his coat and keys, and virtually pushing Harri out of the door. 'Let's go clean!'

The Punto took a sharp left just before the grass triangle on the road towards Greenhill and Little Swinford, and bumped and jostled its way down the steep farm track. 'What made you want to come, anyway?' Harri asked, as Alex held on to the dashboard for dear life.

'I didn't have anything better to do. And it seemed like it might be fun.'

'Blimey, you really don't get out much these days, do you? OK, Mr Brannan, we're here: you can relax and open your eyes now.'

Looking pale, Alex vacated the car as quickly as he could – only to be almost pinned to its door by Fly. 'Whoa – er, hello, doggie.'

Harri smiled at the sight of the black and white furry animal joyously head-butting Alex's knees. 'Alex, meet Fly.'

Footsteps crunched rapidly across the gravel as Emily hurried towards them, flinging her arms around Harri. 'Oh, you're *here*! Wonderful you! And you've brought someone with you.' She held her hand out to him. 'Hi, I'm the crazy woman Harri's probably told you about. Thank you so much for coming – um – Rob, is it?'

Harri rushed to correct her. 'No, Em, sorry. This is my friend Alex – from the coffee shop in Stone Yardley?'

The mention of his name struck a chord with Emily and she blushed. 'I am so sorry! Hi, Alex. Ah, so *you're* the spontaneity guy. Lovely to meet you at last. Right, if you want to come into the farmhouse first I'll make you a cuppa before we all get cracking.'

It transpired that Emily and Stu, during a particularly late night (that might possibly have involved several bottles of Merlot), had excitedly discussed ideas for their embryonic new business. Somewhere along the line, the idea of a Valentine craft weekend had been born and it had seemed like such a brilliant, original plan that Emily and Stu had dashed to their Mac and spent a happy hour designing an advert for the imaginary event. It was only the next morning, with throbbing heads and bilious stomachs, that the true horror of the situation began to reveal itself: the Sent email to the advertising manager of an online crafters' forum and – worse still – their first bookings.

'How come people booked so quickly?' Alex asked.

'Apparently, we offered a twenty per cent discount for a limited period,' Emily replied, still wincing at the consequences of their drunken game. 'I've been a member of that forum for years and I should have remembered how quickly people respond to things on there. Crafters are a determined bunch.'

'No kidding,' said Harri. 'Well, you said you wanted to be spontaneous and seize the moment.'

Emily grimaced. 'Don't remind me. I used to have a good job in a bank. What on earth am I doing?'

Alex laughed. 'Hey, listen, I know exactly how you're feeling. When I walked out of my job I was completely scared by what lay ahead. But it's all part of the thrill ride, Emily. Just roll with it. I lost track of the amount of times I ended up in crazy situations when I was travelling. Like the time I was in Puerto Rico and caught a local taxi in town to Vieques Airport, but my woeful Spanish meant I asked for the wrong destination. The taxi driver thought my panicky pleas for him to turn round were threatening, so he stopped the car and demanded I get out – in a village where nobody spoke English.'

Emily gasped. 'Gracious, what did you do?'

'I found a bar and managed to get an old guy to understand that I'd arrived in the village by mistake. He thought I was amusing so he offered me a bed for the night and his wife cooked me a wonderfully spicy *mole* stew. In the morning, his cousin arrived and gave me a lift to the nearest town, where I met an English teacher from the local school who arranged for his uncle to take me to Vieques. I had to wait there for twelve hours to catch a flight, but at least I was in the right place. Things generally work out – that's what I've found, anyway.'

'Wow, Harri was right about you,' said Emily, eyes wide.

Intrigued, Alex stared at Harri, who quickly stood up from the kitchen table. 'I think we need to get cracking, don't you? I'll go and start unpacking the car.'

Viewed first-hand, the task ahead of them was even more daunting than Harri had anticipated. Stu walked them around the interior of the soon-to-be craft workshop, guiding them around the edges of the rubbish where it had been piled up away from the newly painted walls.

'So this is where the main craft table is going to be – I've a friend working in a reclamation timber yard in Innersley making it for me as we speak. And then there will be a kind of teabreak-slash-lounge area . . . Em and I contacted a friend at the Swinford Hospice charity shop warehouse and they've put aside some donated sofas and chairs for us.'

Alex brushed a cobweb from his leg as they picked their way carefully around rusting bits of metal, wire and rusted remains of farm implements. 'Sounds like it's going to be cool, then.'

Stu wiped his brow with the sleeve of his paint-splattered rugby shirt. 'It'd better be after all this. I'm just glad I replastered and rewired when Em quit her job. If that hadn't been done we wouldn't have had a hope of completing all the work in time. Fourteen hours I've been working since we discovered that blasted email . . . So, if you guys can get cracking on moving this I'll sort out the painting team – well, my parents and their bridge club colleagues, to be exact. They've put aside their regular Saturday night meeting for this. I'm going to be reminded of that fact for years to come.'

Donning old gardening gloves, Alex and Harri set to work, clearing the detritus of years of farm labour from the former milking shed – old tractor tyres, rolls of barbed wire, grain sacks and bag upon bag of rotting rubbish – piling it all in an old skip behind the large barn, where it would be out of view of the guests.

'Hilarious that Emily thought I was Rob, wasn't it?' Alex smirked as they hauled an old splintered beam into the skip. 'We must make a lovely couple.'

Brushing wayward curls from her face, Harri smiled back. 'Either that or she thought you looked like a soft sales executive who doesn't like physical work.'

'Oi! I'm every inch the capable man, thank you very much,' he retorted. 'She was probably amazed at what a captivating specimen of manhood I am.'

'And so humble too!' Laughing, Harri grabbed a handful of old hay from the skip and threw it at him.

'Oh, you are *so* going to regret that! There's only one place for you now,' he exclaimed, grabbing her by the waist and lifting her up over the skip.

Arms and legs flailing, she protested, 'No, Al! Don't you dare!'

He relented and brought her back to the ground, leaning against the skip while he tried to regain his breath. 'Emily was definitely mistaken – Rob would never try to throw you in a skip.'

'Thank goodness!'

Alex smiled at her as he walked past. 'But then, maybe fun stuff like that is what you guys need.'

Harri watched him go, a strange sensation passing through her. For a moment she remained where she was, unsettled by his parting shot. Then, brushing the dust from her shirt, she headed back to the milking shed.

Emily joined them an hour later after taking delivery of the table and some of the charity shop sofas that friends had brought over.

'I can't thank you enough for this,' she puffed as she and Harri carried an enormous tyre out to the skip.

'Hey, it's fine. Glad to help.'

Emily beamed and lowered her voice a little. 'Alex seems nice.'

Harri looked back to where Alex was helping Stu unload pots of paint from the back of someone's car. 'He is.'

'I can see why you're so protective of him,' Emily smiled, the tiniest glint of mischief in her eyes.

'I didn't think I was.'

'Oh, you *so* are! Worrying about him with that plastic

girlfriend of his. Not that I blame you, of course. Talk about spontaneous – if I wasn't with Stu I could more than happily be a bit spontaneous with *him*.'

Harri stared at her. 'Em! I can't believe you just said that!'

Emily shrugged, a wicked grin appearing. 'I'm just saying, that's all. You two seem really close, anyway.'

'Well, Al's a really great mate. And it's nice to get the time to hang out with him – we haven't been able to do that much since Chelsea arrived.' Harri was quick to move the conversation away from Alex after that, his comment earlier still playing on her mind.

By midnight, Stu and the bridge club volunteers had painted the walls and ceilings, constructed flat-pack cupboard units to hold craft supplies and installed the new table and chairs. Meanwhile Harri, Emily and Alex swept, mopped and cleaned every surface until, at precisely one a.m, the work was completed. Celebrating with well-earned mugs of tea or beer, they all stood back to admire the fruits of their labours.

'Well, troops, I think our work here is done,' Stu grinned, raising his mug. 'To the success of the inaugural Greenwell Hill Farm craft weekend!'

Cheering, they all joined the toast.

'Emily and Stu are great,' Alex said as they drove home. 'Crazy, but great.'

'You don't regret volunteering to help, then?' Harri asked.

'No. I had fun.'

'Me too.' Harri slowed to navigate a sharp right-hand bend, which looked a lot scarier with only the headlight beams to illuminate the road. She was aware of Alex looking at her in the darkness, the glow from the dashboard lights barely defining the contours of his face. 'What?'

'I was just wondering what Emily meant when she said you were right about me.'

How on earth had he remembered that? Harri was thankful that he couldn't see the blush claiming her cheeks in the darkened car. 'She was just stirring.'

This was by no means sufficient to satisfy Alex's curiosity. 'No, I don't think she was. So you've talked with her about me?'

'I talk about a lot of people, Al. You, Stella, Viv . . .'

'That's not what I meant and you know it.'

Reaching the roundabout at the lower end of Stone Yardley, Harri drove towards the High Street. As they neared Wātea, she took a deep breath. 'I just told her that you're my best friend and that I envy you.'

'Envy me? Whatever for?'

'Just the easy way you live your life and aren't scared by anything.'

Alex was silent as the car pulled up outside his coffee lounge. Then he turned to smile at Harri. 'It's been a great night. Look, there's something I need your help with.'

'Sure, it's the least I can do after tonight.'

'Excellent. How about dinner on Wednesday?'

'Great,' Harri answered, as an idea presented itself in her mind. 'Tell you what, why don't you come to mine for a change? Chelsea's welcome too, obviously,' she added quickly.

'Oh, Chels is on another girls' night out,' he pulled a face, 'so it'll just be me.'

Despite her better intentions, a guilty thrill raced through her at the prospect of a Chelsea-less Alex. 'Eight o'clock at mine, then?'

He nodded. 'Thanks, H.' He looked at her for a moment, then left the car.

* * *

On Monday, Harri met up with Rob after work at the Showcase cinema in Lornal. Rob had chosen an early film as he was likely to be called upon to work late nights for the remainder of the week. When Harri pulled up next to his VW Passat in the cinema car park he was leaning back in the driver's seat, chatting animatedly on his mobile. Taking the opportunity to look at him while he was oblivious to her arrival, she noted how gorgeous he was looking in his pristine white work shirt, his tie removed and top three buttons undone. His hair had been spiked on top and a faint line of stubble peppered his jaw. Without even being close to him, she could tell he smelled good, too. There was something so intensely appealing to her about Rob in his business clothes – wearing them he was confident, relaxed and in possession of a self-assured swagger that took her breath away.

Just then, he turned, his hazel eyes sparkling as they met hers. He quickly ended the call, swinging out of the car to meet her.

'Hey, gorgeous,' she smiled.

'Hey yourself, beautiful. Ready for the film?'

'Only if you're buying the popcorn.'

The multiplex was buzzing already, large swarms of teens moving *en masse* through the thickly carpeted expanse of the foyer to join the queue for tickets. Harri and Rob followed suit.

'Alex is coming for dinner on Wednesday night. Is that OK?'

Rob moved out of the way as a screaming child ducked under the flexibarrier and made a bid for freedom, hotly pursued by an older sibling. 'Fine by me. Is he bringing the Jordan freak with him?'

'No, she's out that night.'

'Probably the highlight of the poor guy's week then.

342

I couldn't live with *that*, I tell you. Leave her too close to a radiator and she'd melt.'

'Rob, that's terrible,' she chastised him, but her amusement was impossible to hide. 'I think he really likes her.'

Rob pulled a face. 'Each to his own.'

'Absolutely. So how was work today?'

'Busy. There's a new contract we're possibly going to go for when the Preston job's finished.'

Harri stared at him. 'Where?'

Rob fiddled with his phone. 'Damn thing. I can't get a signal in here.'

Recognising his lacklustre attempt at a sidestep with dismay, Harri lowered her voice. 'Where, Rob?'

He didn't look at her, staring defiantly ahead. 'Edinburgh.'

'Are they going to expect you to travel there as much as Preston?'

'It's possible, yeah.'

The queue moved and Rob bought their tickets while Harri fumed quietly by his side. She hadn't considered the prospect that there might be more contracts like Preston, naively assuming that success in securing the elusive business deal would somehow exempt him from further work away.

Rob was well aware of Harri's growing consternation, but he ignored it until they were seated in the cinema. 'Look, Red, you knew my job was important to me when we met. That hasn't changed.'

'But it was never supposed to take over your entire *life*,' she hissed back under her breath.

'Maybe I want it to, have you considered that?'

She stared at him. 'Are you serious?'

His eyes flicked back to the screen. 'Of course not. Watch the film.'

* * *

343

The revelation was still irritating her on Wednesday evening as she prepared dinner. Why did he *always* do something like that just when she was starting to relax in their relationship? Somehow, it seemed to diminish all the good work he had been doing recently, calling every gesture and every loving word into question. Was this what Auntie Rosemary had been alluding to at the weekend? Harri had to admit that she had seen an indefinable sadness in her aunt's eyes whenever she mentioned Rob and its appearance unnerved her. But then, with her experience of men, Auntie Rosemary could be forgiven for being cautious. Her own marriage had come crashing to an end when she discovered that Uncle Nick had not only been having an affair for twelve years, but also that he was starting a family with the woman. As a final kick in the guts, he then emigrated to Australia, breaking contact with Rosemary and – arguably worse – James and Rosie. Whilst she never made an issue of what had happened to her, Harri knew that it had broken her heart to see her own children denied a father. It was only natural, then, for her to project her experience onto Harri. But Harri *wasn't* Auntie Rosemary – and, more importantly, Rob wasn't Uncle Nick. Nevertheless, Rob's almost pathological compulsion for work filled Harri with dread for their future. Was this how it was going to be when they got married and had kids? Would Harri be the one left holding the fort whenever a new shiny contract turned Rob's head?

Realising she had subconsciously taken out her frustration on the carrots – which now lay in jagged, chunky orange lumps, instead of the perfectly dissected identical rounds in Nigella's version – she decided to call them 'rustic' and hope Alex was convinced.

At eight o'clock Alex arrived, bearing a bottle of wine and a preoccupied expression. He refused to discuss what it was that he required Harri's help with until after they had eaten Harri's Provençal Chicken with roasted vegetables, and whilst on the surface he was his usual jokey self, Harri was aware of a deeper narrative going on behind his smile. When the meal was finished and plates washed and stacked in the kitchen cupboards, Harri made coffee and brought it into the living room.

Alex was looking through the collection of travel DVDs by the television. 'You've got half the world in here, haven't you?' he grinned when she sat down. 'It's like Dan Beagle World.'

Harri shrugged. 'He's an amazing writer and presenter, that's all.'

'Crazy that your best friend ended up travelling with him, then. I can't imagine Stella Smith teetering up Tibetan hills in her knock-off Jimmy Choos. Shouldn't that have been you?'

Feeling her stomach lurch, Harri pushed down the cafetière plunger. 'Stel's having a fab time. I think it might just be the making of her.'

'Maybe.' His eyes scanned the rows of DVD spines. 'You know, with the money you spent on these you could have actually visited some of these places.' He looked at her. 'I mean, why pay for somebody else's experiences when you could see it for yourself?'

Dusting off the list of plausible excuses, Harri presented them for his perusal. 'You know why. It just hasn't happened for me yet. There's always something that's stopped me going: nobody else to travel with, Rob wanting to holiday in the UK, the recession . . .'

Alex stood and joined her on the sofa – thus incurring the feline disdain of Ron Howard, who stalked away to sit underneath the coffee table and stare in disgust at him. 'Come on, Harri, be honest with yourself. All those fine reasons you trot out so often mean nothing here. Admit it: you're scared to do it.'

How dare he? 'That's not true . . . It's . . .'

His smile was kind even though his eyes sparked with victory. 'You just need to believe it's possible, that's all.' He placed his warm hand over hers on the sofa cushion. '*I* believe in you.'

The effect that those four words exerted on her was immense – completely unexpected: reaching into the furthest fathoms of her being and setting tiny stars alight, spinning with mirror-ball reflections in the darkness. It was only then that she realised how much she needed to hear that – not just from him, but from anyone. While she knew that Auntie Rosemary, Viv and Stella probably felt that way, none of them had taken the time to say it out loud. And as for Rob . . . well, even in his most thoughtful moments it would have never occurred to him that the sentiment was necessary.

'Thank you. That means a lot.'

'Good.' His fingers lingered on her hand a moment longer and then let go.

Suddenly uncomfortable, Harri changed the subject. 'So, come on then. What's this thing you need my help with?'

'Uh, yeah, *that* . . .' Looking like a shy five-year-old, Alex pulled a crumpled sheet of paper from his back pocket. He took a deep breath.

'I just need your advice, you know – being a *woman* and everything.'

Harri raised her eyebrows. 'Thanks for noticing.'

'Perceptive, me.' He began fiddling with the zip on one of the sofa cushions. 'It's just that – well – I've given this loads of thought and I think the time is right . . . That is to say, I don't know for sure, but . . .'

'Al! Just spit it out!'

'I'm going to propose to Chelsea on Valentine's Day.'

The silence this was met with was so long and weighty it could have had its own series on BBC4. Harri knew she should have been happy for him, as supportive for his dreams as he had just been for hers, but somehow she couldn't muster up anything but a sense of stone-cold loss, like a heavy door slamming shut somewhere. She had been waiting for seven years for Rob to make that decision and yet Alex seemed capable of making it in a matter of months. Angry at her uncharacteristic response, she cajoled a smile to sit awkwardly on her face.

'Wow.'

He looked uncertain. 'Yeah.'

She nodded slowly, calm on the surface masking a frantic battle within. 'So how can I help?'

As he answered, his eyes held a strange sadness, in sharp contrast to the positive expression he wore. 'Would you listen to what I'm planning to say? I've been trying to find the words for a while and I don't know if it's sincere or just pathetic.'

No! screamed the confident version of Harri inside. *Find some other mug to ask. This is beyond what I can offer you* . . . But as she looked at him, so unsure, suddenly so out of his comfort zone, she knew she couldn't refuse. 'Go on, then.'

His face brightened, the relief impossible to conceal. 'Really? Thank you so much, H! Seriously, the hassle this has caused me so far . . . OK, sorry, I'll – er . . .' He nodded at the piece of paper now held aloft in his hands, shaking slightly. 'Right. Well, I thought I'd start by saying how the past few months of my life have been so amazing, etc, then, you know, say it's all down to her, blah, blah . . . Say how alive being with her makes me feel and, I don't know, maybe something about spending the rest of my life with her? Not sure about that bit – borderline cheesy, d'you think? Anyway, then I'll go for the big ending, the one-knee thing, the ring, and then I thought I'd just go for the classic "Will you marry me" line – none of that "Would you do me the honour" stuff . . . OK, *what*?'

Despite the war within, Harri couldn't hide her mirth. 'Al, that's *dreadful*! You sound like you're giving a business presentation, not begging the woman of your dreams to spend the rest of her life with you! I really hope you're not going to do it like that on Monday night.'

He looked aghast at her. 'How else am I meant to do it? I mean, she already knows all this stuff and last week we even ended up talking about what kind of ring she'd like. It's hardly going to come as a surprise to her, is it?'

'Alex, listen. Every girl dreams about the day someone proposes to her. You hope it's only going to happen once in your life, so it needs to be memorable. It needs to come from your heart.'

He stared at his notes, then helplessly back at her. 'But it *is*. Man, I'm going to be rubbish at this. I can't do the whole lyrical, romantic spiel.'

'You don't need to. Just be yourself.' From his perplexed expression, it was obvious that he needed more than this to go on. 'OK, listen. When I was at college and we were learning about selling holidays, the best way for us to learn what to do was to pair up and practise on each other. So, why don't I pretend to be Chelsea and you can say it like you're going to say it to her?'

'Ew! That's just going to be *well* weird.'

Harri sighed. 'Yes, well, it's not exactly how I'd anticipated spending my Wednesday evening either, but it might just put your mind at rest.'

He folded his arms and looked around the room as he mulled it over, his foot tapping nervously. Then he let out a massive sigh and slapped his hands decisively on his knees. 'Oh, what the heck, I'll do it – but you have to promise *never* to tell another living soul about this, all right?'

She nodded and traced a cross on the left side of her breast-bone with her fingers. 'Cross my heart. Now get on with it, before I change my mind.'

'All right.'

'Good. So, I'm Chelsea – ooh, wait . . .' she grabbed a cushion and shoved it up the front of her top, stretching it out to Jordan-esque proportions, '. . . now I'm Chelsea.'

'You're not funny.'

'Sorry.' Removing it, she turned to face him. 'OK, ready.'

Rubbing his hands together, Alex hesitantly took her hand and glanced at his paper. 'Right . . . Chelsea, I—'

'Hang on a minute.'

'*What now?* Come on, H, this is excruciating.'

'Lose the paper.'

'Eh?'

She gently took his script from him and he watched help-lessly as it was placed out of reach. 'You don't need this. Stop panicking, calm down and just speak from your heart. Now . . .' She offered her hand back to him.

Taking it again, he took a deep breath and fixed his dark brown eyes on hers. 'Chelsea . . .' he began, as if securing the mental image of his girlfriend in front of him, 'you know how I feel about you. I . . . *man*, this is hard . . . Er, OK, sorry. Chelsea . . . The past few months have been amazing and it's all down to you. Being with you makes me feel alive.' He paused, gazing into her eyes, the unexpected intensity of this taking her by surprise. 'You understand me in a way that nobody else does. I feel complete when I'm holding your hand . . . like *this* . . . and right now I don't want to be anywhere else than here with you.'

Harri could see the rise and fall of his chest as his breathing quickened, feel the heat in his hand as it cradled hers, his thumb beginning to move in feather-like circles across the top of her fingers. The change in him was phenomenal: gone were the embarrassed, stilted words and, in their place, prose infused with the very beat of his heart began to weave an intoxicating spell around her.

'So, I want to ask you . . . I need to know . . .' he moved deftly from the sofa to his knee, '. . . can this last forever? Because I can't imagine my world without you in it.' A brave smile assumed centre stage and Harri was aware of her own mirroring his. 'Will you marry me?'

Without warning, without thought, instinctively . . . forgetting everything else and for the first time letting her heart lead, Harri bent down and kissed him. The softness of his lips on hers sent shockwaves blasting through her body, rendering rational thought redundant as he began to return the kiss. It was as if they were two magnetic fields, with no other choice than to connect – the urgency and intensity of which was astounding. Locked together, his fingers tangling in her hair while her arms wrapped around his shoulders, they rose slowly to their feet as if the euphoria building within them could lift their bodies clear off the ground. Right there and then, nothing mattered but this beautiful, shocking, world-changing moment . . .

Then, in a heartbeat, the poles reversed, forcing them apart. Harri opened her eyes in bewilderment as she realised Alex was breaking free. Staggering back, face contorted in sheer horror, he faced her – and everything suddenly became horribly clear as the reality of the situation fell full on Harri with sickening weight.

'No! I can't . . . what the *hell* were we just . . .' he stammered, the words dancing elusively around his tongue.

'Al, I—'

'No – don't say it, Harri! Don't even . . .' Looking about him hurriedly, he grabbed his coat and began backing towards the door. 'I can't . . . It's all wrong – we shouldn't have let that happen . . .' Flinging open the door, he ran out and Harri reached the gaping doorway in time to see his car speeding away.

Alone in the freezing night, Harri let out a cry that seemed to come from outside herself, slumping against the door frame as the full force of it all blind-sided her. Razor-raw questions surrounded her conscience, jabbing with devastating accuracy. What just happened? How did they move from a stilted role-play to *that* kiss? Worse still, how could she have allowed *herself* to be so reckless? How could she face Rob now? How could she ever look Alex in the eye again?

Stupid, stupid, *stupid* spontaneity! She had long suspected that following her heart could only end in tears and this had proved the theory. Blankly gazing out at the frigid night, Harri suddenly realised the world-shattering truth: missing the last train home, she stood on the platform of her life, watching Alex disappearing out of view at the very moment she understood what he meant to her. She was falling for him – but it felt like death.

Struggling to contend with the gamut of emotions bombarding her from all sides, Harri pushed the door closed, leaning the full weight of her body against it as if to shut the new and unwelcome questions outside – only to find they had sneaked in behind her back and were now lining up accusingly in her hallway.

This can't be happening, she screamed at herself, standing alone in her hall. *Get a grip* – think . . .

Whatever she thought she had felt could never be allowed to rise to the surface again. She loved Rob, not Alex: Rob who, for all his unreliability and frustrations, had stayed with her for over seven years and, even now, was discussing spending the rest of his life by her side. Alex was a good friend – nothing else. And after the way he had fled from her tonight, he *couldn't be* anything else, not now, not ever . . . Running a hand through her hair, angry tears racing from her eyes, she clutched the memory of Alex's kiss and forced it back to the furthermost reaches of her consciousness.

One thing was certain: she had to forget tonight ever happened. And she had to forget Alex.

CHAPTER NINETEEN

Truth and Dare

'It's getting late, Harri. I would imagine we're the only ones here now. So let's stop this nonsense and get you out of here, eh?'

Maybe Viv is right, Harri thinks. Maybe it's time. She slowly stands, her ankles stiff from being seated for such a long time, and reaches for the door lock . . .

Just then, the door to the ladies' flies open, the pneumatic hinge squealing in surprise. 'Vivienne, what on earth are you doing in here?'

'Mervyn Riley, get out of these toilets! Harri, I'll be back in a min . . .'

Harri pauses, holding her breath. Viv's chair scrapes back and her heels click quickly outside as Merv is bundled out of the door into the corridor beyond. Her irritated voice can be heard lambasting him for his rude interruption.

'. . . and walking into the *ladies*', for pity's sake? What were you thinking?'

Granted a brief reprieve from her inevitable exit, Harri sits back down.

From: armchairtraveller@gmail.com
To: stellababy@danbeagle.co.uk
Subject: I am an idiot

Hi Stella

I don't know if you're likely to get this at all. I'm going out of my mind and if I don't talk about it I'm scared they'll have to cart me off to somewhere padded wearing a nice white jacket that fastens at the back . . .

Three weeks ago, I kissed Alex. I mean, **properly** kissed him – and he kissed me back too, which just made everything a million times worse. It was crazy, like something out of a soap opera. One minute he was practising his proposal speech for Chelsea (long story and I know what your face will be like when you read this) and the next we were all over each other. But then he stormed out and hasn't spoken to me since. The absolute worst thing about it is that it was **wonderful**. Honestly, Stel, I've never been kissed like that before in my life, not even by Rob – and I always thought his kisses were the best. It was only after the event that I realised the terrible truth: I'm falling for him! But it's all wrong and it just can't happen. Worse than that, I can't believe that I cheated on Rob. That looks so terrible written down – I cheated on my boyfriend, who has stuck by me all these years and has been nothing but faithful. How could I do that? I mean, I'm planning to marry him – and, as I mentioned above, Alex is planning to marry Chelsea. Well, actually, there's no planning involved any more. I just heard today from Viv that he proposed and she accepted. They've even set a date – 10th September this year.

It's such a mess, Stel. I miss Al so much as a friend, but how can I ever face him again after this? I have officially thrown away one of the best friendships of my life and for what? For a stupid, stolen moment that never had a hope of becoming anything anyway . . . I keep walking past the coffee lounge and I can't even bear to look in the window to see if he's there. Would you believe I've started crossing the road just to avoid it now?

Rob doesn't suspect anything, of course, but that doesn't make it any better because now I just feel like such a hypocritical bitch. How can I be with him when I have these feelings for someone else? They're not going away, but I know I have to make them.

I don't think I'm asking for advice, here. I just needed to get it out and you are literally the only person I can tell. Auntie Rosemary has been so busy lately that I haven't seen her, and Viv, as you can imagine, is happy to see Al settling down at last.

I hope you don't mind me sending such a huge email.

Got to go. Take care of you.

Harri xx

Stella didn't reply – not that Harri was expecting her to. For all she knew, Stella could be in a Tibetan monastery perched precariously in the mountain mists – and she was pretty sure there wouldn't be an internet café there. The weeks passed by, Easter came and went, and still Alex remained firmly off-limits to her.

At the beginning of April, when a welcome bout of unseasonably warm weather brought the Rose & Slug regulars back to their chairs on the allotment, Viv persuaded her to join them, 'to get you out a bit more'.

Viv, concerned over Alex and Harri's refusal to rebuild their friendship, sat Harri down with a particularly strong glass of elderflower wine, a little way away from the noisy joviality of Merv and the gang.

'Sweetheart, I don't know what's gone on between you and Al, but he misses you. I know he does. He's planning his wedding but his heart isn't in it. He needs a friend – you could help him so much right now.'

Harri shook her head defiantly. 'I can't. And please don't ask me to explain why. I don't think either of us could salvage our friendship if we tried. It's gone too far for that.'

'Strange. That's not how Alex sees it.'

'Well, maybe he wasn't in the same room that I was. Look, I know what you're trying to do and, believe me, I think it's admirable, but you just have to accept that my friendship with Al is over.'

May arrived in the rain, and memories of the April sun were quickly washed away. On a particularly murky Tuesday afternoon at SLIT, Harri received a call from Rob's mother.

'Hi, Clarice, how are you?'

'Good, good,' Clarice replied, her mind obviously dashing from one thought to the next. Rob often joked that his mum was so hyperactive if you filmed her and played it on slow motion, she would still look like she was speeded up. 'I need a favour.'

'How can I help?'

'Well, I popped over to Rob's house this morning to pick up some laundry to iron for him while he's away and there was one of those blasted cards from Royal Mail saying they'd tried to deliver a parcel that requires a signature. The thing is, it's his nan's birthday on Friday and Rob's arranged for some old cine film of her and my dad to be transferred to DVD as a surprise. I think that might be what the parcel is. But if Rob's not coming back until next Monday I'll have to pick it up from Little Swinford sorting office, or else Mum won't have it in time for her birthday. I knew he'd have his driving licence and credit cards with him, so I had a look for his passport but couldn't find it. Do you have any idea where it could be?'

'I didn't realise Rob had a passport,' Harri replied, a little taken aback.

'It was news to me when he mentioned it. He renewed it a while back, apparently – something to do with legal stuff for his job, I think.'

Harri thought for a moment. 'He keeps most of his important papers in an old bureau by the wardrobe in his spare room – if it's anywhere, I'd imagine that would be where he'd keep it.'

'That room is such a tip I daren't even set foot in there. Good thinking, Harriet. The only problem now is, I can't get back to his house today. I've just taken my car to Evans' Garage to have the dent knocked out of it from when I hit that bollard at Sainsbury's.'

'Don't worry. I'll head to his house straight after work. Then I can drop the passport with you on my way home.'

'You're a lifesaver, Harriet. I'll see you later. Thank you!'

At six, Harri opened Rob's front door, pausing briefly to collect his post, before heading up the stairs to the small, third bedroom that Rob sometimes used as an office, but which was, ostensibly, a dumping ground for stuff that hadn't quite made it into the loft yet. Carefully negotiating old fitness equipment, dusty holdalls and stacks of survival magazines, Harri made her way to the bureau. It was a hideous piece of furniture – some eighties designer's ill-judged attempt at 'reimagining a Victorian classic'. Veneered with a layer of too-burgundy mahogany-effect vinyl, with a slatted cover that rolled up jerkily to reveal a range of tiny compartments, the bureau bore more resemblance to a bread bin on stilts than a nineteenth-century gentleman's writing desk.

As with the rest of the room, the bureau was a place to stash piles of paper – Rob's half-hearted attempt at a 'safe place' for his important documents. Creased, coffee-stained bank statements and old gas bills jostled for position with cheque book stubs, old mobile phones, photographs of the Dynamo Stone Yardley team, countless letters and used envelopes with nothing inside them. Harri groaned as she surveyed the task before her of finding Rob's passport in this lot.

Rolling up her sleeves, she began picking her way through the piles, her heart jumping every time she caught sight of something red, only to find it was an old blood donor card, pocket diary or, strangely, hotel sewing kit. Just when she was about to give up, she spotted it, half-stuffed into a brown envelope. Grasping it thankfully, she navigated the floor junk and raced down the stairs.

As she reached the front door, the envelope in her hand slipped and a small rectangle of card fluttered to the carpet. Bending to pick it up, she realised immediately what it was.

A boarding card stub. For a British Airways flight from Birmingham International Airport to Paris Roissy/Charles de Gaulle Airport. In disbelief, Harri read the date aloud: '22nd December'. Clamping a hand to her mouth, she let out a yelp of pain as a crashing realisation hit her head on. *That was the day Rob was meant to be in Preston after cancelling our Christmas break.*

She emptied the envelope, its contents spilling out across the beige carpet and confirming her worst fears. There were more: Vienna, Prague, Milan, Rome, two more for Paris . . . but the most devastating revelation was yet to come. Hidden securely within the pages at the back of the passport was a final stub, one that shattered Harri's heart into a billion tiny pieces: Venice Marco Polo Airport.

'N-no . . .' she stammered. 'That's not possible . . . he . . . No!'

It was as if the whole world were being sucked into a black hole beneath her as the name on the last boarding card repeated louder and louder in her mind. *Venice* . . . The place she dreamed of, the destination her heart most desired. And yet Rob had flown there only two days after her birthday in April last year. Presumably, not alone . . .

Slumping to the bottom step, the shaking in her hands intensified as tears flooded her vision. How *dare* he? How dare he insist on keeping her in the UK when he was travelling to the very places she most longed to see?

Now all of his grand gestures made sense: far from being the heartfelt tokens of love Harri had assumed, they were merely the outward workings of a guilty conscience – Rob absolving himself for the lies he had fed her.

All this time, Harri had been beating herself up for her stolen kiss with Alex, painting Rob as the faithful, betrayed partner. She had lost sleep over her indiscretion, believing herself to be unworthy of his love. But nothing she had ever done could warrant the kind of sustained deception Rob had practised.

The enormity of it was almost too much to comprehend as she sat on the horrible carpet in his horrible house, staring at the crumpled boarding pass in her hand. Now, Rob's apparent enthusiasm for cheap camping weekend breaks was revealed as nothing more than a cost-cutting exercise. It all made sense: with so many European trips to pay for, all he had left for Harri was small change. That was all she meant to him: someone to throw the scraps of his leftover affections. She let out another loud sob. All that time – when she had stood by him, defended his lack of travel imagination and the amount of time he was giving to the mythical contract in Preston, graciously forgiving his every broken promise – Rob had been boarding planes with someone else, heading off for adventures while Harri sat at home. *All that time* – wasted on someone who had never been worthy of her love . . .

Who he travelled *with* was immaterial: the biggest betrayal was his blatant disregard for the thing she loved the most.

How stupid and naïve he must have thought her! As the full weight of the revelation fell on her, Harri's devastation gave way to thundering anger. White-hot fury shuddered through her limbs as she grabbed the damning evidence, opened the door and got into her car. Throwing the envelope on the passenger seat, she grabbed her mobile and fired off a text:

Hey you. Hope Preston is OK. Just picked up your passport for your mum. And the boarding cards. I know you must be busy right now doing much more important things than lying to me. Goodbye. H

She drove to Rob's mother's house, ignoring the insistent ring-tone of her phone all the way. No prizes for guessing who was calling. Clarice's cheery smile faded instantly when Harri handed her the envelope and Harri realised with horror that she already knew what it contained.

'Rob called me,' Clarice said quietly. 'Honestly, Harri, you have to believe me that I didn't know he'd taken *that woman* abroad. He promised me he was going to break it off with her last year, but . . . for what it's worth, my son is an idiot.'

'Yes, he is. You knew, then?'

'Oh, yes, he tells me everything,' she said proudly.

Harri's laugh was bittersweet. 'Shame you didn't tell me. What's her name?'

Clarice folded her arms and looked away. 'Melissa. He works with her. She's married, of course: husband works away a lot. Just so you know, the Preston contract was real, but it was all signed and sealed last July. I'm so sorry, Harri.'

Harri sighed. 'It's not your fault. But there is one thing you can do for me.'

Clarice nodded. 'Anything.'

'Tell your son to stop calling me. I've nothing more to say to him.'

Pulling away from Clarice's road, she suddenly recalled Alex's words before the kiss, the last time she had seen him:

You just need to believe it's possible.

He was right: all her life there had been other things to blame her fear on. But the fact remained that if she was as passionate about travelling as she said she was, *nothing* should stop her from stepping on a plane. Especially not Rob . . .

As she drove home, an idea started to form in her mind, tiny but burning bright: by the time she walked into the cottage her mind was made up. Picking up the phone as Ron Howard made a fussy circumnavigation of her feet, she called George.

'*Harriet?* Is that you?'

'Yes, it is. Sorry for ringing so late, George, but it's a bit of an emergency.'

'Flippin' 'eck, what's up? It's not going to involve hospitals, is it?'

Harri smiled. George's aversion to all things bloody, broken or infectious was nigh on legendary.

'No. I need to take some time off, in a bit of a hurry.' Her heart was banging against the wall of her chest, her palms clammy as adrenalin pumped through her veins.

361

'When?'

'Tomorrow. For two weeks. I know it's short notice, but I really have to go now.'

George paused and Harri could almost hear his mind whirring. 'This isn't like you.'

Her excitement began to sink away. 'I know.'

'So it must be important for you to ask. Oh, what the heck, it'll do Nusrin and Thomas good to have a bit of responsibility thrust upon them. I suppose I'll see you in two weeks.'

'Thank you, George!'

'Wait – where are you going?'

Harri smiled, remembering a conversation that afternoon at work. George had appeared with the new offers for the window and, as happened every week, Tom, Nus and Harri had gathered round to see which destinations were included. One had really caught her eye, not least because she had bought a travel book for the place only a week before.

'Wow – Kefalonia,' Tom had breathed, picking the card up. 'Two weeks, self-catering in a luxury apartment, flying from Birmingham International.'

'Man, how nice would that be?' Nus had said wistfully. 'Kefalonia in May – perfect! Before all the horrible kids go out there for summer holidays, and not too hot.'

'It's meant to be amazing,' Harri had agreed, recalling the pictures of deep blue and turquoise seas around picturesque beaches and hidden coves she had seen in her book.

'You should go,' Tom had beamed. 'Bit of sun, nice apartment, all those friendly towns . . . I'd be there like a shot if my mum hadn't cut up my credit card.'

'Kefalonia,' Harri said now.

'The holiday from the offers? Excellent choice. Want me to book it for you from my wireless connection to the office network?'

362

'Would you?'

'Your wish is my command, *mademoiselle*.'

'What about the money, though?'

'Settle up with me when you get home. When do you want to travel? How about later tomorrow? Give you a chance to pack and that.'

Harri realised she hadn't thought this through. She didn't even have a decent suitcase to pack, let alone suitable clothes. 'I think that might be an idea. I'll have to go to Berryhall first thing tomorrow to buy some things – oh, and pick up some money.'

She heard George laugh. 'When did you get so impetuous, eh? When you get to Berryhall, head to Best Choice Travel and ask for Holly. Tell me how much you want and I'll call her tonight and arrange for some Euros to be left for you – just pay for them when you get there, OK?'

'Thank you. Um, George?'

'Yeah?'

'Why are you being so nice to me?'

He sighed. 'Because I know something big must've happened and you sound like you need a break. And also because, contrary to popular opinion, I am not a heartless ogre from Codsall.'

'Well, right now, I think you're wonderful,' Harri said.

George coughed nervously. 'You can pack that in right now. Just beggar off and have a nice time, OK?'

The next call Harri made was going to be tricky. Ron Howard needed looking after and it was too late to book him into the cattery. There was only one option left . . .

Half an hour later, with a very bemused ginger and white cat in tow, Harri arrived at Viv's house.

The front door flew open as she reached the doorstep and Viv threw her arms around Harri, hugging her tightly.

'Oh my *darling*! My poor, poor girl! What a horrible thing to happen to you!'

Harri had expected this kind of welcome after her phone call, so she said nothing until Viv relinquished her hold. 'It is. But it's done now and I'm not going to give him another thought. So –' she presented the cat carrier to Viv, 'here's Ron. Are you sure you don't mind looking after him?'

'Not at all.' Viv pushed a cat treat through the wire bars, instantly winning over Ron Howard. 'He'll have a lovely time here, don't worry.' She looked at Harri. 'And how are you feeling?'

Harri took a deep breath. 'Good, actually. I'm doing the right thing.'

Viv smiled, her eyes full of compassion for her late friend's daughter. 'Yes, my darling. You are.'

By the time Harri climbed into bed that night, she was utterly exhausted by the day's events. The promise of what lay ahead thrilled and terrified her in equal measure, but the devastation at Rob's affair was still raw. She caught sight of the faded postcard in Grandma Langton's gilt frame on her bedside table and fresh tears filled her throbbing eyes. Gazing at the dome of Santa Maria della Salute, she whispered, 'I haven't forgotten you.'

The dream of Venice was still alive in her soul – but her hope to see it hand in hand with a man she loved remained firmly in place. Kefalonia was a test: if she could do this, then anything was possible. Baby steps, as her mother used to say. Now at least, she knew that Rob wouldn't be the one to take her, but despite all the heartache and betrayal, she was surprised to find an eternal flame of belief burning away inside. The right man was somewhere out there in the world and, when she found him, Venice would be hers. But for now, her first adventure beckoned . . .

CHAPTER TWENTY

Island Life . . .

From the cubicle, Harri can hear Viv's voice – still berating Merv – trailing away into the distance, and she breathes a sigh of relief. Just a little while longer, she tells herself, and then I'll go. She checks her purse to see if she has any Sterling and finds a five-pound note. It looks strange after two weeks of nothing but Euros. She smiles as a business card catches her eye in the card section. Pulling it out, she reads the gold embossed name at its centre: *Blanche Gilmour-Olsen*.

Athens Airport was a frenetic hub of noise, colour and movement, relentless in its assault on the senses. Loud, animated conversations in a multitude of languages were firing left and right across the terminal floor as passengers pushed squeaky-wheeled baggage trolleys laden with luggage across its shiny expanse, like crazy Dodgems in a funfair ride.

The flight had been amazing. Harri loved it, mentally photographing every moment from take-off to landing. Slightly disoriented after her arrival, Harri passed slowly through the terminal following signs for onward flights, checking her travel information as she went. Finally, she found the airport lounge and, thankfully, dropped into a seat.

'You look like I feel, missy,' a deep, gravelly American woman's voice said from behind a copy of American *Vogue*. 'Only you make bewildered look so much better.' The magazine lowered to reveal a large, glamorous-looking redhead in a white linen trouser suit. She extended her perfectly manicured hand, gold bracelets jangling as she did so. 'Hey. I'm Blanche. Blanche Gilmour-Olsen.'

'Harriet Langton. Um – Harri's fine.' They shook hands.

'I see we have the same choice in hair colour,' Blanche beamed, patting her luxuriant bouffant style. 'Yours natural?'

'Yes, it is. Yours?'

Blanche threw her head back and unleashed a cracked, guttural laugh on their unsuspecting fellow passengers, eliciting a mixed reaction. 'Hell, no, honey! But thanks for indulging my ego there.'

'So are you waiting for the transfer flight to Kefalonia?'

'I am indeed. Where are you staying?'

'Fiskardo – in an apartment complex just on the outskirts of the town.'

'You're kidding me? Me too! What's the name?'

Harri pulled the information from her rucksack. 'Emplissi Beach.'

Blanche clapped her hands and let out a whoop. 'It looks like we'll be travelling together, Harri.'

Liking her loud American travelling companion immediately, Harri was glad of the company.

After the forty-five-minute transfer to Kefalonia Airport flew them over the breathtaking turquoise-blue sea as the sun began to dip towards the horizon (with Blanche hardly pausing for breath during the entire journey), they emerged from the busy terminal building into the warm evening sun. Taxi drivers were parked up outside, grinning white smiles in the hope of winning fares. They walked along the ranks of cars until they saw a tall, lean young man holding a sign that read 'Emplissi Beach Apts'. He smiled as they approached.

'*Yásas*, ladies. You are for the Emplissi Beach, yes? Harriet Langton and Blanche . . . er . . .' He stared at the name written on the back of his sign.

'Gilmour-Olsen,' Blanche interjected. 'Don't worry, I'm sure you'll get your tongue round it real soon.' She fluttered her eyelashes vampishly at him. Though he could be her son, Blanche clearly had no intention of letting pass the opportunity to flirt outrageously with their good-looking escort.

'My name is Milos Voukouris. Let me take your bags, please. The minibus is not far away.'

The journey up to the north of the island was stunning – and the low, golden evening light added a lustre to everything as the minibus sped along the coast road towards Fiskardo. She remembered Alex describing this journey to her last year, but experiencing it for herself was so much better. Pushing the thought of him away, she gazed out at the Kefalonian landscape.

'My father owns the apartments,' Milos explained. 'We have a small taverna too, so you must come for dinner. This is your first time here?'

'It's my first time *anywhere*,' Harri laughed. 'I've never holidayed abroad before.'

Blanche looked at her aghast, as if her revelation was tantamount to heresy. 'How on *earth* have you never travelled?'

'Long story. How about you?'

'Why, darling, I've travelled *all* over, believe me. But this is my first time on your beautiful island, Milos.'

His huge white-toothed grin flashed again. 'Well, maybe we

will have to show you around a little. Although I warn you: you will be leaving a piece of your heart here.'

The Emplissi Beach Apartments lay up a track that rose from the main road and headed into the hills. The minibus bumped along, an experience made more hair-raising in the fading light of the evening. Rounding a corner, the apartments suddenly came into view – every window in the traditional, dusky-pink three-storey building alive with soft light.

Milos helped them out, opening the back doors to retrieve their cases. They followed the grey crazy-paved path edged with small garden lights as it rounded the ground floor of the building and up to the pool area. As they did so, a stunning view came into sight below them. Tiny lights from far-off villages over the bay twinkled round the fringes of the inky black ocean, and stars brighter than Harri had ever seen shone in the sky. The warm night air was filled with the scent of wild thyme and hibiscus, while the rhythmic chirping of cicadas lulled the senses into an undulating slow dance, like the waves of the ocean far below the hillside where they stood.

'Isn't it wonderful?' Harri breathed as Blanche slipped an arm through hers and hugged it.

'Awesome. Simply awesome.'

'Come, ladies – this way, please.'

Milos opened a large, wooden door and they walked inside. 'This was a farmhouse originally,' he informed them, taking the role of unofficial tour guide as they began to climb a whitewashed stone staircase to the floor above. 'It is over two hundred years old and has been in my family for four generations. My father and brother converted it into apartments three years ago.' He stopped by another door and pushed it open, revealing a large room with a kitchen at one end, a balcony at the other and separate bathroom and bedroom. 'Miss Langton, this is your apartment,' he smiled. 'Miss Blanche, yours is across the hall. If you would like to rest a while, I will return at eight o'clock – my father has invited you to our taverna for dinner.'

Alone in her room, Harri walked out onto the cream-tiled balcony and inhaled deeply. No book could ever show you the smell, sound and taste of a place – but in one lungful of air, she felt like she had inhaled Kefalonia into her soul. For the briefest moment, she wished she could tell Alex about this – it was a reflex action she still hadn't quite managed to shake the habit of. Stepping back into the room, she put the thought behind her and started to make herself at home.

To Kardiva was a small, single-storey taverna with a vine-canopied terrace overlooking a secluded beach, just off the Fiskardo road. Milos' father, Thaddeus, strode out to meet them when they walked up from the minibus.

'*Kalí spéra*, my honoured guests!' he boomed, kissing Harri and Blanche on both cheeks. 'Tonight you will join my family. Come, come . . .'

Although Harri had tasted Greek food before, it was nothing like the dishes served up by Thaddeus and his tiny wife, Eleni. Crisp fried *saganaki* cheese, with lemon and hunks of home-made bread; simple, grilled sardines, fresh from the sea; tender Greek lamb *souvlaki* and the ubiquitous Greek salad filled the long table. Milos sat next to Harri, while Thaddeus seated himself next to Blanche, who, of course, was delighted to have the broad-shouldered Greek beside her. Eleni never seemed to sit down for more than five minutes, shuffling back and forth between table and kitchen, barking orders at her sons Galen and Zeno, who were preparing the food.

Neighbours passed by and were dragged into the taverna to meet Harri and Blanche, whilst several cats and dogs wandered

369

happily around their feet. It was chaotic and relaxed at the same time – and this, Harri was to learn, was Greek life in a nutshell.

After a few days adjusting to their surroundings, exploring the achingly pretty town of Fiskardo, with its beautiful architecture, green-shuttered pink houses, yachts in the harbour and restaurants lining the quayside, Harri and Blanche began to take in more of the island, hiring taxis or occasionally hitching a lift with Milos or one of his brothers if they happened to be passing. As they did so, Kefalonia unveiled its treasures before their eyes: beautiful secluded coves you could only reach from the sea; lively towns like Sami and Argostoli; ancient ruins like the castle of Agios Georgios; and everywhere the uniquely Greek sights, sounds and smells – whole families crammed onto scooters cruising the streets in the evening, the scents of pine, bougainvillaea, and mouthwateringly fresh lemons, and the ever-present sound of goat bells (even though Harri never actually *saw* a goat during the whole two weeks she spent on the island).

To her great surprise, Harri learned that Kefalonia had a Venetian past: evidence of their architecture was everywhere, like the Venetian fortress at Assos. The original inspiration for Kefalonia's Carnival season came from the opulent masquerades Venice became so famous for. Knowing that this island – chosen, it has to be said, on a whim – was so inextricably linked with the city she dreamed about gave Harri a massive sense of peace, as if her world had just opened up to welcome her to its heart.

Early each morning, Harri would take the steep, winding path that led from the back of the apartments towards a tiny cove. She had found it quite by mistake, rising early on her first morning and venturing out into the lush gardens surrounding the pool. She never discovered its name, but as it seemed like she was the only person who visited it, she decided to call it La Serenissima beach, in honour of the island connection with the place she most longed to visit. Here, as dawn painted the sky with pastel pinks and blues, she would walk slowly along the water's edge, feeling the sand sinking beneath her toes and the warm waves lapping over her feet. For the first time in years, she felt peaceful – as if she was breathing fresh air for the very first time. She thought about the events of the past few months – of Rob, Alex and Chelsea – and it was as if the small cove afforded her a new objectivity to it all. While she had no idea what lay ahead, Harri knew that her decision finally to get on a plane was the vital first step to whatever came next. In those early morning strolls along the silent shore, the cool shadow of the cliff rising behind her, Harri began to make sense of her emotions, coaxing each one out from its hiding place deep in her heart. On the tiny beach she had infinite time and space to consider everything, and each morning she felt stronger, more resolute in her desire to become more like the Harri in her mind.

Most of all, Harri was glad of Blanche's company. The big, boisterous multiple-divorcee, originally from Kentucky but now living in a mansion in New Jersey, was fearless, happily throwing herself headlong into each new experience or challenge that came her way. After days spent exploring the island, they would retire to the coolness of her balcony, gazing out towards the island of Ithaca with the sunset sky arcing magnificently over the Steno – the expanse of sea that separated it from Kefalonia – and talk for hours, usually with a bottle of local Robola wine.

One thing that Harri quickly learned about Blanche was that it was no use trying to be elusive about your life with her. She had a way of getting to the truth eventually, so it was

371

simpler to tell her everything she wanted to know in the first place. Maybe it was because Harri was so far away from Stone Yardley, or maybe the positive outlook of the Kefalonians was rubbing off on her – but she somehow found it easier to talk about herself here.

'Wait, so let me get this straight: you kissed your best friend and then you didn't speak to him again?' Blanche asked, one evening at *To Kardiva*.

Harri nodded and helped herself to some Greek salad. Thaddeus and Eleni had outdone themselves tonight, she mused, looking across the blue and white checked table groaning under the weight of so much food. *Stifado*, thick beef *souvlaki*, plates of fresh tomato and cucumber slices, *tzatziki*, spicy, grilled fish – it was a Greek feast fit for a queen.

Blanche whistled. 'We-ell, that's one you got on me, missy. I kissed a lot of fellas in my time but I never locked lips with my best friend. So was it really that bad a kiss that you had to go all silent on him?'

Harri laughed – and it felt good. 'That was the problem. It was a *great* kiss.'

'Oh yeah?' Blanche took a large forkful of *stifado* and spoke as she chewed. 'OK, I gotta hear this, sister. Spill.'

'I couldn't possibly. Anyway, that's immaterial now. He's marrying someone else and I need to think about where I go from here.'

'Hey, come to New Jersey, girl! You know you're more than welcome. I'll find you a handsome guy who'll top *that kiss* for sure.' Her smile was genuine. 'I think you'll be fine, Harri Langton. You're one gutsy lady.'

Harri sipped her wine, feeling the spicy warm afterglow working its way to her toes. 'I don't feel very gutsy.'

Dropping her fork, Blanche stared at her. 'Well, you are!

Coming all the way out here, all alone, when you've never done it before? I call that gutsy! And if you can do that, well, I pretty much think you can do anything. You just have to believe it. Now tell me more about the guy you kissed . . .'

So Harri told Blanche about Alex, Chelsea, Stella, Dan and Rob – stories that joined together like a patchwork quilt as the days passed by. Blanche's favourite by far was what happened the night of the Christmas Amble, after Harri returned home.

Two Trees Cottage had welcomed her back with its warm yellow porch light throwing a beam across the frosted path as she opened her front gate; when she stepped inside its familiar surroundings she was surprised at how weary she felt. Changing out of her Victorian garb into pyjamas, towelling robe and slippers, she made a mug of milky coffee and curled up on the sofa with a blanket, as Ron Howard draped his warm body over her feet. She flicked through television channels until she found something nondescript to drown out the internal din of her thoughts and was just beginning to drift towards sleep when her mobile rang, bringing her sharply back into the room.

'Hey, matey, how's it going?'

'Al, I just left you an hour ago.' She willed him to take the hint. *Please go away*.

He didn't. 'What are you doing right now?'

Harri closed her aching eyes. 'Talking to you on the phone.'

'Such a comedian – shall I call Jongleurs and book you in?' Harri didn't reply. Undeterred, Alex pressed on valiantly. 'Well, I'll tell you what you're doing, young Harri-me-lass: you're going to eat ice cream with me.'

'I'm not hungry, Al.'

'Since when do you ever have to be hungry to eat ice cream? Don't you know all humans have a secondary stomach specifically designed to store emergency Ben & Jerry's late at night?'

'Mate, look, I appreciate the offer, but it's late and it will be even later by the time you get here.'

'Not much,' Alex replied, as a knock sounded at the front door.

Harri groaned. 'You're kidding, aren't you?'

The knock came again; a bright *dum-dum-dee-dum-dum* reminiscent of the sound heralding amusing next-door neighbours in sickly sweet sixties sitcoms. 'Nope. Let me in – the ice cream's melting.'

Slightly embarrassed about greeting him in her PJs, Harri made her way to the front door. When she opened it, Alex's grin lit up the hallway. 'Phish Food, see? Nobody can refuse Phish Food this close to Christmas.'

Despite her battered emotional state, Harri couldn't help smiling at her friend. 'You are a loon, Al. Come in then.'

Alex followed her into the kitchen, receiving a disdainful stare from Ron Howard *en route*, who was most displeased at being unceremoniously ejected from Harri's lap.

'Are you sure you're OK? You look *terrible*.'

'Cheers,' Harri replied, opening the cutlery drawer and rummaging around for spoons.

'I don't mean it like that. I'm concerned, that's all.'

Harri pushed past him to reach the crockery cupboard over the kettle. 'Well, don't be. I'm fine, honestly. It's just been a really long day.'

'I know,' he replied, eyeing her carefully. 'I just couldn't let you be alone – not after Rob's latest disappearing act.'

Harri's hand slipped and a bowl almost fell from the cupboard, saved only by Alex's quick reactions.

'Why don't we dispense with bowls and just share a tub,

374

eh?' he suggested gently, taking Harri's hand away from the cupboard and closing the door. 'I think our friendship has reached the point where that would be appropriate, don't you?'

She smiled weakly and nodded, following Alex back into the living room. 'I'm sorry, mate. Being tired makes me clumsy.'

'Yeah, yeah, whatever,' he grinned, flopping down on the sofa and patting the cushion next to him. 'So sit down and let's show this ice cream we mean business, shall we?'

Nothing more was said about Rob or the abandoned Scottish trip that night as Harri and Alex sat there: an unspoken understanding between them made further discussion unnecessary. Instead, Alex retrieved the remote control from underneath Ron Howard's generous behind – much to his disgust – and found an old Katharine Hepburn and Spencer Tracy film on TV. It was already almost an hour into its showing, but that was immaterial: what mattered was that words were rendered unimportant as they watched in the darkness. Harri finally allowed herself to relax, pushing concerns about her unreliable boyfriend away – for tonight at least, everything was good: Spencer and Katharine were still hopelessly in love *and* there was a half-demolished tub of ice cream to enjoy. Harri closed her eyes and succumbed to the blissful softness of the sofa . . .

When she woke, daylight was pooling in through the gap between her living-room curtains, and Alex was nowhere to be seen. Blinking away the sleep from her eyes, Harri sat up slowly and realised that she had been sleeping underneath the duvet from her bed. Looking down, she saw a pillow resting on the arm of the sofa where her head had lain. She smiled and shook her head. Alex must have tucked her in before he left. As the blurriness left her vision, she noticed a hastily scribbled note propped up against the empty ice-cream tub on the coffee table in front of her:

Morning sleepy!
Breakfast in the kitchen (amazing what culinary delights
you can source from an all-night garage at 3 a.m.). Sorry
I had to dash but I promised Mum I'd take part in the
annual Brannan family gift-round before she goes away.
I've put a couple of pizzas in the fridge if your other
(non ice-cream) stomach gets hungry.
  Alx
Ps. Thanks for last night. Spencer and Katharine send
their regards (even though you fell asleep during their
film. Tsk).

Harri stood and walked stiffly through to her kitchen, where Alex had placed eggs, a pack of bacon and two English muffins, together with a large carton of orange juice, a can of cat food and another note:

Welcome to your breakfast.
Please treat with respect and do not (a) incinerate on
hob; or (b) attempt crockery juggling re: last night. Also
please see grub duly provided for RH – even though he
hates me.
  Enjoy! X

'Let me get this straight: the guy comes to your rescue, brings you ice cream and leaves you breakfast and you don't understand why you kissed him?' Blanche asked incredulously. 'I'd have married him on the spot!'

In return, Blanche told Harri all about her own life: marrying

376

an oil prospector when she was seventeen, who then became a millionaire, divorcing him when she found him in bed with his secretary; meeting husband number two – a film director – at an oil baron's ball and eventually moving to Los Angeles where they had three kids, but filing for divorce when a newspaper exposé revealed a string of his affairs with aspiring actresses. Marrying husbands three and four within the space of five years – number three (considerably older than she was) dropping dead in their kitchen while making popcorn, and number four divorcing her because he decided he wanted to move in with an eighteen-year-old waitress from Tucson; and finally, number five – a university professor at Harvard who, after three blissful years of marriage, calmly announced to her that he wanted a sex change.

'So, that was the end of that,' she said with a wry smile. 'I got the mansion in New Jersey, he got my wardrobe. Everyone was happy.'

'I bet that put you off relationships for life?' Harri sipped her wine and closed her eyes to inhale the night air.

'Hell, no, missy! Just like that good-for-nothing ex of yours won't make you swear off men either. See, I was *designed* to be loved – and so were you. My mother used to say there are two types of people in this world: those that need somebody and those that are enough of a somebody all by themselves. You and I need to share our lives with somebody else – and that's why you'll move on to someone new in time, and so will I.'

'But don't you want a break? After all those broken relationships and messy divorces?'

Blanche's laughter drowned out the cicadas' song. 'Darling, I'm *having* a break, right now. Two weeks here, a month in London and then I'm back out there, looking for the next great love of my life.'

The more time she spent with Blanche, the more positive Harri felt about her own life. She could feel herself changing as the days passed, and the forward motion felt good. She didn't care what Rob did next; Melissa was welcome to him. But Alex was a different proposition. What if Viv had been right when she said he was missing Harri? As she mulled it over, walking along Fiskardo's harbourside, or reading on its olive-fringed beach, she realised that she needed to make peace with him.

The day before she was due to leave, a text arrived from Viv:

Hi sweetie. Hope the holiday is going well and that you're feeling better. You are well shot of Rob. Alex and Chelsea are having a belated engagement party this Friday night at the village hall. PLEASE COME. I know it would mean the world to Alex if you were there. At least think about it. Lots of love, Viv xxx

'Are you going to go?' Blanche asked as they sat in a restaurant on the promenade at Sami after a morning spent shopping for souvenirs.

Harri took a bite of sweet *baklava* and considered it. 'I honestly don't know.'

'Well, for what it's worth, I think you should go.'

'You do?'

'Most definitely. Show them all who you really are – one gutsy lady!' She raised her coffee cup. 'Here's to life, no matter where it takes us!'

Harri grinned and clinked her cup with Blanche's. 'To life, no matter what!'

They said their goodbyes to Thaddeus, Eleni, Galen and Zeno that night at *To Kardiva*, Eleni in tears as she hugged them goodbye.

'You will come back to Kefalonia,' she sobbed. 'We are family now!'

Milos arrived early next morning to take Harri and Blanche to the airport. Harri watched with a heavy heart, fighting the urge to cry as Fiskardo slipped out of view on the winding coast road. The journey south was a quiet one, Harri and Blanche lost in their thoughts as the beauty of the Kefalonian scenery whizzed past. All too quickly, the minibus pulled up outside the airport terminal. Milos hugged them and kissed them on both cheeks.

'*Efharistó, Milos,*' Harri smiled, 'for everything.'

'You are welcome, Harriet. I think pieces of your heart are scattered over this island,' he grinned. 'I know you will return.'

Harri and Blanche caught the transfer flight back to the hustle of Athens Airport and here they said their goodbyes.

'Now promise me you'll go back looking for the next big love of your life,' Blanche said, hugging Harri as if her life depended on it. 'Make me proud, missy!'

'I'll try. And you have fun looking for Number Six,' she replied, hugging Blanche back.

'Oh, I intend to!' Breaking the hug, Blanche touched Harri's face with her hand. 'Go to the party, darling. What have you got to lose?'

CHAPTER TWENTY-ONE

Raise Your Glasses, Please . . .

The door to the ladies' opens and Viv returns.

'I'm sorry, darling. Merv's being an absolute pain the proverbial. He's had way too much wine and he just challenged the caretaker to a duel. I've had to sit him in the car to calm him down. *Silly* man. I think I need to get him home for his own safety. So . . . so I'm going now. Are you coming with me?'

Inside the cubicle, Harri is less certain about leaving than she has been all evening – the shock from the events leading up to her flight into the ladies' only now beginning to fully assault her mind. 'I'll be fine. Just go.'

Viv hesitates, torn between protecting Harri and preventing Merv from embarrassing himself any further. 'Well – if you're sure?'

'Don't worry about me. Thanks for the company. I'll call you tomorrow.'

The thud of the door closing as Viv leaves resounds with a profound sense of finality. Now Harri knows what she must do . . .

The flight back to Birmingham seemed significantly shorter than the flight out to Kefalonia – but with Harri trying to make up her mind about the party, conscious of time slipping past like the clouds outside the aircraft windows, it was perhaps not surprising.

By the time she passed through customs and collected her case, the answer to her dilemma was clear. The tiny possibility that Viv had broken the habits of a lifetime and *not* exaggerated the truth wouldn't go away. If Alex did want her there then he might be ready to step back into his 'best friend' shoes . . . Whatever else she felt about him, she had to admit that she had been bereft without his friendship. If they could make peace, at least that would be a start to regaining the friendship she thought had died.

She hailed a taxi and leaned against the plush upholstery inside as it took her around the outskirts of Birmingham, on through the Black Country towards Stone Yardley. As they drove through Innersley, Harri suddenly had a thought and asked the taxi driver to stop outside Impress, the small boutique at the end of Oak Street. The purple shoes on the rack just inside the shop immediately caught her eye – gorgeous purple satin with tiny diamanté sparkles all over them. She winced when she saw the price tag, but she needed to feel confident tonight and they were perfect for the occasion.

When she stepped out on the road by her cottage, her mind was made up: she was going to the party.

She showered, then suddenly panicking that she had nothing suitable to wear with her new shoes, she searched through her wardrobe for a dress. Eventually, she discovered the emerald-green halter-neck dress that Stella had bestowed on her and was delighted to find it draped beautifully around her figure. It was a bold colour, but it glowed like a jewel against her wavy red hair and Ionian tan. Realising it was nearly seven o'clock, she ran a brush quickly through her hair, noting with pleasure the strawberry-blonde streaks recently added by the Kefalonian sun, applied a little eyeshadow, some mascara and a slick of lipstick, slipped on her ludicrously expensive shoes, grabbed her handbag and purple cardigan and ran out of the door to another waiting taxi.

When she arrived at Stone Yardley Village Hall, Harri paused on the pavement, seeing the disco lights whirling through the hall's windows and hearing the thud-thud-thud-thud of Disco Dave's music extravaganza already in full swing. How different she felt today from the last time she was here: leaving the Binchams' celebration early before Rob broke her heart over his abandonment of their Scotland break. Now, she even seemed to be walking taller, the spirit of optimism Kefalonia had infused through her glowing with an iridescence that was almost visible.

'Harri! You *came*!' Viv spotted her even before she reached the front steps and came running out, flinging her arms around her. 'You look *amazing*! Have you lost weight? Ooh, it's just *so* good to see you.'

'It's nice to see you, too,' Harri smiled. 'But if Al doesn't want me here then—'

'He does,' said a deep, velvety-soft voice behind her. 'Very much.' Spinning round, Harri came face to face with familiar chocolate-brown eyes – not filled with horror as they had been the last time they had met hers, but wide with anticipation and maybe a little touch of apology.

'Hi, Al.'

'Hey, H.'

'Right, well, I'll just . . . er . . . go inside, then . . .' Viv chirped, clapping her hands together and skipping quickly indoors.

Alex kept his eyes fixed on Harri, as if scared she would

382

disappear if he looked away. 'I apologise for my mother,' he smiled wryly.

'You should thank her, actually. I wouldn't have come if she hadn't asked me to.'

This was news to Alex. 'Seriously? Wow.' His hand moved, and for a moment Harri thought he was going to reach out to her, but he quickly thought better of it, stuffing it in his pocket. 'I'm really glad you did.'

'Me too.' A myriad questions flocked about their heads as they stood there like two uncertain teenagers at a school disco.

'Look, H, this is stupid. I was a total idiot in February and once I'd walked out I didn't know what to say to you.'

Relief broke like a white-crested wave over Harri's mind. 'I'm sorry, too. I was so embarrassed about . . . well, you know . . . and it was easier to hide away than face what happened. I never meant to make you feel uncomfortable or anything.'

'No, you didn't . . . I didn't . . .' He laughed nervously, in spite of his embarrassment. 'Um, I'm not brilliant at this, am I?'

'No, you're not.' The tension between them gone, Harri laughed. 'For heaven's sake, shut up and hug me, will you?'

'Gladly.' He opened his arms wide and she wrapped hers around his waist. The sudden closeness felt strange after so much time apart. At the end of the hug, Alex took a step back. 'I want to say how proud I am of you for just jumping on a plane, H. I always knew you had it in you. Rob is an idiot for not seeing that.'

'Thanks, Al. That means a lot.'

'Harri? Oh my life, how amazing do you look?'

Harri turned to see a familiar face walking towards them.

'Stella? When did you get back?' Harri squealed and they hugged. 'Let me look at you . . .'

Doing a little twirl, Stella happily obliged. Alex stared, open-mouthed. 'Crikey, Stel, what happened to you?'

'Dan. And Tibet. And *truth*,' she answered. 'There's so much I have to tell you about truth. Lama Rhabten taught me so much – I can't believe I ever lived my life without it. Absolute truth, Harri – it's the greatest gift.'

As transformations go, this was pretty impressive. Gone was the uniform bottle-blonde hair, strands of her natural chestnut tones now clearly visible. Gone were the designer-copy clothes and killer heels: now Stella was dressed in a flowing ethnic-print shirt over a plain white vest top with loose-fitting jeans and blue kitten-heeled pumps, and a simple wooden necklace hung at her neck. She was thinner than before and her skin was dewy fresh – in fact, Harri could hardly see any make-up at all. But the most notable feature of her 'Dan Beagle make-over' was the change in her attitude: she was calmer, more relaxed, maybe even more mature.

'I'm glad you could come,' Alex smiled.

'Your mum invited me this afternoon when Dan and I popped into her shop. I went into SLIT too, Harri, but they said you were *abroad*?'

'I've just come back actually,' Harri beamed. 'It was amazing, Al, you should've seen it. And the scent of the place – nobody tells you how wonderful that is, either! I'll definitely go back.'

There was a definite twinkle in his eyes. 'I've missed you. Now I suppose I should be getting back to my fiancée . . . Where is she?'

Harri looked around. 'There she is,' she said, pointing to the hall entrance, where Chelsea was deep in conversation with Jack.

Alex followed her outstretched arm until he saw them. '*Man,* are they nattering *again*?' he groaned. 'Honestly, they're either planning something thoroughly nasty for my stag night or else I'm about to lose a Best Man and gain a Chief Bridesmaid. I'll catch you later, Harri – OK?'

The village hall was packed with guests, mostly sitting at tables around the edges of the hall or crowding together at the bar, although some brave souls were already throwing some dubiously funky shapes on the dancefloor. Stella and Harri found a vacant table and sat down to catch up.

It was so good to see Stella after all this time, and Harri found herself relaxing back into their easy conversation, her mind at peace knowing that Alex didn't hate her. It transpired that Dan and Stella had taken three months off, following the completion of the filming schedule for his great Himalayan odyssey, and were now making plans for their own wedding after an unexpected result of their trip came to light.

'You're *pregnant*?' Harri repeated, as Dolly Parton's 'Nine to Five' elicited a gutsy singalong from the dancing partygoers.

Stella nodded ecstatically. 'I know! And I *hated* children! Who'd have thought it, eh? Me a wife and mother . . .' she lifted one foot and pointed, '. . . in almost flat shoes!'

As the evening progressed, Harri told Stella about Rob and her subsequent spur-of-the-moment decision to go on holiday. Stella listened intently to it all, taking everything in – something virtually unheard of before she had met Dan. Maybe he was what she had been waiting for during all those years of dating unsuitable men.

'So, I take it the stand-off between you and Al is over?' she asked as they watched the long line for the buffet snake its way across the dancefloor.

'Yes, I think so. I just missed him being my friend,' Harri

385

replied, looking over to the table on the opposite side of the room, where Alex and Chelsea were chatting to friends.

'But the kiss was real, right?'

'I honestly don't know what happened, Stel. I'm just so glad it's behind us.'

'Uh-huh.' Stella's expression concealed more than Harri could fathom.

'*Laydeez* and gentlemen,' Disco Dave's voice boomed through the hall, 'please join us on the dancefloor to toast the happy couple!'

Harri and Stella joined the other guests as they formed a circle in the middle of the room. Viv stepped forward and took the microphone from a slightly worried-looking Dave.

'Thank you, Dave, and welcome everybody. Now, as you know, the reason we're all here tonight is to celebrate the engagement of my lovely son Alexander to the lady who has stolen his heart – Chelsea.'

Suitable 'aah's and noises of approval rippled around the room. Chelsea looked like she was in heaven, being the centre of attention.

'We thought it would be a lovely idea if some of you here tonight had the opportunity to offer your own good wishes to Alex and Chelsea,' Viv continued, as trays of sparkling wine were handed out. 'So if you'd like to say something, just raise your hand and I'll bring the microphone over.'

Unlike his fiancée, Alex looked decidedly uncomfortable in the middle of the dancefloor. Catching Harri's eye, he mouthed, 'Help!' as his mother circled the floor, seeking out her first volunteer.

Jack raised his hand and Viv thrust the mic into it. 'Hell-o Stone Yardley,' he said in his best rockstar voice, to the amusement of the onlooking guests. 'OK, listen. I've known Al for a long old time and I know he's the kind of guy that will go out of his way to make *any* woman happy,' he grinned wickedly, 'so watch out for my Best Man's speech in September! And as for Chels – well, what can I say? Top bird, Al, she's the best thing that's happened to you.' He raised his glass. 'Cheers.'

'Cheers!' echoed the guests.

Chelsea feigned embarrassment and blew him a kiss.

'Right, thank you, Jack. Someone else?' Viv looked hopefully around the room as almost every guest dropped his or her eyes to avoid her stare. 'Come on – there must be someone?'

To Harri's surprise, Stella's hand shot up. Delighted, Viv walked over and bestowed the microphone on her. Walking into the middle of the dancefloor, Stella turned and smiled at everyone.

'Hi, everyone. Can I just say what a great honour it is to be here tonight, to celebrate Alex and Chelsea's engagement. Don't they make a wonderful couple?'

The guests agreed and a smattering of applause broke out across the room. Harri was impressed by Stella's self-assuredness with the microphone; she had obviously learned a lot from watching Dan at work.

'I've known Alex since he came back to live in Stone Yardley after all his years travelling this wonderful world. And I must say, having recently returned from the Himalayas, I now understand what all the fuss is about. Now, I have to admit, Alex and I haven't always seen eye to eye on things, but I know the kind of friend he is to my best mate Harri Langton over there . . . come on Harri, give us a wave!'

Harri felt herself shrinking back, willing the crowd's eyes away from her.

'. . . and I know that he really cares about her, which is good enough for me. He's a top bloke – a little insensitive on some things, perhaps, but generally a nice guy. Round of applause for the bridegroom-to-be, please.'

Hesitantly, the crowd obliged.

'Excellent, thank you. As for Chelsea, well, I've only just met her although it feels like I know *so much* about her already . . .'

Chelsea's smile turned into a grimace, willing the hippy limelight-hogger to leave *her* spotlight immediately.

Stella continued, oblivious to anything but her own train of thought. 'And I'm sure she is fully prepared for the responsibilities of being a wife. Aw, round of applause for Chelsea!'

This time, the lukewarm applause was accompanied by confused glances exchanged around the room. Harri watched as the crowd began to get restless, shifting position where they stood and whispering amongst themselves. She tried to summon Stella's attention, but it was no use: she was on a roll and there was no stopping her now.

'So, to my toast . . .'

'Haven't you done that already, love?' a man called from the crowd, as those around him agreed noisily, like a gaggle of backbenchers heckling a speaker.

'Not quite,' Stella smiled serenely. She raised her glass. 'Alex. Chelsea. When I was in the Himalayas, I met an old Tibetan monk called Lama Rhabten. We spent three weeks at his home, talking about the mysteries of life and love. And he said this: "The greatest gift you can give yourself is the truth. Truth sets us free and gives us wings. Truth banishes doubts and fears." So I would like to give you the greatest gift possible for your lives ahead: the truth.'

Harri's heart began to pick up pace. What was she talking about?

'Alex, if you're going to spend the rest of your life with Chelsea, you need to fully understand her – not just what you see on the outside, but the secret, hidden aspects of her life. A good husband knows who his wife is and loves her anyway.'

Wincing, Harri stared at Stella. Where on earth had she got that little gem of wisdom from? A fridge magnet?

'So the truth is, Alex, that Chelsea is more interested in your best friend than she is in you.'

Silence clamped its hand firmly across the mouths of the astonished guests. Chelsea looked at Jack, panic washing across her face, mirroring his own expression.

Angrily, Viv stepped towards Stella and made a bid for the microphone. 'I really don't think this is appropriate for—'

'Mum, hang on a minute.' Alex's voice was low and serious. 'What do you mean by that, Stella?'

'I saw them kissing earlier this evening, round the back of the hall.'

Chelsea yelped and Jack sprang forward. 'Mate, she's a loon. You're not going to believe her, are you?'

'I – I don't know . . .' Alex's stare switched between Chelsea and Jack like a spectator at a tennis match.

'Alex, you of *all* people should know about hidden truths,' Stella continued, a note of reproach in her voice. 'I mean, when you kissed *Harri*, you—'

'You kissed *her*?' Chelsea demanded, as Harri shot to her feet.

'Stella, *enough!*'

'But it wasn't enough, was it, Harri? Face it – you're head over heels in love with him, aren't you?'

'Stop it, Stel! Just stop this!'

Stella moved the microphone away from her face and shouted loud enough for everyone else to hear. 'But I'm only telling the truth, Harri! You said as much in your email – you said you were going out of your mind with it all and that you loved him!'

It was as if the floor beneath Harri's feet was giving way. She slumped back into a chair as the whole room began to fill with noise and movement.

Viv wrenched the microphone from Stella's hands. 'That's quite enough interfering from you, young lady!'

Stella folded her arms coolly, unfazed by the murderous look in Viv's eyes. 'Interfering, eh? Well, from *you* I take that as a compliment.'

'I *beg* your pardon?'

'It was your idea to nominate Alex for that magazine column that started all of this, wasn't it? It was because you thought he was so pathetic at dating that he needed a helping hand. But you need to learn to complete each task you undertake, Viv. I mean, getting Harri to do all the work of going through those letters without ever helping was a bit tough, wasn't it?'

Viv opened her mouth to speak, but shut it when she saw her son's expression. 'Darling, I . . . I only had your best interests at heart . . .'

'So why didn't you help Harri?' Alex demanded.

'Yes, Viv, why didn't you? Maybe then Harri wouldn't have been tempted to set Alex up on the *worst possible date*.' Stella looked pointedly at Chelsea, who was being comforted – perhaps ill-advisedly – by Jack.

'What do you mean?' Alex looked from Stella to Harri, who had begun to shake uncontrollably. 'Harri?'

'Chelsea was meant to be revenge,' Stella said, 'for what you said to Jack.'

'How *dare* you?' Chelsea screamed like a banshee. 'I'm *not* the worst possible date. I'm the best he's ever likely to get! If it wasn't for me, he'd be *nothing* – still stuck in his crummy coffee shop with no ambition, no dress sense . . . *I* made him what he is, I mean, look at him!'

Obediently, all eyes in the hall swung to Alex, who was fuming dangerously. 'Is that what you think of me, Chelsea?'

Defiantly, Chelsea wrapped her arm around a startled Jack. 'Yes, actually. She's right: I *am* more interested in Jack than I ever was in you. Jack takes me to nice, expensive places. Jack spends serious cash on making me happy. He doesn't have a lousy business to "save his money" for.'

'You should have chosen Harri when you had the chance!' Stella shouted, as Viv swung for her. 'She's always loved you!'

At that moment, all hell broke loose. Alex lunged at Jack and hit him with a hefty right hook, sending him careering backwards into the bar, glasses and onlookers scattering in all directions. Chelsea jumped onto his back, kicking and screaming like a madwoman, and Alex yelped in pain, shrugging her off onto the buffet table. Rising to his feet, Jack punched Alex in the stomach, bending him double and Viv, incensed by this, ran over to Jack and laid him out cold with one seriously scary uppercut. Women screamed and men shouted as smaller disputes began breaking out all over the hall, vol-au-vents and sandwiches grabbed as ammunition and thrown at offending opposers.

In the middle of it all, Alex staggered, bloodied, through the wrecked remains of his engagement party towards Harri. His dark eyes – which earlier had been so happy to see her – now filled her with fear . . . because this time the look he gave her was *real* pity.

Hurt, scared and angry, Harri chose the only sensible thing left to do. She fled out of the hall, down the corridor, pushed open the grey-green door to the ladies' loo and locked herself in the middle cubicle, sitting on the wobbly plastic seat with her head in her hands, sobbing uncontrollably.

CHAPTER TWENTY-TWO

Stepping Out

It's time.

Rising to her feet, Harri takes her bag off the hook and reaches for the lock. It slides open with a loud click. Swinging the door open, she walks out into the washroom area. It's colder in here than she realised and she is glad of Viv's pashmina still wrapped around her shoulders. Stepping over to the wash basins, she catches sight of herself in the mirror. Blimey, she looks rough. Glancing at the pale stripe across her left wrist, she remembers that she left her watch at home tonight. Even so, she can tell it's late.

She leans against the ladies' loo door, listening carefully for any signs of life. But all is silent: the commotion that drove her in here is now audible only in her memory. Confident that she is alone, she pulls the door open and steps out into the corridor.

The light is still on and Harri wonders if someone has stayed behind to wait for her. The heels of her too-expensive shoes click-clack loudly down the parquet floor of the corridor until she reaches the main hall. Far from the scene of carnage she left, most of the debris has now been tidied away, leaving an empty space behind. Nobody is here, either. Secretly, Harri had entertained a hope that Alex might be waiting for her – even if it was just to have the last say before walking away forever – but the emptiness of the hall confirms her worst fears: she has lost him, for good this time.

Just as she is about to leave, a flicker of movement out of the corner of her eye catches her attention, spinning her back round. A figure is standing by the entrance to the kitchen. Squinting, she tries to make out their features, her heart in her mouth.

'Hello?'

'You the last of 'em, are you?' A short, wiry-limbed man steps forward.

Harri's hope plummets. 'Oh, hi, Ned. Yes, I think I am.'

'Proper bostin' punch-up it was in 'ere tonight,' he observes drily. 'I 'aven't seen one that good since the Silver Jubilee.'

Harri smiles politely and makes her escape into the cold night.

It's too late for a taxi now – and she doesn't have the number of a local rank, anyway. The only way to get back to her cottage is to walk. In reality, it isn't far – only a mile and a half – a journey she has made countless times before on pleasant summer evenings. But tonight it seems to take an eternity. Her feet feel leaden, dragging her downwards, making every step an immense effort . . .

As she walks, she remembers the harbourside in Fiskardo at night: the warm breeze swirling around her arms as she passed row upon row of tables and chairs in the waterfront restaurants; the lights of the town reflecting in the indigo-black waters of the harbour; above her, the full moon she had watched rise quickly from the sea like Venus in an old master painting. Now it feels almost as if she dreamed Kefalonia – the cold breeze numbing her fingers as she draws the ends of Viv's pashmina ever closer.

If only she hadn't confided in Stella. She should have known that information like that wouldn't have stayed hidden for long once Stella was in possession of it. Yet at the time the thought of her friend thousands of miles away and unlikely to return gave her reassurance to divulge it. How wrong she had been . . .

As she opens the gate from the field and walks out onto Waterfall Lane, her thoughts inevitably shift to Alex and her heart contracts with a long, dull ache. She had come so close to regaining her friendship with him – how had it all been taken away from her again so easily?

'Do you love him, Harri?' Blanche had asked one night as they ate a dessert of Greek yoghurt with walnuts and thick honey under the vines at *To Kardiva*.

'I honestly hope not,' Harri had answered truthfully. But inside, she knew the answer to the question; and so, she suspected, did Blanche.

Not that any of that matters now, of course. Alex is gone and she needs to move on, like Blanche said: *Just keep looking out for the next great love of your life . . .*

At least – she muses as she walks – with the complications of her heart removed, she can set about creating the kind of life *she* wants to live. She will definitely take more holidays abroad: Blanche has invited her to New Jersey later in the year, 'when my break from looking for Number Six is over . . .' and Harri plans to combine it with a trip to New York, visiting her cousin Rosie and seeing the sights. Before she left for Kefalonia, Emily had asked her to help with the art and craft holidays at Greenwell Hill Farm too – a prospect Harri still likes immensely. Getting through the past few months and taking her first steps into the big wide world that she has always wanted to experience has brought about a vital change within her: the fear of the unknown has gone.

She walks the final stretch of Waterfall Lane, passing her neighbours' houses as she nears her own. Reaching the gate at the bottom of her garden, she lifts the latch – and stops dead...

Someone is waiting for her. He is leaning against the front door, shoulders hunched against the cool night.

'Alex?'

Slowly, she walks up the garden path towards him. He says nothing, eyes scrutinising her, cold and emotionless. He has come for the last word.

Harri has had enough drama and tension tonight to last her for several lifetimes. Wearily, she stops in front of him. 'Do you want to come in?'

Nothing. No response, not even a flicker.

'OK, well, if you don't mind, I've had a horrible day and I want to go to bed.' She waits for him to move, but he remains stoically in the porchway. It is too much. 'Al,' she pleads, emotion constricting her words, 'just say what you came here to say and then let me get on with my life. There's nothing you can say that I haven't already beaten myself over the head with.'

He breathes out, his breath a cloud of warm steam rising in the cool atmosphere that surrounds them. 'Is it true?'

'Is what true?'

'What Stella said tonight. Do you love me?'

'Why on earth does it matter?'

His eyes sear into hers. 'Because I want the truth.'

She stares back at him. 'I would have thought you'd had more than enough "truth" tonight.'

'I want to know, Harri. Do you love me?'

Perhaps the quickest way to get him to leave her alone is to be honest, Harri reasons. 'Yes, I do. And I really wish I didn't, but there it is. Now can I get into my house, please?'

'See, the thing is, Harri, I can't believe you told Stella all this stuff. She humiliated me – she humiliated all of us – for what purpose? I'm sure we could have survived blissfully unaware of all of that for the rest of our lives. I mean, why rake it all up now?'

Harri rubs her eyes. 'You know what, Al? I don't need this. I've just spent I don't know how many hours trying to get my head round it all and I've failed miserably. You just need to deal with it too, and move on. And I'm sorry I had to inconvenience you so much by falling in love with you. Believe me, I didn't plan it. But you needn't worry: I won't inconvenience you any longer. Thanks for being my friend, but I think you'll agree it's run its course. So just go home and let me get on with my life.'

Alex shakes his head. 'Ah, but I don't want to.'

With a cry of frustration, Harri steps forward. 'OK, what do you want from me, Alex?'

He reaches inside his jacket pocket and pulls out a long, white envelope. 'I want you to have this.'

Surprise sweeps aside her anger. 'What is it?'

'This is what I was going to give Chelsea tonight, only I really don't think there's much point doing that now, is there? Seeing as she's having an affair with my best friend. She probably wouldn't have appreciated it anyway.'

'I am sorry about that, Al,' Harri replies softly. 'I know what it feels like.'

'Yeah, I'm sorry to hear about Rob. You didn't deserve that. Go on, open it.'

Harri carefully unseals the envelope and takes out a plane ticket. Twisting it round, her eyes read the destination. Her heart leaps – then tumbles. Carefully, she replaces the ticket in the envelope and calmly hands it back. 'I can't. Sorry.'

His frow furrows. 'You can, it's yours.'

She pushes it back towards him. 'No, I can't.'

'But it's *Venice*,' he protests, refusing to accept it from her.

'And that's why I *can't*. Not on my own.'

There is a long silence. Harri's eyes brim with tears and the pain forces her eyes away from the ticket in her hand.

Then, Alex speaks, his voice unsteady. 'I know. That's why I have one too.'

Looking up, Harri searches his face. 'What do you mean?'

'Come to Venice with me.'

'I don't understand . . . I . . .'

'See, I've tried to put you out of my mind, Harri. I moved things on with Chelsea, proposed and started planning the wedding. I even bought tickets to the one place you love the most, thinking it would put you out of my head for good if I saw it with Chelsea. But nothing worked. All I can think about is the way we kissed that night. It changed everything. Don't look so shocked, H; you can't be totally surprised by this?'

'Forgive me, but I am. What you said then – the way you looked at me – you were horrified. I saw it in your eyes again this evening. How can that be love?'

'You saw *fear*, Harri! This whole thing scares the life out of me because you're my friend and I depend on you – and I don't want to risk losing you. That night I was an idiot and I ran away because I couldn't cope with how I felt.' He takes a step closer, his hands closing around hers as she grips the Venice ticket. 'You blew me away when you kissed me. I've never felt like that with anyone before – not even Chelsea, who I was convinced was the One. And it shook everything up.'

Questions are building like skyscrapers inside her – layer upon layer of issues, fears and disbelief cementing themselves together, blocking the way forward from view. At a loss for how to respond, Harri shrugs. 'So where do we go from here?'

Warmth ignites Alex's expression, a fire she has never seen before burning in his eyes. 'Venice. Me and you. I know we don't have the answers yet, but I'm willing to work it out if you'll help me?'

Heart beating wildly, Harri bows her head and whispers: 'So take me to Venice . . .'

Then his hands are stroking her face, his eyes are melting into hers and, when their lips meet, it's like a billion shooting stars colliding, filling every atom of darkness with shimmering light . . .

Venice: *La Serenissima* – the serene city where love and dreams walk its streets, hand in hand. On a stone bench overlooking the Grand Canal, two lovers kiss, each embrace answering another question in their hearts.

This is where Harri and Alex chose to begin the greatest journey of their lives – together. And all around them, the city smiles.

Read on for an exclusive extract from Miranda's next novel,
It Started With a Kiss **coming in 2010.**

ONE

The Most Wonderful Time of the Year?

When it comes to telling your best friend that you love him,
there are generally two schools of thought. One strongly advises
against it, warning that you could lose a friend if they don't
feel the same way. The other urges action because, unless you
say something, you might miss out on the love of your life.

Unfortunately for me, I listened to the latter.

The look in Charlie's eyes said it all: I had just made the
biggest mistake of my life . . .

'*Sorry?*'

'Maybe I should say it again? I said I love you, Charlie.'

He blinked. 'You're not serious, are you?'

'Yes.' I could feel a deathly dragging sensation pulling my
hope to oblivion.

'H-how long have you . . . ?'

I dropped my gaze to the potted plant beside our table. 'Um
– a long time, actually.'

'But, we're *mates*, Rom.'

'Yeah, of course we are. Look, forget I said anything, OK?'

He was staring at his latte like it had just insulted him. 'I
don't know how you expect me to do that. You've *said it* now,
haven't you? I mean it's – it's *out there.*'

I looked around the overcrowded coffee shop with its

uniformly disgruntled Christmas shoppers, huddled ungratefully around too-small tables on chairs greedily snatched from unsuspecting single customers. 'I think it's safe to assume that none of that lot heard anything.'

As attempts at humour go, it wasn't my finest. I took a large gulp of coffee and wished myself dead.

Charlie shook his head. 'That doesn't matter. *I* heard it. Oh, Rom – why did you say that? Why couldn't you just have . . .?'

I stared at him. 'Just have what?'

'Just *not said anything*? I mean, why me? Why put this on me now?'

I hated the look of sheer panic in his eyes. He'd never looked at me that way before . . . In my perennial daydream about this moment it had been so very different:

Oh Romily – I've loved you forever, too. If you hadn't told me we could have missed each other completely . . .

'We're fine as we are, aren't we? I mean, if it's good then why change it? I can't believe you actually thought that declaring your undying love for me would be a good idea.'

Well, *excuse me*, but I did. Somewhere between my ridiculous, now obviously deluded heart and my big stupid mouth, my brain got pushed out of the picture and I – crazy, deranged *loon* that I am – found myself persuaded that I might be the answer to his dreams. That maybe the reason for the many hours we'd spent together – cheeky laughter-filled days and late night heart-to-hearts dripping with chemistry – was that we were destined to be more than friends. Everyone else noticed it: it was the running joke amongst our friends that Charlie and I were like an old married couple. We'd lost count of the number of times complete strangers mistook us for partners. So if it was this blindingly obvious to the world, how come Charlie couldn't see it?

Of course, I couldn't say any of the above to him. Only much, much later, staring at the wreck that was my reflection in the bathroom mirror through mascara-blurred eyes, did I deliver my Oscar-worthy performance. But then and there, in the crowded café packed with people who couldn't care less about what I was saying, I found that – to my utter chagrin – all I could say was:

'I'm sorry.'

Charlie shook his head. 'I did *not* see this coming. I thought we were friends, that's all. But this – this is just *weird . . .*'

'Thanks for the vote of confidence, Charlie.'

He stared at me, confusion claiming his eyes. 'I – I didn't mean . . . Heck, Rom, I'm sorry – you've just got to give me a moment to get my head around this.'

I looked away and focused on a particularly harassed couple talking heatedly at the next table over enormous mugs of cream-topped festive coffees. 'You don't appreciate me,' the woman was saying. Right now, I knew exactly how she felt. 'The thing is,' Charlie said, 'you're just Rom – one of the guys, you know? You're a laugh, someone I can hang out with . . .' He gave a massive sigh.

'I'm really not sure how to deal with this . . .'

I'd heard enough. I rose to my feet, intense pain and crushing embarrassment pushing my body up off the chair. I opened my mouth to deal a devastating parting shot, but nothing appeared. Instead, I turned and fled, stubbing my toe on a neighbouring customer's chair, tripping over various overstuffed shopping bags and almost taking a packed pushchair with me as I beat an ungraceful retreat from the coffee shop into the bustling shopping mall beyond.

'Rom! Where are you going? *Rom!*' Charlie's shouts behind me blended into the blur of crowd noise and Christmas hits of yesteryear as I ran through the shopping centre, making my way blindly against the tidal flow of bodies, countless faces looming up before me, unsmiling and uncaring.

As I passed each shop the Sale signs began morphing into condemnatory judgments on my actions, screaming at me from every window:

Insane!
Stupid idiot!
What were you thinking?

Paul McCartney was singing 'Wonderful Christmastime' like it should have an ironic question mark at the end, as the jostling crowd propelled me involuntarily towards the upward escalator. Unable to wriggle free, I found myself moving along with the throng. But I felt nothing; my senses numbed by the faceless bodies hemming me in and my heart too beset by ceaseless repeats of Charlie's words to care any more. At a loss to make sense of the total catastrophe I'd just caused, I surrendered to the welcoming blandness of my surroundings and, quite literally, went with the flow.

What was I *thinking* telling my best friend in the whole world that I loved him? Perhaps it was the impending arrival of the *Most Wonderful Time of the Year* (thanks for nothing, Andy Williams) or the relentlessly festive atmosphere filling the city today that caused me to reveal my feelings to Charlie like that. Perhaps it was the influence of watching too many chick-flick Christmas scenes that had tipped my sanity over the edge and made the whole thing seem like such a great idea (Richard Curtis, Norah Ephron, guilty as charged). Whatever the reason, I had completely ruined everything and was now undoubtedly facing my first Christmas in fifteen years without him.

Unceremoniously dumped onto the next tier of the mall by the escalator, I managed to squeeze through the slow-moving shoppers to emerge breathless into a small pocket of relatively fresher air by a large, over-decorated artificial Christmas tree. Tears stung my eyes and I swallowed angrily in a vain attempt to keep them at bay. *What was the matter with me? How did I get it so devastatingly wrong?*

All the signs had been there, or so I thought: hugs that lingered a moment too long, snatched glances and shy smiles in the midst of nights out with our friends, moments of unspoken understanding during conversations begun in the early evening and ending as birdsong heralded a new day. Then there were his unexplained silences – times when I felt he had something more to say, where unresolved question marks sparkled magnificently in the air between us and the room held its breath – ultimately in vain. There had been more of these lately, peppering almost every occasion we spent together with an irresistible spice of intrigue. Only last Wednesday, Charlie had stopped the car in a country lay-by on our way to meet friends at our favourite bistro, specifically to give me a hug – with no words, no explanation. It was an intensely warm, lingering embrace, his cinnamon scent pervading my senses and his neck soft against my cheek, while his fingers traced slow circles across my shoulder blades. Once it ended, he started the car and we drove on as if it had never happened. If it didn't mean what I thought it did, then what on earth was that all about?

My mobile phone rang in my bag, but I couldn't face answering the call, so Stevie Wonder continued his tinny rendition of 'Sir Duke' unhindered by my usual intervention. Reaching into the crummy depths of my coat pocket, I retrieved a half-screwed up shopping list and read down the list of scribbled names: my To-Do list for the afternoon. It was the last Saturday before Christmas and my final chance to buy everyone's presents. Christmas shopping waited for no one, it seemed – not even thoroughly embarrassed owners of newly-shattered hearts.

Mum & Dad
Auntie Clara
Wren
Jack & Soph
Freya & Niall
Elliot & Millie
Tom & Anya
Charlie

Charlie. My breath caught in the back of my throat as my eye fell on the last name. *No need for that one to be there,* I hissed under my breath, *I think he's had quite enough surprise gifts from me this year.* I stuffed the list back into my pocket and turned as I prepared to dive back into the undulating ocean of people.

And that's when it happened.

It was so fast that I almost didn't realise what was going on. Even now, the details remain frustratingly sparse in my mind. But here's what I know:

As I was about to step out, a hurrying shopper slammed into my shoulder from behind, the force of it stealing my balance and propelling me forward. I braced myself for the inevitable impact as I headed towards the polished mall floor, but instead found myself suddenly supported by strong arms, lifting me back to my feet. My eyes first met a striped scarf, then headed north to reach quite the most gorgeous face I had

404

ever seen. His hazel eyes caught the light from white fairy lights strung overhead, whilst wavy strands of his russet-brown hair picked up the twinkling blue light from the lavishly decorated Christmas tree beside us. A slight shadow of stubble edged his jaw-line and his cheekbones were quite defined. Tiny details, really. But what I remember most – apart from what happened *next*, of course – was the expression on his face.

It was the kind of look you see in movies when a bridegroom turns to see his bride walking towards him for the first time; a heady, overpowering mix of shock, surprise and all-encompassing, heart-stopping love. It was the look that Charlie *should have* given me when I told him I loved him. But this wasn't Charlie: and that, in itself, was part of the problem. Because – apart from *not* being the man to whom I had publicly expressed my undying love not fifteen minutes beforehand – *this* person was almost perfect: from the woody scent of his cologne and the smile making its unhurried progress across his lips, to the strong, safe arms cradling me like a precious gem.

But most of all because of what happened next . . .

He only said two words, but they were enough. Two simple, amazing words that were just about to change *everything*.

'Hello beautiful,' he said.

I was about to say something in return when his head turned and I could hear a voice calling from the melee of faceless shoppers behind him.

'We've got to go . . . *Now!*'

His eyes returned to mine, now widening as he debated his next move. He stepped back, his hands slipping from my shoulders to my elbows, maintaining their hold on my arms. When they reached my hands, he took another look behind him, then back at me. Shaking his head, he drew both my hands towards him until we were face-to-face. I held my breath as the sudden intensity of the moment seemed to suspend time around us . . .

. . . and then, he lifted my hands up between us to meet his lips, and kissed them.

Although it was only the smallest of gestures, it was unlike anything else I've experienced. It was the kind of moment you only expect to see in Hollywood films – finally uniting the two leads as the credits start to roll over the delicious tones of Nat King Cole. In fact, even the soundtrack was perfect – because, at that very moment, Mr Cole himself began crooning 'Have Yourself a Merry Little Christmas' from the muffled speakers of the shopping mall, as I closed my eyes and gave in to the unexpected gift of the stranger claiming my hands.

It was almost perfect. *Almost*. But not quite. Because, as suddenly as he had appeared, he was gone: swallowed up by the heaving, unyielding mass of shoppers. So there I stood alone once more, dazed yet elated by the Christmas tree, my heart thumping wildly and my whole life altered irrevocably.

And that's why I have to find him.

Win a trip to Venice!

AVON are offering 1 lucky reader the chance to win a 3-night break for two adults to Venice, including flights and accommodation.

To enter this free prize draw, simply visit www.harpercollins.co.uk/avon to answer the question below. The closing date for this competition is March 31st 2011.

In *Welcome To My World* what is Harri's occupation?

A) A cleaner
B) A travel agent
C) A florist

Competition Terms and Conditions

1. This competition is promoted by HarperCollins Publishers ("HarperCollins"), 77-85 Fulham Palace Road, London, W6 8JB.
2. This promotion is open to all UK residents except employees of HarperCollins (or their parent, subsidiaries or any affiliated companies) and their immediate families, who are not allowed to enter the competition.
3. To enter this free prize draw go to www.harpercollins.co.uk/avon
4. Closing date and time for entries is midday on March 31st 2011. No entries received after this date will be valid. No purchase necessary. Only one entry allowed per household.
5. The prize is a trip to Venice, Italy for two adults including international return flights (economy class) and three nights accommodation at a 3 star hotel on a board only basis. Prize must be taken between 1st April 2011 and 31st October 2011 (excluding travel on UK bank holiday weekends). Meals are not included. Transfers to and from the hotel are not included.
6. The prize is non-refundable, non-transferable and subject to availability. No guarantee is given as to the quality of the prize.
7. No cash or prize alternatives are available.
8. HarperCollins reserve the right in their reasonable discretion to substitute any prize with a prize of equal or greater value.

9. The winner of the competition will be drawn at random from all correct entries and notified by telephone no later than the 30th April 2011.

10. Any application containing incorrect, false or unreadable information will be rejected. Any applications made on behalf of or for another person or multiple entries will not be included in the competition.

11. HarperCollins' decision as to who has won the competition shall be final.

12. To obtain the name of the prize winner after the closing date, please write to Welcome To My World/AVON, HarperCollins Publishers, 77-85 Fulham Palace Road, Hammersmith, London, W6 8JB.

13. The entry instructions are part of the Terms and Conditions for this competition.

14. By entering the competition you are agreeing to accept these Terms and Conditions. Any breach of these Terms and Conditions by you will mean that your entry will not be valid, and you will not be allowed to enter this competition.

15. By entering this competition, you are agreeing that if you win your name and image may be used for the purpose of announcing the winner in any related publicity with HarperCollins, without additional payment or permission.

16. Any personal information you give us will be used solely for this competition and will not be passed on to any other parties without your agreement. HarperCollins' privacy policy can be found at: http://www.harpercollins.co.uk/legal/Pages/privacy-policy.aspx

17. Under no circumstances will HarperCollins be responsible for any loss, damages, costs or expenses arising from or in any way connected with any errors, defects, interruptions, malfunctions or delays in the promotion of the competition or prize.

18. HarperCollins will not be responsible unless required by law, for any loss, changes, costs or expenses, which may arise in connection with this competition and HarperCollins can cancel or alter the competition at any stage.

19. Any dispute relating to the competition shall be governed by the laws of England and Wales and will be subject to the exclusive jurisdiction of the English courts.